PRAISE FOR

"No one digs into . . . with the zest that Robert J. Sawyer . . . thriller framework, but the . . . exploring the details of t . . ."
—*Milwaukee Journal Sentinel*

"A turbo-charged techno-thriller . . . Sawyer offers an escape from the recent run of near-future dystopias in a combination of classic and contemporary science fiction." —*Publishers Weekly*

"First and foremost, Robert J. Sawyer is a rip-roaring good storyteller . . . *Triggers* operates on both a global and a personal scale . . . By juxtaposing the problems of the entire world with the problems of individuals, Sawyer allows each equal importance. It makes for a rich and compelling narrative . . . There are few authors writing today that bring such a strong combination of literate storytelling and complex ideas to the page. Robert J. Sawyer is one of the best in the business right now, and *Triggers* is him at his finest." —*The Maine Edge*

"A tense, race-against-the-clock adventure with a surprise ending."
—*Library Journal*

"Enthralling . . . Despite the near-dystopian setting, *Triggers* is haunting in its optimism. It was a joy to read."
—*Tulsa Book Review*

"[Robert J. Sawyer] pulls together elements of a gripping political thriller with cutting-edge psychological insights to create a story that works on many levels . . . *Triggers* has the pacing of an episode of *24* and the philosophical sensibilities of an Isaac Asimov novel, so any readers who were introduced to Sawyer through his television series *FlashForward* will find it particularly interesting."
—*Black Gate*

continued . . .

"*Triggers* is constantly gripping on the surface and seriously pro-vocative deep down." —*The Wall Street Journal*

"[*Triggers*] fully justifies the title of a techno-thriller . . . There are chases and standoffs, terrorist threats, bombs, and hostage situations. But they are never allowed to dominate the novel, because *Triggers* is also a medical drama, with many of the legal ramifications of medical accidents discussed. And it's a love story, as people learn that barriers are sometimes things that we simply create for ourselves. It's also a treatise on memory, identity, and perception . . . You come away with a lot of new viewpoints and ideas to think about . . . Verdict: Not to be missed."

—*Sci-Fi Bulletin*

"A thriller's pacing and a chilling near-future world . . . Sawyer's strength is in the overarching ideas of his stories, and he certainly delivers here." —*Booklist*

"Sawyer's body of work, though it covers a myriad of subjects, is uniformly optimistic in tone . . . [*Triggers*] slides comfortably into that body of work, optimistic while attempting to address an inordinate number of social and racial issues."

—*The Globe and Mail*

"[*Triggers*] is an imaginative and technical tour de force . . . A fascinating book that makes its bizarre situation seem real and possible and the people linked so strangely and sometimes unhap-pily to one another quite true. It's hard to put down."

—*The StarPhoenix* (Saskatoon)

"[*Triggers* is] about issues and social commentary . . . such as empathy among humankind . . . and the brutal trauma of war. Sawyer is a pacifist at heart, and it's refreshing to hear a voice advocating peace in a genre that often glorifies war . . . [*Triggers* is] an action movie with a big science-fiction finish and an opti-mistic message." —*Mississauga Life*

"Sawyer's novel not only posits new ideas on the workings on the mind, but also offers a unique viewpoint on the roots of terrorism, not to mention a possible solution."

—*Fast Forward Weekly* (Calgary)

"It's a national security nightmare—someone has access to the secrets lodged in the brain of the most powerful man in the world. There's lots of fascinating stuff here about how human memory works, and Sawyer expertly explores the personal as well as political consequences of his high-concept premise."

—*Financial Times*

PRAISE FOR THE WWW TRILOGY

"Unforgettable. Impossible to put down."
            —Jack McDevitt, Nebula Award–winning author of *Firebird*

"A superb work of day-after-tomorrow science fiction; I enjoyed every page."   —Allen Steele, Hugo Award–winning author of *Hex*

"Not just an adventure story, *Wonder* is also (like its predecessors) a starting point for speculations on ethics and morality, the meaning of consciousness and conscience, and the place of intelligence in the cosmos. This is Robert J. Sawyer at his very best."
            —*Analog Science Fiction and Fact*

"Cracking open a new Robert J. Sawyer book is like getting a gift from a friend who visits all the strange and undiscovered places in the world. You can't wait to see what he's going to amaze you with this time."
            —John Scalzi, *New York Times* bestselling author of *Redshirts*

"The thought-provoking first installment of Sawyer's WWW trilogy explores the origins and emergence of consciousness. The thematic diversity—and profundity—makes this one of Sawyer's strongest works to date."   —*Publishers Weekly* (starred review)

"Strong characterizations; thoughtful 'what if' scenarios . . . An excellent read."   —*SF Signal*

"Fun . . . [An] intelligent and compassionate approach . . . to the nature of consciousness."   —*Sacramento News & Review*

"When people call science fiction a literature of ideas, they mean Robert J. Sawyer . . . It's heady stuff. But Sawyer provides plenty of food for the heart as well."   —*Sci Fi* magazine

BOOKS BY ROBERT J. SAWYER

NOVELS

GOLDEN FLEECE
END OF AN ERA
THE TERMINAL EXPERIMENT
STARPLEX
FRAMESHIFT
ILLEGAL ALIEN
FACTORING HUMANITY

FLASHFORWARD
CALCULATING GOD
MINDSCAN
ROLLBACK
TRIGGERS
RED PLANET BLUES

THE QUINTAGLIO ASCENSION TRILOGY

FAR-SEER
FOSSIL HUNTER
FOREIGNER

THE NEANDERTHAL PARALLAX TRILOGY

HOMINIDS
HUMANS
HYBRIDS

THE WWW TRILOGY

WAKE
WATCH
WONDER

COLLECTIONS

ITERATIONS
(introduction by James Alan Gardner)
RELATIVITY
(introduction by Mike Resnick)
IDENTITY THEFT
(introduction by Robert Charles Wilson)

For book-club discussion guides,
visit **sfwriter.com**

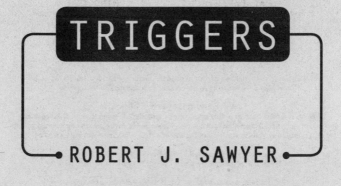

TRIGGERS

ROBERT J. SAWYER

ACE BOOKS, NEW YORK

THE BERKLEY PUBLISHING GROUP
Published by the Penguin Group
Penguin Group (USA) Inc.
375 Hudson Street, New York, New York 10014, USA

USA / Canada / UK / Ireland / Australia / New Zealand / India / South Africa / China

Penguin Books Ltd., Registered Offices: 80 Strand, London WC2R 0RL, England
For more information about the Penguin Group, visit penguin.com.

TRIGGERS

An Ace Book / published by arrangement with SFWriter.com, Inc.

This novel was serialized in four parts in the January–February, March, April,
and May 2012 issues of *Analog Science Fiction and Fact* magazine.

Ace Books are published by The Berkley Publishing Group.
ACE and the "A" design are trademarks of Penguin Group (USA) Inc.

For information, address: The Berkley Publishing Group,
a division of Penguin Group (USA) Inc.,
375 Hudson Street, New York, New York 10014.

ISBN: 978-0-425-25652-7

PUBLISHING HISTORY
Ace hardcover edition / April 2012
Ace mass-market edition / April 2013

PRINTED IN THE UNITED STATES OF AMERICA

10 9 8 7 6 5 4 3 2 1

Cover art by Stephan Martiniere.
Cover design by Diana Kolsky.

ALWAYS LEARNING   **PEARSON**

For
Randy McCharles and **Val King**

Wonderful writers
Wonderful friends

ACKNOWLEDGMENTS

Huge thanks to my lovely wife **Carolyn Clink**, to **Ginjer Buchanan** at Penguin Group (USA)'s Ace imprint in New York, to **Adrienne Kerr** at Penguin Group (Canada) in Toronto, to **Malcolm Edwards** at Orion Publishing Group in London, and to **Stanley Schmidt** of *Analog Science Fiction and Fact* magazine. Many thanks to my agents **Christopher Lotts**, **Vince Gerardis**, and the late, great **Ralph Vicinanza**.

Thanks to my writing colleagues who saw this project through multiple drafts, especially **Paddy Forde** and **Herb Kauderer**. And thanks to **James Alan Gardner** for being there early on and getting me on the right track.

Thanks, too, to all the other people who answered questions, let me bounce ideas off them, or otherwise provided input and encouragement, including: **Chris Barkley**, **Asbed Bedrossian**, **Ellen Bleaney**, **Ted Bleaney**, **Linda Carson**, **David Livingstone Clink**, **Marcel Gagné**, **Shoshana Glick**, **Julie Marr Hanslip**, **Larry Hodges**, **Al Katerinsky**, **James Kerwin**, **Brian Malow**, **Christina Molendyk**, **Kirstin Morrell**, **Kayla Nielsen**, **Virginia O'Dine**, **Sherry Peters**, **Alan B. Sawyer**, **Sally Tomasevic**, **Jeff Vintar**, and **Romeo Vitelli**. And a tip of the hat to **Danita Maslankowski**, who organizes the twice-annual "Write Off" retreats for Calgary's Imaginative Fiction Writers Association.

Many thanks to **Lisa McDonald** and **Nicole Pokryfka** of the George Washington University Hospital in Washington, DC, and to **Bettina Trotter** of the Woman's Hospital of Texas in Houston.

Finally, thanks to **Pauline Martin**, Librarian/Archivist,

The Sixth Floor Museum at Dealey Plaza in Dallas; to **Ian Randal Strock**, author of *The Presidential Book of Lists;* to **Zachary Wiita** of the office of Congressman Maurice Hinchey, Washington, DC; and to The New America Foundation, Arizona State University, and *Slate* magazine, which jointly brought me to Washington in February 2011 to speak at their "Future Tense" conference entitled "Here Be Dragons: Governing a Technologically Uncertain Future"—I piggybacked much research for this novel on that trip.

E pluribus unum
Out of many, one

CHAPTER 1

Friday

THIS is how we began . . .

SUSAN Dawson—thirty-four, with pale skin and pale blue eyes—was standing behind and to the right of the presidential podium. She spoke into the microphone hidden in her sleeve. "Prospector is moving out."

"Copy," said the man's voice in her ear. Seth Jerrison, white, long-faced, with the hooked nose political cartoonists had such fun with, strode onto the wooden platform that had been hastily erected in the center of the wide steps leading up to the Lincoln Memorial.

Susan had been among the many who were unhappy when the president decided to give his speech here instead of at the White House. He wanted to speak before a crowd, he said, letting the world see that even during such frightening times, Americans could not be cowed. But Susan estimated that fewer than three thousand people were assembled on either side of the Reflecting Pool. The Washington Monument was visible both at the far end of the pool and upside down in its still water, framed by ice around the edges. In the distance, the domed Capitol was timidly peeking out from behind the stone obelisk.

President Jerrison was wearing a long navy blue coat, and his breath was visible in the chill November air. "My fellow Americans," he began, "it has been a full month since the latest terrorist attack on our soil. Our thoughts and prayers today are with the brave people of Chicago, just as they continue to be with the proud citizens of San Francisco, who still reel from the attack there in September, and with the patriots of Philadelphia, devastated by the explosion that shook their city in August." He briefly looked over his left shoulder, indicating the nineteen-foot-tall marble statue visible between the Doric columns above and behind him. "A century and a half ago, on the plain at Gettysburg, Abraham Lincoln mused about whether our nation could long endure. But it *has* endured, and it will continue to do so. The craven acts of terrorists will not deter us; the American spirit is indomitable."

The audience—such as it was—erupted in applause, and Jerrison turned from looking at the teleprompter on his left to the one on his right. "The citizens of the United States will not be held hostage by terrorists; we will not allow the crazed few to derail our way of life."

More applause. As she scanned the crowd, Susan thought of the speeches by previous presidents that had made similar claims. But despite the trillions spent on the war on terror, things were getting worse. The weapons used for the last three attacks were a new kind of bomb: they weren't nukes, but they did generate super-high temperatures, and their detonation was accompanied by an electromagnetic pulse, although the pulse was mostly free of the component that could permanently damage electronics. One could conceivably guard against the hijacking of airplanes. But how did one defend against easily hidden, easily carried, hugely powerful bombs?

"Each year, the foes of liberty gain new tools of destruction," continued Jerrison. "Each year, the enemies of civilization can do more damage. But each year we—the free peoples of the world—gain more power, too."

Susan was the Secret Service agent-in-charge. She had line

of sight to seventeen other agents. Some, like her, were standing in front of the colonnade; others were at the sides of the wide marble staircase. A vast pane of bulletproof glass protected Jerrison from the audience, but she still continued to survey the crowd, looking for anyone who seemed out of place or unduly agitated. A tall, thin man in the front row caught her eye; he was reaching into his jacket the way one might go for a holstered gun—but then he brought out a smartphone and started thumb-typing. *Tweet this, asshole,* she thought.

Jerrison went on: "I say now, to the world, on behalf of all of us who value liberty, that we shall not rest until our planet is free of the scourge of terrorism."

Another person caught Susan's attention: a woman who was looking not at the podium but off in the distance at—ah, at a police officer on horseback, over by the Vietnam Veterans Memorial.

"Before I became your president," Jerrison said, "I taught American history at Columbia. If my students could take away only a single lesson, I always hoped it would be the famous maxim that those who fail to learn from history are doomed to repeat it—"

Ka-blam!

Susan's heart jumped and she swung her head left and right, trying to spot where the shot had come from; the marble caused the report to echo. She looked over at the podium and saw that Jerrison had slammed forward into it—he'd been shot from *behind*. She shouted into her sleeve microphone as she ran, her shoulder-length brown hair flying. "Prospector is hit! Phalanx Alpha, shield him! Phalanx Beta, into the memorial—the shot came from there. Gamma, out into the crowd. Go!"

Jerrison slid onto the wooden stage, ending up facedown. Even before Susan had spoken, the ten Secret Service agents in Phalanx Alpha had formed two living walls—one behind Jerrison to protect him from further shots from that direction; another in front of the bulletproof glass that had shielded him from the audience, in case there was a second assailant on the Mall. A male agent bent down but immediately stood up and shouted, "He's alive!"

The rear group briefly opened their ranks, letting Susan

rush in to crouch next to the president. Journalists were trying to approach him—or at least get pictures of his fallen form—but other agents prevented them from getting close.

Alyssa Snow, the president's physician, ran over, accompanied by two paramedics. She gingerly touched Jerrison's back, finding the entrance wound, and—presumably noting that the bullet had missed the spine—rolled the president over. The president's eyes fluttered, looking up at the silver-gray November sky. His lips moved slightly, and Susan tried to make out whatever he was saying over the screams and footfalls from the crowd, but his voice was too faint.

Dr. Snow—who was an elegant forty-year-old African-American—soon had the president's long coat open, exposing his suit jacket and blood-soaked white shirt. She unbuttoned the shirt, revealing the exit wound; on this cold morning, steam was rising from it. She took a length of gauze from one of the paramedics, wadded it up, and pressed it against the hole to try to stanch the flow of blood. One paramedic was taking the president's vital signs, and the other now had an oxygen mask over Jerrison's mouth.

"How long for a medical chopper?" Susan asked into her wrist.

"Eight minutes," replied a female voice.

"Too long," Susan said. She rose and shouted, "Where's Kushnir?"

"Here, ma'am!"

"Into the Beast!"

"Yes, ma'am!" Kushnir was today's custodian of the nuclear football—the briefcase with the launch procedures; he was wearing a Navy dress uniform. The Beast—the presidential limo—was five hundred feet away on Henry Bacon Drive, the closest it could get to the memorial.

The paramedics transferred Jerrison to a litter. Susan and Snow took up positions on either side and ran with the paramedics and Phalanx Alpha down the broad steps and over to the Beast. Kushnir was already in the front passenger seat, and the paramedics reclined the president's rear seat until it was almost horizontal, then moved him onto it.

Dr. Snow opened the trunk, which contained a bank of the president's blood type, and quickly set up a transfusion. The doctor and the two paramedics took the rearward-facing seats, and Susan sat beside the president. Agent Darryl Hudkins—a tall African-American with a shaved head—took the remaining forward-facing chair.

Susan pulled her door shut and shouted to the driver, "Lima Tango, go, go, go!"

CHAPTER 2

KADEEM Adams knew he was in Washington—God damn it, he *knew* it. When they'd brought him here from Reagan, he'd seen the Washington Monument off in the distance giving him the finger, but . . .

But in every fiber of his being, he felt like he was in another place, another time. A cruel sun hung high overhead, and countless bits of burnt paper, ash, and debris swirled about him—a ticker-tape parade commemorating the destruction of the village.

Not again.

Sweet Jesus, why couldn't it stop? Why couldn't he *forget?*

The heat. The smoke—not quite the smell of napalm in the morning, but bad enough. The relentless drone of insects. The horizon shimmering in the distance. The buildings torn open, walls collapsed to rubble, rude furniture smashed to kindling.

His right arm ached, and so did his left ankle; it could barely support his weight. He tried to swallow but his throat was dry and his nostrils were clogged with sand. His vision was suddenly obscured, so he wiped a hand in front of his eyes, and his palm came away wet and red.

More sounds: helicopters, an armored vehicle moving along the dirt road crunching wreckage beneath its tracks, and—

Yes, always, overtop of everything, unending.

Screams.

Babies crying.

Adults wailing.

People shouting—cursing—praying—in Arabic.

The cacophony of a ruined place, a ruined culture.

Kadeem took a deep breath, just like Professor Singh had taught him to. He closed his eyes for a second, then opened them and picked an object in the room here at Luther Terry Memorial Hospital, focusing his attention on it and nothing else. He selected a vase of flowers—clear glass, with fluted sides, like a Roman column that had been squeezed in the middle—

—by a fist—

And the flowers, two white carnations and three red roses—

—blood-red roses—

And . . . and . . .

Glass could cut.

And—

No. No. The flowers were . . .

Life. Death. On a grave.

No!

The flowers were . . .

Were . . .

Beautiful. Calming. Natural. Unspoiled.

Deep breaths. Trying to relax. Trying to be *here,* in this hospital room, not there. Trying, trying, trying . . .

He *was* here, in DC. *That* other place was the past. Done. Finished. Dead and buried.

Or at least dead.

Professor Singh entered the room. As always, the Sikh's eyes went first to the vital-signs monitor, and he doubtless noted Kadeem's elevated pulse, his increased respiration, and—Kadeem looked himself and saw that his blood pressure was 190 over 110.

"Another flashback," Singh said, as much diagnosis as question.

Kadeem nodded. "The village again."

"I am so sorry," Singh said. "But, if we're lucky—and we both deserve some of that—today's the day we may be able to do something about this. I've just come from seeing Dr. Gaudio. Your final MRIs are fine. She says we can go ahead with the procedure."

THE same hospital, but another room: "Ready, Mr. Latimer?" asked one of the two orderlies who had just entered.

Josh Latimer was more than ready; he'd been waiting many months for this. "Absolutely."

"What about you, Miss Hennessey?" the other orderly asked.

Josh lolled his head, looking over at the daughter he'd recently been reunited with after a thirty-year separation.

Dora seemed nervous, and he couldn't blame her. He'd be better off after this operation, but—there was no denying it—she'd be worse off. Parents often made sacrifices for their children, but it was a rare child who was called upon to make a sacrifice as big as this for a parent. "Yes," she said.

One orderly went to the head of each gurney. Josh's was further from the door, but his orderly started pushing him first, and he passed close enough by his daughter to reach over and touch her arm. She smiled at him, and just then she reminded him of her mother: the same round head, the same astonishingly blue eyes, the same lopsided grin. Dora was thirty-five now, and her mother would have been sixty-one, the same age as Josh, if breast cancer hadn't taken her.

They made an odd train, he knew, as they were pushed along: him as the locomotive, thin, with white hair and beard; her as the caboose, still a little on the hefty side despite dieting for months to get in shape for the operation, her long brown hair tucked into a blue cap to keep it out of the way. They happened to pass the door marked "Dialysis." Josh had spent so much time in there he knew how many tiles were in the ceiling, how many slats in the blinds, how many drawers in the various cabinets.

They continued down the corridor, and Josh was pushed feet-first into the operating room, followed by Dora. The orderlies joined forces to transfer him to one of the surgical tables and then her to the other. The second table wasn't normally here; it was mounted on wheels. Overhead was a glassed-in observation gallery that covered two adjacent sides of the room, but its lights were off.

The surgeon was present, along with her team, all in their green surgical garb. Her eyes crinkled as she smiled. "Welcome, Josh. Hello, Dora. We'll start by putting you both under. All right? Here we go . . ."

SECRETARY of Defense Peter Muilenburg—a broad-shouldered sixty-year-old white man with silver hair and hazel eyes—stood looking at the giant illuminated world map stretching the length of the subterranean room at the Pentagon. Above the map, a large red digital timer counted down. It currently read 74:01:22. In just over three days, Operation Counterpunch would commence.

Muilenburg pointed at the big screen, where the string "CVN-76" was displayed in the middle of the Arabian Sea. "What's the status of the *Reagan?*" he asked.

"She's making up for lost time," replied a female analyst, consulting a desktop monitor.

"We need the aircraft carriers in position within sixty hours," Muilenburg said.

"It'll be tight for the *Reagan* and even tighter for the *Stennis,*" the aide replied, "thanks to that hurricane. But they'll make it."

Muilenburg's BlackBerry buzzed, and he pulled it out of his blue uniform pocket. "SecDef," he said.

"Mr. Secretary," said a woman's voice. "This is Mrs. Astley." The next words were always, "Please hold for President Jerrison," followed by silence, so he lowered the handset a bit, and—

He quickly brought the phone back to his ear. "Repeat, please."

"I said," the president's secretary replied, and Muilenburg realized that her voice was shaking, "Mr. Jerrison has been shot. They're rushing him to LT right now."

Muilenburg looked up at the bank of red digits, just in time to see it change from 74:00:00 to 73:59:59. "God save us," he said.

CHAPTER 3

THERE were always two members of the Secret Service Countersniper Team on the roof of the White House; today one of them was Rory Proctor. The chill wind cut through him. He was holding his rifle in gloved hands and walking back and forth, scanning the grounds between here and the Ellipse, the fifty-two-acre public park south of the White House fence. The Washington Monument was visible, but even from this elevated position, Proctor couldn't see the Lincoln Memorial, where all of the action had been taking place, although he was listening intently to the chatter in his earpiece.

Proctor was so used to scanning for things in the distance, he didn't pay much attention to the rooftop, which had a stunted colonnade around its edges and a few potted shrubs. But a dove happened to catch his eye as it flew into view. It landed a few yards from him, by a squat metal enclosure at the base of one of the rectangular chimneys on the south side. There was some odd scuffing of the white roofing tiles in front of the enclosure. He took one more look at the grounds on the south side, saw nothing of interest, then walked over to look at the enclosure.

The padlock had been jimmied, and although it had been closed, it wasn't locked. He swung the lid of the enclosure up, leaning it back against the white chimney, and—

Oh, shit. Inside was a hexagonal contraption of squat metal about two feet in diameter and, judging by the depth of the enclosure, about a foot thick; it looked like someone had taken a slice through one of the lava pillars from the Devil's Causeway. Proctor recognized the device from intelligence briefings. The attacks on Chicago, San Francisco, and Philadelphia had been successful—meaning the bombs used there had been utterly destroyed when they exploded. But a planned attack on Los Angeles International Airport had been averted ten days ago when a terrorist from al-Sajada, the al-Qaeda splinter group that had risen to prominence after the death of Osama bin Laden, had been intercepted with a device just like this one in the trunk of his car.

Proctor spoke into his headset. "Proctor, Central. I'm on the White House roof—and I've found a bomb."

THE doors to the operating room burst open, and Dr. Mark Griffin, the CEO of Luther Terry Memorial Hospital, strode in, wearing a hastily donned green surgical smock, surgical hat, and face mask. "Sorry, Michelle," he said to the startled surgeon. "You've got to clear out."

Michelle sounded shocked. "I'm in the middle of a kidney transplant."

"We've got a priority patient," Griffin replied, "and no other operating room is available."

"Are you *nuts?*" Michelle said. "Look at this woman— we've opened her up."

"Can you stop?"

"Stop? We've just begun!"

"Good," said Griffin. "Then you *can* stop." He looked at the assembled team. "Clear out, everyone."

"What about the patients? They're intubated and we've put them both under, for God's sake."

"Sew her up, then move them out to the corridor," Griffin replied.

"Mark, this is crazy. The donor flew in all the way from London for this, and—"

"Michelle, it's the president. He's been shot, and he'll be here any minute."

AS soon as the bullet hit President Jerrison, Secret Service agents swarmed into the Lincoln Memorial. The interior was divided into three chambers by two rows of fifty-foot-tall columns. The large central chamber contained the giant statue of a seated Abe made of starkly white Georgia marble, mounted on a massive oblong pedestal. The small north chamber had Lincoln's second inaugural address carved into its wall, while the small south one had a carving of the Gettysburg Address.

Agent Manny Cheung, the leader of Phalanx Beta, looked around. There were only a few places to hide: behind the columns, in the narrow space behind the statue's pedestal, or somehow clambering up to perch on Lincoln's back. Cheung held his revolver in both hands and nodded to Dirk Jenks, the thickset young agent on his left. They quickly determined that there was no one else in here, but—

But the elevator door was now *closed*. It was in the south chamber, in the wall adjacent to the Gettysburg Address, and had been locked off here at the top with the door open; Cheung knew that Jenks had checked it before the president had arrived. The elevator—used to provide handicapped access to the statue—went from here down to the small exhibit hall in the lower part of the memorial. Cheung barked into his sleeve. "He's in the elevator heading down."

There were security people guarding the entrance to the basement gallery anyway, but Cheung took off, running on the hard marble floor and down the wide outside steps. He passed between the two signs that flanked the entrance. The white one on his right said, "Warning: Firearms Prohibited," and showed a silhouette of a pistol with a barred red circle over it. The brown one on his left said, "Quiet" and "Respect Please."

Cheung hurried down the steps past the seating area that

had been erected for the presidential party, rounded a corner, and headed down again to the narrow entrance to the lower level. He had looked through the gallery just yesterday, as part of the preparations for the president's speech. It had been his first time in it—like most Washington residents, he tended to visit the sites only when he had company from out of town, and there were so many things to see on the Mall, he'd never bothered with this little museum before.

The exhibit hall, opened in 1994 and occupying just 560 square feet, had been partially paid for by school kids collecting pennies. Since the back of the penny had depicted the Lincoln Memorial then, it had been called the "Pennies Make a Monumental Difference Campaign." Cheung had read the Lincoln quotes carved into black marble slabs, including one that had startled him: "If I could save the Union without freeing any slave, I would do it; and if I could save it by freeing all the slaves I would do it; and if I could save it by freeing some and leaving others alone, I would also do that."

He tore past the exhibits, heading to the little elevator lobby in the back. Of course, by the time he got there, the elevator had completed its descent. Three other men—two uniformed DC cops and another Secret Service agent—were already there, with guns aimed at the elevator door. But there was no sign of anyone else, and the brass door was closed; whoever was inside must have a key for the elevator's control panel, which would explain how he'd started it after it had been locked off on the upper level.

"Anybody try pushing the button?" Cheung asked. There was just one button, since the elevator could only go up from here.

"I did," said one of the uniforms. "Nothing happened."

Cheung pushed the button himself. The door remained shut. "He's definitely got a key, then," he said.

"And he's armed," noted the other Secret Service agent.

Cheung judged the brass door sufficiently sturdy that the would-be assassin probably couldn't shoot through it. He rapped his knuckles loudly against one of the metal panels. "Secret Service!" he shouted. "Come out with your hands up!"

CHAPTER 4

"EVERYONE, attention please! We need to evacuate the White House and the surrounding buildings immediately. Do *not* assemble at your fire-muster stations; just keep going. Get as far from the building as you can. Exit right now in an orderly fashion. Don't stop to take anything; just get out. Move!"

"ARE we sure he's in there?" Agent Manny Cheung asked.

"There were guards at the outside door the whole time," replied the other Secret Service man, "and we've looked in the exhibit space and the restrooms. He's got to still be in the elevator."

Cheung spoke into his sleeve. "Cheung to Jenks: make sure the elevator shaft is guarded at the top, in case he tries to ride up again."

"Copy," said a voice.

"Sir," said one of the DC cops, "this is bullshit. There are three of us, and dozens more if we need them. Look at that door." Cheung did so. It was an old-fashioned elevator, and the door consisted of two parts—but they didn't separate in the middle. Rather, the left part tucked behind the right part as the door opened, and both parts slipped into a pocket on the right side of the elevator shaft. "If we pull on the right-hand part in the middle, there, the left-hand part will draw away from the wall."

Cheung wondered at the wisdom of talking just outside the elevator; although the heavy door probably muffled the sound, whoever was inside could doubtless hear some of what they were saying. Nonetheless, the plan made sense. He nodded at the officer, who was the biggest of the three of them, easily six-five and 280 pounds. The man grabbed the right-hand panel by its edge, near the centerline of the door, and put his back into it, pulling it aside so that it slid with a grinding sound into the pocket hidden behind the beige wall. Cheung, the other Secret Service agent, and the other cop, had their guns trained on the left side, which was now showing a crack, then a sliver, then a strip of light from within. The big cop grunted and pulled again, hard, and the door opened to eighteen inches—but no gunfire hailed from the interior.

Another yank, and the right-hand leaf was now all the way into its pocket, leaving the entire left-half of the elevator's width open now, and—

And there was no one inside.

Cheung looked up, and—*ah hah!* There was a service door in the roof of the elevator. He tried to reach it but wasn't tall enough. He gestured to the big cop, who had no trouble pushing the roof door aside. The cop then immediately stepped out of the way, and Cheung craned his neck to hazard a peek. It was dark in the shaft, but—Christ, yes, there was someone there, illuminated from below by light coming out of the elevator. He was shimmying up the thick cable.

"Cheung to Jenks: the suspect is climbing the elevator cable. He's about ten feet shy of the top."

"Copy, Manny," Jenks replied.

The elevator door started shuddering shut. Cheung wheeled around, going for the rubber bumper at its edge at the same time the tall cop moved for the "Door Open" button; they collided, and the cab lurched into motion—

—and through the open roof Cheung could see the cable

moving. There was a massive thud, and the cab shook violently. The assailant must have lost his grip and fallen the twenty feet or so he'd climbed. One of his arms flopped down through the roof hatch.

There was no stopping the elevator's ascent now, and Cheung hoped there was enough clearance to keep a downed man from being squeezed against the top of the shaft.

But, yes, there *must* be enough clearance! The assailant must have entered the elevator yesterday, when it was announced that Jerrison would give a speech here, and had simply hauled himself up onto the cab's roof and waited; doubtless when they did finally get to examine the roof, they'd find blankets and whatever else he'd needed to survive overnight in the shaft.

The elevator came to a stop, and the door opened, revealing a crowd of agents and dour Lincoln off to the right.

"Who the hell pushed the button?" Cheung demanded.

"I did," said Jenks. "I thought—"

"Jesus Christ," said Cheung, cutting him off. "You!" he pointed at a female agent. "In here."

The woman hurried forward, and Cheung motioned for the tall cop to boost her up. She placed a finger on the wrist that was dangling through the hatch and shook her head. The cop lifted her higher so she could stick her body through the roof hatch. After a moment, she signaled that she wanted down.

"Well?" Cheung demanded as soon as she was standing again.

"It's not pretty," she said.

AGENT Susan Dawson spoke into her wrist microphone. "Dawson to Central: Prospector secured in the Beast. Tell Lima Tango that he's got a severe gunshot wound—shot in the back. His physician, Captain Snow, is with us."

The Beast had bulletproof windows and five-inch-thick hull plating. There was a presidential seal on each of its rear doors. A small American flag flew from the right side of the hood, and the presidential standard flew from the left. The vehicle had a blue emergency light that could be attached to the roof; the driver—himself a Secret Service agent—had already deployed it. Motorcycle escorts with sirens blaring were out in front and following behind.

The car took a hard right onto 23rd Street NW. It was only 1.3 miles to Luther Terry, Susan knew, but the traffic was heavy with the tail end of Friday-morning rush hour.

Dr. Snow was still trying to stop the flow of blood, but it was all over the president's gray-haired chest; even with the transfusion, it seemed clear he was losing blood faster than it was being replaced.

"Where's the vice president?" asked Agent Darryl Hudkins.

"Manhattan," said Susan, "but—"

A male voice came over their earpieces: "Rockhound is *en route* to *Air Force Two*. Will be at Andrews in ninety minutes."

Despite the siren—and the driver leaning on the horn— they'd slowed to a crawl. Those motorists listening to the radio might already have heard that the president was being rushed to the hospital, and that might make them slow down for a look: would-be Zapruders hoping to catch the moment of presidential demise.

"This is ridiculous," the driver said over his shoulder. "Hold on." He pulled a hard left onto E Street, and Susan did her best to keep the president from sliding out of his seat as the car careened onto its new course. They were now heading directly toward the Kennedy Center. The limo then took a sharp right onto 24th, and the president pressed against Susan. She gently pushed him back into place, but the hip of her dark jacket was now soaked with his blood.

A voice came over Susan's earpiece: "They've got a stretcher waiting at the ambulance entrance, a thoracic team is assembling, and they're clearing an operating room."

"Copy," Susan said. They were doing better than when Reagan had been shot decades ago. Back then, the Secret Service had started taking the president to the White House, not realizing he'd been hit until he began coughing up bright, frothy blood.

Mercifully, some cars were pulling aside to let the Beast pass. Susan looked into the rearview mirror, catching the driver's eyes there. "Maybe two more minutes," he said.

At last the car made the forty-five-degree turn onto New Hampshire Avenue, paralleling the longest side of the hospital, which was shaped like a right-angle triangle. After some deft maneuvering, the driver got the Beast up the ramp into the ambulance emergency bay. There was indeed a team waiting at the side of the curved, covered driveway with a stretcher.

Susan jumped out into the cold air, but by the time she was around to the other side, Darryl Hudkins and the two paramedics were heaving the president onto the stretcher. As soon as Jerrison was secure, they rushed him through the sliding glass doors. Susan put a hand on the stretcher and ran—experiencing an eerie echo of all the times she'd run alongside the Beast, holding on to it with one hand.

"Susan Dawson," she called across the stretcher to the tall, handsome black man on the opposite side. "Secret Service special-agent-in-charge."

"Dr. Mark Griffin," he replied. "I'm the hospital's chief executive officer." He looked behind Susan at the president's physician. "Captain Snow, good to see you."

They hustled the stretcher into Trauma, which had two beds separated by an incongruously cheery purple, yellow, and blue curtain. There was a patient in the other bed—a white teenage boy, who, despite having a mangled leg, sat up to try to get a glimpse of the president.

"On three," said one of the doctors. "One, two, three!" He and two other men transferred Jerrison to the bed.

"The bullet obviously missed his heart," Griffin said to Susan, as a swarm of doctors, including Alyssa Snow, surrounded Jerrison. "But it looks like a major vessel has been clipped. If it's the aorta, we're in real trouble; the mortality rate for that is eighty percent."

Susan couldn't see what was being done to Jerrison's chest, but a new transfusion bag had already been set up on a stand beside him; of course, they had Jerrison's records on file here and knew his blood type. Four more pint bags were on a tray next to the stand, but she guessed he'd already lost more than that; the backseat of the limo had been sodden.

A DC police helicopter deposited a bomb-disposal robot onto the roof of the White House. Secret Service sharpshooter Rory Proctor was now on the far side of the Ellipse, along with a hundred White House staffers who had decided they had evacuated far enough; many others, though, had headed further south, crossing Constitution Avenue onto the Mall.

Proctor looked north across the grass at the magnificent building. He'd had binoculars with him up on the roof, and still had them: he used them to watch as the squat robot, visible through the columns of the balustrade, rolled on its treads toward the second chimney from the left. Listening to the chatter on his headset, he gathered that the original notion—just winching the bomb into the sky—had been vetoed, out of fear that there might be a switch on its underside that would detonate it as soon as it was lifted.

"Stand by, everyone," said the calm male voice of the bomb-squad leader, who was operating the robot remotely from a police truck parked on the far side of the Eisenhower Executive Office Building, which had also been evacuated, along with the Treasury Building and the buildings on the north side of Pennsylvania Avenue. "I have the bomb in sight . . ."

"LET'S get him into the O.R.," said one of the doctors.

The trauma bed was on a wheeled base. Susan Dawson followed as they rolled it out of the room and down a corridor. They came to a metal door with a sign next to it that said, "Trauma Elevator—DO NOT BLOCK." Susan made it inside with the president, Dr. Griffin, and two other physicians, and they rode up to the second floor. Dr. Snow—who wasn't a surgeon—headed to the ICU to make arrangements for Jerrison, who would eventually be taken there if the surgery was successful.

The president was wheeled out of the elevator, down another corridor, and into an operating room. More Secret Service agents were already up here. Susan took a moment to deploy them. Rather than piling them all in front of the door to the operating room, she spread them out along the corridor; she didn't want any unauthorized personnel getting anywhere near Jerrison. When Reagan had been shot, a dozen Secret Service agents had crammed into the O.R., but they'd gotten in the way of the surgical team and represented an unnecessary infection risk; protocol now called for only a single agent to actually go in—and she designated Darryl Hudkins, who had the most EMT training.

Susan pointed to two occupied gurneys a short distance away, one with a thin white-haired man in his sixties, the other with a plump younger woman; they were attended by a nurse. "I want them out of here."

"They'll be gone in a few minutes," Griffin said. He led Susan up a steep narrow staircase to the observation gallery. As they settled in, she heard, "Rockhound is airborne" in her ear, and then, a moment later, she received a report about the discovery of a bomb at the White House. She looked down at Darryl Hudkins just as he looked up at her, his face a question. She shook her head: no point distracting the surgical team with this awful news; they needed to focus. Darryl nodded.

People in the operating room were working rapidly. The anesthesiologist was the only one sitting; she had a chair at the head of the surgical bed the president had been transferred to. A nurse was cleaning the president's chest with antiseptic soap.

"Which one is the lead surgeon?" Susan asked.

Griffin pointed at a tall white man, who, now that the nurse had stepped aside, was applying the surgical drape over the president's chest. The doctor's features were mostly hidden by a face mask and head covering, although Susan thought he perhaps had a beard. "Him," said Griffin. "Eric Redekop. A doctor of the first water. Trained at Harvard and—"

They were interrupted by the sound of a bone saw, audible even through the angled glass in front of her. The president was being cut open.

Susan watched, fascinated and appalled, as a chest spreader was used. Jerrison's torso was a mess of blood and bone, and her stomach churned looking at it, but she couldn't take her eyes off the spectacle. One of the doctors replaced a now-empty bag of blood with a fresh one.

Suddenly, the whole tenor of the room changed: people rushing around. Griffin stood up and leaned against the glass with splayed hands. "What's happening?" demanded Susan.

Griffin's voice was so low, she almost didn't hear it. "His heart's stopped."

The O.R. had a built-in defibrillator, and another doctor

was adjusting controls on it. With the open chest, they didn't have to use the paddles; the doctor applied electrical stimulation directly to Jerrison's heart. A nurse in a green smock was obscuring Susan's view of the vital-signs monitor now, but she saw the woman shake her head.

The man administered another shock. Nothing.

Susan rose to her feet, too. Her own heart was pounding—but the president's still wasn't.

Something else happened—Susan didn't know what—and various people changed positions below. The defibrillator operator tried a third time. The nurse watching the vital signs shook her head once more, and that famous phrase echoed through Susan's mind: *a heartbeat away from the presidency* . . .

The nurse moved, and Susan could at last see the flat green line tracing across the monitor. She spoke into her wrist. "Do we know where Hovarth is?"

Griffin looked at her, his jaw falling. Connally Hovarth was chief justice of the United States.

"He's in his chambers," said a voice in her ear.

"Get him out to Andrews," Susan said. "Have him ready to administer the oath as soon as *Air Force Two* touches down."

CHAPTER 5

KADEEM Adams desperately wanted the flashbacks to end. They came all the time: when he was out for a walk, when he was in the grocery store, when he was trying to make love to his girlfriend. Yes, Professor Singh, and Dr. Fairfax at the DCOE before him, had told him to avoid triggers—things that might set off a flashback. But anything—everything!—could provoke one. A chirping bird morphed into a baby crying. A car horn became a wailing alarm. A plate falling to the floor turned into the *rat-a-tat* of gunfire.

Kadeem knew better than to hope for the best. If things had worked out for him in the past, he wouldn't have failed to get that scholarship, he wouldn't have been working at a McDonald's, he wouldn't have enlisted because it was the only halfway-decent-paying job he *could* get, he wouldn't have ended up on the front line in Iraq.

Still, he was grateful for Professor Singh's attention. Kadeem had never met a Sikh before—there'd been none in the 'hood—and he hadn't known what to expect. At first, they'd had trouble communicating; Singh's accent was thick, and his speech was rapid-fire, at least to Kadeem's ears. But slowly he'd gotten used to Singh's voice, and Singh had gotten used to his, and the seemingly endless alternation of him saying "What?" and Singh saying "Pardon?" had fallen by the wayside.

"Okay, guru," Kadeem said. He knew it amused Singh when he called him that, and Singh's beard lifted a bit as he smiled. "Let's do this."

Kadeem walked over to the low-back padded chair and sat down. Next to it, on an articulated arm, was the latticework sphere. Kadeem had once quipped that it looked like the skeleton of God's soccer ball, but he knew that wasn't quite right. It was about two feet in diameter, and it was, as Singh had told him, an open geodesic, made up of triangles fashioned from lengths of steel tubing. Singh unclipped its two halves and opened it. The hemispheres, joined by a hinge, swung apart.

There was an open section at the south pole of the sphere. As Singh jockeyed the articulated arm to move the hemispheres closer to Kadeem's head, that opening allowed for his neck. Singh rejoined the two halves, enclosing Kadeem's head. There were about eight inches of clearance on all sides, and Kadeem could easily see through the open triangles. Still, it was unnerving, as if his head were now in some bizarre jail cell. He took a deep, calming breath.

Singh loomed close—like an optician adjusting glasses even Elton John wouldn't wear. He moved the sphere on its arm a bit to the left, and a bit up, and then, apparently deciding he'd gone too far up, a bit down. And then he nodded in satisfaction and stepped away.

"All right," Singh said. "Relax."

"Easier said than done, guru," replied Kadeem.

Singh's back was to him, his turban piled high. But his voice was warm. "It will be fine, my friend. Let me just calibrate a few things, and—yes, yes, okay. Are you ready?"

"Yeah."

"All right, then. Here we go. Five. Four. Three. Two. One. Zero."

Singh pushed a button; it made a loud click. At the vertices of each triangle in Kadeem's vision, blue-green lights appeared, like laser pointers. In the demos Singh had done for him, colored dots had shown up on the dummy head. They'd stood out brightly against the white Styrofoam, but were doubtless hard to see against Kadeem's dark skin. He'd thought there might be some sensation associated with them: heat, maybe, or a tingling. But he felt nothing at all. The lights weren't strong enough to blind him, but he did nonetheless shift slightly to stop one of them from hitting his left eye.

Singh moved around, looking at Kadeem again. He seemed satisfied, and said, "Okay. I'm going to run the program now. Remember, if you feel any discomfort, tell me and we can abort."

Kadeem nodded. Since the sphere was supported by the articulated arm, it didn't bob at all as he did so. Singh reached over to a laptop computer sitting on a surgical-instrument stand, moved the cursor with the trackpad, and finished off with a rapping of his forefinger.

The program started executing. The blue-green lights began to dance; they were on tiny gimbals and moved in patterns Singh had programmed. It was impossible to keep the teal points from hitting his pupils every few seconds, and rather than fight that, Kadeem just closed his eyes. The beams were bright enough that he could still tell when one was touching his eyelid, but it wasn't irritating, and the darkness helped him clear his mind.

This was going to be hard, he knew. He'd spent years trying to avoid triggering flashbacks—and now Singh was going to find whatever switch in his brain caused them and throw it, hopefully for the final time. The only small mercy there'd been with the previous flashbacks was never expecting them— they just hit him upside the head, with no warning. But now Kadeem felt dread, knowing one was coming. He was hooked up to a vital-signs monitor, and he could hear the soft ping of his pulse accelerating.

The intersecting lasers were specially tuned to pass through bone and flesh; the teal dots were mere markers for invisible beams that coincided with them. The beams entered his skull without having an effect, but when two or more beams criss-crossed inside his brain, they stimulated the neural net at the intersection and caused it to fire, providing, as Singh had explained to him, the equivalent of an action potential. First one net was brought to life, then another, then another. Singh's equipment bypassed the usual excitatory disinhibition that frustrated other brain researchers: normally, if a neural net had fired once recently, it was disinclined to fire again. But Singh could make the same net fire as often as possible, until it had, at least temporarily, exhausted its supply of neurotransmitters.

Singh was doing that just now, and—

A picnic, one of the few happy moments of Kadeem's childhood.

Five big kids taking his lunch from him on the way to school.

His mama, trying to hide her bruised eye from him, and his rage at knowing she was going to let that man back in their home.

His first car.

His first blowjob.

A sharp pain but—but no, only a memory of a sharp pain. Ah, it was when he broke his arm playing football.

More pain, but of a good kind: the short, sharp shock of Kristah playfully biting his nipple.

A flock of birds blocking the sun.

The sun—

The sun.

Hot, beating down. The desert sun.

Iraq.

Yes, Iraq.

His heart pounded; the sound from the monitor had the tempo of the Bee Gees' "Staying Alive."

Singh was homing in, getting close, circling his prey.

Kadeem gripped the padded arms of the chair.

Sand. Tanks. Troops. And, in the distance, the village.

Shouts. Orders. The roar of vehicle engines fighting against the drifting sand and the heat.

Kadeem's breathing was ragged. The air he was taking in was cool, but his memory was of searing hotness. He wanted to shout for Singh to *abort, abort, abort!* But he bit his lower lip and endured it.

The village was growing closer. Iraqi men in desert gear, women who must have been sweltering in their robe-like black abayas, children in tattered clothes, all coming to see the approaching convoy. Greeting it. *Welcoming it.*

Kadeem tasted vomit at the back of his throat. He fought it down and let the memory wash over him—all the screams, all the pain, all the *evil*—one last time.

SHARPSHOOTER Rory Proctor continued to watch the activity on the roof of the White House from what he hoped was a safe distance. He was angry and worried: the nation had been pounded for months now by al-Sajada. How much more was yet to come? How much more could this great country take?

He'd tuned his headset to pick up the appropriate police channel and was listening to the running commentary from the man operating the bomb-disposal robot: "I'm going to try cutting into the side of the enclosure so that we can get at the device. In five, four, three, two . . ."

AGENT Susan Dawson kept flashing back to an episode of *Columbo* she'd seen years ago, in which Leonard Nimoy had guest-starred as a surgeon who'd tried to arrange the death of someone while supposedly saving his life: when installing an artificial heart valve, Nimoy's character had used dissolving instead of permanent suture. But as far as she could tell, Eric Redekop and his team had worked fervently to save Seth Jerrison.

"Central to Dawson," said the voice in her ear. "Justice Horvath is *en route* to Andrews, but says he can't proceed without an official death notice. Has the president actually—"

Screeeeech!

Susan yanked her earpiece out; the wail from it was unbearable. The lights in the observation gallery flickered, then died, as did the ones down in the operating room. A few seconds later, emergency lighting kicked in below. Mark Griffin bounded up the steps in the small gallery and opened the door at the back. More emergency lighting spilled in from a ceiling-mounted unit containing what looked like two automobile headlamps.

"Those are battery-operated lights," said Griffin. "The main power is off—meaning so is that defibrillator, as well as the perfusion pump." Susan saw someone run out of the O.R., presumably to get a crash cart with a portable defibrillator.

Eric Redekop, starkly illuminated from the upper left by the harsh emergency lights in the O.R., reached his gloved hand into the president's chest and began squeezing Jerrison's heart. The surgeon glanced at the paired digital wall clocks—the actual time and the event timer—but their faces had gone dark.

After a moment, the regular lighting flickered back to life. Susan looked down at the surgical bed. Redekop continued to squeeze the heart once per second. Other doctors were frantically trying to reboot or readjust equipment. She turned to Griffin. "What the hell happened?"

"I don't know," he said. "The emergency power is supposed to kick in automatically. An operating room should never go dark like that."

Susan picked up her earpiece and, after making sure it wasn't still wailing, put it back in her ear. "Dawson," she said into her sleeve. "Whiskey tango foxtrot?"

A deep male voice: Secret Service agent Darryl Hudkins, looking up at her from down in the operating room. "Could it be an electromagnetic pulse?"

"Christ," said Susan. "The bomb."

"Agent Schofield cutting in," said another voice in Susan's ear. "Affirmative. The bomb at the White House has gone off."

"Copy that," replied Susan, stunned.

"How are they managing with Prospector?" asked Schofield.

Susan looked through the angled glass at the chaos below. Redekop was still squeezing the president's heart, but the vital-signs monitor continued to show a flat line. "I think we've lost him."

RORY Proctor had been using his binoculars when the bomb went off. As soon as he saw the flare of light, he lowered them—just in time to see the entire curved back of the White

House blow out toward him. A plume of smoke started rising into the gray sky, and gouts of fire shot out of the shattered windows of the east and west wings. Screams went up all around him.

SETH Jerrison's deep, dark secret was that he was an atheist. He'd managed to secure the Republican nomination by lying through his teeth about it, by periodically attending church, by bowing his head when appropriate in public, and—after numerous reprimands from his wife and campaign director— finally breaking himself of the habit of using "Jesus" and "Christ" as swearwords, even in private.

He believed in fiscal conservatism, he believed in small government, he believed in taking a strong stand against America's enemies whether nations or individuals, he believed in capitalism, and he believed English should be the official language of the United States.

But he did not believe in God.

The handful of RNC members who knew this sometimes chided him for it. Rusty, his campaign manager, had once looked at him with a kindly smile—the sort one might bestow on a silly child who had claimed that when he grew up he was going to be president—and said, "Sure, you might be an athe- ist *now,* but just wait until you're dying—you'll see."

But Seth was dying right now. He could feel his strength fading, feel his *life* draining away.

And still he felt secure in his atheism. Even as his vision contracted into a tunnel, the thoughts that came to him were of the scientific explanation for that phenomenon. It was caused by anoxia, and was, after all, commonly experienced even in situations that weren't immediately life-threatening.

He was momentarily surprised not to be feeling any panic or pain. But, then again, that was normal, too, he knew: a sense of euphoria also went with oxygen deprivation. And so he managed a certain detachment. He was surprised to be con- scious at all; he knew he'd been shot in the torso. Surely they'd given him a general anesthetic before performing surgery, and he *must* be in surgery by now, but . . .

But there was no doubt his mind was active. He tried, and failed, to open his eyes; tried, and failed, to sit up; tried, and failed, to speak. And, unlike some horror stories he'd heard about patients feeling every scalpel cut and stitch while supposedly knocked out, he was experiencing no pain at all, thank—well, thank biochemistry!

Ah, and now the white light had begun to appear: pure, brilliant, but not at all painful to . . . well, not to *look* at; he wasn't seeing with his eyes, after all. But to *contemplate*.

A pristine, bright, soothing, inviting light . . .

And then, just as those who'd come back from the brink said it sometimes does, his life began to flash in front of his eyes.

A kindly female face.

A playground.

Childhood friends.

A public school.

But he didn't remember all the graffiti, all the litter, the broken stonework, and—

No, no, that was ridiculous. *Of course* he remembered it—or he wouldn't be seeing it now.

But . . .

A knife. Blood.

Tattered clothes.

The air shimmering. Unbearable heat. Screams. The stench of . . . yes, of burning flesh.

No, no, he'd been a good person! He *had*. He'd done his best always. And even with him agreeing to Counterpunch, he couldn't be going to hell!

A metaphoric deep breath; he had no control over his body, but it *felt* like he was inhaling.

There is no hell. No heaven, either.

But the *heat*. The flames. The screams.

There is no hell!

All of it was explicable, a natural phenomenon: just the way the brain responded to oxygen starvation.

The images changed, the smells changed, the sounds changed. The hellish vista was replaced by a city street at night.

Another woman's face.

And much more, in rapid succession: people, incidents, events.

It *was* a life review flashing before him.

But it wasn't *his* life that he saw.

CHAPTER 6

"EEG is erratic!"

"BP continues to fall!"

"We're losing him!"

Eric Redekop lifted his head to look at his team as he continued the manual heart massage. A nurse named Ann January daubed his forehead with a cloth, picking up the sweat. "No," he said simply. "We are *not*. I'm not going down in history as the surgeon who couldn't save the president."

NIKKI Van Hausen looked at her hands—and an image of them covered with blood filled her mind. She shook her head, trying to dispel the grisly sight—but it came back to her even more forcefully: her hands red and dripping, and—

My God!

And she was holding a knife, and its blade was slick and crimson.

More images: cutting into skin, blood welling up from the wound.

Again: another cut, more blood. And again: another thrust, this time blood spurting.

She sat down and looked—really looked—at her hands: the smooth pale skin, the tiny scar along the side of her right index finger from a wineglass that had broken while she was washing it, the silver ring she wore with a turquoise cabochon, the painted nails—red, yes, but not blood-red.

But again images of her hands covered in blood came to her. And beneath the blood, peeking out here and there: gloves. Like a murderer who knew that fingerprints would otherwise be left behind.

Her heart was pounding. "What's happening?" she said softly, although no one was paying any attention to her. She raised her voice. "What's happening to me?"

That caught the interest of a doctor who was walking past her here on the fourth floor of Luther Terry Memorial Hospital. "Miss?" he said.

"What's happening to me?" she asked again, holding her hands in front of her face, as if he, too, could see the blood on them. But, of course, they were dry—she knew that; she could *see* that. And yet visions of them glistening and red kept coming to her, but—

But her real hands were shaking, and the bloodied hands *never* shook; she somehow knew that.

The doctor looked at her. "Miss, are you a patient here?"

"No, no. Just visiting my brother, but—but *something's wrong.*"

"What's your name?" the doctor asked.

And she went to answer, but—

But *that* wasn't her name! And *that* wasn't where she lived! And *that* wasn't her hometown! Nikki felt herself teetering. She was still holding her hands up in front of her, and she fell against the doctor, her palms pressing into his chest.

More strange thoughts poured into her head. A knife slicing through fat and muscle. Being tackled in a football game—something that had never happened to her. A funeral— oh God, a funeral for her mother, who was still alive and well.

Her eyes had closed when she'd fallen forward, but she opened them now, looked down, and saw the doctor's little engraved plastic name badge, "J. Sturgess, M.D.," and she knew, even though she'd never seen him before, that the *J* was for Jurgen, and she suddenly also knew that M.D. didn't stand for "Medical Doctor," as she'd always thought, but rather for the Latin equivalent, *Medicinae Doctor*.

Just then, two nurses walked by, and she heard one of them spouting medical gobbledygook. Or it should have been gobbledygook; she shouldn't even have been able to say, a moment later, what words the nurse had used but . . .

But she'd heard it clearly: "Amitriptyline." And she knew how to spell it, and that it was a tricyclic antidepressant, and . . . *My God!* . . . she knew that "tricyclic" referred to the three rings of atoms in its chemical structure, and—

Her flattened hands balled into fists and pounded into the doctor's chest. "Make it stop!" she said. "Make it stop!"

The doctor—Jurgen, he played golf badly, had two daughters, was divorced, loved sushi—called out to the passing nurses. "Heather, Tamara—help, please."

One of the nurses—it was Tamara, she *knew* it was Tamara—turned and took hold of Nikki's shoulders, and the other one, Heather, picked up a wall-mounted phone and dialed four digits; if she was calling security . . .

How the hell did she know all this?

If she was calling security, she'd just tapped out 4-3-2-1.

Nikki half turned and pushed Tamara away, not because she didn't want help but because it welled up in her that it was wrong, wrong, wrong to touch a nurse during duty hours.

She felt dizzy again, though, and reached out for support, finding herself grabbing Dr. Sturgess's stethoscope, which was hanging loosely around his neck; it came free and she was suddenly falling backward. Heather surged in to catch her. "Is she stoned?" the nurse asked.

"I don't know," said Sturgess, but Nikki was incensed by the suggestion.

"I'm not stoned, damn it! What's happening? What's going on here? What did you *do?*"

Tamara moved closer. "Security is on its way, Dr. Sturgess. They're sending someone down from five; everyone normally on this floor is downstairs, helping guard the president."

The president.

And suddenly she saw *him,* Jerrison, his chest split wide, and her hands plunging into his torso, seizing his heart, squeezing it . . .

And that name again: *Eric Redekop.*

"Make it stop!" Nikki said. She moved her hands to the top of her head and pushed down, as if she could somehow squeeze the alien thoughts out. "Make it stop!"

"Tamara," said Sturgess, "get some secobarbital."

And *that,* Nikki found she knew, was a sedative.

"It'll be okay," Sturgess said to Nikki, his tone soothing. "It'll be fine."

She looked up and saw a middle-aged white man: lean, bald, bearded, wearing green surgical garb, and—

"Eric!" she called. "Eric!"

He continued to close the distance but had a puzzled expression on his face.

Sturgess turned and looked at Eric, too. "Eric! My God, how's—" He glanced at Nikki. "How's your, um, your special patient?"

Eric sounded weary. "We almost lost him, but he's stable now. Jono is closing."

"And you?" asked Sturgess, touching Eric's arm briefly. "How are you?"

"Dead," said Eric. "Exhausted." He shook his head. "What's the world coming to?"

Nikki was reeling. She'd never seen Eric before, but she knew exactly what he looked like, and—God!—even what he looked like naked. She knew him, this Eric, this man who—

—who was born fifty years ago, on April 11, in Fort Wayne, Indiana; who has an older brother named Carl; who plays a killer game of chess; who is allergic to penicillin; and who—yes!—had just performed surgery, saving the president's life.

"Eric," she said, "what's happening to me?"

"Miss," he replied, "do I know you?"

The words struck Nikki like a knife—like a *scalpel.* Surely he must know her, if she knew him. But he didn't. There was no hint of recognition on his face.

"I'm Nikki," she said, as if that should mean something to him.

"Hello," Eric said, sounding bewildered.

"I know you," Nikki said, imploringly. "I know you, Eric."

"I'm sorry, um, Nikki. I don't think we've ever met."

"Damn it," said Nikki. "This is crazy!"

"What's wrong with her?" Eric asked Sturgess.

Tamara was gesturing to someone; Nikki turned to see who. It was a uniformed security guard.

"No," she said. "No, I'm sorry I hit you, Jurgen."

Sturgess's eyebrows went up. "How did you know my name?"

How the hell *did* she know his name—or Eric's?

And then it came to her: she knew Jurgen's name because Eric knew it. They were old friends, although Eric found Jurgen a tad brusque and a bit too humorless for his taste. She knew . . . well, *everything* Eric knew.

"It's all right," Eric said, motioning for the guards to halt their approach. "Nurse Enright here will look after you. We'll get you help."

But that was even worse: suddenly a flood of memories came to Nikki: recalcitrant patients, patients screaming obscenities, a heavyset man throwing a punch, another man breaking down and crying—a cascade of disturbed patients Eric had dealt with over the years.

"I—I'm not like that," Nikki stammered out.

Eric narrowed his eyes. "Like what?"

Christ, she was a real-estate agent, not some fucking psychic. Her sister believed in that shit, but *she* didn't. This was impossible—she must be having a stroke, or hallucinations, or *something*.

"Come with me," said Heather Enright. "We'll get you taken care of."

"Eric, please!" implored Nikki.

But Eric yawned and stretched, and he and Jurgen started walking away, talking intently about the surgery Eric had just performed. She resisted Heather's attempts to propel her in the opposite direction until Eric had turned the corner and was out of sight.

But not out of mind.

CHAPTER 7

THE secretary of defense continued to study the wall-mounted deployment map; it had flickered off for a few seconds but now was back on. The aircraft carriers were mostly on station, and, as he watched, the *Reagan* moved a little closer to its goal.

"Mr. Secretary," said an analyst seated near him, looking up from her workstation, "we've lost the White House."

Peter Muilenburg frowned. "If primary comm is down, switch to aux four."

The analyst's voice was anguished. "No, sir, you don't understand. We've *lost* the White House. It's—it's *gone*. The bomb they found there just went off."

Muilenburg staggered backward, stumbling into a table. As he flailed to steady himself, he knocked a large binder onto the floor. His eyes stung, and he tasted vomit.

An aide burst into the room. "Mr. Secretary, they're asking if we should evacuate the Pentagon as a precaution."

Muilenburg attempted to speak but found he couldn't. He gripped the edge of the table, trying to keep on his feet. The Oval Office, the Roosevelt Room, the Press Room, the

Cabinet Room, the State Dining Room, the Lincoln Bedroom, and so much more . . . could they really be gone? *God . . .*

"Mr. Secretary?" the aide said. "Should we evacuate?"

A deep, shuddering breath; an attempt to regain his equilibrium. "Not yet," Muilenburg replied, but it was doubtless too soft for the aide to hear. He tried again. "Not yet." He forced himself to stand up straight. "Have them continue to sweep for bombs here, but we've got a job to do." He looked again at the deployment map and found himself quaking with fury. "And no one can say they don't have it coming."

BESSIE Stilwell looked down at her wrinkled hand; the skin was white, loose, and translucent. She was gently holding the hand of her adult son, which was smoother and not quite as pale.

Bessie had often imagined a scene like this: the two of them in a hospital room, one lying in bed and the other providing comfort. But she'd always expected it to be her in the bed, waiting to die, and Mike sitting next to her, doing his duty. After all, she was eighty-seven and he was fifty-two; that was the way the scene was supposed to be cast, their parts ordained by their ages.

But she was well, more or less. Oh, there was a constant background of aches and pains, her hearing was poor, and she used a cane to walk. But Mike should have been vigorous. Instead, he lay there, on his back, tubes in his arms, a respirator covering his nose and mouth.

His father had made it to sixty before having the heart attack that took his life. At least the coronary Mike had suffered hadn't killed him—although it had come close. The stress of a Washington job had doubtless been a contributing factor; he should have stayed in Mississippi.

Mike had no family of his own—at least, not anymore; his marriage had ended over a decade ago. He was a workaholic, Jane had said when she left him—or, at least, that was the story Mike had conveyed to Bessie.

"Thanks for coming, Mom," Mike said, each word an effort for him.

She nodded. "Of course, baby."

Baby. She had always called him that. It had been five decades since he'd been as helpless as one, and yet he was again.

She moved over to his bed and leaned in—painfully, her back and knees hurting as she did so—and kissed him on the top of his bald head.

"I'll come back tomorrow," she added.

"Thanks," he said again, and closed his eyes.

Bessie regarded him for another half minute; he looked like his father had at the same age. Then she started the slow walk out of the hospital room and down the long corridor, heading toward the elevator.

Her eyesight wasn't as good as it used to be, but she read the signs on the doors, noting landmarks so that she could easily find Mike's room again tomorrow; she'd gone down the wrong corridor earlier and, when every step hurt, that was the sort of thing she didn't want to have happen again. There were a lot of people further down the corridor, but the stretch she was in now was empty. As she passed a door labeled "Observation Gallery," the lights in the corridor suddenly went off, startling her. Emergency lighting soon came on, but she was terrified that the elevators would be off; she was on the third floor, and doubted she could manage that many stairs.

She continued to shuffle along, and after a short time the overhead lights spluttered back to life. Up ahead, she saw the elevator door open, several people get off, and several more get on; everything seemed to be back to normal.

She finally made it to the elevator and rode down to the lobby. To her surprise, there were uniformed hospital security guards and several men in dark blue suits there, but they seemed more interested in who was trying to come into the hospital than who was leaving. She headed out into the cool air, and—

—and the world had changed since she'd entered earlier today. Thousands of car horns were honking, the sidewalk outside the hospital was packed with people, there was the smell of smoke in the air. A fire, perhaps? A plane crash? Reagan was only a short distance away . . .

Numerous TV crews crowded the sidewalk. Near her, a

reporter—a colored man wearing a tan trench coat—was holding a microphone, waiting for a signal, it seemed, from another man who was balancing a camera on his shoulder.

It came to her that the reporter's name was Lonny Hendricks—although why she knew that, she didn't know. But, well, this *was* Washington, and stories from here often got national exposure; she supposed she must have seen him on the news back in Mississippi at some point.

She'd had trouble finding her way inside the hospital—the corridors took odd bends. But now that she was outside, she found herself feeling confident. Her hotel was *that* way, down New Hampshire Avenue, and—well, if she continued up there, she'd run into Dupont Circle, although . . .

Although she didn't know why she knew that, either; she hadn't had cause to go that way yet. She supposed she must have seen it while flipping through a tourist guidebook.

She slowly made her way over to the taxi stand, wondering what all the panic, all the commotion, all the *noise,* was about.

SETH Jerrison opened his eyes. He was lying on his back, looking up at a ceiling with fluorescent tubes behind frosted panels; one of the tubes was strobing in an irritating fashion. He attempted to speak, but his throat was bone-dry.

A face loomed in: black, perhaps fifty, gray hair, kind eyes. "Mr. President? Mr. President? Can you tell me what day it is?"

Part of Seth recognized that this was a test of competency— but another part wanted his own questions answered. "Where am I?" he croaked out.

"Luther Terry Memorial Hospital," said the man.

His throat was still parched. "Water."

The man looked at someone else, and a few seconds later, he had a cup of ice chips in his hand. He moved it over and tipped it so that a few went into Seth's mouth. After they'd melted, Seth asked, "Who are you?"

"I'm Dr. Mark Griffin. I'm the CEO here."

Seth nodded slightly. "What happened?"

The man lifted his eyebrows, wrinkling his forehead in the process. "You were shot, Mr. President. The bullet ruptured the pericardium—the sac that contains the heart—bruised the right atrium, and clipped the superior vena cava. A centimeter to the left and, well, we wouldn't be having this conversation."

Seth wanted to speak again, but it took him several seconds to find the strength. "Anyone else hurt?"

"Not by gunfire. Some members of the crowd were injured in the panic that ensued—broken bones, bloody noses—but nothing life-threatening." Griffin paused for a moment, then: "Sir, forgive us for waking you up. Normally, we'd keep you under as long as possible while you heal, but, well, you *are* the president, and you need to know. First let me assure you that no one was hurt—the First Lady, as you know, is in Oregon. She's fine, and so is everyone else. But there's been an explosion at the White House. The bomb was spotted before it went off, and they got everyone out."

Seth's head swam. He'd long lived in northern California; he'd felt the ground literally shift beneath his feet before—but this was more disorienting, more terrifying: the whole world shifting, changing, *crumbling*. His heart pounded, every beat a knife thrust.

"They're relocating most of the White House staff to a facility in Virginia, I'm told," said Griffin. Mount Weather was an underground city there, built during the Cold War; there were contingency plans for running most of the executive branch from it.

"Take me . . . there," said Seth.

"Not yet, sir. It's not safe to move you. But your chief of staff will be at the Virginia facility soon. He can be your eyes and ears there; we'll get you a secure line to him." A pause. "Mr. President, how do you feel?"

Seth closed his eyes; everything went pink as the overhead light filtered through his eyelids. He tried to breathe, tried to hold on to his sanity, tried not to let go—not to let go *again*. At last, he managed to speak. "Were . . . were my . . . injuries . . . life-threatening?"

"Yes, sir, to be honest. We almost lost you on the operating table."

Seth forced his eyes open. To one side, he saw Susan Dawson and another Secret Service agent whose name he didn't know. He felt weak, still parched, emotional agony layered atop all the physical pain. "Did you . . . open my chest?"

"Yes, sir, we did."

"Did my heart stop?"

"Sir, yes. For a time."

"They say . . . if you're about to die . . . your life . . . flashes in front of your eyes."

Griffin, still looming over him, nodded. "I've heard that, sir, yes."

Seth was silent for a few moments, trying to sort it all out, trying to decide if he wanted to confide in this man—but it *had* been the damnedest thing. "And, well," he said at last, "something like that happened to me."

Griffin's tone was neutral. "Oh?"

"Yes. Except . . ." He looked at the doctor for a moment, then turned his head toward the windows. "Except it wasn't *my* life that I saw."

"What do you mean, sir?"

"Someone else's memories," said the president. "Not mine."

Griffin said nothing.

"You don't believe me," Seth said, with effort.

"All sorts of weird things can happen when the brain is starved for oxygen, Mr. President," Griffin said.

Seth briefly closed his eyes—but the images were still there. "That's . . . not it. I . . . have someone else's . . . memories."

Griffin was quiet for a moment, then said, "Well, you're in luck, sir. As it happens, we've got one of the world's top memory experts here—a fellow from Canada. I can ask him—"

Griffin's BlackBerry must have vibrated because he fished it out and looked at the caller ID. "Speak of the devil," he said to Jerrison, then into the phone: "Yes, Professor Singh? Um, yes, yes. Wait." He lowered the handset and turned to Susan Dawson. "Is your middle name Marie?"

Susan's eyebrows went up. "Yes."

"Yes, that's right," Griffin said into the phone. "What? Um, okay. Sure, I guess. I'll tell her. Bye."

Griffin put the BlackBerry away and turned to face Susan. "Our resident memory expert would like to speak to you up in his office."

CHAPTER 8

ERIC Redekop continued down the hospital corridor, accompanied by Dr. Jurgen Sturgess. They were both still a bit rattled from their encounter with the distraught woman named Nikki, and Eric was exhausted from the hours of performing surgery on the president. Sturgess soon headed off in another direction, leaving Eric walking alone. In the middle of the corridor was the nurses' station, and he smiled as he saw Janis Falconi there. She was thirty-two, and she was a knockout: leggy, stacked, with long straight platinum blonde hair and icy blue eyes.

He normally saw her only in her nurse's uniform, but he'd run into her on the street once during the summer when she'd been wearing a tank top, and he'd been surprised to discover she had a large, intricate tattoo of a striped tiger stretching its way up her left arm onto her shoulder. As a doctor, Eric had an instinctive dislike for tattoos, but this one had been so elaborate, with such subtle shading and vibrant coloring, he'd had to admire it; he admired it even more when Janis told him that she herself had done the original art it had been made from.

Of course, right now, he could see no sign of the tattoo as he approached, but his memories of her on that summer day, arms and shoulders exposed, came to the fore, and—

And—*ouch!*

Getting a tattoo hurt!

And getting one as elaborate as Janis's *really* hurt.

Eric found himself looking for a way to steady himself. An empty gurney had been pushed against the corridor wall next to him; he grabbed one of its tubular metal railings, and—

And he couldn't take his eyes off Janis.

She hadn't looked up yet, hadn't noticed him, but—

But he found himself reliving that summer's day—that *August* day, standing outside Filomena, a restaurant he'd never heard of or even noticed, he was sure, but he *knew* that was its name.

His grip on the tubular railing tightened.

Cute.

Yes, yes, *she* was—very. But it wasn't just the word "cute" that had popped into Eric's brain. No, no, no, there was a pronoun in front of it.

He's cute.

And, although Eric had thought this before about some babies or toddlers, this wasn't a reference to a tyke with a teddy bear. It was about a man, a grown man. And yet Eric was, as he himself liked to say, flamingly heterosexual. But this thought was about an adult man with a bald pate and a graying beard, and—

Oh!

It was a thought about *himself.*

Yes, he kept his beard neat with a barber's electric razor, and, sure, he did try to hit the gym a couple of times a week, but he was no narcissist; he didn't think of himself as cute. In fact, if anything, he thought he was kind of funny-looking with beady eyes and a nose so short it might fairly be called "pug."

And, hey, he's checking me out.

Eric was so discombobulated that he was about to turn on his heel and head back the other way when Janis looked up and smiled a huge, radiant smile at him, and—

It's her, he realized. *It's what* she *thought about* me, *back on that August day, but—*

But *how?*

The pain of the tattoo.

A house—small, cramped.

A dachshund waddling along.

Pink cross-country skis.

He continued walking toward her, drawn to her.

He knew how much she made. Knew her birth date. Knew all kinds of things.

"Hello, Jan . . . iss." He paused, having to force the second syllable out, it coming to him in a flash that only people at work ever called her "Janis." Everyone else in her life called her just "Jan."

"Dr. Redekop," she said. "Good to see you."

His eyes dropped—not to her breasts, although they were certainly noteworthy, but to her shoulder; he was thinking of the tattoo, and—

And the bruise . . .

Not bruising from having the tattoo made, but—

My God!

But bruising from . . . from *yesterday.*

She saw where his gaze had gone, and she turned a little, as if to hide her upper arm from his sight, but then she must have realized that her nurse's smock covered it completely, and yet, when she turned back to him, it was a long moment before she met his eyes again.

"Um," he said, "you look well." And as soon as the words were out, he realized it was an odd thing to say, but—

But his mind was filling now with thoughts that—God!—that *must* be hers.

He'd never believed in telepathy, or mind reading, or any of that garbage. Jesus!

But, no, wait. It wasn't that; not quite. She was looking at him quizzically now, and he had no idea what she was currently thinking. But as soon as he thought about the day he'd run into her in the tank top, memories of *that* came to him—from *her* point of view.

And other things kept coming to him, too—information about patients in this wing; details about some online game called EVE; a bit from *The Colbert Report,* which he never watched; and—yes, yes—more thoughts, more *memories,* about him. About the first time they'd met. He didn't remember the specific day, but *she* did; it was her first day on the new job here, nine months ago. It had been—ah, yes, now that he thought about it, he *did* remember . . . or *she* did. All the decorations: it had been Valentine's Day.

And she'd thought, after meeting him, of this bald, thin man, "Slap a British accent on him, and he's everything I've been fantasizing about since I was fifteen." She liked older men. She liked Patrick Stewart and Sean Connery and—

And Eric Redekop.

He'd always liked Janis, but he'd had no idea—none!—that she felt that way about him, and . . .

And she was speaking, he realized, and he'd been so lost in thought he hadn't heard what she'd said. "Sorry. Um, could you repeat that?"

She gave him another quizzical look, then: "I said, that was quite a surprise when the power went off, wasn't it? I didn't think that could happen here."

"Oh, yeah. Yes, it was." He was only about three feet away from her now, and he could see that her makeup was perfect— a little eyeliner, a little blue eye shadow—and her eyebrows had been recently and expertly plucked; in fact, he had a flash of seeing herself as she'd leaned toward a bathroom mirror, and he recalled a constellation of pain-points as she'd done the deed.

But thinking about her eyes brought forth other memories— memories of her *crying*—crying as someone screamed profanity at her. It was so shocking, so *wrong,* that Eric instinctively stepped backward.

"Janis," he said, this time getting the full name out without hesitation—although he realized at once that it wasn't the *full* name; her full name actually was Janis Louise Falconi, and Falconi was her *married* name; her maiden name was Amundsen, and—

And he had to finish the sentence he'd begun! "Janis, um, are you okay?"

"As well as can be expected," she said. "Why do you ask?"

"No reason," he replied, but he found himself backing further away.

CHAPTER 9

SUSAN Dawson had an odd feeling as she came into the room on the third floor, and it took her a moment to identify it; it was something she'd heard of but never experienced. The incongruity of having *déjà vu* for the first time made her head spin.

And it was indeed that: this room, this little office tucked away inside a hospital she hadn't visited before, seemed familiar. It wasn't just that many institutional offices looked alike—neutral colors, venetian blinds, tiled floors, fluorescent lights. No, there was more to it. The desk, the top of which seemed to be made of pine and was a distinctive kidney shape, looked . . .

She shook her head slightly, but . . .

But there was no denying it: it looked *exactly as she remembered it.*

And yet she'd never seen it before. She *couldn't* have.

Oh. Maybe she'd seen one like it in the IKEA catalog; they sold lots of stuff with pine veneers. But the silver-gray roller chair also looked familiar—as did the blue tennis racquet leaning against the wall, and the trophy, there. She knew what it was for, even though she couldn't read the engraving on it from this distance: it was the top prize from the recent LT tennis tournament.

And the wide bookcase, with its dark green shelves and rows of journals with identical spines, somehow were familiar, too. A memory came to her, and this one she did recognize as her own: her anger many years ago when *National Geographic* had done a special issue on oceans and had given the magazine a blue cover and spine instead of the traditional yellow one, breaking up the lovely set she'd been collecting ever since her grandfather had started sending her gift subscriptions when she was a little girl. And here, in this office, one of the journal volumes had a green spine instead of the wine-colored ones all the others had.

She looked at the wall. On it were three diplomas, including one from McGill University; she was pleased with herself for knowing that it was in Montreal. There was also a framed photograph of a brown-skinned woman and three similarly complexioned children, and—

And the woman's name was Devi, and the children were Harpreet, Amneet, and Gursiman.

But she'd never met them before. She was sure of that. And yet—

And yet *memories* of them were pouring into her consciousness. Birthday parties, vacations, Harpreet getting in trouble at school for swearing, and—

"Are you Agent Dawson?" The voice was richly accented.

She spun on her heel and found herself facing a Sikh wearing a jade green turban and a pale blue lab coat. "Ranjip," she said, the name blurting out of her.

His brown eyes narrowed slightly. "Have we met?" He looked to be perhaps fifty; his beard had wisps of gray in it.

"Um," said Susan, and "ah," and then, at last, "no—no, I don't think so. But . . . but you *are* Ranjip Singh, right?"

The man smiled, and Susan belatedly realized that he was quite handsome. "As my son would say—"

"'That's my name; don't wear it out.'" The words had come to Susan in a flash. She found her hand going to her mouth, startled. "I, um—he *does* say that, doesn't he?"

Singh smiled again, his friendly eyes crinkling. "So do lots of kids his age. He also likes the one about the chicken going halfway across the road to—"

"To lay it on the line," said Susan. Her heart was pounding. "What in hell is going on?" She found herself taking a half step backward. "I don't know you. I don't know your son. I've never been in this room before."

Singh nodded and gestured at the office's single chair—the familiar and yet unfamiliar silver-gray roller. "Won't you have a seat?"

She normally would have stayed standing—it was a stronger position. But she was feeling unsteady, so she took him up on his offer. For his part, Singh leaned against the dark brown bookcase with the green shelves. "As you say," he said "something is going on. And I do fear it may be my fault."

Susan felt her eyebrows going up. "You were doing an experiment here," she said. "Well, not here; down the corridor, in room, um, 324. It's—damn, it's too technical; I don't know what you're talking about."

"I haven't said anything."

Susan stopped. "No, you haven't. What in hell is happening?"

Singh blew out air. "I'd initially thought just my patient and I had been affected, but I see *you* have been affected, too. I didn't anticipate that. And it seems you can access my memories?"

"'Abso-freakin'-lootely,' as your son would say." She paused for a second. "God, it's *strange.*" And then it hit her. "So, can you read *my* memories?"

"No," said Singh. "Not me. My patient—he's accessing your memories. That's how I knew you were here with Dr. Griffin; he told me."

"What about you? Are you . . . how did you put it? Are you accessing someone?"

"Yes. I know his name, but it's no one I've ever met."

"Is it someone here at the hospital?"

"Yes. A surgeon named Lucius Jono."

"But—but how did this happen?" Susan asked.

"I was doing an experiment, attempting to modify a young man's memories. The lights went off—which should *never* happen in a hospital—then there was a power surge of some sort."

"More than that," said Susan. "There was an electromagnetic pulse."

"Ah," said Singh. "Perhaps that explains it. In any event, *this* seems to be the result."

Susan looked around, getting her bearings. "Room 324 is just down this hall, isn't it? I was right next door, in the observation gallery above one of the operating rooms. I was maybe a dozen feet from you when the lights went off while you were doing your experiment."

"Yes," said Singh. "So I guess people within a certain radius were affected."

Susan felt her eyes go wide. "But the president—God! The president was even closer, but down below—maybe eight or ten feet down, on the second floor."

Ranjip nodded solemnly. "Yes. I know all about the operation—because Dr. Jono, the person I'm linked to, was there; he was one of the people assisting in the procedure."

"Shit! If someone's reading the president's memories—Christ, national security goes right out the window." Susan ran out the door and down the corridor to the third-floor nurses' station. She whipped out her ID. "Susan Dawson, Secret Service. I want this building locked down immediately. No one gets in or out."

The stocky nurse looked flabbergasted. "I—I don't have the authority . . ."

"Then get me Dr. Griffin—*stat!*"

The nurse scooped up a telephone handset.

Susan caught a movement out of the corner of her eye. She wheeled. A broad-shouldered white man was walking briskly toward the elevator. "Freeze!" she shouted.

The man had doubtless heard what Susan had said to the nurse, but now was pretending not to hear. He reached the elevator station and pressed the down button.

"I said *freeze!*" Susan snapped. "Secret Service!" She unholstered her SIG Sauer P229.

The man turned; he was perhaps thirty-five, with light brown hair and round rimless glasses, and was wearing a blue business suit. "I'm just a visitor here," he said.

"No one is leaving," Susan said.

The man at the elevators spread his arms. "Please. I've got a crucial meeting across town. I *have* to be there."

Susan shook her head. "No way. Step away from the elevator."

The phone on the nurse's desk rang; the nurse picked it up. "Yes, ah—good. Hang on." She offered the handset to Susan, but Susan was holding her pistol with both hands and had it trained on the man.

"Is that a speakerphone? Put it on."

The nurse shook her head. "No."

Susan frowned, then motioned for the nurse to give her the handset. She used her left hand to hold it while keeping the gun in her right. "Dr. Griffin? It's Susan Dawson. I want this hospital locked down."

"I can't do that," Griffin said. "There's been an explosion only a mile from here, for God's sake. We're an emergency-services facility."

"They evacuated the White House in time."

"Regardless," said Griffin. "There's been a terrorist attack. We need to be open."

"*Mister* Griffin, the president is in danger. Lock this building down!"

Just then, an orderly pushing a gurney crossed in front of Susan's line of sight—and line of fire. The elevator doors opened, and the man who'd been standing by them hurried inside, just as the orderly was eclipsing him from Susan's view. Susan dropped the phone and started to run, but the elevator's door closed before she got to it.

"Where are the stairs?" Susan barked over her shoulder.

"There!" the nurse shouted, pointing.

Susan found the door, pushed it open, and pounded down the two flights, almost colliding with a startled doctor who was climbing up.

The elevator must have stopped on the second floor on the way down because she arrived in the lobby just as it did. A portly woman was waddling out of the car, followed by the man she'd seen upstairs.

"Freeze!" Susan called.

The woman did just that, but the man still kept walking.

Susan moved herself between him and the doors leading outside and pointed her pistol at him. "I said freeze!"

People in the lobby screamed, and another man tried to make it out the front door, running toward it. But the automatic door didn't slide away, and he collided with the glass.

A deep voice came over the intercom: Dr. Griffin. "Attention, everyone. Attention, please. We have a situation here in the hospital, and I'm locking all the doors."

The guy who'd come out of the elevator mouthed the word, "Fuck."

Susan strode over to him. "Come with me."

"There's seven figures on the line here," he said imploringly. "I have to get to that meeting."

"No, you don't. What you have to do is precisely what I tell you to do." She pulled out her handcuffs and snapped them on his wrists.

CHAPTER 10

THE man who had tried to escape the hospital turned out to be a lawyer named Orrin Gillett. Susan Dawson took him to a room on the third floor. There was a TV in the room, and she put it on and turned to CNN. She'd hoped for an update on the attempted assassination, but the current story was about the destruction of the White House. Susan watched, mesmerized, horrified; she'd spent most of the last three years in that historic building.

The camera was panning left and right. The mansion reduced to rubble. The two wings gutted by fire. Billowing smoke.

Susan fought back tears. Gillett looked on in shock, too, his jaw hanging loosely open. The voice-over was talking about echoes of 9/11, and Susan flashed back to how stunned and terrified she'd felt when the Twin Towers had collapsed. Back then, she hadn't yet ever held a gun, hadn't yet ever fired a shot, hadn't yet been trained to be cool and calm during a crisis. But she felt no better able to handle this now than she had in 2001; it was just as overwhelming, just as heartbreaking.

At last, the ruins of the White House disappeared, replaced

by the lined face of a news anchor, himself looking as devastated as Susan felt. She forced herself back to the here and now, back to her duty. She got a security guard to lock Gillett in the room, then she half walked, half staggered down the hall to see Professor Singh in his office. "Your research subjects," she said as she entered, more of Singh's memories bubbling up in her consciousness, "suffer from post-traumatic stress disorder."

Singh was seated in his roller chair. "That's right. They have terrible flashbacks, mostly related to events from whatever war they were in."

Singh's patients weren't the only ones suffering from post-traumatic stress, she thought: the whole damned world had to be experiencing flashbacks today. Still, information about Singh's technique came to her. "And you were trying to erase those bad memories?"

"Yes."

"But the . . . the *effect* wasn't well contained, was it?"

"Something happened," said Singh with an amiable shrug. "I honestly don't know what. When the electricity came back on, there was an enormous power surge through the equipment. And these—these *linkages*—are the result."

"Terrorists blew up the White House," Susan said. "That's what caused the electromagnetic pulse I mentioned."

Singh sagged back in his chair and his bearded jaw dropped. "The White House is . . . gone?"

It was still almost impossible to contemplate. "Yes," Susan said softly.

Singh lifted a questioning hand, but it was shaking badly. "A nuke?"

Susan struggled to stay focused, stay in command. "No. Same kind of bomb as in Chicago, SF, and Philly. Non-nuclear and with a very limited E1 component to the pulse. They disrupt electronics but don't do much permanent damage. The pulse is just a side effect; the real destruction is done by the intense heat."

Singh's lab had no window, but he was looking in the direction of where the White House had been, as if trying to visualize it. "How . . . how many died?"

"Fortunately, this time the bomb was discovered in time to evacuate the building."

"Still," said Singh. He shook his head. "I'd thought I was starting to get over the shock of what happened in Chicago, but . . ." He looked up at her, his brown eyes moist. "It never ends, does it?"

"No," said Susan softly. She gave Singh—and herself—a moment. Then, gently, she said, "It looks like President Jerrison has been affected by your experiment, too. He almost died on the operating table, and he claims someone else's life flashed before his eyes. He should be briefed about this. Come with me."

"To see the president?" asked Singh, sounding astonished at the notion.

"Yes." Singh shakily got to his feet, and they exited his office. Susan would normally take the stairs for a single flight, but Singh was clearly still in shock; at one point, he reached out to steady himself against the wall. They took the elevator down, and, when they came out on the corridor on two, she caught sight of Darryl Hudkins's shaved head. He was now standing guard outside the president's door.

"You okay?" Susan asked, once they'd closed the distance. Darryl's face was slack and his eyes wider than normal.

"I'm—I'm holding up."

"Who is in there?" she asked, tilting her head toward the nearest door.

"Just Michaelis, the president, and a nurse," said Darryl. "Dr. Griffin has gone off to deal with the lockdown."

Susan nodded and went to push the door open, but Darryl held out his arm, blocking Professor Singh.

"Forgive me, sir," Darryl said, rallying now, "but are you carrying a knife?"

"A kirpan, yes," Singh replied.

Darryl shook his head. "You can't take it into the president's room."

Susan was mortified—first, that the issue had come up, and, second, because it hadn't even occurred to her; she'd been about to let an armed man approach the president.

Singh's voice had regained its steadiness. "I didn't catch your name."

"Darryl Hudkins."

"Darryl," Singh said, "the kirpan is a defensive weapon."

He opened his lab coat and revealed the cloth belt he was wearing; the ceremonial knife was attached to it. "It is an instrument of *ahimsa*—of nonviolence; a tool to prevent violence from being done to a defenseless person when all other means have failed." He looked directly at Hudkins. "You'll forgive me, but given the current circumstances, I rather suspect I could do no worse than the Secret Service already has in protecting the president."

Susan thought about the kirpan, leafing through Singh's memories related to the artifact—and it came to her. He would never, ever use it to hurt anyone. "Let him pass," she said to Darryl.

"If you say so, ma'am," Darryl replied—but he moved a hand to his holster, just in case.

SETH Jerrison was resting with his eyes closed. He'd insisted that Jasmine—the First Lady—stay in Oregon today. She'd wanted to rush back, but the last time terrorists had attacked Washington, on 9/11, they'd targeted multiple buildings; the current attack might not be over.

Seth opened his eyes when he heard the door to the room swinging inward on its hinges. A white Secret Service agent named Roger Michaelis was in the room already, as was Sheila, a stern-looking Asian nurse. Coming in was the leader of his Secret Service detail, Susan Dawson, and accompanying her was someone Jerrison had never seen before.

"Mr. President," Susan said, "this is Professor Ranjip Singh. He's a memory researcher, and, well, he thinks he has an explanation—sort of—for what happened to you."

"Good," Seth said weakly. "Because it didn't end when my near-death experience did. I keep remembering things that couldn't possibly be my own memories."

Singh stepped closer. "Forgive me, Mr. President, but if I may: what sort of things?"

"Just now, I was recalling a basketball game."

"Watching one on TV?" asked Singh. "Or as a spectator in a stadium?"

"No, no." It took Seth a second to rally the strength to go

on. "Playing basketball. Me and three other men." He paused; his body just wanted to sleep. "But it wasn't *my* memory."

"Then what brought it to mind?" asked Singh, sounding intrigued.

"I don't know," Seth replied, still struggling to get each word out. But then he lifted his eyebrows. "Oh, wait. I *do* know. I'd been thinking about previous times surgery had been performed on a president."

"Yes?" said Singh.

"Last time was in 2010." He gathered some strength, then: "Obama got an elbow in the face while playing basketball with friends. Needed twelve stitches on his upper lip."

Singh frowned. "I don't remember that."

Nurse Sheila spoke up. "I do. It was done by the White House Medical Unit, under a local anesthetic."

Seth nodded ever so slightly. "Yes. Still . . ."

"Still," said Singh, "you were thinking of that, and that led you to think of the last time *you* played basketball. Except that the memory that came wasn't your own."

"Exactly," said Seth. "Explain that." He'd meant for his voice to have a challenging tone, but he was still too weak to speak in anything much above a whisper.

"I will try," said Singh. "But—forgive me, Mr. President, I'm . . . words fail me. I never thought I'd be speaking to the president of the United States!"

"It's all right," said Seth.

Singh smiled. "I know, but . . . again, forgive me. I have to push a little here, and, ah, I'm not comfortable doing that—not with you."

"It's fine," Seth said.

Singh closed his eyes for a moment, nodded, and went on. "Very well. These three men you saw—can you describe them?"

"Twenties. One was fat and bald—shaved bald—and the other two were thin and had short hair."

"Forgive me, sir, but do you really mean 'thin'? Or do you just mean they were of normal weight?"

"Sorry. Normal weight."

"And their hair color?"

"Dark, I suppose."

"You suppose?"

"Dark."

"And eye color?"

"I didn't notice."

Singh paused for a moment, then: "So, blue then, like yours?"

"Maybe."

"Any other details? Clothing, perhaps?"

"T-shirts on all three. One was wearing green track pants; another, red gym shorts; and the third—the fat guy—cutoff jeans."

"And they were playing basketball?"

"Well, shooting hoops."

"And you were participating?"

Seth rested for a moment, then: "Yes, but . . ."

"What?"

"I haven't played basketball for, God, forty years. I wrecked the tendons in my left foot, taking a tumble down a staircase at college."

"Ah," said Singh. "Do you know the other players' names?"

"No. Never met them, and—*hmmm*. Well, *that's* strange." He let himself breathe for a moment, then: "Yes, now that I think about it—now that you ask—I *do* know their names, but . . ."

Singh prodded him with a "Yes?"

Seth looked at Susan for a moment. "Well, they're unusual names. Deshawn, Lamarr, and, um—Kalil. But . . ." He fell silent. Singh was looking at him expectantly, but, damn it all, he'd put his foot in it by calling them "unusual names."

Singh was all over it. "You mean, they're unusual names for white people. They're common enough African-American names, though."

"Well, yes."

"But you saw white people?"

Seth managed a small nod.

Singh's eyebrows climbed toward his turban. "Fascinating. Mr. President, do you know the name of the person whose memories you're accessing?"

"No."

"Think about it."

"Nothing is coming to me."

Susan and the other Secret Service agent were watching intently, as was Sheila the nurse.

"All right," said Singh. "Try this: everyone is made fun of at school. My last name is Singh, and the students at my school in Toronto called me 'Singh-Song.' And my first name is Ranjip, but the mean boys at high school always called me 'rancid'—although I took some pleasure in the fact that some of them didn't even know what that meant. What did they call you?"

The president frowned. "Fairyson."

Singh tried to suppress a smile. "Any other names you were called?"

"No."

"Nothing is coming to you?"

"Nothing, but . . ."

"Yes?"

"'Firstman' just popped into my mind. Like 'First Man,' but all run together."

"'Firstman,'" repeated Singh, excitedly. "Adam, no? Does the name Kadeem Adams mean anything to you?"

"No. Oh, wait. Yes—yes! Sure, Kadeem Adams—that's him."

"Well, that was easy," said Singh, turning to Susan. "He's reading the memories of my patient, Private Kadeem Adams."

"Is that the guy who is reading me?" Susan asked.

"Yes," said Singh.

"So he's not the person reading the president?"

"What's that?" said Seth. "Somebody's reading *my* memories?"

Susan nodded. "We think it's possible, sir. We've locked down the hospital because of it. Don't worry—no one is getting in or out." She turned to Singh. "But it isn't this Adams who is reading the president, right?"

"He certainly has given no indication of that," said Singh. "We don't have a lot of data yet, but it seems the links are not reciprocal. Rather, they appear to form a chain. The president is reading Kadeem Adams; Kadeem is reading you, Agent Dawson; you are reading me; and I'm reading Dr. Lucius Jono."

"So then this Jono is the one reading the president?" Susan asked.

"Let us hope," said Singh. "We don't know how long the chain is, or whether it closes into a circle. However, from what I've seen, the linkages are first-order, shall we say? That is, you can remember what *I* remember, but you can't remember through me to what Dr. Jono remembers, isn't that right?"

Susan frowned. "Yes, I guess that *is* the case. I can't recall any of this Jono person's memories."

"And, Mr. President, is it safe to say that you recall what Private Adams recalls, but not what Agent Dawson remembers, even though she is the one Private Adams is reading?"

Jerrison considered, then: "Yes, that's right. Even looking at you, Susan, I can't recall your memories."

"Okay, good," said Singh. "At least we don't have a cascade." A pause. "I would like to speak to Private Adams and see how accurate the president's recollections are. If you'll excuse me for a few minutes . . ."

Susan nodded, and she moved aside so he could leave the room.

Seth was grateful for a chance to stop talking—it was all so much to take in, and he was more exhausted than he'd ever felt in his life. Sheila came over and adjusted one of the drip bags attached to his arm. He looked over at Susan and saw her touch a finger to her earpiece. "Copy that," she said at last. She then looked at Seth. "I'm sorry, Mr. President. We didn't tell you yet that the would-be assassin is dead. But they've positively ID'd the body now, and—" Seth saw her glance at Roger Michaelis, who looked shocked; he'd presumably just heard the same thing Susan had through his own earpiece.

"Yes?" Seth prodded.

"It was Gordon Danbury," Susan said. "He was one of us— a Secret Service agent."

CHAPTER 11

ONCE he'd left nurse Janis Falconi, Eric Redekop went by his office and got his Bose noise-canceling headphones. He'd originally bought them for long flights, but now used them at the hospital when he needed to sleep. Eric liked to sleep on his side, and he'd thought there'd be no comfortable way to wear the headphones when doing so, but the hospital had a supply of donut-shaped pillows for people with broken tailbones or hemorrhoids to sit on, and he'd found that the hole nicely accommodated the large earpiece.

He headed down to the staff sleep room on the first floor, turned the headphones on, turned off the lights in the room, and lay down on one of the cots. He'd hoped to fall right to sleep, but . . .

But being here, on his side, in a semifetal position, made him think of . . .

. . . of lying next to a man like this, turned away from him, trying to pretend the man wasn't there, and—

And it was Tony Falconi, Janis's husband. She lay like this every night, trying to ignore him, hoping he wouldn't touch her, wouldn't initiate the ninety seconds of pounding away that was his idea of sex, wouldn't leave her unfulfilled.

Damn it, damn it, damn it. He did *not* want to know any of this. He had no idea what the hell was going on, but—

But there had to be a rational explanation.

He was so tired—the surgery on the president had been grueling.

The headphones were doing their job—eliminating the actual background noise of the hospital. But the background noise of Janis Falconi's memories continued unabated, and there didn't seem to be anything he could do to shut them out.

SUSAN Dawson had to sit down. She'd known Gordon Danbury for years. He'd been a military sharpshooter in Afghanistan, and, upon his return to the States, had decided to try his luck with the Secret Service. That meant taking the ten-week Criminal Investigator Training Program at the Federal Law Enforcement Training Center in Glynco, Georgia, followed by the seventeen-week Special Agent Training Course at the James J. Rowley Training Center, just outside DC.

Susan had first met Danbury at Rowley; active agents spent two weeks every two months there honing their skills. He'd seemed like a nice enough guy although he didn't drink. Still, he was buff with a great face. Or, she supposed, he'd *had* a great face; apparently, he'd landed on it when he fell in the elevator shaft, which was why it took so long for anyone to recognize him.

She looked over at Agent Michaelis; he'd known Danbury, too. He was shaking his head slowly back and forth as if he couldn't believe the news.

President Jerrison was lying flat on his back, tubes going into his arm from drip bags, a small oxygen feed tucked into his nostrils. "Danbury," Jerrison said. "I don't think I knew him."

"You wouldn't normally have run into him, sir," Susan said. "He was one of the sharpshooters deployed on the roof of the White House."

"The bomb," Jerrison said.

Susan nodded. "Yes, it seems likely he was the one who

planted it. He'd have had easy access to the White House roof—although how he got a large metallic device through security to get up there, I don't know." She listened to her earpiece again, then: "Anyway, they're sending investigators to his house; see what they can find."

They were all silent for a time, until Agent Michaelis spoke. "This is crazy."

Susan thought he was referring to Danbury. "Yeah. You think you know a guy . . ."

"Not that," said Michaelis, "although that's crazy, too. I mean this memory stuff."

"Are you experiencing any outside memories?" Susan asked.

"Me?" said Michaelis. "No."

"Professor Singh's memories are coming more easily for me all the time," Susan said. "His phone number, his employment history. I even think, if I thought about it hard enough, that I could speak a little Punjabi—not to mention some bad Canadian French." She paused. "Why would the president and I have been affected and not you? We were all pretty close together. You were just outside the O.R., right?"

"Yeah," said Michaelis.

"Did you leave that area at any point?"

"No. Well, no, except to go to the washroom. In fact, that's where I was when the lights went out."

"And you stayed there through the blackout?"

"Sure. It didn't last long."

"No, it didn't," said Susan. "I'm no scientist, but—"

"The blackout?" said the president.

"Um, yes, sir. There was an EMP when the bomb went off at the White House—same as what happened in Chicago and Philadelphia." She turned to Michaelis. "How far was the washroom from the O.R.?"

"Halfway down the corridor. Maybe fifty feet."

"Did anybody take your place outside the operating-room door?"

"No. I signaled Dougherty, who was on my right, and Rosenbaum, on my left, that I was going off station for a moment; they had line of sight to each other, so . . ."

Susan nodded, then: "Singh's lab was more or less above

the operating room. So the effect probably was limited in radius—and you'd stepped outside it at the crucial moment."

Singh came into the room, accompanied, coincidentally, by Agent Dougherty, whom Michaelis had just mentioned.

"Well, *that's* interesting," Susan said to Singh. "I can even access your most recent memories, including new ones since the power surge."

"Really?" said Singh.

"Yes. I know all about what just went down between you and Private Adams."

"Fascinating," Singh said. "That means it wasn't a dumping of memories—you didn't just get a copy of my memories transferred to you when the power surge hit; you're still somehow connected to me on an ongoing basis." He frowned, clearly thinking about this.

"Anyway, it's interesting what Private Adams said to you just now," Susan said. She gestured to indicate it was all right for Singh to move closer to the president.

"Thank you," Singh said, coming further into the room. "Mr. President, those gentlemen you recall playing basketball with: you said one of them was named Lamarr. Please think about him, and see if you can conjure up anything else about him."

Seth's eyebrows rose. "Oh. Um. Sure, Lamarr. Lamarr . . . um . . ." The president seemed to hesitate, then: "Lamarr Brown."

"And his skin color?"

He took a moment to breathe, then. "He's . . . oh, well, um, okay. Yes, he's black. I've got a mental picture of him now, kind of. Black . . . short hair . . . gold earring . . . a scar above his right eye."

"His right eye?"

"Sorry, my right; his left."

"Private Adams described the same man, and added another detail. Something about Lamarr's smile."

The president frowned, concentrating. "Big gap between his two front teeth." He paused. "But . . . but I don't . . . I've never met . . ."

"No, you haven't. And you don't play basketball, either." Singh tried to inject a little levity. "It's not actually true that white men can't jump, but you, a *particular* white man, can't, because of your foot injury, isn't that right?"

"Right."

"And when you first recalled these men, you saw them as white," said Singh. "Now you see them as black."

"Um, yes."

"My patient upstairs, as you've doubtless guessed, is African-American. And, unlike you, he knows all three of the gentlemen—who also are African-American."

Seth said nothing.

Singh went on. "With due respect, Mr. President, let us not dance around the issue. If I ask you to picture a man—any man, an average man—you picture a white face, no doubt. It might interest you to know that a goodly number of African-Americans, not to mention Sikhs like myself, picture white faces, too: many of us are acutely aware that we are a minority in our neighborhoods and workplaces. Your default person is white, but my patient on the floor above grew up in South Central Los Angeles, an almost exclusively black community, and *his* default person is black."

"So?" said the president, sounding, Susan thought, perhaps slightly uncomfortable.

"The point," said Singh, "is that in storing memories of people, we store only how they *differ* from our default. You said one of the men was fat—and my patient described him the same way. But then you volunteered that the other two were thin, which might mean scrawny, which is why I asked you to clarify. If these people were notably thin, that detail might have been stored: scrawny is noteworthy; normal is not. Likewise, for my patient, his friends' skin color was not noteworthy. And when you are reading his memories, all you have access to is what he's actually stored: distinctive features, such as the gap between Lamarr's teeth, or the scar above his eye, interesting items of clothing, and so on. And out of those paltry cues, your mind confabulated the rest of the image."

"Confabulated?"

"Sorry, Mr. President. It means to fill in a gap in memory with a fabrication that the brain believes is true. See, people think that human memory is like computer memory: that somewhere in your head is a hard drive, or video recorder, or something, with a flawless, highly detailed record of everything you've seen and done. But that's just not true. Rather, your brain stores a few details that will allow it to build a memory up when you try to recall it."

"Okay," Susan said, looking at Singh. "And you're linked to this Lucius Jono fellow, right—and he might be the one linked to the president?"

"Yes."

"What's your most recent memory of him?"

"It's hard to say," said Singh. "No, wait—wait. He is—or quite recently was—down in the cafeteria, eating . . . um, a bacon cheeseburger and onion rings." He paused. "So *that's* what bacon tastes like! Anyway, it's got to be a recent memory; he's talking about the destruction of the White House and the electromagnetic pulse."

"All right," said Susan. "I'm going to go speak to him. If we're lucky, the circle only contains five people."

The president said something, but Susan couldn't make it out. She moved closer. "I'm sorry, sir?"

He tried again. "We haven't had much luck so far today."

She looked out the large windows and saw smoke in the sky. "No, sir, we haven't."

SECRET Service agent Manny Cheung hadn't recognized Gordon Danbury after his fall in the elevator shaft; it was, as the female agent who had first looked at his body on the roof of the elevator had said, not a pretty sight. But Danbury's fingerprints had been intact, and running them had quickly turned up his identity. Cheung had known "Gordo"—as he was called—pretty well, or so he'd thought, although he'd never been to his house.

That was being rectified now. Although the Secret Service protected the president, it was the FBI that investigated attacks on him. But the two FBI agents dispatched to Danbury's home had asked Cheung to join them since he'd been familiar with the deceased. Gordo lived an hour's drive southwest of DC, in Fredericksburg, Virginia—far enough away that his place hadn't been affected by the electromagnetic pulse.

It didn't take long to find what they were looking for. Danbury had an old Gateway desktop computer, with a squarish matte-finish LCD monitor, an aspect ratio that was hard to get these days; both were connected to a UPS box. He'd left them on, with a Microsoft Word document open on the screen. The document said:

Mom,

You'll never understand why I did this, I know, but it was the right thing. They won't let me get away, but that doesn't matter. I'm in heaven now, receiving my reward.
    Praise be to God.

Cheung glanced around; there was no sign of a printer. "He expected to die today," he said. "And he knew we'd find this."

The FBI agents were both white, but one was stocky and the other thin. The stocky one said, "But he ran."

"If he hadn't, he'd have been gunned down," said Cheung. "Sure, Gordo was a sharpshooter, but he'd have been facing a swarm of armed Secret Service agents; they'd have had no trouble taking him out, and he had to know that. Once he shot the president, he knew he'd be neutralized."

"Did you know he was religious?" asked the thin FBI man, whose name was Smith, as he pointed at the glowing words.

"No," said Cheung. "Never heard him mention it."

"'Praise be to God,'" Smith said. "Odd way to phrase it."

Cheung frowned, then gestured at the computer. "May I?"

"Just a minute," said the heavier agent, Kranz. He took a series of photos of the computer as they'd found it and dusted the keyboard for prints, on the off chance that the note hadn't actually been typed up by Danbury.

"Okay," Kranz said when he was done. "But don't change or close the file."

"No, no." Cheung looked at the screen. The document name, showing in the title bar, was "Mom"—and since it had a name, he must have saved the file at least once. He brought up Word's file menu, which listed recently opened documents at the bottom, and he noted which folder "Mom" was in. He then hit the Windows and *E* keys simultaneously to bring up Windows Explorer, navigated to that folder, and found

"Backup of Mom." "An older version of the file," he said to the two FBI men, "prior to the last save." He clicked on it, and it opened.

"Looks the same," said Smith, then, "Oh!"

Oh, indeed, thought Cheung. There *was* a difference: one single word, the very last word in the file. Instead of ending with "Praise be to God," in his earlier draft, Gordon Danbury of the United States Secret Service had written, "Praise be to Allah."

CHAPTER 12

ERIC Redekop woke with a start in the staff sleep room. The door had opened, and someone else had come in to use one of the other cots. He rolled onto his back, resting his head on the donut-shaped pillow, and looked up at the ceiling.

Eric knew that dreams were a key part of the brain's process of consolidating memories—of determining which of the day's events were important enough to store permanently. He only remembered his dreams when, as now, he awoke during them. But this dream was—

It was the most astonishing thing. He never recalled colors from his dreams. He'd always imagined that was because the act of dreaming predated the advent of color vision in primates. Dogs dreamed, after all, and they didn't see in color. He'd read about the experiment that had eliminated the part of a dog's nervous system that caused sleep paralysis—the effect that kept one from acting out one's dreams. Not surprisingly, it revealed that dogs dreamt about running and hunting and humping.

But he had just dreamt about . . . well, it was hard to say.

The imagery was the usual surreal dreamscape mishmash, but there was vibrant color in it: a scarlet dress, an azure sky, someone with striking emerald eyes, someone else with copper-colored hair.

He'd heard that artistic people were more likely to have vivid dreams, and, of course, Jan Falconi had made the original tiger illustration that a tattoo artist had faithfully transferred to her skin. He guessed that he was now consolidating her latest memories, flying through them the way she herself would have: Janis and the amazing Technicolor dream float.

He opened his eyes and saw a short, thin Asian woman: Christine Lee, the anesthesiologist who had worked on Jerrison. She said something, but he couldn't make it out; he moved one of the noise-canceling earphones off his ear. "Pardon?"

"Sorry to wake you," Christine said. "Who'd have thought putting other people to sleep could be so exhausting?"

Eric interlaced his fingers behind his head. "That's okay."

"I just need to lie down," Christine said, apologetically.

"No problem," Eric replied. He was still tired but was grateful for the intrusion; anything was better than the craziness swirling through his head.

Christine moved over to another cot and sat on its edge, holding her head in her hands.

"Are you okay?" Eric asked. The room was dimly lit, and he couldn't quite make out Christine's expression.

"I guess," she said.

Eric removed the headset and propped his head up with a crooked arm. "You did great earlier today, Christine."

"What?" she said. "Oh. Thanks. It's not that."

He didn't say anything more, but after a minute she went on. "You know David January?"

Eric did his best Peter Lorre impression. "You despise me, don't you, Rick?"

He'd hoped for a smile, but all he got was a nod. "That's him. Little bug-eyed man."

"Yeah?"

"I've known him for a few years," Christine said. "But not well. But now I know all sorts of things about him. It's like . . ."

She trailed off. Eric felt his heart pounding. He wanted to

say, "It's like you can access his memories, right?" But he couldn't say that—that was *crazy*.

Christine didn't say anything else, and Eric stared at her, wondering what to say. He felt like he was going out of his mind, but—but—

It hit him. *God, yes.* He'd been so discombobulated by his encounter with nurse Janis Falconi that he'd forgotten what had happened earlier. But suddenly he recalled Nikki, the distraught woman who had accosted Jurgen Sturgess. She had known his name. He sat up on the cot. "Christine?"

She was still sitting there, head in her hands. "Hmmm?"

"Something very weird is happening."

SUSAN Dawson went to the round lobby, which had a very high ceiling; people on the second floor could look down on the comings and goings. Except of course that, right now, there were no comings *or* goings. Susan had a brief word with the uniformed security guard who kept individuals from getting into the hospital proper without showing ID, then she crossed over to the cafeteria, passing people who looked dazed, people who looked inconsolable, people who looked scared to death.

Inside the cafeteria, there were hospital staff and visitors with food in front of them, but they mostly weren't eating. Rather, they were talking in low tones about what had happened. She saw one man comforting a woman who was sobbing softly, and another man with his head down on the table in front of him; he seemed to be crying, too.

The first couple of people Susan asked didn't know Dr. Lucius Jono, but the third person, a woman with eyes wide open as if still half in shock, did, and she pointed to a compact man with wild red hair sitting with three other men; they were all wearing white hospital smocks. Just as Singh had said, a discarded half of a bacon cheeseburger and most of an order of onion rings were still on a plate on the brown tray in front of Jono.

"Dr. Lucius Jono?" Susan said as she came up to the table. She pulled out her ID. "Susan Dawson, Secret Service. Might I have a word with you in private?"

Jono lifted his eyebrows—he really should trim those things, Susan thought; they looked like orange caterpillars that had been given electroshock therapy. He crammed one final onion ring into his mouth, excused himself from his colleagues, and stood. "What's up?"

"This way, please," Susan said. She led him across the wide lobby, past the security guard, and into the hospital. They took the elevator up to the third floor. Susan had decided to co-opt Professor Singh's office for her use—after all, crazy as it seemed, it was intimately familiar to her; she knew, for instance, where to find the paper clips if she needed one. When they got there, she sat behind the kidney-shaped desk and motioned for Jono to take the other chair.

Susan hesitated, not quite sure how to pose the insane questions she needed to ask. Finally, she simply dove in. "Something odd is going on here at the hospital involving memories, and—"

"You mean it's not just me?" asked Jono, looking relieved.

"It's not," said Susan. "Tell me about what you've experienced."

"It's like—God, it's like I know all sorts of things I shouldn't know, like, um—where do you live?"

Susan was startled by the question, but answered it. "Kenilworth."

"Interesting neighborhood," he said at once. "Average house price this past quarter was $223,000. Some wonderful old homes, although they tend not to have enough bathrooms— but I know a couple of excellent fixer-uppers."

"What are you talking about?" Susan said.

"Real estate," said Jono. "It's like I suddenly know all about real estate. And I've never known *anything* about that. I moved here five years ago, after having a long-distance relationship with the woman I live with now; she already had a house here. I've never bought a home in this part of the world, but I know all the districts, average selling prices, and so on, not to mention a whole bunch of techniques for closing a deal."

"What do you know about the president of the United States?" Susan asked.

"Medically?" said Jono. "Tons now, of course. He's in good shape internally for a man his age."

"No, I mean about him personally."

"What everyone knows, I suppose. Came out of nowhere to win the Republican nomination. Likes sports fishing. And so on."

"Nothing more intimate?"

"I'm not sure what you're getting at."

"Do you know, for instance, his wife's birthday?"

"The First Lady's? Haven't a clue."

"Or maybe the name of his high school?"

"No."

Susan nodded. "Okay. Tell me: how do you think you came by all this information about real estate?"

"I haven't stopped to think about it. I really haven't had many quiet moments since the surgery on Jerrison. But . . ."

"But?"

"Well, there's this woman I know . . ."

"Yes?"

"I *know* her. I know all about her, but I don't *know* her." Jono's freckled face conveyed that he was aware he wasn't making sense. "I mean, I seem to know her, but I'm sure I've never met her. A real-estate agent."

"Her name?"

"Nikki Van Hausen," said Jono. "Well, Nicola, but she goes by Nikki. N-I-double-K-I."

"And she's here at the hospital? A patient?"

"Not a patient. Oh! Well, not originally, anyway."

"What do you mean?"

"She was here to visit her brother, but they've locked her up."

"Where?"

"The psychiatric ward."

"Where's that?"

He told her, and she headed toward it. As she approached the main door to it from one direction, a thin, bald man wearing a doctor's smock arrived there from another. Susan was always absorbing everything around her and habitually read name badges; this fellow's said, "E. Redekop, M.D." She hadn't recognized his face—because, she suddenly realized, she hadn't yet seen it, except for the eyes, and those only from a distance.

"You're Eric Redekop."

He lifted his eyebrows. "Not again!"

"Pardon?"

"Sorry. It's just that you're the second person today to recognize me that I don't know."

"Actually," said Susan, "I just read your badge—and Dr. Griffin had told me your first name. I'm Susan Dawson, the Secret Service agent-in-charge here. I watched you save the president today." She paused, trying to think of what else to say, but couldn't come up with anything better than, "Thank you."

"My pleasure," said Redekop, looking a bit relieved.

Susan's job was all about noticing things that were out of place. "What's a surgeon doing in the psychiatric ward?"

Redekop's handsome face was still for a few moments, as if he was thinking about what—or how much—to say. Finally, he lifted his narrow shoulders a bit. "Well, it's like I said. Someone recognized me earlier, but I didn't know her. She seemed quite upset."

"Let me guess," said Susan. "Nikki Van Hausen, right?"

Redekop looked astonished. "I don't know her last name, but, yes, her first name is Nikki."

"Come with me."

SECRET Service agent Dirk Jenks slipped away from the crowd of fellow agents swarming the interior of the Lincoln Memorial. He headed down the wide marble stairs and then went around to the back. Only three thousand people had come out on this cold morning to hear Jerrison's speech, but now that he'd been shot, many thousands more were swarming onto this part of the Mall, hoping to see the site of the assassination attempt—and an even greater number were scurrying to see the ruins of the White House: lemmings rushing headlong into dust and nothingness, into the end of history.

Jenks briskly walked the hundred-odd yards to the nearest road and caught a cab that had just disgorged two people. He told the driver to take him to Reagan National Airport, four miles away in Virginia.

"Hey," said the driver, "were you here earlier? Did you see the guy take a shot at Jerrison?"

"No."

"What about the White House? Did you see that go up? Jesus!"

Jenks shook his head, and, mercifully, the driver shut up. Traffic was almost at a standstill—the journey was going to take forever. Jenks glanced anxiously out the car's right side and saw the Jefferson Memorial for what he imagined would be the last time.

CHAPTER 13

NIKKI Van Hausen was supposed to show two houses this afternoon, but that wasn't going to happen. After her encounter in the hallway with Drs. Sturgess and Redekop, the security guard had taken her to a room that she only belatedly realized was in the psychiatric ward. A few other people seemed to have been here for a while, and two more were brought into the ward shortly after her—wailing and screaming over the terrorist attack.

Her room was cubic, with a high ceiling, and was empty except for a couch bolted to the wall. She wasn't suicidal—but this was where they put people who were, so there was nothing that a makeshift noose could be hung from, no glass over pictures that might be smashed and used to slit wrists—and no way to open the door from the inside. There was also no bathroom. She was just about to press the buzzer that would summon a guard to let her out so she could use the one across the hall when the door opened and in came Eric Redekop accompanied by a pretty blue-eyed brunette with shoulder-length hair. She was wearing a black jacket, black pants, and black leather shoes with flat heels.

"Hello, Ms. Van Hausen," Eric said.

She tried to match his formality—after all, she wanted out of here. "Dr. Redekop," she replied, and nodded politely.

Eric indicated the woman. "This is Susan Dawson, a Secret Service agent."

Nikki felt her heart beginning to pound. "Hello."

"You seemed to know me out in the corridor earlier," Eric said.

Nikki nodded. "I know we've never met, but . . ."

"But you knew things about me—or was it Dr. Sturgess?—that you wouldn't normally know."

She had a brief moment where she thought she should lie: letting them know that she *sensed* things had gotten her into this booby hatch in the first place. But, no, no, she had to tell them; she had to get this *fixed*.

"It's you," she said, looking at Eric. "I only know the things about Jurgen that you know."

Susan Dawson spoke. "What has happened to you has happened to several others. There's been a linkage of minds. We're going to try to find a way to break the links, but for now we must acknowledge that they exist."

Eric nodded. "I'm affected, too, and so is Agent Dawson."

Nikki felt a wave of relief—it *wasn't* just her; as crazy as all this sounded, she wasn't nuts. Suddenly, she was angry. "But if it was happening to you, too, why didn't you speak up when you first saw me? Why'd you let them lock me up here?"

Eric spread his arms. "I'm so sorry, Nikki. I probably did become linked to the person I'm reading at the same moment you became linked to me. But nothing brought her memories to mind for me until I actually saw her, *after* I saw you—first, because I was exhausted and preoccupied with the president's health, and, second, because we both work here, she and I; this building is mostly background noise for the two of us. But for you being in a hospital is unusual, and the sights and sounds of this place immediately brought my memories of it into your consciousness."

"Oh," said Nikki. "But—wait!—does that mean somebody can read *my* mind, too?"

"Your memories, yes," said Agent Dawson.

"But my memories are private!" said Nikki.

"So are mine," said Eric. "So, um, if you'd not share them with anyone else, please . . ."

"Of course," said Nikki. "Of course. But how long is this going to last?"

"We don't know," Agent Dawson said.

"I want to meet the person that's linked to me," said Nikki.

Susan Dawson shook her head. "I don't think that would be advisable. Some of those who are linked already knew each other, and there's nothing we can do about that, but others are strangers, and I think it's best we keep it that way. But of course we'll get you out of the psychiatric ward. Do you have a cell phone with you?"

"Yes."

"Give me the number so that I can find you easily later. You're free to roam the hospital—there's a cafeteria in the lobby—but we're not letting anyone leave."

"LESHIA, it's Darryl. Are you okay?"

"I'm . . . I'm fine. God, Darryl, are *you* all right?"

"Yes."

"You heard about the White House? My God . . ."

"Awful. Just . . . awful."

"They say no one was hurt, but . . ."

"But *everyone* was hurt."

"I saw you on TV just now. They were showing what went down at the Lincoln Memorial. I'm so proud of you. Where are you now?"

"Still at LT."

"How's—how's the president doing?"

"He's stable, but Sue has locked the hospital down. Leshia, listen, something super-unusual is going on here. It's happened to me, and it's happened to other people. We're—we're reading each other's memories somehow."

"What?"

"I know it sounds crazy, baby. It *is* crazy. But it's happening. So I need you to go online and change the PINs for our bank accounts and things like that."

"But—"

"Just do it. Don't you see? Somebody else knows them

now; I don't know who. But we've got to change them before they clear us out. Do it, and don't pick anything I'd easily guess."

"Darryl, um, are you *sure* you're okay?"

"Yes, I'm fine. I know it sounds insane, baby, but do it—do it right away. Okay, look, I gotta go. Love you!"

THE cab dropped Secret Service agent Dirk Jenks at Reagan. He paid the fare in cash, didn't wait for his change, and didn't ask for a receipt. He checked the departures board and saw that there was a flight to LaGuardia in sixty-five minutes. In the wake of the explosion at the White House, FBI agents were already swarming the airport, but so far there'd been no sign that flights were going to be suspended as they had been back on 9/11.

There was a line at the Delta ticketing counter, but Jenks flashed his Secret Service ID at people and moved to the front.

"The next flight to LaGuardia, please," he said.

"One-way or round-trip?" asked the woman behind the counter.

"One-way."

SUSAN Dawson headed from the psychiatric ward to Professor Singh's laboratory, which, she knew, was six doors down the third-floor corridor from his office. As she entered the lab for the first time, it was, as Yogi Berra had famously said, *déjà vu* all over again.

Singh was talking on his phone. He quickly finished his call.

"Who were you talking to?" Susan asked.

"My wife. Why?"

"Did you tell her about the memory linkages?"

"Of course. It's fascinating."

"I wish you hadn't done that," she said. "We should keep this quiet."

He gestured at his computer monitor, which was showing Twitter.

"You tweeted about this?"

"No, no. I just searched Twitter for 'Luther Terry' while I was talking to my wife, and those came up."

Susan loomed in. There were several about Jerrison being brought here after the shooting and five about the lockdown. But there was also one that said, "Weird things going on at Luther Terry Memorial Hospital." Another declared, "Memories being linked at Luther Terry Hosp in DC." Someone else had chimed in with, "I'm at Luther Terry Memorial Hospital. Anybody know anything about telepathy?" Twitter was helpfully informing Ranjip that there were now four new tweets that matched his search. Instead of clicking on the link for those, though, he put in a new search: "LTMH." Two tweets came up: One said, "Saw a woman freak at #LTMH, berating the surgeon who saved the prez. She must have been a Democrat." And the other said, "Heard craziest story at LTMH just now about reading memories. Anybody else?"

"God damn it," said Susan. "We should put a lid on contact with the outside world."

But Ranjip shook his head. "There's been a terrorist attack here in the city, Agent Dawson. People need to keep in touch. They need it on a human level; they need to know their loved ones, wherever they are, are well—and to let them know that they themselves are safe."

Susan said nothing; there was no rule book, no protocol, for a situation like this.

"And, anyway," continued Singh, "besides the hospital's phone system, there are hundreds of cell phones here. Patients have them, and staff, too. And, of course, hundreds of laptops and iPads and the like, not to mention all the hospital's computers. By the time you could confiscate them all, even if you could find legal grounds to do so, the whole world will know about the memory linkages. And if a bomb hits here—the terrorists must know where the president is, after all, and that he's still alive—you'll want people to have as many ways to communicate as possible, in hopes that some will function after the EMP."

"You're right," Susan said. Just then, the door to Singh's office opened and in came Kadeem Adams. Susan knew him at once, although—

Well, *that* was interesting. There was no doubt that this was indeed Kadeem; he easily matched Ranjip's memories of him. But she was now looking at him with her own trained agent's eyes, and seeing details Ranjip had never noted. For starters, Ranjip had had no idea how tall Kadeem was, but Susan immediately pegged him at six-one; agents learned to take the measure of a man even when he was seated. She also noted he was wearing a T-shirt advertising Brickers, a rap group that Ranjip had apparently never heard of; that he had creased ear-lobes; and that he was a nail-biter.

A memory—her own—of one of her favorite writers flashed through her head: *You have been in Afghanistan, I perceive.* But that was the *other* war; she knew, because Ranjip knew it, that Kadeem had actually been in Iraq.

"Kadeem Adams," said Singh, "this is Agent Susan Dawson. As you know, she's with the Secret Service."

Kadeem shook his head. "All this shit that's goin' down. I can see it from your point of view—the president bleeding on the steps, you and him in the limo, you looking down on him on the operating table. Been one hell of a day."

"Yes," said Susan.

"And—well, *damn,* girl! You had a hell of night last night, too, didn't you, Agent Dawson?" Susan felt herself blushing. Kadeem went on. "Although, given how well I now know you, maybe we should be on a first-name basis, don't you think . . . Sue?"

Ranjip picked up a lined notepad. "I think we need to start writing this down. Agent Dawson is reading my memories. Kadeem, you're reading Agent Dawson's. And . . ." He paused.

"And?" said Kadeem.

Ranjip looked at Susan, asking permission with his eyes.

Susan thought about it, then said, "I don't think I'm actually in a position to keep secrets from Kadeem."

And as soon as she said it, Kadeem's eyes went wide. "And—God!—the president is reading my memories."

Susan knew there was no point denying it.

Kadeem looked at Ranjip. "I knew *somebody* was, from the questions you asked, guru, but . . ." He shook his head. "No shit! The president!" He smiled slightly. "Guess he knows now I didn't vote for him." He then looked at Ranjip. "What about you, guru? Who are you reading?"

"A doctor here named Lucius Jono," said Ranjip—and he took a moment to jot this fact on the chart he was making.

"And he's reading a real-estate agent named Nikki Van Hausen," said Susan. She gestured for the pad and wrote the name down. "And Nikki's reading Eric Redekop, who was the lead surgeon for the president. And Redekop is reading a nurse, Janis Falconi." She wrote these names down, too. "The chain just keeps getting longer and longer—which raises the question of exactly how many people are affected. Agent Michaelis wasn't—he was too far away from your equipment, it seems. But how many were?"

"Good question," Singh said. He consulted a PC on a work-table. "Huh," he said, and then, "Hmmm."

"Yes?" said Susan.

Ranjip moved to his apparatus, a padded chair and a geo-desic sphere two feet in diameter. "Well," he said, "this equipment can edit memories, but the effective field is normally constrained to the interior of this sphere. According to the diagnostics, what happened, it seems—and this certainly was unanticipated—was that during the electromagnetic pulse, the field expanded while maintaining its spherical shape. It got to be about thirty-two feet in diameter, so presumably everyone in that sphere was affected."

"That's a radius of sixteen feet," Susan said. "Enough to reach up to the fourth floor and down to the second, no?"

"Exactly," said Singh.

Susan considered. "The president was there." She pointed down and to her left. "And I was right next door in the obser-vation gallery." She pointed directly to her left. She turned to Singh. "Are you sure the field didn't get any bigger than that? And you're sure no one outside that radius could have been affected?"

"We're not sure of much," Singh replied. "But the field size is directly proportional to the power used to generate it, and the equipment recorded the magnitude of the surge in its syslog file. Assuming we're right, and it's my equipment that caused all this, then, yes, I'd say the effect was limited to people in that bubble."

"I can't keep the hundreds of people in this hospital locked up indefinitely," said Susan.

"Given the size of the bubble, it shouldn't be more than one or two dozen who were affected," replied Singh. "Anyone who was on the lobby level or below, or on five or above, probably isn't affected. And anyone on two, three, or four who was more than a couple of rooms away from here probably wasn't, either."

"Assuming nobody has moved to a different floor," said Susan.

"Ah, right," replied Ranjip.

"Still, it does narrow the list of suspects," Susan said.

"Suspects for what?" Kadeem asked. But then he looked at Susan and nodded. "Ah. For who's reading the president's memories. Guess you gotta find that dude soon, huh, Sue?"

CHAPTER 14

DARRYL Hudkins and Mark Griffin sat in the security office at Luther Terry Memorial Hospital, along with Deanna Axen, the hospital's director of security. They were in front of a bank of twelve flatscreen monitors, arranged in three rows of four. Eleven of the monitors were doing what they normally did: cycling through the endless array of security cameras secreted inside the hospital and on its grounds, including the plaza connecting to the Foggy Bottom metro station on the south side of the triangular building. But the twelfth—the lower-right one—was showing footage from just before and just after the lights went out. Darryl and Dr. Griffin were making a list of who was within the critical radius of Singh's machine at the key moment, starting with those in the operating room. It was almost impossible for Darryl to distinguish the members of the surgical team; nothing but their eyes were visible. Griffin, who knew them all to one degree or another, fared better, and Darryl wrote down the names:

President Seth Jerrison
Lead surgeon Dr. Eric Redekop

Surgeon Dr. Lucius Jono
Cardiac specialist Dr. David January
Anesthesiologist Dr. Christine Lee
Surgical nurse Ann January
Secret Service agent Darryl Hudkins

Next, they looked at footage from the corridor outside the O.R. The two patients who had been removed to make room for Jerrison were there, as well as a nurse who had been tending to them. Griffin identified them as:

Intended kidney recipient Josh Latimer
Intended kidney donor Dora Hennessey
Nurse Janis Falconi
Security guard Ivan Tarasov

They then turned their attention to the third floor, starting with the observation gallery above the O.R.:

Hospital CEO Dr. Mark Griffin
Secret Service agent-in-charge Susan Dawson

And next door, in Singh's lab:

Ranjip Singh, Ph.D.
Private Kadeem Adams

They continued on, identifying others on the third and fourth floors, including some visitors to the hospital. They were aided by the records kept by the security checkpoint in the lobby, where IDs were examined and recorded. It took a while to compare the hundreds of faces that had gone through the various entrances to the faces spotted near Singh's equipment, but finally they had completed their list of all those who had likely been affected. As it happened, only Susan and Darryl from the Secret Service detail were within the sphere; the rest of the agents on-site had been further north or south in the corridor on two, or down on one, guarding the building's entrances.

Darryl spoke into his sleeve. "Hudkins to Dawson. Sue, we're done here."

"Great," said Susan. "Come on up to Singh's lab. It's room 324."

"'PRAISE be to Allah,'" said Manny Cheung, reading from the computer screen in Gordo Danbury's house.

"Danbury must have been a plant," said Smith, the skinny one of the two FBI agents.

"But he'd been with the Secret Service for two years," Cheung said.

Smith nodded. "They're nothing if not patient."

"No one has claimed responsibility for the White House bombing yet," said Cheung, "but it was the same type of device they intercepted at L-A-X—so it's probably al-Sajada."

Kranz, the other FBI agent, looked at him. "But how would they recruit an all-American boy like Danbury?" They had gone over Danbury's personnel file before coming here; he'd been born in Lawrence, Kansas, and had earned school letters in baseball and track.

"He was ex-army," Cheung said. "Stationed in Afghanistan. He could have been compromised there."

"They probably promised him seventy-two virgins," sneered Smith.

"He wouldn't be the first soldier they'd turned," said Cheung. "Lots of grunts feel disenchanted with the US and wonder what we're doing there. Give them enough drugs and money, maybe some women, and . . ." He gestured at the screen. "But whatever Danbury thought he was going to receive in heaven was presumably contingent on him taking out Jerrison. He probably planted the bomb on the White House roof during his last shift up there, with the timer set to blow up the building shortly after Jerrison was scheduled to finish his speech."

"That would have been pretty fucking demoralizing," Smith said, "on top of all the demoralizing kicks in the balls they've already given us. Jerrison gives a speech about how we're going to win the war on terror and—*boom!*—he's killed as the White House blows up. Classic al-Sajada."

"Yeah," said Kranz. "But when Jerrison decided to move his speech to the Lincoln Memorial . . ."

Cheung nodded. "With the bomb's timer already set, and no clearance for him to go back up on the roof until his next shift on Sunday, Gordo must have been scrambling for a Plan B. But as a sharpshooter, he figured he could take Jerrison out *while* he was giving the speech. He might have thought it was even better, a one-two punch: Jerrison assassinated during his speech about the war on terror, and an hour later the White House is destroyed."

Danbury's house was small. Kranz was nosing around, looking on the bookshelves, which, from what Cheung could see, contained mostly military nonfiction and Tom Clancy novels.

Smith nodded, then said, "I guess when Danbury heard that agent calling out that Jerrison was still alive, Danbury must have realized he wasn't going to be a martyr—his mission to take out the president was a failure. He probably hadn't even planned an escape route at the Lincoln Memorial; he was all set to go out in a blaze of glory. Guy like that, a crack shot, probably never even occurred to him that Jerrison would survive."

"I suppose," said Cheung. "But when Jerrison *did* survive, Gordo panicked and ran—hoping to get away and find another way to earn his heavenly virgins."

"But now that fucker is in hell," said Smith.

Cheung found himself a chair, dropped into it, and looked out the window, out at the changed world. "Aren't we all?"

THE year Ranjip Singh's family had moved from Delhi to Toronto, US television, which spilled over the border into Canada, was filled with "Bicentennial Minutes," celebrating America's past.

Years later, Canada started its own series of similar television spots called "Heritage Minutes." Singh fondly remembered several of them, including Canadian Joe Shuster creating Superman, paleontologist Joseph Burr Tyrrell discovering dinosaur bones in Alberta, Marshall McLuhan electrifying his students at U of T with a lecture during which he coined the phrase "The medium is the message," and a moving monologue by an actress portraying Emily Murphy, the first woman magistrate in all of the British Empire, who fought for the rights of Canadian women to be recognized as persons under the law.

But the one that caught teenage Ranjip's attention most of all was about pioneering Canadian neurosurgeon Wilder Penfield, performing in 1934 what came to be known as "the Montreal procedure." By touching electrodes to particular parts of his patients' brains, Penfield could apparently reliably elicit specific memories. A phrase from that Heritage Minute—"I can smell burnt toast!" uttered by a female patient in astonishment when Penfield identified the source of her ongoing seizures—became a catchphrase in Canada, and Ranjip had been so fascinated by that little film, he'd ended up choosing memory research for his career.

All of this came to Susan Dawson as she waited in Professor Singh's lab for Darryl and Dr. Griffin to get there. As soon as they arrived, she asked, "What's the tally?"

Darryl showed her the list of names. "Nineteen, including you, me, Prospector, Dr. Griffin, Professor Singh here, and—" He looked at the other man in the room. "You're Private Adams, right?"

"That's me," said Kadeem.

Darryl nodded. "We checked and double-checked: that's everybody. Your runner—Orrin Gillett—was the only borderline case, as it happens; if he's affected, the total is twenty."

Susan frowned and turned to Professor Singh. "Do you see any rhyme or reason to the linkages we've already uncovered? Anything like, oh, say, you're linked to the person who was closest to you, whether or not in line of sight? Or you're linked to—I don't know—the person who's closest to you in age, or something?"

Singh shrugged; it seemed, Susan noted, to be his favorite gesture. "I've been looking for correlations, but none leap out. Certainly, it's not simply distance. The attending surgeons were much closer to the president than Private Adams was, for instance. And if distance were the factor, the links would be reciprocal: *A* linked to *B,* and *B* to *A.*"

"So," said Mark Griffin, standing up—he was a good ten inches taller than Susan, and he clearly wanted the advantage his imposing stature gave him—"once we isolate all the people on this list, we can end the lockdown and let everyone else come and go as they please, right?"

Susan looked up at him—and hated that she had to do that. But she supposed one didn't get to be the head of a major hospital without learning a few power-game tricks. "Until we've actually identified who is reading President Jerrison's memories, I don't want to take any chances."

"Agent Dawson," said Griffin, "the record will show that Luther Terry Memorial Hospital immediately complied with your lockdown request. Our staff have been fully cooperative. However, this cannot go on indefinitely; if necessary I'll call your superior. I believe that would be Director Hexley, no?" Susan had to give him his due: he was good at this; he'd prepared for the confrontation. "This is a hospital. We provide emergency services to a wide area, as well as extensive outpatient care. We can't remain closed. And, my God, after what's happened today, people here have a right to go to their homes, be with their loved ones, and try to find some way to get on with their lives."

"They also have a right to have their national-security interests protected," Susan said.

"Perhaps so. But you can't keep *everyone* locked up, and we have to start letting new patients in. We've already had one near tragedy, Agent Dawson: a patient who would have been easily saved here was almost lost *en route* to Bethesda, when her ambulance was diverted there. And we're extraordinarily lucky that no one was hurt in the explosion at the White House, but we have to be prepared to treat casualties if another bomb goes off here in DC."

"I hear you, Dr. Griffin. Now, you hear me: we'll try to get this done quickly; we'll interview everyone on the list until we find out who is linked to the president. But I'm not letting you unlock the doors until we do, understand?"

Before Griffin could answer, Susan's BlackBerry rang; her ringtone was the theme music from *Inside the Beltway.* "Dawson, go!"

"Hello," said a male voice. "My name is Dario Sosso. I'm an FBI agent and I'm out at Reagan."

"Yes?" said Susan eagerly.

"We got him."

She blew out air. As Secret Service agent-in-charge of the presidential detail, she'd been getting continual updates about the situation at the Lincoln Memorial. Dirk Jenks's absence had been noted, and she'd ordered him found and detained. Jenks, after all, was supposed to have checked the elevator at the Lincoln Memorial before Jerrison arrived; he might well have been an accomplice of Danbury. And it had been Jenks who had started the elevator when Danbury had gone off-script and tried to escape—apparently getting just the result he'd hoped for, bringing Danbury plummeting to his death.

"Thanks," Susan said. "That he ran is proof enough that he was involved, but let me know if he reveals anything under interrogation, please."

"Will do," said the FBI agent. Susan terminated the call, looked at the people in the professor's lab, and suddenly found she couldn't meet Darryl Hudkins's gaze. One rogue Secret Service agent was bad enough. But two constituted a conspiracy. And it was anyone's guess how big the conspiracy was.

CHAPTER 15

SUSAN enlisted Professor Singh to help her interview the other potentially linked people: he'd speak individually to half of the remaining group, and she'd take the other half. They could have gotten through everyone even more quickly if she had the other Secret Service agents do interviews, too, but she didn't know who among them she could trust. But Singh, who she recalled had enough psychology courses under his belt to know how to effectively question people, had no secrets from her, and she could access his memories of each interview once it was done; it was almost as good as being in two places at one time.

Susan's next interviewee was a young woman named Rachel Cohen, who worked in accounts receivable here at Luther Terry Memorial Hospital; she'd happened to be on the fourth floor, passing directly above Singh's lab, when the memory-linking effect occurred.

"I don't understand," Rachel said, sounding quite distraught. "This doesn't make any sense."

"We're all still trying to get a handle on it," Susan said. "It was an accident."

"But it's . . . God, it's *freaky*. I mean, I wasn't aware that anything was wrong until just now."

"It seems the foreign memories don't come to mind unless something triggers them, or unless you actually think about them. Some people knew at once that they'd been affected; others, like you, didn't know until they were asked about it."

Rachel shook her head in dismay. "But now that you *have* asked me about it, I can't stop recalling things he knows."

"He?" said Susan, leaning forward. "Do you know his name?"

"Sure. It's Orrin."

The chances of there being two Orrins around struck Susan as pretty slim, but: "Orrin what?"

"Gillett."

Susan hoped she was keeping her face from showing distaste; Orrin Gillett was the lawyer who'd tried to run at the beginning of the lockdown. She asked Rachel a few questions about Gillett, just to be sure: the names of his law partners, which law school he'd gone to, and so on, and then she verified the answers on the law firm's website.

"How—how long is this . . . this pairing . . . going to last?" Rachel asked, when Susan was done.

"I honestly have no idea."

Rachel shook her head again. "This is *so* strange. God, it feels weird. I mean, he's a man, you know? I've always wondered what it'd be like to be a man instead of a woman."

"Maybe when this is all over, you'll write a book about it," Susan offered.

Rachel seemed to consider this. "Maybe I will, at that. It's . . . it's fascinating." And then, after a moment, almost to herself, it seemed, she added, *"He's* fascinating."

"Okay," said Susan. "Thank you for your cooperation, Miss Cohen. We're still keeping people here at the hospital for a while, but please give me your cell number, so I can find you easily again if I need you."

Rachel dictated it, then left Singh's office. Just as she did so, Susan's earpiece buzzed. "Hudkins to Dawson."

"Go ahead, Darryl," Susan said.

"We've located nineteen of the twenty people," said the

voice in her ear. "But one seems to have gotten out of the building before you initiated the lockdown."

"Shit," said Susan. "Who?"

"Bessie Stilwell, a woman who was visiting her son. And *I'm* the one reading her—which is strange, I gotta say. She's visiting from Pascagoula, Mississippi—at least, that's what I recall."

"Do you know who she's linked to?"

"No. And I'm not sure where she's gone; I'm trying to recall it, but it hasn't come to me yet. I just went to see her son, Michael Stilwell, but he's pretty much out of it; he had a major heart attack. He's got no idea where she might have gone today."

"If you're linked to her, why can't you just recall it?"

"I asked Singh about that. His guess is that it's because she's elderly—she's eighty-seven, her son said. Bessie has trouble recalling things herself; she's not senile, or anything, just *old*. Singh thinks it may clear up for me; he suspects I might to index her memories as time goes on, using my younger brain. But at the moment, well, let's say I now know how my grandma feels when she's struggling to recall something. It's frustrating."

"What hotel is she staying at?"

"She isn't. She's staying at her son's place. I've got the address, and will get the DC police to stake it out."

Susan didn't want to become paranoid—and she'd known Darryl for four years now—but it *was* suspicious that he was both claiming *not* to be linked to Jerrison *and* was having trouble corroborating that he was linked to someone else. Still: "Copy," Susan said. "But find her. Oh, and Rachel Cohen is linked to Orrin Gillett—can you tell Singh to add that to his chart? And I guess I better speak to Gillett now; might as well do this in some kind of order. Can you get him and bring him to 312? I've got him locked up in 424."

"Copy," said Darryl.

RACHEL Cohen was fascinated by Orrin Gillett, the man she was linked to. A lawyer—and a rich one, at that. Certainly a good start! And he was handsome, too, if his own memories of his driver's license and passport photos were anything to go by. Not that he thought of himself as handsome—but the photos showed a man who *was:* lots of light brown hair, a great face, and beautiful brown eyes behind round rimless glasses. Still, Rachel wanted to see for herself, and—

And another memory of his came to her, one of a black Secret Service agent with a shaved head coming to get him, and—yes, yes—and bringing him down here, and—

And the memory must be of only a minute or two ago, because here they came, coming down this corridor, and—

And Orrin Gillett was *hot.* She found herself saying an ebullient "Hi!" to him, like she was greeting an old friend—and, in a way, she supposed she was.

He looked at her, startled, but then smiled a terrific open-mouth smile at her. "Hello," he said. "Nice day." She had a strange feeling that his voice didn't sound quite right—which, she suddenly realized, was the same feeling she had when she heard recordings of her own voice; he remembered his voice as he himself heard it, resonating in his sinus cavities. "Do I know you?" he added.

"No," said Rachel. "But I know you."

His tone was affable but baffled. "I don't understand."

Rachel nodded toward the door of the office Agent Dawson was using. "You will."

Rachel knew she should get back to her desk, but work here had slowed to a crawl because most of the staff was still shell-shocked by the assassination attempt and the destruction of the White House; people were just sitting at their desks staring into space, or softly crying, or endlessly chatting to others, trying to make sense of it all.

Rather than heading down the corridor, Rachel instead took a seat in a little waiting alcove just past the room Agent Dawson was using. If her own experience was anything to judge by, Orrin Gillett would be coming out again in twenty minutes or so.

Whenever Rachel was considering doing business with a new company, she ran a simple test. She put the company name and the word "sucks" into Google. Every giant corporation had its detractors: "Microsoft sucks" yielded 285,000 hits,

"FedEx sucks" produced 568,000, and "Disney sucks" served up a whopping two million pages. But for local businesses or obscure web companies, she'd found it a useful barometer.

Likewise, whenever she was interested in dating someone, she'd do a quick search on his name and the word "asshole": "Devan Hooley asshole" had helped her dodge a major bullet!

But now, in this particular case, she had something even better than Google. There was no doubt that Orrin Gillett was attractive. And he seemed like a nice guy: he had a warm, friendly smile, and teeth that either hadn't seen a lot of coffee, cola, or tobacco, or had been whitened, and—

And, yes, whitened. The Zoom! process, to be precise. Cost him six hundred bucks.

But he hadn't been a smoker since high school, he didn't like carbonated beverages, and his coffee intake was pretty average. But he *had* been treated with tetracycline as a kid, and it had left his teeth a pale tan, and he'd been self-conscious about it for years. And so he'd had the problem corrected.

Rachel thought about *my girlfriend,* but no memory came to her. And then—well, he *was* pretty buff, and impeccably dressed to boot!—she thought about *my boyfriend.* But the only memories that came were of her own exes, the most recent of which had left her life—or, at least, her bed—ten months ago.

And speaking of exes—ah.

Melinda.

And Valerie.

And Jennifer.

And Franca.

And Ann-Marie.

And that bitch Naomi.

She thought about them, but—

No, that wouldn't work. She couldn't think about them collectively; she had to pick one, and think about just her. Say, Valerie.

Ah. Blonde. Brown-eyed. Big-breasted. Rachel glanced down at her own chest: well, two out of three ain't bad. And— oh, my! Our Val liked it a little rough, didn't she? But . . .

But Orrin actually *didn't.* He played it up that way, because Val asked him to, but—

Ah, in fact that was one of the reasons they'd broken up.

She tried another one. Jennifer.

Hmmm. Long straight hair, blue eyes, and . . . a very strong chin—

Oh my God! It was Jennifer Aniston! Orrin had dated Jennifer Aniston!

But no. That was crazy. Aniston lived in Los Angeles and she dated movie stars and—

Of course. Thinking about Jennifer now, her last name was Sinclair, not Aniston. But Rachel was conjuring up the only long-haired, blue-eyed Jennifer she herself knew, or knew of—and, of course, the character Jennifer Aniston was most famous for playing had also been named Rachel.

Jennifer and Orrin had dated for only a couple of months. And, at least as Orrin remembered it, they had parted on good terms—although he'd not heard from Ms. Sinclair since.

Rachel picked up a magazine—the cover story, like so many magazines of late, was related to the spate of terrorist attacks; the cover photo was of the smoldering remains of the Willis Tower, the building Rachel had always called the Sears Tower until the day it fell. But she didn't put on her glasses even though she thought her new pair with the mauve frames looked great on her. Instead, she stared at the pages of fuzzy type, concentrating not on them but on Orrin's past.

Prostitutes.

The memories were of streetwalkers seen in bad neighborhoods—but no direct interaction with them. Although those memories did slide into strippers, and he'd seen a bunch of them over the years, mostly while entertaining clients. The best place in DC, in his opinion, was the Stadium Club.

She turned the page; there was an ad for some pharmaceutical or other, and—

Rape.

Nothing.

I know she said she didn't want it, but you could tell . . .

Nothing.

And, finally, just to be sure . . .

I can be a real asshole when it comes to . . .

She took a deep breath, and lifted her gaze now, looking at the featureless pale green wall in front of her.

  . . . those damn telephone solicitors who call during dinner.

Rachel smiled, put down the magazine, folded her hands, and waited.

CHAPTER 16

"THANKS, Darryl," Susan said to Agent Hudkins, as he deposited Orrin Gillett in the office she was using.

Darryl nodded and left, closing the door behind him. Susan turned to the lawyer. "Mr. Gillett, you were in quite a hurry to leave earlier." She was still sitting in the roller chair behind the kidney-shaped desk; Gillett had taken the seat opposite her.

"Yes, as I said, I had a meeting to get to." He looked her in the eye and added, defiantly, "An *important* meeting."

"I do apologize," Susan said, in a tone that she hoped conveyed that she didn't really; she was still pissed at this clown. "Still, let me ask you a few questions. Can you tell me what you were doing here at the hospital?"

"I was visiting a friend, a partner in my law firm. He was in a car accident yesterday."

"And where were you when the lights went out?"

"In the corridor. I'd just left my friend's room."

"And tell me, Mr. Gillett, have you had any unusual experiences since 11:06 A.M. this morning?"

"Yes," he said flatly. "I had a Secret Service agent pull a gun on me."

Susan had to admire the man's moxie. She allowed herself a half smile. "Besides that, I mean."

"No."

"No unusual thoughts?"

Gillett narrowed his eyes. "What do you mean?"

"Just that: any unexpected visions, or memories, or . . . ?"

"That's a very strange question," Gillett said.

"Yes, it is," replied Susan. "Do you have a very strange answer?"

Gillett spread his arms. "What would you have me say?"

"Well, President Jerrison is in the building, and—"

"Yes, I know."

Susan was about to let that pass; after all, there were lots of TVs in the hospital, and hundreds of smartphones that could have been used to look at news reports, not to mention doctors and nurses buzzing about what was going on. But something in the way Gillett had said "I know" struck her. "How?" she asked. "How do you know?"

He looked like he was at war with himself, trying to decide how much to share. She asked again: "How exactly do you know?"

Finally, Gillett nodded. "All right, okay. You mentioned visions. Well, I was—it was like I was in the corridor, as the president was rushed into surgery. I was—I had a gun, but I swear to you, Miss Dawson, I had nothing to do with what happened to the president. There were these two people on gurneys, an older man and a younger woman, and there was a nurse—a, um, forgive me, but a stacked nurse—and . . ."

Susan thought for a moment. There'd been a security guard with the two people in the corridor; she'd since learned the two people had been scheduled for a kidney-transplant operation, and she guessed the guard had been summoned in case they got unruly at being bumped to make room for Prospector. She consulted her notes for the security guard's name. "Ivan Tarasov—does that name mean anything to you?"

"Yes," said Gillett. Then, more enthusiastically, "Yes! I don't know how, but I know all about him. He's been a guard here for four years, and he's got a wife named Sally and a three-year-old daughter named Tanya."

Susan asked him a few more questions, just to be sure he

really was linked to Tarasov. When she was done, Gillett said, "So, can I leave the hospital now?"

"No," said Susan. "I'm sorry, but you're going to have to stay a while longer."

"Look, unless you're going to charge me with something—"

"*Mister* Gillett," Susan said sharply. "I don't have to charge you with *anything.* This is a national-security matter. You're going to do what I say."

ERIC Redekop walked along a hallway at LT, wanting nothing more in the world than to go home. He was exhausted, and . . .

And, damn it all, he kept accessing Janis Falconi's memories. He didn't want them. He didn't want them at all. Yes, it was flattering—and surprising!—to know that she found him attractive. But he felt like a stalker, like he was invading her life, like a total fucking *creep.* That they both worked at LT just made matters worse: so many things here triggered him to recall *her* memories. That painting on the corridor wall: he'd never really noticed it before, but she'd stopped and looked at it repeatedly. Of course: she was an artist in her own right, he knew. And that orderly, there, walking toward him, whose name he'd never known before, was Scott Edwards, who had hit on Jan repeatedly.

He didn't need to know that. He didn't need to know any of it. But he knew it *all;* for any question he wondered about, the answer instantly came to him. How much she made, when and where she'd lost her virginity, and—Christ—what her menstrual cramps felt like. He hadn't wondered about that—what man would?—but seeing the wall calendar, there, had brought to mind that her period had just ended, and *that* had led to the recollection of the pains.

He tried not to think about anything intrusive, but that was impossible. Telling himself *not* to wonder about her sex life had the same effect *as* wondering about her sex life: it immediately brought memories to mind of her and her husband Tony, and—

Damn it.

Tony pushing into her, even though she wasn't wet.

And his inability to keep from ejaculating almost at once.

And his rolling off her, and lying on his side, his back to her, ignoring her after he was done, leaving her sad and frustrated and unfulfilled, and—

Damn it, damn it, damn it! He didn't want *any* of this, and—

And he was passing a woman's washroom now, and—

Oh, Christ, no.

But it came to him.

Her, in there.

At night.

No one else around.

And—

And Janis was a nurse, and she had access to all sorts of drugs, including ones designed to make pain go away, and she'd been in so much pain because of Tony for so long now. He saw her tattooed arm, recalling it in much greater detail than he could have on his own, knowing the pattern of stripes on the tiger, the deployment of its claws, the glint in its eyes. He knew it like—well, yes, the cliché applied—like the back of his own hand. But that arm was holding a syringe, and Janis was injecting herself.

For once, he did try to search her memories, looking for any sign that she was a diabetic, but—

But no. He knew what he was seeing, what he was recalling. She was shooting up. To make life bearable, to get her through the day.

He was sympathetic. He knew drug addiction was common among nurses and doctors, but he did *not* wish to know her secrets, damn it. And, for God's sake, he was obligated to report this, but—

But what would he report? That he thought he remembered her shooting up? She hadn't willingly shared that with him, and he hadn't stumbled upon evidence. It was just in his head.

He continued to walk the corridors of the hospital, hating himself for invading her privacy and wishing it would all come to an end.

CHAPTER 17

ORRIN Gillett came out of the room Agent Dawson was using for interviews. Rachel Cohen closed the magazine and put it back on the little table next to her chair, walked the short distance to where he was, and smiled her sweetest smile. "Hi," she said.

Orrin looked startled that she was still here. "Oh, hi," he replied. It wasn't nearly as sunny a greeting as before. "So I'm guessing from what you said before that you're the person who's reading me, right?"

Rachel nodded. "Right. Care to go for a walk?"

"They're not letting us leave the hospital yet."

"No. But we can go down to the lobby; the cafeteria's there. Maybe get a bite to eat."

"All right," Orrin said, but he sounded distracted.

"'Kay," she replied. "Just a sec." She went to a nearby drinking fountain and bent over to get some water, her jeans pulling tight as she did so. It was a bit tricky to glance at him from this posture, but—yes—Orrin was checking her out. She allowed herself a smile that he couldn't see, then walked back to him. "Shall we go?"

• • •

PETER Muilenburg and a half-dozen senior strategists were poring over weather forecasts for the target sites. The door opened, and a male aide came in. "Excuse me, Mr. Secretary."

"Yes?" replied Muilenburg.

"I've just gotten off the phone with the Secret Service agent-in-charge at Lima Tango, a Susan Dawson. They're getting a better handle on what's happening there. Yes, it seems clear that someone has access to Jerrison's memories, but they're just like *any* memories. Unless something brings a specific one to mind, you're not even aware you have that memory. It takes something to trigger it."

Muilenburg looked up at the display board, and he saw the call sign CVN-74, representing the U.S.S. *John C. Stennis,* move a bit closer to its target position.

"Well," said Muilenburg, "let's hope whoever it is doesn't read a newspaper or watch the news between now and the zero hour, because I can't see that stuff without thinking it's high time someone did *something*—and if they think that, they'll know what that something is, right?"

"Yes, Mr. Secretary," said the aide. "I imagine they will."

KADEEM Adams knew that President Jerrison was confined to his room in the ICU. But the man was gregarious by nature; Kadeem had seen that often enough on TV. And he was doubtless lonely. It was no fun being hospitalized, as Kadeem himself well knew. But, more than that, Jerrison was a politician; he wouldn't be able to resist the photo op. Even bedridden by an assassin's bullet, the president would make time to see an Iraq War vet, to have his picture taken shaking the young man's hand, and—yes, Kadeem knew the stats—given how poorly Jerrison was doing with African-Americans in the polls, to be seen congratulating a black soldier would be the best of all.

And so he went to Professor Singh's office and waited patiently outside the closed door until the man Susan Dawson had been questioning came out. Before she could bring someone else in, he entered himself.

Susan looked slightly flustered. "Hello, Kadeem."

He smiled his warmest smile. "Hey, Sue."

She didn't return the smile. "It's awkward, you knowing my memories."

"Sorry 'bout showing off earlier. I don't mean to pry."

She nodded. "No worse than what I've been doing with Professor Singh's mind, I guess. I just hope these linkages aren't going to last forever."

"I dunno," said Kadeem. "It be cool, in a way. I never got to go to college. But now I got a college-level education, kinda: whatever you remember of your classes, I can remember. Don't think geography would have been my choice of major, but I know things now I'd never have known."

"I guess," said Susan. "Anyway, what can I do for you, Kadeem?"

"Ma'am," he said, "I got a favor to ask."

She tilted her head slightly, apparently noting that he'd dropped the overly familiar "Sue."

"Yes?"

"The president, he's just downstairs, right?"

She looked for a moment like she was going to deny it—a reflex security concern—but there was no point; it had been mentioned on newscasts that he was on the second floor. She nodded.

"I'd like to see him. Meet him. Y'know? Something to tell my grandkids about someday."

Kadeem had no doubt that Susan, or one of her associates, had already been through his service record in minute detail. They'd know it was exemplary, and that he even had a degree of security clearance because of the weapon systems he'd worked with. There was no reason at all to think he presented a risk.

"He's still quite weak. He's in intensive care."

"I know, ma'am. And I know you've gotten to see him every day for years. But for a guy like me, I'll never get another . . ." He stopped himself; saying "shot at this" would hardly be the right phrasing just now. ". . . chance. Would mean the world to me."

Agent Dawson didn't reply at once, and so, Kadeem added, smiling as nicely as he could, "Please, ma'am."

He suspected she was weighing the new reality: that he'd *know* whether or not she actually tried to get him an audience;

that she couldn't get away with just saying she'd asked, but someone higher up had denied his request. Finally, she nodded. "I'll see what I can do."

SETH Jerrison had been fascinated by codes ever since he'd stumbled across Herbert S. Zim's classic *Codes and Secret Writing* in his school library when he was ten. Zim had outlined all sorts of ways to conceal written communication: everything from language tricks such as Pig Latin and Oppish to making invisible ink with lemon juice. He'd also demonstrated lots of substitution-cipher systems; the tic-tac-toe code had long been one of Seth's favorites.

Shortly after reading the book, Seth had invented his own encryption system that he called the "13 Code." He used it to share secret messages with his fourth-grade friend Duncan Ellerslie about Brenda Jackson, who they both agreed was the cutest girl in their class. One message he remembered sending looked like this:

```
3-6-4
ELBHA DROQB WGBEB XXBLX NDHUI Y!
```

Zim had recommended clustering letters into groups of five, lest word lengths provide clues to their meaning; he also suggested using all capitals, so that proper nouns or the pronoun *I* couldn't be easily detected.

The key to the 13 Code was to pick any three numbers that added up to 13, and put them at the beginning of the message. The recipient would then write down the letters of the alphabet in three paired columns, the lengths of which corresponded to the three numbers given. For the key of 3-6-4, the recipient would produce a decryption table that looked like this:

A=D	G=M	S=W
B=E	H=N	T=X
C=F	I=O	U=Y
	J=P	V=Z
	K=Q	
	L=R	

And then he'd use that table to substitute the appropriate letters to yield the plain text of the message. Thus:

ELBHA DROQB WGBEB XXBLX NDHUI Y!

would become:

BREND ALIKE SMEBE TTERT HANYO U!

or, with word spacing corrected and normal capitalization:

Brenda likes me better than you!

Hah! A perfect "Take that!" delivered by secret code! Seth had loved sending messages that only he and Duncan could read.

But that was then. Now there were no secrets; there was no privacy. He couldn't encrypt his thoughts and—

Well, yes, he supposed they *were* encrypted, sort of, in the way he'd heard Singh talk about. Only bits and pieces were stored. In fact, it was sort of like the 13 Code: even after decoding the message, the recipient had to rebuild it by adding to it: guessing at where to put in the spaces, converting characters to lowercase except where it seemed sensible to retain the capitals. Whatever the person reading his memories would recall would be filtered through his or her own experiences, conjuring up something not quite the same as what Seth himself would—but it would be close enough to do damage.

And the damage could be considerable. Whoever was sharing his memories knew what legislation he was planning to veto, what campaign promises he intended to break, what he really thought of the Speaker of the House.

And yet those things were *small,* in so many ways. But if news about Operation Counterpunch got out early, there might be enormous American casualties. He shifted his head slightly—it was painful to do so—and looked at the large windows. The ever-present nurse was seated by them, and beyond her, through the glass—which he'd now been told had been reinforced with a bulletproof layer—he saw a plume of gray smoke. That smoke contained the ashes of his clothes, his books, all his wife's things, and priceless mementos of US history: the *Resolute* desk, centuries-old oil paintings, the artifacts in the Lincoln bedroom, and more.

He wasn't a monster; none of those who had put Counterpunch together were. They were just people—husbands and wives, fathers and mothers, sons and daughters—who had had enough. Even before today's terrorist attack, they'd had enough.

He remembered a joke that had gone around the Internet in the fall of 2001: "What's the difference between Osama bin Laden and Santa Claus?" And the answer, which had seemed so funny back then when people had been forwarding the joke endlessly: "Come Christmas, Santa Claus will still be here."

But bin Laden had survived an entire decade. Indeed, as today's events had proved, it was easier to put a bullet in the president of the United States than it was to take out a religious zealot, especially when he had powerful allies.

Seth had taught history for twenty years. The US had had a chance—a brief window—during which it could have preemptively struck the Soviet Union, wiping it from the map. The governments of the day—JFK's regime, and then Johnson's—hadn't had the balls. And so the US had instead endured decades of living in fear of the Soviets' attacking first, and had spent trillions—*trillions!*—stockpiling weapons.

And it was the same damn thing again.

San Francisco.

Philadelphia.

Chicago.

And now Washington.

A whole nation—a whole planet—living in fear.

He watched the smoke rise and swirl.

CHAPTER 18

SUSAN finished another interview, speaking with Dora Hennessey, the woman who'd come here to give her father a kidney. Sue took a bathroom break, then stopped by Singh's lab, which was where he was conducting his interviews. A squat white man was leaving just as Susan arrived. "Any thoughts about how to sever the links?" she asked Singh.

"I don't even know what *caused* them," the Canadian replied. "I mean, memory is *chemical*. It's based on molecules squirting across the synaptic cleft from one neuron to the next. How a memory could leap many meters is beyond me." He shook his head. "That's why most people with scientific training think claims of telepathy must be junk: there's nothing your brain puts out that can be read at a distance."

"What about brain waves?" asked Susan, sitting on the experimental chair next to the articulated stand holding up the geodesic sphere.

"There aren't any brain waves in the sense you're thinking," Singh said. "The brain doesn't radiate electromagnetic signals the way, say, a Wi-Fi source or radio broadcaster does. And, even if it did, the signals would be weak, and get weaker, as all signals do, over distance—usually according to the inverse-square law. By the time a signal has traveled three times as far away, it's only got one-ninth the power. Before you knew it, any signal would be lost in the background noise of all the other signals."

"Then what are EEGs recording, if not brain waves?"

"Well, they *are* recording brain waves—but, like I said, the name gives the wrong idea. See, the brain contains billions of neurons. When one neuron gets a signal from a neighbor, it can respond by releasing ions—which are charged atoms, right?"

Susan nodded.

Singh went on. "Ions with like charges repel each other, and when a bunch of neighboring neurons release a bunch of similarly charged ions, they all push each other away, creating a physical wave—an undulation—in the material of the brain, which has the consistency of pudding. EEGs measure those actual waves bumping against the skull."

"Oh."

"So, you see, there's no way to read brain waves across a large spatial gap."

"Your mother's name is Gurneet and your father's is Manveer."

Singh tipped his head in a small sign of concession. "I admit I have no explanation for your knowing that."

"So, I'm what, six feet from you?"

"About two meters, yes."

"And this square-inverse law you mentioned—"

"Inverse-square."

"If I went to the far end of the building, the signal should drop off to almost nothing, right?"

"The building is—I don't know—a hundred meters on its longest side perhaps. So, yes, if we were as far apart as we could get in this building, the signal strength would be one over one hundred squared, or one one-ten-thousandth as strong, assuming there *is* a signal, and assuming it is broadcast in all directions."

"What if it isn't? What if the linkage is just that—a link, like, you know, a line drawn between you and me?"

Singh stood up and spun in a circle. "And did the link

maintain itself during that? What mechanism would there be to keep a beam focused from my head to yours, or from yours to Private Adams's? It's inconceivable."

"All right. Still, let's test it. I'm going to go as far from you as I can without leaving the building, and we'll see if the signal, um . . . attenuates? Is that the right word?"

"Yes."

Susan left the lab and headed down the long corridor, passing patients on gurneys, doctors, nurses, and other people—several of whom tried to question her about how much longer the lockdown was going to last. She made it to the far end of the building as quickly as she could—and then, for good measure, she entered the stairwell and headed up to the sixth floor, which was the highest level.

She found a janitor there in a blue uniform, pushing a mop. "You!" Susan said, pointing at him. "Name a topic."

"Excuse me?"

"A topic—something, anything—to think about."

"Ma'am?"

"Oh, come on, man! It's not that hard a question. Any topic."

"Umm, like, um, baseball, do you mean?"

"Baseball! Fine. Thank you!" And then she turned her back on the no-doubt-bewildered man, closed her eyes, and concentrated on the first time she'd ever seen a baseball game live, and . . .

And a memory of her father taking her to Dodger Stadium came to her. She'd spilled her Pepsi all over him, and he'd laughed it off and squirted water at her. She shook her head, clearing her own memory, and tried to summon another, and—

And she was watching the Toronto Blue Jays play, and from a private box, something she herself had never done.

More details: others in the booth. Sikhs, remembered not because they *were* Sikhs but because the colors of their individual turbans had been noted; Sue had previously had no idea that such choices were individual fashion statements. A party, a celebration of . . . of . . .

Ah, yes. Of Ranjip's brother's eighteenth birthday, which—yes—had actually been the day before, but there'd been no game that day. A wonderful memory, a happy memory—and no sense at all that it was more difficult to access or recall than Singh's memories had been when they'd been much closer together. She didn't have to strain, didn't have to cock an ear as if listening to something faint, didn't have to do *anything* differently. It just came to her when she thought about it, as easily as when she'd been right next to Singh.

She headed along the sixth-floor corridor until she got to the stairwell near the elevator station, then went down to three.

Professor Singh was still in his lab. "The first baseball game you saw live was in Toronto, wasn't it?" asked Susan. "For your brother's eighteenth birthday? Your dad rented a private box at the SkyDome."

Singh nodded. "Although they don't call it that anymore. It's the Rogers Centre now."

"You remember it as the SkyDome."

"No doubt." He blinked. "So you had no trouble reading my memories, even from far away?"

"None."

"I don't understand that. There should have been attenuation, unless . . ."

"Yes?"

He swiveled his chair, turning his back on his computer. "It's . . . no. No, it can't be that."

"What?"

Singh thought for a moment, then, seemingly out of the blue, said, "Do you ever watch *Saturday Night Live?*"

"Not since I was a teenager."

"Remember when Mike Myers used to be on? He'd play a Jewish woman named Linda Richman, who had a call-in talk show. When she got emotional, she'd put her hand on her chest, and say, 'I'm all *verklempt.* Talk amongst yourselves. I'll give you a topic.' And then she'd say something like, 'The Civil War was neither civil nor a war—discuss.'"

"No, I don't remember that. Oh, wait—um, yes, now I do."

Singh smiled. "Exactly."

"I think the one when the character said, 'The peanut is neither a pea nor a nut' was funnier."

Singh nodded slightly. "Perhaps. But the point is, if I tell you to remember something that you don't actually have memories of, but I do, *you* remember it, too. So, let me give you a topic—but don't discuss it. Think about it; *recall* it. Okay?"

She nodded. "Okay."

"Quantum entanglement," he said.

Her first impulse was to pull a Linda Richman and say, ". . . is neither quantum nor entangled," but she didn't even know if that made sense, and—

And it *didn't* make sense. Quantum entanglement was a property of quantum mechanics, and it *did* involve entangling things, and—

And it was *weird*. She'd never heard of anything like it. When pairs of particles are created simultaneously under the right circumstances, they can become linked in such a way that they continue to be connected no matter how far apart they become.

"Wow," said Susan.

"Wow indeed," said Ranjip. "Okay. Another topic—well, not really; it's the same topic, but a different way of looking at it. Ready?"

Susan nodded.

"Spooky action at a distance," Ranjip said.

Susan was startled that she knew this was something Einstein had said. And, yes, it *was* spooky. Change the spin of one entangled particle, and the spin of the other changes instantaneously; they are bound together in an almost magical way— again, no matter how far apart they get from each other.

"Got it," said Susan, and then she surprised herself by asking a question. "But if it's quantum entanglement, why aren't the linkages symmetrical? I mean, if *A* can read *B,* why can't *B* read *A?*"

"The linkages probably *are* symmetrical," Singh replied. "That is, either *A* or *B* could change any specific shared memory for both of them—the shared memories are entangled, and changes to them at one location would change them at both. But symmetry doesn't imply reciprocity. *A* and *B* have symmetrically shared memories that happen to have originally belonged to *A*. Meanwhile, *B* and *C* have symmetrically shared memories that happened to originally belong to *B*. And so on."

"Ah," said Susan. "I guess."

"Okay," said Singh. "New topic, sort of: Penrose and Hameroff."

And that came to her, too: physicist Roger Penrose—a sometimes-collaborator with Stephen Hawking—and the anesthesiologist Stuart Hameroff had proposed that human consciousness was quantum mechanical in nature.

It was astonishing: to know something so complex and yet never have even *heard* of it before. It wasn't like university lectures were running through her head at high speed, and it wasn't like playing Trivial Pursuit, where she had to dig deeply to find the answers; these were things that Singh knew well, and so she knew them well, too, and they came effortlessly to mind as soon as he said the trigger words.

"Got it," she said again.

"Okay, new topic: the design of my apparatus."

And she now knew all about that, too: a device that used tuned lasers—which emitted photons, which were a type of particle that could indeed be entangled—to selectively excite neurons. His design actually *displaced* the photons that were already there and *substituted* new ones.

Then . . .

"Cytoskeleton."

And:

"Microtubule."

And:

"Bose-Einstein condensate."

She shook her head, as if somehow that would get the pieces to sift out of the swirling jumble they were in and fall into place. And, after a moment, they did. "And this is legit?" Susan said at last.

"Well, it's a legitimate theory," replied Singh. "Penrose and Hameroff say the actual seat of consciousness, which, of course, must somehow interact with memory, is not in the chemical synapses but rather in quantum effects in the microtubules of the cytoskeleton—the internal scaffolding—of brain cells. Their theory has its passionate advocates—and passionate detractors. But if we *are* dealing with quantum entanglement, that could explain why the linkages don't weaken over distance."

"And does it suggest how to break them?" asked Susan.

"Well, um, no—no, I don't have a clue how to do that. Entanglement is a tricky thing, and normally it's quite fragile. But I'll keep trying to find the answer."

"Do that," Susan said.

"I will. What about you? Any progress?"

Susan shook her head. "I still don't know who's reading the president."

"What are you going to do if you can't identify who it is?" Singh asked.

Susan said nothing.

"You can't keep all the people here prisoner indefinitely."

Again: nothing.

"They've committed no crime!" said Singh.

"One of them has in his or her possession classified information."

"Not deliberately."

She shook her head. "Doesn't matter. *Possession* of such information is a felony, and they're all suspects."

"You'd like to . . ." Singh began, and then, not able to give voice to it, he tried again: "You'd like to have them *disappear,* wouldn't you?"

Susan lifted her eyebrows. "It's an option."

"They've done nothing wrong!"

"Professor Singh," Susan said, "look at me. My job is to die for the president, if need be; my life instead of his. I didn't vote for him, I don't agree with most of his policies, I don't even particularly *like* him, but none of that matters. We live in a system in which the president is more important than *anyone,* and this president has been compromised in a way that has to be contained or eliminated. In fact, even breaking the link may not be enough. Yes, once it's severed—if it ever is—the person may not be able to access new memories, but presumably they'll still remember anything they've recalled while the link was intact, right?"

"I don't know," Singh said. "Honestly. No one has any experience with this."

"Which means," Susan said, "that we may indeed have to lock these people up indefinitely."

"You can't," said Singh. "I'll go public."

"It's not my call to make," said Susan. "But don't count on having that option. In fact . . ."

Singh narrowed his eyes. "Yes?"

"Your work may end up being classified. You have to recognize that you've developed the ultimate interrogation technique. Replicate the linking effect, but with only two people within the sphere. They'd each link to the other, right? An interrogator would know everything a prisoner knew—plans, names, dates, codes, whatever."

"And vice versa, Agent Dawson. Don't forget that."

"Yes, you'd have to carefully choose your interrogator—make sure *he* doesn't know anything vital . . . that is, if you ever expected to let the prisoner go free again."

Singh had a shocked expression on his face, but Susan pressed ahead. "Let's update the chart," she said. The Sikh had redrawn his chart on the lab's whiteboard. The grid had twenty columns and three rows; the rows were labeled "Name," "Can Read," and "Is Read By."

Susan pointed to the column for Orrin Gillett. "Gillett can read Ivan Tarasov, a security guard."

Singh filled in this information with a blue dry-erase marker.

"Ah," said Singh. "I interviewed this Tarasov. He can read Dora Hennessey, who was here to donate a kidney to her father." He wrote this in.

"Yes, I know who she is," said Susan. "I interviewed Dora just before coming here. She's able to read the memories of Ann January. Mrs. January is a surgical nurse, and—"

"Excuse me," said Singh. "I'm sorry, but—are you sure?"

"Well, Dora didn't tell me Ann's exact job title," Susan said, "but she's *some* kind of nurse."

"No, no. I mean, are you sure that Dora Hennessey is reading Ann January?"

"Oh, yes. No question."

Singh pointed at a square on his whiteboard. "Because David January is reading Ann January, too. I just interviewed him."

Susan came over to look at the board. "Husband and wife? Or brother and sister?" But before Singh could reply, she had the answer from his memory. "Husband and wife, right?" she said.

"Yes."

"That's very strange," said Susan.

"Indeed it is," said Singh. "We haven't had two people linked to the same person before, and . . ."

"Yes?" prodded Susan.

Singh looked frustrated. "Well, I thought I was making progress puzzling this out. But multiple linkages wouldn't work with the kind of quantum entanglement we were just talking about; a double linkage would require a complex superposition that I should think would rapidly decohere."

Susan was astonished that talk like this actually now made sense to her. She thought about Singh's theory—not so much the details, but his level of confidence in it. He *had* been sure he was on the right track, and—

"He's lying," Susan said.

"What?" said Singh.

"He's lying. This David January fellow is lying."

"Why would he lie about who he's linked to?" asked Singh. But then he got it: "Oh! The president!"

"Exactly," said Susan. "I'm going to have a word with Mr. January myself." She looked at Singh. "Cheer up, Ranjip. Maybe we'll only have to eliminate one person."

CHAPTER 19

SUSAN left Singh's lab and walked the short distance to his office, sitting down behind his kidney-shaped desk. She pored over the handwritten notes Singh had made on David January: he was, it turned out, the doctor who had operated the defibrillator that had been used on Prospector, and he'd been married for twenty-three years now to Ann January, who was indeed a surgical nurse. Susan googled his name, just to see what would come up, and then checked up on his wife. She then called hospital security and asked them to locate David January and bring him to Singh's office.

A few minutes later, Dr. January arrived, accompanied, to Susan's surprise, by a security guard whose nameplate read "Tarasov"—he was the person being read by Orrin Gillett. Tarasov was behaving oddly: he wouldn't meet her gaze, and he seemed generally uncomfortable to be talking to her. She wondered if he was trying to hide something; she'd grill him next. But for now David January was her priority. She dismissed Tarasov.

January turned out to be the squat man she'd seen leaving

Singh's lab earlier. He was forty-four, according to Singh's notes, and had hyperthyroid bulging eyes; he looked a bit like Peter Lorre.

"Have a seat, Mr. January," Susan said. She deliberately chose not to call him "Doctor"—you never elevate an interrogee above the interrogator. "I'm just following up on the conversation you had with Professor Singh. I understand you told him you are linked to your wife."

The big eyes got even bigger for a moment. "To Annie, yes."

"How convenient, that," Susan said, her tone neutral.

January smiled amiably. "I don't know if it's convenient, but there's no one else I'd rather be linked to."

"Well," said Susan, trying on a disarming smile of her own, "I guess it's what every woman wants in a man if you believe the magazines. You'll no longer be able to say to her, 'I can't read minds,' when she expects you to do something but doesn't explicitly tell you, right?"

His smile now seemed forced. "I guess. It still seems so . . . so *fantastic*." He spread his arms a bit. "I gotta tell you, it's funny seeing myself as *she* sees me."

"Funny?"

"You know, to have memories from her point of view, memories in which she sees me instead of me seeing her."

Despite her suspicions, Susan was intrigued. "How closely do the memories match? I mean, do you see an almost three-dimensional scene, shifting from her perspective to your own and back again? Do they synch up that well?"

"Depends on the memory, of course. Some are more detailed than others—and some are more detailed for me and hazy for her, and vice versa." He made an indulgent little smile. "She doesn't like hockey nearly as much as I do; she can barely remember what *teams* are playing, let alone individual plays."

"All right," Susan said. "Let me ask you a question."

"Go ahead."

"What is Ann's lover's name?"

"She doesn't have a lover," January said, sounding miffed. "Other than me."

"Oh?" said Susan. "Think back to last month—October.

She dropped you at Reagan, and you flew to—where was it now? Ah, yes. Denver, for a conference on defibrillation technology, right?" Her Google search had found his name on the program. "You settled in for a long flight and maybe watched a movie."

"I did. On my laptop."

"But continue that memory from her point of view," said Susan. "What did *she* do the moment she dropped you off?"

"My wife drops me off all the time at the airport; I attend a lot of meetings. There was nothing special about that day that I recall—that *she* recalls."

"No? October eighteenth? Unseasonably cold and windy. And you were going to be gone for an entire week that time."

"I don't . . ."

"Remember it?" asked Susan. "Remember that day?"

"Nothing comes to mind."

"All right. I'll tell you. Stop me when this begins to sound familiar. She left Reagan and drove on to Dulles, leaving her car in long-term parking. She then took the shuttle to the terminal, and there she met a man named William Cordt—although she called him Willie."

"Then there's no way you could know that. There's nothing exceptional about my wife; there's no way you'd have been watching her back then."

"That's true," said Susan. "We weren't watching her. We were watching William Cordt. This *is* Washington, after all. We watch a lot of people—especially those who have illicit ties to foreign defense contractors, as Mr. Cordt does. When he takes a trip out of the country, we know—and he did, with your wife, to Switzerland, for a skiing vacation."

"Bullshit," he said. "Annie was never involved with any arms smuggler, or anything like that."

"Now, that I actually believe," Susan said. "That is, I believe that she never knew that that's what he was and so would have no memories of it. But you must surely have other memories of this event, from her point of view. The trip to Switzerland. The hotel they stayed in there, the Englischer Hof. The evenings they spent there."

January narrowed his eyes, as if concentrating on something small. And then he made a short, sharp intake of breath.

"Oh, my . . . Oh, God." He slumped in the chair. "I—I had no idea . . . We . . . she . . . I . . ."

Then he looked at her, and his face was contorted in rage. "That was *cruel,*" he said. "Making me see that. Making me *know* that."

"It would have been cruel, Mr. January, if any of it had ever really happened. But it didn't. There is no William Cordt. Your wife hasn't left the United States in over three years; I checked her passport records."

January's eyes went wide. "You . . . *bitch!*"

"And you're under arrest."

"For what?"

"For espionage. Spying on the president is a felony."

"The president!" said January.

"Don't play games now," Susan said. "Yes, the president." She stood up. "Extend your arms."

"What for?" asked January.

"So I can cuff you."

"I demand to see a lawyer."

"Oh, you will. Before this is over, you'll have seen more of them than you can count. But for now, not only do you have the *right* to remain silent, you have the *obligation.* Spying on the president is bad enough. Revealing what you've learned is . . . well, I'm glad we never got around to closing Gitmo."

"Wait!" said January as Susan went to cuff him. "You're wrong! You're wrong!"

Susan closed the metal loops around his wrists. "Tell it to the judge."

"No, no. Listen to me! You're wrong. I'm not linked to the president, honestly. God, it never even occurred to me that anyone might be linked to him—he wasn't conscious, after all, when all this went down; he was under general anesthesia."

"Then why'd you lie about being linked to your wife?"

He hesitated. Susan put the flat of her hand against his back and propelled him toward the door.

"All right!" he said. "All right. I'm telling you the truth. I'm not linked to President Jerrison. I'm linked to Mark Griffin."

"The hospital CEO?" she said. "Why lie about that?" They

were at the closed door to Singh's office; Singh's black bomber jacket was hanging from a hook on the door's back.

"Because I'm president of the staff association here, and he's the hospital's chief executive officer—and my opponent. I'm facing off against him over contract negotiations, and, well, this will give me the edge, so long as he doesn't know I'm reading him. I figured it would be easy to fake that I was linked to my wife; we already have so many memories in common."

"Prove it," Susan said. "Prove you're linked to Griffin. When did he and I first meet?"

"When you arrived here this morning with the president. He was on the right side of the gurney, and you were on the left. You had blood smeared on your jacket."

"Who was behind me?"

"The president's personal physician. Griffin greeted her, although he called her by her military rank: Captain Snow."

"And what did he say about Dr. Redekop?"

"Nothing, then."

"Later, I mean. What did he call him when we were in the observation gallery?"

"He said Redekop was 'a doctor of the'—well, I don't know what this means, but it's what he said: 'a doctor of the first water.'"

"Fuck," said Susan.

"I'm sorry," said January. "I really am. I—this all just sort of fell into my lap, you know? I didn't know what to do."

"Rule number one, asshole: don't lie to the Secret Service." She took off the handcuffs. "Get out of here."

"You mean I can go home?"

"No, you cannot. Not until I choose to end the lockdown. But get out of my sight."

"Yes, ma'am," he said, and he scurried out the door.

SUSAN was livid as she walked down to Singh's lab. The Canadian was sitting at his computer, and Darryl Hudkins had now joined him. He was looking at a city map spread out on a table.

"Any luck tracking down the woman who went AWOL?" she demanded.

"Not yet," Darryl replied, looking up. "Problem is, the old thing has cataracts, I think. She's *somewhere* today—I just can't make out where; the visuals in her memories of this afternoon are indistinct. It's noisy—she doesn't like that—but I still don't know where it is. She's just not paying any real attention to her surroundings."

"Indoors or out?"

"Indoors. But it's not a museum or a gallery or a store. She's just wandering around in a daze, it seems—she was already preoccupied with her son's having a heart attack, and then someone told her about the president being shot, and later about the White House. When I think about this afternoon, the only memories of hers I get are of her worrying about, well, about *everything.*"

"Damn it," said Susan. "Keep trying." She went over to the whiteboard and corrected the information on it, now that they knew that David January was really linked to Mark Griffin.

"Agent Dawson?" said Singh.

She wheeled around. *"What?"*

Singh looked startled by the sharpness of her tone. Susan took a deep breath; she wasn't mad at him, and she shouldn't take it out on him. "Sorry, Ranjip. What is it?"

"Have a look at this, please." Singh gestured at his monitor.

Susan came over and stared at the screen, which was showing a complex graph. It felt strange to be seeing it. For the first second or two, it appeared to be just a random shape, with numbers and letters marking certain points, but as she looked at *this* part, she suddenly understood it, and shifting her attention *here* caused that part to make sense, as well, and all at once the numbers at the bottom of the screen conveyed meaning for her, too. She'd originally opened her mouth to say, "What is it?," but the words that came out were, "Are you sure?"

"I'm positive," said Singh. "It's based on the data from my equipment's diagnostic files, and it's the only configuration that works."

"Twenty-one nodes, not twenty?" asked Susan.

"Exactly. Twenty-one people were affected."

Darryl Hudkins walked over and stood with his arms crossed in front of his chest. "Dr. Griffin and I were careful in reviewing the security-camera recordings. There's no way someone was in the affected sphere that we didn't see."

"There was an electromagnetic pulse," Susan said.

"Well, yeah . . ." replied Darryl.

"Which means there could have been an interruption in the recordings, no?"

"Sure, yeah," said Darryl. "There was. But according to the timecode, it lasted less than a minute."

"A good runner," Susan said, "can cover a thousand feet in a minute." She looked at Singh's grid of linkages on the whiteboard, then picked up a marker and drew in a twenty-first column at the far right. In the spot for the person's name at the top of the column, she put an "X" for unknown.

CHAPTER 20

SETH Jerrison lay on his back. His chest ached, and it hurt to breathe, but he'd insisted the doctors keep him awake as much as possible; he couldn't risk the Speaker or anyone else trying to move for a forced handover of power under the Twenty-Fifth Amendment—not this close to the initiation of Counterpunch.

He'd just spent half an hour on the phone with his chief of staff, who was holding things together at Mount Weather, and he'd also spoken to his science advisor, who was currently at a conference at CERN but was cutting that short to return to the States.

The phone calls had been enough to exhaust Seth, and so he stared up at the ceiling and the irritating strobing fluorescent tube there. Jesus Christ, he was leader of the free world; all he had to do was *mention* it to someone, and it would be fixed. He looked over at Nurse Sheila, who was ever vigilant.

He knew he was in good hands here—and not just because the hospital was named for the man who had saved more American lives than anyone else in history, even though a recent survey had shown that less than one percent of

Americans knew who he was. In fact, Jerrison had to admit, he himself hadn't—the only holder of the same office that he could name prior to becoming president was the one immortalized by the B-Sharps, Homer Simpson's barbershop quartet: *"For all the latest medical poop, call Surgeon General C. Everett Koop—koop koop a koop."*

But Luther Terry was responsible for more people knowing *of* the office of Surgeon General than anyone else, for he was the one who in 1964 had released the report linking smoking to cancer, and in 1965 had instigated the "Surgeon General's Warning" on cigarette packs.

Seth had recently reviewed proposed new warnings, designed to prevent teenagers who see themselves as invincible from picking up the habit. "Smokers become slaves to Big Tobacco." "The maker of this product intends to addict you to it." "Smokers are pawns of heartless corporations." And his favorite, short and sweet: "You are being used."

The fluorescent tube continued to flicker, and—

An Inside Job.

Seth had taught American history for twenty years—including all about the previous presidential assassination attempts. He'd read the whole damn Warren Commission Report, as well as the myriad conspiracy theories. Earl Warren and his colleagues got it right, in his view: Oswald had acted alone, not in cahoots with the CIA. It was crazy to think a conspiracy could reach so far into the government; a lone nut was far easier—and far less scary—to contemplate. Hell, Nixon couldn't keep Watergate a secret; Bill Clinton couldn't keep a blowjob a secret. How could anyone keep a plan within the Secret Service to eliminate the president under wraps?

Seth didn't know what he should do. He thought about dismissing the entire Secret Service, but there were dozens of protectees that would be affected: the First Family, Flaherty and his family, the living ex-presidents, visiting foreign dignitaries, and so on.

But, damn it all, at least he could get *this* fixed. "Sheila," he said as loudly as he could—which he supposed was about half a normal speaking volume.

Sheila moved immediately to his bedside. "Yes, Mr. President?"

"That light," he said softly, and he managed to lift his free hand a little to point at it. "Can you get it replaced?"

She looked up at it. "Of course, sir."

Just then, the door opened, and in came Susan Dawson. "Mr. President, how are you feeling?"

His voice was still weak, he knew, but Ronald Reagan had set a high standard for banter on occasions like this, and so he tried his best. "Like someone shot me in the back, and someone else carved my chest open. Oh, and like someone blew up my house."

Susan rewarded him with a small smile, and Seth supposed he *was* feeling slightly better, despite all those horrors; she was a beautiful woman, and it pleased him to have her smiling at him. Actually, he liked it better when she was wearing her Secret Service–issue sunglasses; there was something really sexy about women in dark glasses, and—

The Secret Service.

The people who were supposed to protect him.

He still couldn't believe it.

"What happened to the . . ." He kept wanting to call him "the assassin," but that wasn't right; he'd failed at his job. ". . . the assailant?"

"He was trying to escape, sir. He'd been in the elevator at the Lincoln Memorial and—"

"What elevator?" Seth said.

"There's one for handicapped access, sir. It was installed in the 1970s."

"Oh."

"He was shimmying up the elevator cable, trying to get away, and the elevator started up and he fell. Broke his neck."

"That's the passive voice," he said.

"Sir?"

"'The elevator started up.' Surely someone pushed the button."

"Yes, sir."

"Who?"

"Agent Jenks, sir. Dirk Jenks."

Shit, Seth thought. Maybe the assailant *hadn't* been acting alone after all. "Investigate him," he said.

But Susan nodded. "Way ahead of you, sir. The FBI apprehended him at Reagan. He hasn't broken yet under interrogation, but it seems almost certain that he was in cahoots with Gordo."

Seth would have sat up if he could. "Gordo?"

"Sorry. That's what most of us called Agent Danbury. Not Gordon but Gordo."

That name was ringing a bell. He'd heard it recently . . . somewhere. From someone.

No, no, he hadn't heard it—he'd *overheard* it. At the White House . . . in the Oval Office. He'd come in through his private door while Leon Hexley, the head of the Secret Service, was talking on his BlackBerry, but . . .

But what had he said? It was just a couple of days ago. Damn it, what had Hexley said? "Tell Gordo to . . ."

Tell Gordo to . . . what?

It had been intriguing, he remembered that much, even not knowing then who Gordo was. But, damn it, he couldn't dredge it up.

THE door to Singh's lab burst open, and in strode lawyer Orrin Gillett. "Dr. Griffin told me I might find you here, Agent Dawson. How long until you let us go?"

Susan had been busily thumb-typing to her boyfriend Paul on her phone, bringing him up-to-date on what was going on. She finished the message she was sending, pocketed the device, and let Gillett wait in silence for five seconds, then said, "I haven't made that determination. Frankly, I'm not sure it's safe for people to leave the hospital."

Gillett stared at her through his round glasses. His tone was cool, measured. "You actually don't have the power to detain people indefinitely."

Susan looked over at Professor Singh, who was running simulations on his computer, then back at Gillett. "We're dealing with an unprecedented situation," she said.

Gillett helped himself to a chair, crossing his long legs and leaning back. "That's right, Agent Dawson. But in the law, precedents are what matters—precedents and regulations. And so I did some research." He pulled out his iPhone and consulted its screen. "Under Title 18, Section 3056, of the

United States Code, Secret Service agents have very limited powers. You can execute warrants issued under the laws of this country—but no warrants have been issued in this matter." He looked up. "You can make arrests without warrants for any offense against the United States committed in your presence, or for any felony recognizable under the laws of the United States, if you have reasonable grounds to believe that the person to be arrested has committed such a felony. But you have no reason to believe *any* offense or felony has been committed in this matter. Beyond that, all you're allowed to do is"—he read from the screen—"'Investigate fraud in connection with identification documents, fraudulent commerce, fictitious instruments, and foreign securities.'"

"Don't gloss over that so quickly, Mr. Gillett. The Secret Service does indeed deal with cases of identity theft."

He slipped his phone into his breast pocket. "But no one here has committed any such crime, have they?"

"Not yet, but they're all surely capable of it now. They know every personal detail, every possible answer to any security question—mother's maiden name, first-grade teacher, what have you."

"This is the United States of America, Agent Dawson, not some third-world police state. You can't imprison people because you think they might someday commit a crime; indeed, you slander them by suggesting they might do so."

"I'm not talking about imprisoning," Susan said, folding her arms in front of her chest. "I'm talking about, well, protective custody."

"What for?" demanded Gillett.

"We simply don't know what's going to happen to you, to me, or to anyone else who has been affected. Our brains have been messed up; we might have seizures—anything could happen."

"For your own part, you may take whatever personal precautions you see fit," Gillett said. "And you may certainly advise all affected parties of the potential dangers. Indeed, I urge you to do so. But you also have to be honest with them: you have to say you have no reason whatsoever to think people will undergo seizures, lose touch with reality, or otherwise have any difficulties beyond the ones they've already experienced."

"This is a medical matter," Susan said.

"Indeed it is," replied Gillett, "and Luther Terry's lawyers will certainly advise people to stay under medical supervision and get them to sign waivers should they decide to leave, but there's no infection here. They can't compel people to stay; there's nothing that justifies an involuntary quarantine. And, besides, given that the linkages may be permanent, you're talking about what amounts to life sentences without due process. No court will stand for that."

Susan knew she was fighting with Gillett for the sake of fighting; he was probably right legally—and he might well be right morally, too. She exhaled and tried to calm down.

Professor Singh spoke up. "Mr. Gillett, since you're a lawyer, may I ask you a question?"

Gillett had been glaring at Susan, but as he turned to look at the Sikh's kindly face, his features softened. "Who are you?"

Singh stood up. "I'm Ranjip Singh, a memory researcher." He paused, then: "You see that?" He pointed to the padded chair and the stand with the geodesic sphere on a multi-jointed arm. "That's my equipment; it was involved in the linking of memories."

Susan noted that Gillett was as quick on the draw as she herself was: he had his business card out in the blink of an eye. "Have you retained counsel?" he asked.

Singh's eyebrows shot up. "What for?"

"As it happens, Mr. Singh, I'm not at all upset about what has occurred, but others doubtless are. You can count on lawsuits."

Singh looked aghast, Susan thought, but he took the card and slipped it into the pocket of his lab coat.

"You had a question?" Gillett prodded.

"Um, yes," said Singh, still flustered. "It's this: do we let people know who they are being read by?"

"In many cases, those of us who have been affected already know," replied Gillett. "For instance, I'm being read by Rachel Cohen."

"How do you know that?" Singh asked.

"Besides looking at that whiteboard, there, you mean?" Gillett replied with a wry smile. "She told me."

"Oh," said the professor. "But what about those who don't

already know? Do they have the legal right to know who is reading them? After all, it's an invasion of privacy of rare proportions."

Gillett spread his arms. "It's not just those who are being read who have rights, Mr. Singh. Those who are doing the reading have rights, too."

"How do you mean?"

"Well, suppose someone decides he can't abide the notion of somebody else knowing his innermost secrets, and so he tracks down the person who is reading him and kills that person. If you reveal who is reading whom, you might be putting the person doing the reading at risk. Are you prepared to take responsibility for that?"

"I—I don't know," said Singh.

"What about you, Agent Dawson?" asked Gillett, swiveling his chair a bit to face her.

"I don't know."

"No, you don't. You'll need a legal opinion from the Secret Service's counsel, and that will take days to research and render. There are no exact parallels, of course, but I suspect your attorneys will advise against revealing what you've uncovered, just as they'd advise against revealing anything the government discovers in its normal operations; there's an implied covenant of confidentiality when speaking to a government employee, and without signed waivers from those you've interviewed, you'd be on very thin ice legally if you divulged anything you learned."

"But what about the threat Agent Dawson mentioned of identity theft?" asked Singh.

"Advise people to take suitable precautions without revealing who they are being read by."

"And then just let them go?" asked Susan, resting her bottom now against the edge of a desk.

"It's a free country, Agent Dawson. The affected individuals are entitled to make their own decisions about what they want to do. You cost one of my clients enormously when you detained me earlier today, preventing me from getting to a crucial meeting. He may well direct me to file suit over that. Are you prepared for other lawsuits for wrongful imprisonment? Are you going to pay the people who have jobs if you don't let them go perform them, or compensate them for missed vacations? I want to leave, Miss Cohen wants to leave, and I'm sure many of the others want to leave, especially given today's horrific events. They want to get back to their families, their children, their careers, their lives. And you have no legal option except to let them do that."

CHAPTER 21

DAVID January was pleased that the bitch from the Secret Service had let him go. He was even more pleased that she'd believed him when he'd said he'd hidden being linked to Mark Griffin because accessing Griffin's memories would give him an advantage in negotiating the new collective agreement.

But that wasn't the real reason; not at all.

No, what had come to David, just after the operation on the president, was something far more interesting.

He'd been cleaning up, throwing his bloodied gloves and gown into the disposal unit. Other members of the surgical team had been there, too, including his wife Annie. And Annie had made a joke, saying she wondered who was going to pay President Jerrison's hospital bill.

Christine Lee, the anesthesiologist, had quipped, "I don't think he's quite old enough for Medicare."

And—*bam!*—it had come to him, the first foreign memory he'd accessed. It was crazy, bizarre—but the memory was vivid, and he knew in his bones that it was *true*.

Ten years ago, long before he'd joined LT, Dr. Mark Griffin

had worked for a health-insurance company. And that company had bilked Medicare out of close to a hundred million dollars, with claims related to a worthless pharmaceutical that supposedly treated Alzheimer's. Griffin, who had been in charge of government billing for the company, masterminded the whole thing.

David January hated health-insurance companies. His father had had no health insurance, because no one would insure him. And Griffin had taken many millions out of the system that was supposed to provide care for those over sixty-five who didn't have coverage—people like David's dad.

Who knew how long these linkages would last? Who knew how long he'd have these memories? After that Secret Service woman finished grilling him—how dare she suggest that Annie had cheated on him!—he headed to Griffin's office. Griffin's secretary, Miss Peters, looked up as he entered. "Is he in?" David asked.

"He's got an appointment in just a couple of minutes, Dr. January. Can I schedule you for later?"

Which meant he *was* in. David marched past her.

"Excuse me!" Miss Peters said, standing up. "You can't go in there!"

David opened the inner door.

"Dr. January!" Miss Peters said, exasperated.

Inside, Griffin was seated behind a wide wooden desk polished so brightly it gleamed. He looked up, startled.

"I'm sorry, Dr. Griffin," Miss Peters said.

Griffin nodded. "It's okay, Sherry," he said. "What is it, Dave?"

David turned and glared at the secretary. She retreated, closing the heavy door behind her.

"I know what you did," David said.

"What?" replied Griffin.

"Ten years ago. At the insurance company. The Medicare fraud."

Griffin seemed to consider this. His natural impulse might have been to say something like, "I don't know what you're talking about," but his face conveyed that he knew the rules had changed. And so he tried a different tack. "You think that because you've got a memory that you don't recognize, it must be mine? And, even if it is, that it's not just a fantasy I had or the plot of a movie I saw or a book I read?"

"It's real," David said. "You did it, and you know it. And, more importantly, *I* know it."

"You've got no proof I did anything—none. And for all I know, you've got an iPhone or a BlackBerry in your pocket, recording every word I say. So, for the record, I assert my innocence."

"I know what happened," David said. "I even know where the records are stored."

Griffin was wearing a red necktie. It was already loosened, and he pulled it out of his blue shirt collar and held it in front of him. "A nice tie," he said. "Silk. Since you can read my memories, I'm sure you know my wife gave it to me." He then moved over to a counter at the side of his large office, where a Mr. Coffee was set up next to a tree of coffee mugs. He picked up one of the mugs and turned it so that David could see the writing on it. "'World's Greatest Dad,'" he said. "My son assures me it's the only one in existence." And then he did something bizarre: he looped the red tie through the handle of the mug and tied it in a bow. He held it up, as if pleased with his handiwork, and said, "What do you want?"

"You took a hundred million or so out of Medicare. I figured it's worth a lot to keep me silent."

"Not one penny ever went into my pocket for anything unethical," Griffin said.

"Not directly. But you had stock options, and you got a huge bonus that year."

Griffin spread his arms. "Dave . . ."

"As soon as this stupid lockdown is over, you're going to start paying me to keep quiet."

"So that's it? Blackmail?"

David smiled mirthlessly. "Think of the payments as insurance premiums."

Griffin's tone was perfectly even. "You've just made the worst mistake of your life, Dave."

"I don't think so."

"You're right, you can read my memories. But someone else is reading *yours*. And—well, let's see who it is?" Griffin moved back to his desk and without sitting down, he made a call. "Ranjip?" he said, after a moment. "Mark Griffin. Can you have a look at that chart of yours for me? Tell me who is reading the memories of David January, the cardiologist?" A pause. "Really? Yeah, I know her. Okay, thanks. No, no, we're still on; I'm almost finished here. Come on up when you're ready. Bye."

Griffin put down the handset and folded his arms in front of his chest. "Professor Singh has just informed me that Dr. Christine Lee, an anesthesiologist, can read your memories. And all I'll have to do is say to Christine, hey, remember that time I tied my red silk tie into a bow through the handle of my 'World's Greatest Dad' mug? What did David January say just after that?" He paused. "You see, David? There's a witness—she's somewhere else in the hospital right now, but she's a witness all the same. And the linkages are only first-order, did you know that? That means she'll remember you trying to blackmail me, but she won't remember what you claim to remember of my past; she has access only to your memories, not to mine."

David felt his blood boiling. First, that Secret Service woman had manipulated him—that bullshit about Annie! And now Griffin was fucking with him, too. Well, if he was going to go down for this, he'd at least give Griffin something he'd remember, something all of them would remember. He lunged forward, startling Griffin, and punched the tall man in the stomach. Griffin doubled over, and David got him in a headlock.

"You'll keep your mouth shut," David said. "You won't speak to Christine."

Griffin was struggling, and David found them moving sideways across the room, toward the same counter that held the coffee service. Griffin broke out of the headlock, but David managed to get a choke hold on him. Griffin flailed his free arm, and he knocked the coffeemaker to the floor, the glass parts shattering.

They continued to struggle, but Miss Peters must have heard the sound of the breaking glass because she opened the office door and stood there, mouth agape—and behind her, just entering the outer office, was Professor Singh.

Singh surged forward. "Let him go."

"He attacked me," David said. "Went nuts. Tried to kill me."

The syllable "no"—mostly just raw breath rather than a word—came from Griffin.

"I said, let him go!" Singh demanded.

David looked at the guy: he was fifty if he was a day and slight of build; David was sure he could take him, too, if he had to. "Back off," he said.

Singh exploded into movement, rushing forward then pivoting on his left foot while he brought his right foot up into a powerful karate kick, catching David in the side. Griffin seized the chance and managed to twist himself free from David's grip. Singh pivoted again and kicked with his other leg, catching David in the solar plexus, and as David doubled over, Singh delivered a sharp karate punch to the back of David's neck. David slumped face-first to the floor. He was still conscious, but, try as he might, he couldn't get back up. He lolled his head to the side to watch.

Griffin was struggling to get his breath and was still doubled over. He held on to the edge of the counter for support.

"Do you need a doctor?" Singh asked.

Griffin huffed and puffed a few more times, then shook his head. "No. I'll be okay." He straightened up partway, and nodded again. "Good thing you know karate, Professor Singh."

David looked up at Singh, his head still spinning. Singh said, "I don't."

"Well, or whatever martial art that was," said Griffin.

"I don't know any martial arts," Singh said, his voice full of wonder. "But I guess Lucius Jono—the man I'm linked to—*does.*"

Griffin got out, "Well, thank God for that."

Singh was excited. "Indeed. This is fascinating. I wouldn't have anticipated skills being accessible like that."

Griffin straightened and made it over to his desk. He asked Miss Peters to have a security guard and an ER doctor come up here. Then he loomed in to make sure that David wasn't mortally wounded.

"There are two kinds of human memory," Singh went on, huffing a bit from exertion. "One is declarative or explicit memory, which is all that I'd thought had been linked between any of us here. Declarative memory consists of those things that can be consciously recalled and easily put into words—memories of facts or events." He looked down in apparent astonishment at what he'd done to David. "The other kind is what you just saw me access. It's called non-declarative or procedural memory; laypeople sometimes call it muscle memory. Non-declarative memories are the ones that you obviously have but are not conscious of: how to ride a bicycle, how to tie a shoe, how to play tennis—which is something I happen to do well—or how to perform martial arts. Declarative memory is associated with the hippocampus, whereas the dorsolateral striatum is associated with non-declarative memory."

Griffin rubbed his throat. "So?"

The door opened, and a security guard entered, along with a doctor. The doctor immediately went down on one knee to examine David.

"So," said Singh, "the linkages are much more thorough than perhaps they first appeared to be."

"Or maybe they're growing stronger over time," Griffin said.

Singh said, "Maybe they are at that. Who knows where it will all end?"

CHAPTER 22

THE interviews with the affected people continued; several more "Can Read" and "Is Read By" squares had been filled in on Singh's grid. Susan was back in Singh's office, this time interviewing a woman named Maria Ramirez. She was twenty-seven with black hair tumbling down her back, and she was wearing a loose-fitting top.

"By this point, I imagine you've heard some of the gossip that's going around," Susan said to Maria, who was seated on the convex side of the kidney-shaped desk. "All that stuff about memories being shared. Are *you* sharing anyone's memories, do you think?"

"I don't want to get in trouble," said Maria.

Susan's heart skipped a beat. "You won't get in trouble," she replied. "I promise you. We simply want to identify who's linked to who, that's all. It's not your fault this happened."

Maria seemed to consider this. "What if I say I'm not linked to anyone?"

"You'd be the first person inside the sphere who wasn't," Susan said. She let Maria digest this. Better that she decide on her own not to lie than that Susan accuse her of being a liar; that would just make her more defensive.

"I didn't ask for this," Maria said.

Susan nodded. "None of us did."

"You're affected, too?" Maria asked, but then she answered her own question. "*Sí.* You are. You can read the memories of someone here. A scientist named Singh."

Susan sat up straighter. Only Prospector and a few others should have known that. "Maria, who are you linked to?"

"I know I know things I shouldn't. Secret things; secure things. National-security things. I swear to you that I haven't shared them with anyone."

Bingo! "That's fine," Susan said, encouragingly. "I'm sure the president is very grateful for that."

"Poor *Señor* Jerrison," Maria said. "All that blood spilling everywhere." She shook her head. "It was awful."

"Yes, it was," said Susan. "Maria, thank you for being honest about this. Of course, others will be interested in what you know. I'll assign you protection; we won't let anything happen to you."

"*Gracias,*" said Maria, sounding distracted. She was looking not at Susan, but past her. Susan didn't have to turn around to know that there was nothing but a bookcase behind her; she had Singh's vivid memories of this place. Maria's voice was full of wonder. "Watching that man squeeze the president's heart . . ."

Susan nodded, recalling it herself from her vantage point in the observation gallery. "That was incredible, wasn't it?" But then her eyebrows shot up. "You remember that?"

"Well, *he* remembers it."

Susan was amazed. She knew Jerrison had had a near-death experience, and those did sometimes involve seeing oneself from outside the body, usually from up above. But those were hallucinations, she'd always thought: a mind that knew it was dying imagining what was happening to the body that contained it. And yet she'd been with Griffin when he'd briefed Prospector about his brush with death—and Griffin hadn't mentioned the manual stimulation of the heart. Could it be that Jerrison really had, somehow, departed his body and seen Eric Redekop at work?

"If you are going to assign protection to me," Maria said, "it might as well be him."

"Who?" said Susan, baffled. "The president?"

"What?" replied Maria. "No, no. Him. Darryl Hudkins."

Oh, Christ. "Is that who you're reading?"

"*Sí*, of course. I know he knows all sorts of secret things—I guess that's why they call it the Secret Service. But, like I said, I promise you I haven't told any of them to anyone."

Susan was disappointed—but then her heart started beating quickly again. "Maria, I want you to understand something. I'm the Secret Service agent-in-charge here. I'm Darryl's superior, okay?"

"If you say so."

"No, think about it. Ask yourself if that's true."

She narrowed her brown eyes for a moment, then: "Yes, okay, it's true." She smiled ever so slightly. "He thinks you're a good boss."

"Good, fine," said Susan. "Now, I'm going to ask you another question, and I want you to think very, very carefully about it. Your answer is extremely important."

Maria nodded.

"Okay. Here's the question. Did Agent Hudkins have anything at all to do with the attempt on President Jerrison's life?"

Maria narrowed her eyes again then shook her head. "No."

"Are you sure? Are you positive?"

"*Sí*. He had nothing to do with it, but—oh!"

"Yes? Yes?"

"It was an inside job, wasn't it? Another agent—Gordo Danbury—he did it, *sí?*"

"I can't confirm or deny anything at this point. These are national-security matters."

"Darryl can't believe Gordo did it. And—oh! He's been wondering if you're involved."

"Me?" Susan was momentarily shocked, but she supposed his suspicion was as natural as her own. "No, I'm not. And you're totally sure Darryl isn't either, right?"

"I'm sure," said Maria.

Susan nodded; she could use an ally—someone she could trust—and Darryl was now the only other agent she could be sure of. "Okay, thank you," Susan said.

"Can I go home now?" Maria asked.

"I'm afraid not. But soon, I hope."

"Good. Because I can't wait to tell my husband the news."

"About the president being shot?" asked Susan, surprised. "Or about the White House?" Surely everyone outside the hospital knew about those things by now.

"No, no. *My* news. Our news."

"Which is?"

Maria smiled broadly. "That it's a girl."

"I beg your pardon?"

"Our baby. I was here for an ultrasound today."

"You're pregnant?" asked Susan.

"Four months."

Susan surged to her feet and ran down the corridor to Singh's lab.

"ALL right," said Ranjip Singh, writing on the whiteboard in his lab. "Mark Griffin, the hospital CEO, can read Maria Ramirez. Of course, Griffin's been running around all day—hasn't had much time to probe her memories; he didn't even know she was pregnant until I just asked him about it."

Singh continued. "Maria herself can read Agent Darryl Hudkins." He filled in the appropriate squares.

"I spent hours modeling the linkages," Singh added, "looking for a pattern to them—and I kept rejecting one my computer kept spitting out, because it seemed to have two nodes in one. But now that I know about the unborn baby, it makes sense. The linkage pattern of who is linked to whom is an artifact of the sequence of laser firings I'd programmed into my equipment: the paths of the beams traced out the pattern of connections. Not every pulse resulted in a link, and we're not exactly sure of where everyone was deployed within the building when the linkages occurred. Still, here's what I propose." He erased the X in the name field of the twenty-first column and wrote in *Baby Girl Ramirez*. "Based on the beam paths, Maria's unborn baby is linked to Rachel Cohen, although what, if anything, a fetus could make of Ms. Cohen's memories, I have no idea. The baby girl probably lacks the referents to confabulate the cues Ms. Cohen is providing into anything meaningful . . . which I suspect is all to the good. Our Ms. Cohen is rather wanton; she formed a liaison with that lawyer, Orrin Gillett, with unseemly haste."

"'Wanton'?" said Susan, smiling at the choice of word. "Horny as all get-out, I'd say. But, yeah."

"And now, as for the rest," said Singh. "I spoke to Josh Latimer, the intended kidney recipient. He kept insisting he wasn't detecting any foreign memories. He *could* be lying; he could be the one linked to President Jerrison. But my guess is that he's telling the truth about this, as he sees it. The beam paths suggest he's not linked to Jerrison, but rather to the unborn baby, whose memories are simply not remarkable enough for him to have noticed." He wrote in those connections. "Which means it's down to three possibilities." He pointed at the names above the three remaining blank squares in the *Can Read* row. "This person, this person, or this person—one of them is reading the president."

CHAPTER 23

THE DC police had been given copies of the security-camera photos of Bessie Stilwell, but so far they'd failed to turn her up. And Darryl Hudkins kept trying to recall her activities today, to figure out where she'd gone, and—

And memories came to him, of Richard Nixon, of all people. Although Nixon had resigned the presidency before Darryl had been born, he'd seen film of him declaring, "I am not a crook," and him flashing a pair of V-for-victory finger signs at the crowd as he left the White House for the last time, but . . .

But he'd never felt sympathy for Nixon; Darryl's dad, whenever he spoke of him, referred to him as "Tricky Dick." And in all Darryl's years working at the White House, he practically never heard Nixon's name; in an almost Soviet-style rewriting of history, the thirty-seventh president had seemingly been expunged from memory.

But, suddenly, he was thinking about Nixon, recalling things he'd never known about him—like him speaking to the first astronauts on the moon . . . Buzz something, and that other guy. *Back when we'd been proud of him.* And him going to China, and meeting Mao. *Such a smart move!*

But then it had all come tumbling down. First his vice president—Agnew, the name came to Darryl, although he didn't think he'd known it before—had had to resign although over unrelated matters, and then Nixon himself had stepped down.

Unrelated matters.

That was the thought that had popped into Darryl's head, and as he considered it, more details came to him: the "unrelated matters" were charges of extortion, tax fraud, bribery, and conspiracy either when Agnew had been governor of Maryland or Baltimore County Executive.

And those were unrelated to . . .

To Watergate, and—

And—

Yes, yes, yes! *That's* where she was staying! Not at her son Mike's place, but at the Watergate Hotel, which had recently reopened after major renovations. It came to Darryl now: she'd told Mike she was staying in his apartment, and indeed had gone by it once now, but she preferred a hotel, where housekeeping would find her no later than the next morning if she slipped and fell. She hadn't told Mike that, though; she didn't want him to be worrying about her running up expenses.

The Watergate was a great choice for someone who was visiting Luther Terry; it was only three blocks away, straight down New Hampshire Avenue, the diagonal street that constrained the LT building into a triangular shape. The Watergate complex was on the shore of the Potomac, opposite Theodore Roosevelt Island and just north of the Kennedy Center.

And—yes!—Bessie was looking around the grounds, as much as she could look at anything with her dim vision, and thinking *this is where it all began,* and—

And her thoughts were interrupted by a siren, and Darryl had heard a siren himself not five minutes ago. Normally, he'd expect to hear ambulance sirens in the vicinity of a hospital, but LT was under lockdown, and so Darryl had looked out the window and he'd seen a fire truck barreling north, and—

And Bessie had seen—or at least heard!—the same fire truck; this was a very recent memory.

Darryl spoke into his sleeve even as he broke into a run.

"Hudkins to Dawson. I know where Bessie Stilwell is; I'm leaving the building to retrieve her."

"Copy," said Susan's voice in his ear. "I'll make sure hospital security knows; go out the ambulance bay, not through the lobby."

Darryl could have commandeered a car to drive to the Watergate, but it was less than a thousand yards away. He made it down to the first floor and found himself retracing the path by which they'd brought in the president this morning, going past the staff sleep room, past Trauma, turning right, and heading out through the sliding doors that led to the ambulance driveway. A uniformed hospital security guard was indeed there. He checked Darryl's ID, then unlocked the door for him; Darryl nodded thanks at the man and ran out into the chilly evening.

He hadn't bothered to get his coat—that would have cost him a couple of minutes. He ran past the news crews, and one camera guy tried to follow him, shouting questions—Darryl was, after all, the first person to emerge from the building in hours—but the man, carrying a large camera, wasn't able to keep up with Darryl as he ran along the building's longest side, heading toward Eye Street, then—his heart pounding a bit—H Street, and then—sweating now—under the Potomac River Freeway, emerging at the Watergate complex. The hotel, he knew, was off to his right along Virginia Avenue, and he continued to run until he got there, making his way into the swanky lobby.

The aristocratic white man behind the front desk looked askance at Darryl, who was breathing hard, but Darryl whipped out his ID and said, his voice ragged, "Secret Service. What room is Bessie Stilwell in?" but then it came to him before the man answered: *room 534*. "Give me a passkey."

The desk clerk hesitated for a second, but then programmed a keycard and handed it to Darryl, saying, "She just got back, actually."

Darryl took the plastic card and dashed to the bank of elevators. He stabbed the up button and caught his breath as he waited. Then he rode up to the fifth floor, and—

—and that must be her, down near the end of the corridor,

moving slowly away from him; there was no one else in the carpeted hallway.

"Wait!" he called.

She slowly turned around, and Darryl came bounding down the corridor, and she was fumbling to open her purse, and—

—and suddenly he realized how it must look to her: late in the evening, all alone in a long corridor, a large, sweaty black man, huffing and puffing, running right at her.

She soon had a tiny pistol in her hand. Darryl stopped dead in his tracks; he could have easily drawn his own gun and blown her away—he had no doubt his reflexes and aim were better than hers—but instead he raised his hands a little.

"Mrs. Stilwell," he said, hoping the fact that he knew her name would calm her a bit. She peered at him; there were maybe twenty feet between them. Darryl noted the "Do Not Disturb" sign on the door next to him. "I'm a Secret Service agent. Maybe you saw me today at the hospital?"

And saying that triggered him to recall her seeing him for the first time. She had indeed noticed him at the hospital, and—

What's that—

Darryl was stunned as the rest of the thought tumbled into his consciousness: *What's that nigger doing over there?*

And: *Up to no good, I suppose.*

And: *My God, is that blood on his sleeve? Well, there you have it! Been in a knife fight or something. Probably over drugs . . .*

He found his head shaking, and he felt furious. He wanted to say that it was the president's blood, that he'd gotten it on him trying to save the man's life, that she was so totally full of *shit*.

Bessie still had the gun aimed at him, and still looked terrified because . . .

. . . because he was black. Because he was *colored*. Because he was a—

That fucking word again.

Jesus!

She looked back over her shoulder now, but of course there was no way she could outrun him; he was a third her age.

"Mrs. Stilwell," he said, "please lower the gun."

She looked down, as if surprised that the little pistol was in her hands. Darryl actually hadn't put away his ID since showing it to the desk clerk; it was still in his left hand, and he flipped it open and held it out in front of him as he slowly started closing the distance. "I just need to ask you a few questions."

"Sorry," she said. "I thought you were . . . I thought . . ."

"Well, I'm not," said Darryl. He considered suggesting they go into her room to talk, but he realized she'd freak if he did that, so instead he said, "Would you mind coming back to the hospital with me? There's a small matter we need to clear up . . ."

"You really are a Secret Service agent?"

"Yes, ma'am. And I think you should give me that gun."

She thought about it for a moment, then handed it to him. He escorted her down to the lobby and brought her back to the hospital in a cab; the cabbie was not thrilled about such a short trip, but Darryl tried to make up for it by telling him to keep the change from the twenty-dollar bill he handed him. He and Bessie re-entered the hospital through the ambulance-bay doors, and then he walked her to the conference room on one, told her to have a seat in there, called Susan Dawson to come do the questioning, and went off to wash his hands.

Fortunately, he thought, there was *lots* of disinfectant in a hospital.

CHAPTER 24

SUSAN Dawson entered the conference room. Its only occupant was sitting in a chair, staring off into space. "Mrs. Stilwell?" Susan said.

No response. Susan tried again, speaking more loudly. "Mrs. Stilwell? How are you?"

The old woman turned in her chair. "Still breathing," she said. "At my age, that's about all you can hope for."

Susan smiled. "I understand you were here earlier today to visit your son, is that right?"

Mrs. Stilwell nodded. "He had a heart attack a couple of days ago."

"I'm sorry to hear that," Susan said.

"Works too hard. I wish he'd come back to Mississippi with me, but he's like his father that way. Stubborn."

"Will he be all right?" Susan asked.

"So they say."

"It was nice of you to come visit him."

"You never stop being a mother," Bessie said, "no matter how old your children get."

"I imagine so," said Susan.

"You don't have children?"

Susan shook her head.

"Are you married?"

In a normal interrogation, Susan would say, "I'll ask the questions, ma'am," but she had a hard time being disrespectful to the elderly. She shook her head again.

"A pretty young thing like you?" said Bessie. "There must be lots of men who are interested."

"You'd be surprised, ma'am," Susan said. She thought about leaving it at that, then, with a small shrug, added: "Many men are intimidated by strong women. When they find out what I do for a living, they tend to get scared off."

"You're a Secret Service agent, too?"

"Yes, ma'am."

"How old are you?"

"Thirty-four, ma'am."

"And you don't feel the old biological clock ticking?"

"I feel it," Susan said, simply. Then: "Mrs. Stilwell, I need to ask you a few questions."

"All right."

"There's something strange going on here at the hospital, ma'am. People are reading other people's memories."

Mrs. Stilwell frowned. "What nonsense."

"I can understand your thinking so, ma'am. It does seem odd. But it has to do with an experiment that went awry here. As it happens, I'm linked to the experimenter; there's no question about it. And one of the other Secret Service agents— Darryl Hudkins—is linked to you; that's how he knew where to find you."

"That colored man?"

Susan felt her eyebrows going up. "Um, yes."

Bessie frowned again. "I don't think I like that."

Susan let that go. "And so *you* should be linked to somebody, too. Do you have any strange memories?"

"No."

"Are you sure?"

"Of course, I'm sure. This is all nonsense."

Susan decided to try another tack. "Do you know the ZIP code for the White House?"

"Gracious, Miss Susan, I don't even know my own

ZIP code. I always have to look at where I have it written down."

"What about the name of the president's hometown, do you know what that is?"

"Haven't a clue."

"Are you sure? It's in northern California."

"No idea."

Susan made a face. The problem was obvious: Mrs. Stilwell wasn't even *trying* to remember things. She didn't narrow her eyes, or wrinkle her brow, or take even a second before answering. It was all foolishness to her; she had no reason to think she knew the answer, and so wasn't making any effort to see if she did.

"I really need you to *try*," Susan said.

"How old are you, Miss Susan?"

Susan frowned. "Um, I'm—"

But Bessie raised a hand. "Yes, yes, I know I just asked you that—but I don't remember your answer. See? You get to be my age, you don't remember much of *anything*. And it's no fun being reminded of that. So, if you'll forgive me . . ."

Susan thought about letting her get away with it. Maybe, just maybe, she wasn't a security risk even if she were the one linked to the president. And, she thought, Jerrison actually was lucky—well, as lucky as a man who recently got shot could be!—in that, even if the linkages turned out to be permanent, Bessie Stilwell would pass away sometime in the next few years, while Susan might be stuck with Kadeem Adams reading her memories for the rest of her life.

But that would never satisfy Director Hexley—or Prospector. She had to know for sure, and—

Her earpiece bleeped. She lifted her arm. "Dawson, go."

"Sue, it's Darryl. I'm with Singh. We've questioned the other two possibilities, and it's neither of them. Mrs. Stilwell must be the one."

"Copy that," said Susan into her sleeve. "Out." She turned to the old woman. "Mrs. Stilwell, you're it—there's no doubt. You're linked to President Jerrison."

"I tell you, Miss Susan, I'm not."

"Think about the question I'm about to ask you, ma'am. Really think about it. It's important, okay?"

The old woman nodded.

"All right, now. Think about this. What is today's day-word?"

"'Dayword'? I don't know what that means."

"Just ask yourself, Mrs. Stilwell, what is today's dayword? And really think about it."

She pursed her thin lips. And then she lifted her frail arms in exasperation. "I don't know!"

"Guess," said Susan. "Say the first word that pops into your mind. Today's dayword is . . ."

"Oh, for Pete's—all right, all right. Um, 'potbelly.'"

Susan's heart skipped a beat. It wasn't today's word, which Prospector would have memorized this morning; it was the one from three days ago. Still, if this woman was somehow reading Susan or Darryl, she could be accessing the dayword from their memories rather than the president's.

"All right," Susan said. "One more question: what high school did President Jerrison attend?"

"Land's sake, I don't know these things!"

"Guess. Just guess. Please, ma'am."

Maybe that final bit of courtesy did the trick, because Bessie stopped protesting and frowned in concentration. "Nord-hoff High," she said, then, after a second, she added, "Go, Rangers!"

Susan pulled out her BlackBerry, went to the president's Wikipedia page, and checked; the old lady was correct. She put away the phone and spoke into her sleeve. "Dawson to Hudkins. You're right, Darryl. I'm here with our threat to national security."

NOW that they'd found the person reading President Jerrison's memories, Agent Dawson conceded that there was no longer any legal basis for continuing the lockdown. Still, before they would be allowed to leave the hospital, each of the affected people was individually briefed by LT's director of risk management, by Professor Singh, and by one of the hospital's psychiatrists. They were all advised that they were welcome, nay encouraged, to stay at the hospital, as no one could predict what impact or side effects the memory linkages might have.

They were also told that, if they stayed, they would be admitted for free, and they'd be kept under observation and have immediate access to whatever care they might need. Still, those who did want to leave—which turned out to be just about everyone except Joshua Latimer and his daughter Dora Hennessey, who'd had their transplant operation rescheduled for Monday—were required to sign Refusal of Care Against Medical Advice forms. Also, everyone's contact information was collected and verified, and follow-up medical examinations were booked for five days hence.

While that was being done, Mark Griffin sat down in front of the large microphone attached to the public-address system, took a deep breath—and paused; his throat was still raw from being throttled by David January. He swallowed, coughed, then tried speaking into the mike again. "Your attention, please. Your attention, please. I have an important announcement to make. Your attention please."

He waited for a couple of seconds, then: "This is Dr. Mark Griffin, and I'm the chief executive officer here at Luther Terry Memorial Hospital. As doubtless most of you know by now, President Seth Jerrison was shot this morning, and he was brought here for surgery. I'm delighted to tell you that his condition is stable."

There were always lawsuits following any lockdown; the next paragraph had been carefully crafted to hopefully at least somewhat reduce their number.

"The lockdown of this building was implemented at the request of the United States Secret Service. We and they thank you for your cooperation in this time of national crisis, and President Jerrison himself has asked me to pass on his personal gratitude to each and every one of you."

Another pause to let that sink in, then: "We will shortly end the lockdown." Even in this closed office, he could hear the cheers going up. "Because we may need to get in touch with you again, we will be recording your names and contact information as you leave. There are hundreds of people in the building, so we have to process you in an orderly fashion. Staff members may leave through the staff exit whenever their shifts end. For visitors and outpatients, if your last name begins with the letters A, B, C, or D, you may head down to the lobby now."

Griffin swallowed, then went on. "We will, of course, provide you with a free parking voucher good through the end of the night. Please calmly make your way out, and, again, many, many thanks for your understanding."

He paused, then began over again in Spanish: *"Su atención, por favor. Su atención, por favor. Tengo un anuncio importante que hacer . . ."* He was surprised at how fluent he sounded; he wasn't usually this good. But then it came to him: Maria Ramirez, the young woman he was linked to, was bilingual.

"WE found her," Susan Dawson said, coming into the president's room.

Seth lolled his head slightly to look at Susan, and Sheila, his nurse, also turned to face her. "Who?"

"The person reading your memories," Susan said. "Her name is Bessie Stilwell, and she's eighty-seven."

"Did she . . . ah, has she . . . ?"

"Revealed anything? Nothing crucial. And we're hoping it'll stay that way, of course. We'll keep her away from the press and so forth."

Seth managed a small nod, then: "I'd like to speak with her."

Susan's eyebrows went up. "Sir, if I may, I don't think that's wise. She's a huge security risk. Seeing you will doubtless trigger more memories to come back; you really don't want to have anything sensitive brought to her mind."

Seth looked at the Secret Service agent, wondering just how much she herself knew; she shouldn't know *anything* about Counterpunch, of course, but . . .

But maybe she did—and maybe Gordo Danbury had known, too.

Gordo. Damn it, if only he could remember what Leon Hexley had been saying on the phone. *"Tell Gordo to . . ."*

But no matter how much he racked his brain, it wasn't coming back to him. But maybe this woman, this—what had

Susan said her name was? This Bessie? Maybe *she* could remember the conversation. "Bring her here," Seth said.

"Sir, I really—"

"Bring her."

Susan nodded. "As you wish, sir."

CHAPTER 25

IVAN Tarasov was satisfied with his job as a security guard at Luther Terry Memorial Hospital. He was less happy about reading the memories of Dora Hennessey, the woman who'd come here from London to donate a kidney to her father. Ivan tried to keep her memories from coming to mind, but there really was no way to avoid them. Most of them were uninteresting to him. She was a guidance counselor, and he'd always preferred things involving hard science or math but had done too poorly in school to ever get a job in those areas. Today, there'd be a diagnosis for his condition, but twenty-five years ago, when he'd been in high school, they just said he didn't work hard enough.

Dora was a fan of British football; he didn't care for contact sports—years of working here at LT had left him unable to abide people purposefully engaging in behaviors that would result in concussions, hernias, damaged joints, and bruised organs. She was active in clubbing and bar-hopping; he preferred to curl up with his Kindle and read books about the Civil War—he was working through Shelby Foote's history of it for the fifth time.

Now that the lockdown was over, Ivan was pleased to leave

the hospital. Still, he paused just outside it for a time, looking east. The whole sky was dark now, but he could make out the smoke billowing from where the White House had been.

He got on the metro. Normally, he ignored other people, but today he found himself looking at them—looking *right* at them, their faces haunted, gaunt, drawn. It was the same thing on the bus: lost souls, some still softly crying.

Finally, he made it to his house. His wife Sally came down to the entryway along with his three-year-old daughter Tanya. They knew he didn't like to be touched, but today was an unusual day, and they needed whatever he could offer them. He accepted a kiss from Sally and then picked up Tanya and carried her into the small living room, where he set her on the couch. He then sat himself down beside her.

Ivan was devastated by today's terrible events—but also couldn't help being upset that his daily routine had been interrupted. He should have been here hours ago to watch *Wonder Pets* with Tanya; it was their ritual every day when he got home from work. Of course, he'd planned for such contingencies; their DVR was set to record *Wonder Pets*. He found the remote and started it playing. He briefly spared a thought for the person who was linked to him—some lawyer named Orrin Gillett—who now must also know the plots of all forty-two episodes by heart, not to mention every trivial fact about Linny the Guinea Pig, Turtle Tuck, and Tanya's favorite, Ming-Ming Duckling.

He looked at his daughter and—

God.

He shook his head, looked away, but—

But the images were still there.

Horrific images.

Images of . . .

No. No. He did *not* want to see this!

But . . .

God. God. *God.*

The sight of Tanya, sitting on the couch in her little pink dress, made him think of—

No, no. It was *awful*. To do that to a child! To touch a little girl that way!

The image of a man came to him, but it was no one he

knew. A narrow head, brown hair, brown eyes behind unfash-
ionably large lenses.

The face loomed in at . . . at *her,* shushing her, telling her
it would all be all right, telling her to never breathe a word
about this, telling her that it was their little secret that he liked
her so much, that she was so special, and—

He shook his head again, but the images were still there,
the memories.

Memories. Yes, plural. Another time, the same man, but
wearing different clothes. Or, at least, starting out wearing
different clothes, until he unzipped . . .

No!

Ivan stood up, left his daughter, left the room, and closed
his eyes, desperately trying to shut the images out.

"MR. President," said Susan Dawson, "this is Bessie
Stilwell."

Seth still had tubes going into his left arm, and a small
oxygen intake plugged into his nostrils. But he rallied some
strength and extended his right hand toward Bessie, who
responded with an astonished expression.

"What?" said the president, looking at his own hand to see
if it were dirty or something.

"Sorry, Mr. President," said Bessie. "I'm—it's just a flood
of images. All the people whose hands you've shaken with that
hand. The British prime minister. The Russian premier. The
German chancellor. The Chinese president. And—" She took
a half step back, as if daunted. "And the movie stars. Angelina
Jolie and Johnny Depp and—oh, he's always been one of my
favorites!—Christopher Plummer."

"And now," said Seth Jerrison, who, even in his current
state, had an ability almost as good as Bill Clinton's to make
whomever he was talking to feel like the most important person in the world, "it's going to shake your hand." He extended
his arm again.

Bessie hesitated for another moment, then moved closer
and took Seth's hand in hers. "A pleasure to meet you, Mr.
President."

"The pleasure is all mine." He turned toward Susan. "Agent

Dawson, won't you give us a moment? I'm sure I'm safe with Mrs. Stilwell."

Susan looked like she was going to protest, but then she nodded and headed out into the corridor, closing the door behind her. Seth motioned for Bessie to take a seat. She did so; there was a vinyl-covered chair next to the bed. But she was shaking her head.

"What?" asked Seth.

"Nothing, sir. Just memories."

"I understand, believe me. I'm recalling strange things, too, from the person I'm linked to."

"Yes, but . . ."

"But what?"

Bessie averted her eyes but said nothing more.

Seth nodded. It was like the WikiLeaks scandal: all those embarrassing State Department emails. "You don't just recall me shaking, say, President Sarkozy's hand at the G8. You also recall what I thought of him then, right?"

Bessie nodded meekly.

Seth's energy ebbed and flowed, but one of his doctors had recently given him a stimulant. He found he could speak at greater length, at least for the moment, without exhausting himself. "I'm a human being," he said. "And so are all the other national leaders. So, yes, I've got opinions about them, and they've doubtless got opinions about me."

"You really hate the Canadian prime minister."

Seth didn't hesitate. "Yes, I do. He's a weasely, petty man."

Bessie seemed to digest this. "So, um, what happens now?" she asked, looking briefly at the president, then averting her gaze again.

"If word gets out that you're linked to me, lots of people are going to come after you."

"Gracious!" said Bessie.

"So, as of right now, you're under the protection of the Secret Service."

Seth had anticipated that she'd answer with, "Oh, I'm sure that's not necessary," or maybe with, "Well, I hope they do a better job of protecting me than they did of protecting you," but what she actually said was, "My son, too, please."

"Sorry?"

"My son Michael. He's here in the hospital; he's the reason I'm in town. If people want to get at me, they might go after him."

Seth managed another small nod. "Absolutely. We'll protect him, too."

"Thank you, sir."

He found it slightly amusing to be called "sir" by someone a quarter of a century older than himself, but he let it pass; Mrs. Stilwell was from the South, and manners still counted down there.

"And," he said, "speaking of the Secret Service, there's an agent named Gordo Danbury."

Bessie frowned. "You mean there *was* an agent by that name."

"Exactly. Do you know who Leon Hexley is?"

Another frown, then: "The director of the Secret Service."

"That's right. A few days ago, I came upon him in the Oval Office, and he was talking to someone on his phone . . ." Seth paused to catch his breath, then: ". . . and I think he was talking about Gordo Danbury. Do you remember me hearing that conversation?"

"This is so strange," Bessie said.

"Yes," agreed Seth. "But do you remember it?"

"I don't remember a conversation about Gordo Danbury."

"No, Leon didn't say his last name. Just 'Gordo.' He said, 'Tell Gordo to . . .' *something*. Do you remember that?"

"No."

"Please try."

"Gordo. That's a funny name."

"It's short for Gordon. 'Tell Gordo to . . .'"

"I sort of remember it," Bessie said, "He said, 'Tell Gordo to aim . . .'"

To aim! Yes, that was right! It was one more word than he himself had initially been able to remember. But Jesus: to aim! "There was some more," Seth said. "Some numbers, maybe?"

"That's all I can recall," Bessie said.

"If any more of it comes to you . . ."

"Of course," she said. "But . . ."

"Yes?"

"I'm trying *not* to recall your memories," she said. "I don't like knowing your thoughts, sir. I don't like it *at all*. I voted for you. I'll tell you the truth: I was hoping one of the others would get the Republican nomination; you're too middle-of-the-road for my tastes. Still, I always vote Republican—always have, always will. But a lot of what you said on the campaign trail was lies."

"I admit it perhaps wasn't always the full truth, but—"

"It was *lies*," Bessie said. "In many, many cases. You said whatever you had to say to get elected. When I recall your memories, I feel ashamed." She looked directly at him. "Don't you?"

Seth found himself unable to meet the eyes of this woman who could see right into his mind. "It's not an easy thing, getting elected," he said. "There are compromises to be made."

"It's a dirty business," said Bessie. "I don't like it."

"To tell the truth, I don't, either. I'm not sorry I ran, though, and I'm going to do as much good as I can while I'm in office. But you're right: I compromised to get here. And you know what? That was the right thing to do."

"Compromises are one thing," Bessie said. "Lies are another."

"No one who told the truth all the time could get elected—and so we bend the truth on small matters to accomplish the important things. An evil politician is one who lies all the time; a good one picks and chooses when to lie."

"Horsefeathers," she snapped.

He paused. "Well, then, think of it this way, Bessie—may I call you Bessie? Think of it like this: you're my conscience from now on, for as long as these links last. I won't be able to lie because you'll know that I'm lying. You'll keep me honest."

She responded immediately. "You can count on it."

ERIC Redekop was delighted the lockdown was over. He headed down to the staff entrance on the first floor, and—

And there was Janis Falconi; she was heading out, too.

She hadn't noticed him yet, and he took a moment to look at her and think. The flood of her memories continued unabated. He knew now how the rest of her day had gone, what she'd had as an afternoon snack—who'd have guessed pork rinds?—and . . .

And she was clean, at least at the moment. She hadn't shot up since . . .

Well, good for her! It'd been three days, but . . .

But she was dreading going home, dreading going back to Tony, dreading her whole damned life. He thought about whether she'd yet told Tony that the lockdown was over; she hadn't.

The staff had to check out with the Secret Service, just like the visitors to the hospital, although they had a separate line down here. Jan was in that line.

"Great work, Eric," said a doctor as he crossed the room. "Heard all about it."

"Thanks," Eric said, his eyes still on Jan.

Another person touched his arm as he continued to close the distance. "Congratulations, Dr. Redekop!"

"Thanks," he said again. There were eight people behind Jan and twice as many in front. She still hadn't noticed him, and if he just joined the end of the line, she'd get out long before he did.

Which shouldn't matter. Which should be *fine*.

But . . .

But . . .

He walked up to her. "Hey, Janis," he said.

She turned and smiled—a radiant smile, a wonderful smile. "Dr. Redekop."

"Hey," he said again, disappointed by his own repartee. Then he said, "Um." And then he turned to the man behind them. "Do you mind if I . . . ?"

The man smiled. "You saved the president today. I think that entitles you to cut in."

"Thanks." He looked at Jan and lowered his voice. "So, um, I guess you're also one of those affected by that experiment."

She glanced around, as if this was something she'd been trying to keep under wraps, then said softly, "Yeah."

"Who are you linked to?"

"His name's Josh Latimer. He's a patient here, waiting for a kidney transplant."

"Ah."

She looked at him. "How'd you know I was affected?"

It was his turn to look around, but the guy he'd spoken to was now talking to the person behind him, and the woman in front was wearing white earbuds; she seemed oblivious to their conversation. "Because," he said, "I'm reading you."

Jan immediately dropped her gaze.

"So," said Eric, "um, are you in a hurry to get home, or . . . ?"

She didn't look up, but she did reply. "No," she said. "I'm not."

CHAPTER 26

BESSIE Stilwell left the president's room accompanied by a Secret Service agent. Once she was gone, Seth asked for Professor Singh to be brought to his room.

"Mr. President, what can I do for you?" Singh said, upon arrival.

"I take it you've worked out all the linkages, right?"

"Yes, sir. We've got a chart."

"So, I can read Kadeem, Kadeem can read . . . Susan, is it?"

"Yes, that's right. And Agent Dawson can read me, and I can read Dr. Lucius Jono, who helped save your life. Dr. Jono can read Nikki Van Hausen, a real-estate agent. And so on."

"And Darryl?"

"Agent Hudkins? He's the one who can read Bessie Stilwell's memories."

"No, I mean, who is reading him?"

"Maria Ramirez—the pregnant lady."

"Good, okay." A pause, then: "How do you remember all that?"

"I wouldn't be much of a memory researcher if I didn't

know various tricks for memorizing things. A standard method is to use 'the memory palace.' Take a building you know well and visualize the things you want to remember inside that building in the order you'd encounter them as you actually walked through it. In this case, I think of my own house back in Toronto. There's an entryway, and I picture myself there, making me the starting point. In the entryway, there's a door to the garage. I picture Lucius Jono—who's got crazy red hair—in a clown car in there, with a bunch of other clowns, but he's trying to get out, because it's dark in the garage, and he wants to be in the light; 'Lucius' means 'light.' Next to that door is a small washroom. Lucius Jono can read Nikki Van Hausen, and—well, forgive me, but I think of rushing to the washroom in an emergency, and making it in the nick of time. A play on her name. Next to the washroom is the staircase leading up to my living room. Nikki can read the memories of Dr. Eric Redekop, the lead surgeon. I picture bodies stretched out on each of the four steps, and him operating on all four of them simultaneously, scalpels in each of his hands, and also, monkeylike, in each of his feet, as well."

"Good grief!" said Jerrison.

"The more bizarre the image, the more memorable it is."

"I suppose," Seth said. "Anyway, I need your help. There's something important I have to recall but can't."

"One of your own memories, or one of Private Adams's?"

The question would have been nonsensical just twenty-four hours ago, Seth thought. "One of my own."

"Well, I understand they've located the woman who was linked to you—Mrs. Stilwell, I believe. Perhaps she can recall it?"

"No. I already thought of that. She can't. So I was wondering if your equipment could help either her or me to dredge it up."

"What was the memory?"

"A conversation I overheard."

"Forgive me, but can you perhaps be more specific?"

Seth considered how much to tell Singh. "I overheard one end of a phone conversation—Leon Hexley, the director of the Secret Service, talking on his cell."

"Well," said Singh, "if it had been me, that'd be an easy

memory to isolate—because an encounter with such a high-ranking official would be a remarkable thing. But for you, sir? An everyday occurrence. My equipment would have a hard time pinpointing it."

"Damn. It's crucial that I recall what he said."

"Recall is a tricky thing, sir. It requires something to bring it to mind."

"I suppose."

"People always get frustrated when other people can't remember things. In fact, my wife was mad at me a couple of weeks ago because I couldn't remember something that had happened on our honeymoon. She'd snapped, 'But it's important! Why can't you remember?' You know what my reply was?"

Seth managed a small shake of his head.

Singh exploded in mock-anger. *"Because I was loaded, okay?"*

Despite the seriousness of the situation, Seth couldn't stop himself from smiling. "I used to love that show."

"Me, too," said Singh. "But, actually, I'm not making a joke. Not that I was loaded—I don't drink. But declarative memories are best recalled under the same circumstances as they were laid down. Memories formed while drunk—or underwater, or at a hotel—come back best when drunk or underwater or back at that hotel."

"Damn," said Seth.

"What?" replied Singh.

"The conversation took place in the Oval Office—and that doesn't exist anymore."

"Ah, I see," said Singh. But then he smiled. "Still, perhaps there *is* a way."

KADEEM Adams didn't have a room at LT; he'd come to the hospital yesterday morning as part of his work with Professor Singh and was staying in a small hotel Singh had arranged. But although the lockdown was now over, he'd hung around, hoping for a call from Susan Dawson, who had said the president was sleeping intermittently. Kadeem was sitting in Singh's little office on the third floor, doodling on a pad of paper.

He knew he might never have a chance like this again. The linkages had persisted for hours now, but no one knew if they were permanent. And, even if they *were,* he hoped—he prayed—Professor Singh would finish what he'd started in treating him. But for now—for right now—he had something that people jockeyed for, fought for, bribed for, begged for: he had the attention of the president of the United States. It was an opportunity not to be wasted, and, if Singh did figure out how to break the linkages, an opportunity that wouldn't come again.

Kadeem understood how it worked: the president didn't think the same thoughts at the same time as he did, but he could recall anything that Kadeem knew, just as Kadeem could recall anything that Susan Dawson remembered.

And so he knew, because he'd been pondering the question, that Sue had indeed pushed for him to be allowed to visit the president. And, at last, the call came. He told Agent Dawson where he was, and she came to get him, escorting him down the stairs. His footfalls and hers echoed in the stairwell; she was behind him. They exited on the second floor and headed along the corridor. A photographer—a Hispanic man of maybe forty—was waiting; he had two big cameras on straps around his neck. The three of them continued on into the president's room. Two Secret Service agents stood on either side of the closed door. They nodded curtly at Agent Dawson, and one of them opened the door, holding it while first Kadeem, then Susan, entered.

It was shocking to see Jerrison like this. He was looking haggard and wan. It was almost enough to make Kadeem stop, but—

But no. He *had* to do this; he owed it to the others.

As he looked at the president, more details registered. He was surprised, for instance, at how much white there was in the president's hair. Kadeem remembered him from the campaign, mostly, when his hair had been mixed between gray and sandy brown. He imagined that being leader of the free world aged you more rapidly than just about any other job.

Kadeem glanced at the nurse sitting across the room, then looked again at Jerrison. The back of the president's bed was elevated so that he could sit up a bit. He was wearing Ben Franklin glasses, but they had slid down the considerable length of his nose. He looked over them, smiled, and managed a small wave. "Come in"—*flash!*—"young man!"—*flash!*—"Come in!"

The photographer jockeyed for position, now getting shots of Kadeem. Kadeem was surprised to hear his voice crack; it hadn't done that since he was thirteen. "Hey, Mr. President."

The president extended—*flash!*—his hand—*flash!*—and Kadeem closed the distance—*flash!*—and shook it—*flash!* Jerrison's grip was weak; it was clearly an effort for him to shake hands at all.

"Please," the president said, gesturing now to a vinyl-covered chair next to his bed. "Won't you have a seat?"

Kadeem sat down, which put his head and the president's at roughly the same level. "Thank you, sir."

"So, Miss Dawson tells me you're in the Army?"

"Yes, sir."

"Your rank?" But then he smiled. "Private, first class, right? Serial number 080-79-3196, isn't it?"

"That's it, sir."

"It's so strange, having your memories, young man."

"It's strange to me, sir, knowing you have them."

"I'm sure, I'm sure. I'm not deliberately snooping, you know. I'm not saying to myself, 'Gee, I wonder what Kadeem and Kristah's first date was like?,' or—" Then he frowned. "Oh. Well, I'm with you. I thought *Tropic Thunder* was a funny film, even if she didn't."

Kadeem felt his head shaking slowly left to right; it was amazing.

"Anyway, sorry," said the president. "The point is that I'm *not* deliberately doing stuff like that. You're entitled to your privacy, young man."

"Thank you, sir."

"So you were overseas?"

"Yes, sir. Operation Iraqi Freedom."

To his credit, the president's gaze didn't waver. "But you're home now," Jerrison said in a tone that Kadeem was sure was meant to elicit gratitude.

Kadeem took a deep breath, then: "Not exactly, sir. My home is in Los Angeles. But I'm being treated here."

Jerrison frowned, perplexed. "I'm sorry. I didn't know you were injured."

And perhaps he *had* already recalled what Kadeem was about to tell him—but had simply forgotten, what with the mountain of other things he had to think about. Kadeem sighed slightly. If only everything could be so easily forgotten. "I've got PTSD."

The president nodded. "Ah, yes."

"Professor Singh's been helping me. Or he was, until we got interrupted; he's still got a lot of work to do."

"You're in good hands, I'm sure," said Jerrison. "We always try to look after our boys in uniform."

The comment seemed sincere, and although Kadeem indeed hadn't voted for Jerrison—he hadn't voted for *anyone*—he again had second thoughts about what he intended to do. No one should have to go through this.

But he had; Kadeem had. Hundreds of times now. And if the pleas of service moms hadn't succeeded, if the sight of flag-covered coffins hadn't done it, if the bleak news reports out of Baghdad hadn't been enough, maybe, just maybe, *this* would be.

"Thank you, sir," Kadeem said. The president was hooked up to a vital-signs monitor like the one Kadeem had been connected to before; it was showing seventy-two heartbeats per minute. Kadeem imagined his own pulse rate was much higher. The president of the United States! Kalil and Lamarr would never believe this. But then Kalil and Lamarr had stayed in South Central; they probably didn't really believe—or, at least, didn't fully appreciate—the stories Kadeem had brought back from Iraq.

But the president could be made to believe.

To appreciate.

To *feel*.

"Mr. President, I have to say it's a pleasure to meet you, sir. My mamma, sir, she'll be amazed."

The president gestured toward the photographer, who quickly snapped three more shots. "We'll send her pictures, of course." And then the president's eyebrows went up. "Your mamma—she's a nice lady, isn't she?"

"She's the best, sir."

He nodded. "This is so strange. Tanisha, isn't it? I see you love her very much."

"I do, sir. She done her best by me."

"I'm sure, I'm sure. And—oh!—it's her birthday next week, isn't it?"

"Yes, sir."

"Won't you give her my regards?"

Kadeem nodded. "She'd be thrilled, sir." Out of the corner of his eye, he saw Agent Dawson looking at her watch. He doubtless didn't have much time left, and—

And even the mere thought of what he was going to do set his stomach to churning, and he could feel perspiration breaking out on his brow.

"Well," Kadeem said, "I'm sure you've got matters of state"—a phrase he never thought he'd utter in his whole life—"to attend to." He stood up, and the chair's four legs made a scraping sound against the tiled floor as he pushed it back a bit. He took a deep breath and swallowed, trying to calm himself, then, finally, he blurted it out: "But I hope you'll think about babies after I leave, sir."

The president looked at him, his eyebrows pulled together. "Babies?"

"Yes, sir. Crying babies." Kadeem felt his own pulse racing, and he reached out to steady himself by holding on to the angled part of the president's bed, which caused Agent Dawson to surge forward. "Crying babies," Kadeem repeated, "and the smell of smashed concrete."

The president made a sharp intake of breath, and although the volume on his vital-signs monitor was turned almost all the way down, Kadeem could hear the heartbeat pings accelerating.

It happened with astonishing quickness: footfalls outside the door, then a woman came in—black, elegant—ah, one of Sue's memories: it was Alyssa Snow, Jerrison's private physician. "Mr. President, are you okay?" she asked.

All the eyes—the photographer's, Agent Dawson's,

Kadeem's, the nurse's, and Dr. Snow's—were on Seth Jerrison. There were whites visible all around his irises, as if he were seeing something horrific.

And he *was.* Kadeem had no doubt. Yes, just because they were linked didn't mean their recollections were in synch, but the flashback trigger would have had the same effect on the president as it was having on him. They might be experiencing different parts of it just now—Kadeem was seeing the half-track rolling over a corpse; the president might be seeing another wall shattering under mortar fire. But they were both *there,* Kadeem for the thousandth time, and Seth Jerrison for the very first.

"Mr. President?" asked Dr. Snow, desperately. "Are you okay, sir?"

The president was shaking his head slowly left and right, a small arc of what looked like disbelief, and his mouth had dropped open. Dr. Snow was now standing on the opposite side of the bed from Kadeem and using two fingers to check the president's pulse.

Kadeem staggered backward and ended up leaning against the wall for support.

Fire.

Smoke.

Screams.

He could barely see the real world, the hospital room, the president, but he turned his head and tried to make out the great man's expression. His face showed not shock and awe, but shock and horror. The doctor was moving now to wipe the president's brow.

Explosions.

Babies crying.

Gunfire.

"Mr. President?" Snow said. "Sir, for God's sake!"

Agent Dawson moved in, too, and also said, "Mr. President?"

Kadeem knew, of course, that neither of them noticed, or, if they *did* notice, that neither of them cared that he was in distress, too. That was normal here in Washington, the way it had been not just since the start of this war but going right back to Korea.

But maybe, just maybe, that would change now. He tried to shunt aside his own fear so that he could see Jerrison's face contort, see him recoil from some invisible blow or explosion, see him, the president of the United States, be the first person holding that office in decades to walk in a soldier's shoes, share a soldier's burden, and feel a soldier's terror at the things those back home had ordered soldiers to do.

CHAPTER 27

SUSAN Dawson spoke into her sleeve mike. "Get Singh in here right away!" She wheeled on Kadeem Adams. "What did you do to him?"

"Nothing," said Adams, but he seemed to be struggling to get even that single word out.

Susan looked over at the president, lying on his bed, his head propped up, his eyes wide with terror, sweat beading on his forehead. Dr. Alyssa Snow was listening to his chest with a stethoscope.

"Nothing my ass!" said Susan. "What did you do to him?"

But Kadeem's eyes were closed and he was swaying erratically from side to side, as if having trouble keeping his balance. He hadn't touched him. He hadn't done anything, and yet—

"For God's sake, Kadeem," Susan exclaimed, "he's recovering from heart surgery!"

She heard rapid footfalls in the corridor outside, and then the door burst open, revealing Ranjip Singh in the company of one of the Secret Service agents. Susan pointed at Jerrison.

"Kadeem did something to the president's mind, and now he's having a seizure."

Susan watched Ranjip turn to look at Kadeem, and she followed his gaze. Kadeem had his eyes scrunched tightly shut and was shaking his head rapidly in a small arc from left to right. His forehead was slick with sweat.

"Oh, shit," said Singh, the first time Susan had heard him swear. He went over to Kadeem and guided him—Kadeem's eyes were still closed—to the chair next to the president's bed, and gently, almost lovingly, he eased Kadeem into it. And then he took one of Kadeem's hands in his, light brown against dark brown, and, to Susan's surprise, he reached over and took one of the president's in his other hand, beige against light brown, and he stood between the two men, a human bridge, and he said, "All right, both of you, listen to me—listen to me! You're having a flashback. It's me, it's Ranjip Singh, and you're at Luther Terry Hospital. You're home, you're in the United States, and you're safe. You're safe!"

Susan started toward the bed; she didn't like that Singh had brought Kadeem so close to Jerrison. But Dr. Snow motioned for her to stay back. Susan could see the sheet over the president's chest heaving up and down. Above the rapid beeping of his heart-rate monitor, she could hear Kadeem whimpering softly.

"You're *safe*," Ranjip said again. "You're safe. That was thousands of kilometers away and many, many months ago. It's over. Kadeem, it's over. And Mr. President—Mr. Jerrison—*Seth*—it's *over*."

Susan felt helpless—and furious; she never should have allowed Adams in here. Christ, he might end up as the guy who'd managed to succeed at what Gordo Danbury had failed to do. The president's heart was still racing, and Dr. Snow was busily preparing a hypodermic.

"Take a deep breath," Ranjip said, looking at the president, whose eyes were still wide, and "Take a deep breath," he said to Kadeem, whose grip, Susan saw, was so tight now on Singh's hand that it must be hurting them both. "Hold it in," Ranjip said. "Just hold it, for a count of five: one, two, three, four, five. Now, let it out, slowly, slowly—that's right, Seth, that's right. Kadeem, you can do it, too: slowly, gently, let the air out, let the memory out, release it, let it go . . ."

There was an extended silence from the president's monitor as his heart skipped a beat, and when that happened, Susan's own followed suit. Dr. Snow looked at him with concern, but when the beeps started again, they were progressively further apart.

"Again," said Ranjip. "Take a deep breath again, both of you. Relax. Now, concentrate on something peaceful: a clear blue sky. That's it; that's all—just that. The sky, blue and clean and bright; a beautiful summer's day, not a cloud to be seen. Peaceful, calming, relaxing."

It looked to Susan as though Kadeem's grip was lessening a bit, and he'd stopped making sounds. The president's eyes were no longer wide, and he was blinking rapidly—perhaps as he imagined looking up at a sunny sky.

Jerrison turned at last to Singh and seemed to recognize him. "Thank you," he said softly. "Thank you."

Singh nodded and let go of the president's hand. He looked at Kadeem, and Dr. Snow immediately moved in and mopped the president's brow. She then placed her stethoscope back on the president's chest and nodded, apparently satisfied with what she was hearing.

Kadeem was shaking, Susan saw, as if he were freezing to death. Ranjip was now facing him directly. He took both his hands and looked straight into Kadeem's eyes, which had finally opened. "It's all right," Ranjip said again. "It's all right."

Ranjip had a puzzled expression. Susan realized the Canadian wanted to ask Kadeem what had triggered the flashback, but, of course, he couldn't; asking him that would bring the trigger to mind and might set off another episode. "He did it," Susan said, pointing at Kadeem. "Deliberately."

"No," said Ranjip, shaking his head. "Surely not."

"He did it," Susan repeated. "He did that to the president."

Ranjip looked at Kadeem, as if expecting a denial, but when none was forthcoming, Ranjip said softly, his tone conveying he was stunned by what the young man had done. "Kadeem . . ."

Susan spoke into her sleeve. "Dawson to Hudkins and Michaelis: come to Prospector's room right away." She looked at Kadeem. "You've made the mistake of your life," she said. "This was the stupidest thing you—"

"Agent Dawson." The voice was weak but oh-so-familiar. She turned to face Prospector. "Yes, Mr. President?"

"Go . . . easy . . . on the . . . young man," Jerrison said.

"But, sir, he—"

Jerrison silenced her with a hand gesture and he turned his gaze to Kadeem just as the door opened, revealing the two agents Susan had called for. "Private Adams," Jerrison said, still weak, "was that . . . what it was . . . really like?"

Kadeem nodded once. "Yes, sir, Mr. President. I'm sorry I had to—"

Susan saw the president make the same silencing gesture at Kadeem as he had at her, and Seth Jerrison was a hard man to disobey. "You went through all of that?"

"Yes, sir, Mr. President." Kadeem paused, then: "And not just me, sir. Lots of us went through it, or something similar."

Jerrison seemed to consider this for a time, then, at last, he slowly nodded, and, to Susan's surprise, he said, "Thank you, Private Adams. Thank you . . . for sharing that with me."

And then Kadeem Adams surprised Susan. He stood up ramrod straight and crisply saluted his commander in chief. "Thank *you*, sir."

ERIC Redekop and Janis Falconi exited the building, Eric carefully avoiding the reporters who were camped out front. It was a cold night, and he found himself feeling an urge to put his arm around Jan's shoulder, but he didn't. They walked along Pennsylvania Avenue. Things were eerily silent for a Friday night; doubtless, after today's bomb blast, many people were staying indoors. Eric remembered it had been the same way after 9/11, when an American Airlines 757 had crashed into the Pentagon.

In the first block west of LT, they had a choice between the Foggy Bottom Pub and Capitol Grounds Coffee; thank God the pubs and cafés were keeping their doors open. They opted for the pub and found a booth near the back where they could talk.

"So," Eric said, after they'd sat down, and "So," said Janis.

A middle-aged waitress looking worn down by the day's events took their orders: two draft beers.

"I don't know how long these linkages will last," Eric said, "but . . ."

"Yeah," said Jan. "But."

"I . . . ah, I didn't know . . . I don't mean to pry. Really, I've been trying not to, but . . ."

"But you can't help it. I know; I keep getting Josh Latimer's memories, too."

"At work, sometimes . . . when you're alone, you . . . to . . . to ease the pain, you . . ."

She lowered her eyes. "Are you going to report me?"

"No, no. I'd like to see you get help, though. You know there are confidential programs . . ."

"Thanks." She paused. "There's a lot of bad stuff in my life."

They were seated on opposite sides of the booth; her hands were on the table between them. He found his hand moving over to cover one of hers. "I know."

Their beers arrived.

"ALL right," said Susan, after Kadeem had finished saluting the president. "That's enough. Private Adams, you're under arrest." She'd not only have to lock him up, but also sedate him to make sure he didn't try something similar again.

To his credit, Kadeem lifted his hands slightly. "Yes, ma'am."

But the president stirred on his bed. "No."

"Sir, he *assaulted* you."

Jerrison managed some more strength. "I said no, Susan."

"Sir, we can't let him debilitate you at will." She indicated that Kadeem should move toward the closed door.

"No," said Jerrison again. "Private Adams stays, but I want the rest of you out of here. All of you: Alyssa, Sheila, Susan, Professor Singh, Agent Michaelis, and you, there, the photographer. Out."

"Sir!" said Susan.

"Do it. And find Maria Ramirez, the pregnant woman, if she hasn't yet gone home. I want to speak to both of them."

"But, Mr. President, I—"

"Right away, Agent Dawson."

Susan nodded. "Yes, sir."

SETH Jerrison found it odd to be talking with Kadeem Adams. They'd only just met, but he had all the young man's memories. Normally, Seth didn't have much patience for people telling him things he already knew, but listening to Kadeem go on about his life in Los Angeles was actually relaxing; as soon as Kadeem started to tell a story, the episode came to Seth's mind, just as it had come to Kadeem's, although he doubtless was reconstructing it differently. And so while Kadeem spoke, Seth let his mind concentrate on the problem at hand.

Agent Dawson opened the door to the president's room, she looked relieved to see him simply lying there, listening to Kadeem.

"Mr. President," she said, indicating a young woman with long brown hair, "this is Maria Ramirez. You're in luck; she was still waiting for her husband to come pick her up."

"Thank you," Seth said weakly. "That will be all, Susan."

She blew out air, clearly unhappy, then looked meaningfully at Kadeem. "I'll be just outside."

Seth waited until she'd left, then indicated for Maria to take a chair; Kadeem was already sitting in the one closest to the bed.

"Maria, thank you for making time for me."

"It's an honor, *Señor Presidente*."

"I understand you and your husband are expecting a baby."

"*Sí.*"

"Congratulations. That's wonderful."

"Thank you, sir."

"I have a favor to ask of you, Maria." Seth turned to Kadeem. "I need a favor from you, as well, please; I need help from both of you." He caught his breath, then went on. "Professor Singh tells me that you're linked to Susan Dawson,

Kadeem. And, Maria, I'm told you're linked to Darryl Hudkins, the other Secret Service agent who was affected by all this."

"Yeah," said Kadeem, and *"Sí,"* added Maria.

"What I'm about to tell you very few people know so far. The person who shot me was named Gordon Danbury. He was a Secret Service agent. Agents Dawson and Hudkins know this—can you find it in their memories?"

Kadeem looked astonished, but he nodded. But Maria said, "I already knew this. Agent Susan asked me about it."

"Really?" said Seth.

"Yes. She wanted to know if she could trust Agent Darryl."

"Ah. Yes, well, that's what I want to know, too. Whether I can trust him—and whether I can trust Susan. If the two of you search your memories, you can tell me if Agent Dawson or Agent Hudkins are compromised. Just ask yourselves if you knew anything in advance about a plot to kill the president—because if they knew about it, you'd know about it, too. Kadeem?"

The young man frowned. "Nothing, sir."

"Maria?"

"No. Like I told Agent Susan, Agent Darryl is not involved."

"Secret Service agents use my code name: Prospector. Any memories of a plan to kill—or assassinate—or take out—Prospector? Or to eliminate POTUS? That's P-O-T-U-S: president of the United States. Anything?"

"Well, there's all kinds of stuff about the investigation since that guy shot you," Kadeem said. "Sue's been getting constant updates. But I'd swear she didn't know about it beforehand."

"You're sure?"

"Mr. President, I know her like I know myself. I'm sure."

"And Maria? What about Agent Hudkins? Again, any inkling that he might have known in advance, or been involved in any way?"

"No, sir. Nothing like that."

"All right," said Seth. "Thank you. I'm glad to know I can trust Agents Dawson and Hudkins. There's already one other agent who has come under suspicion, a man named Jenks.

But if Danbury and Jenks were part of a larger conspiracy, and if that conspiracy involves others in the Secret Service, well, I . . ."

"You be fucked," said Kadeem. "Sir."

"Yes, exactly, Private Adams. I be fucked."

CHAPTER 28

AGENTS Dawson and Michaelis stood outside the door to President Jerrison's room, along with Dr. Snow and Sheila the nurse; Singh had gone back to his lab. Susan looked left and right down the corridor, nodding at the other Secret Service agents she could see at either end.

At last, the door opened, and she looked at the two people who were emerging: Private Kadeem Adams and Maria Ramirez.

"It's cool, Sue," said Kadeem, lifting his hands a bit. "Big man's fine—but he wants to see you."

Susan nodded and spoke into her sleeve mike. "Dawson to Hudkins. I'm returning to Prospector's room."

"Copy," said Darryl's voice in her ear.

She went in and closed the door behind her. The president did indeed look no worse for wear.

"Sir?" Susan said.

"You knew Gordon Danbury, right?" asked Jerrison.

"Sure. Of course."

"You said he was called Gordo by the other agents?"

"Yeah, most of the time." She shrugged a little. "Off duty,

we get a bit informal. The Susanator—that's what they call me. Darryl Hudkins is sometimes called Straw; you know, after Darryl Strawberry, the baseball player. And Gordon Danbury, he was Gordo."

Jerrison managed a slight nod. "Leon Hexley was talking on his BlackBerry on Wednesday in the Oval. He said, 'Tell Gordo to aim . . .' but I don't remember what came after that. But if it was related to what happened—well, it means there's a conspiracy, and it goes pretty high up."

"But you've known Mr. Hexley for years," said Susan.

Seth managed a philosophical movement of his shoulders. "What I've discovered today is that I don't know *anybody*—well, anybody except Kadeem Adams. I mean, seriously: you and I work together practically every day, Susan, and I know almost nothing about you—where you live, what hobbies you have, whether you're seeing anyone, what you were like as a little girl." He paused and caught his breath. "I've long been *acquainted with* Director Hexley, but I don't know him. And yet there are forty-four hundred sworn members of the Secret Service, and Hexley knew Danbury well enough not only to be on a first-name basis with him, but a nickname basis."

Susan frowned; that *was* curious. "But you don't remember what Mr. Hexley said?"

"No—because it didn't make sense at the time, and I had other things on my mind. I've racked my brain, but . . . no. It was weird, what he said, I remember that. But I just can't recall it. I *do* remember he shut up and turned off his phone the moment he realized I had entered. Didn't even say good-bye."

"Forgive me, sir, but that's not necessarily suspicious. People are conscious of how busy you are. You don't make the president wait while you finish a personal call." She paused. "A thought, sir. Did you have the Oval Office set up to record conversations the way Nixon did? And were they maybe backed up off-site?"

Seth shook his head. "Didn't work out so well for Nixon, that."

"True enough." Susan replied. "So now what?"

"First, I need you to get Hexley's cell-phone records."

"Will do—but they're almost certainly encrypted and scrambled. After Obama insisted on getting to keep his

BlackBerry, all sorts of extra security was instituted on the units issued to high-level government officials. I suspect it'll take days to decrypt them, if it can be done at all."

"Damn," said Jerrison.

"Is there anything else, Mr. President?"

"Yes," he said. "I want to send Mrs. Stilwell on a little trip in the morning."

"IT'S so strange," Jan Falconi said as she sipped her second beer, "having a man's memories." She shook her head. "And, I gotta say, Josh Latimer is *pissed.*"

"About what?" asked Eric.

"He was supposed to receive a kidney transplant this morning, and the surgery was canceled after it had begun, to make room for the president. He and his daughter—she's the donor—were being dealt with in the corridor outside your O.R. while you were working on Jerrison; I was tending to them."

"Good Christ," said Eric. "I saw them there when I went in, but I didn't know what it was about."

"He's thinking about suing."

"I can't say I blame him, but . . . well, most kidney transplants aren't time-sensitive, and the president *had* to be treated immediately."

"Still," said Jan, shaking, "the last thing I need is someone being angry inside my head."

"I know," Eric said gently.

Jan clearly wanted to change the subject. "Somebody must be reading your memories, too."

"Yeah," Eric replied. "Her name's Nikki Van Hausen. She's a real-estate agent."

Jan smiled. "That's funny."

"It is?"

"Sure. Her name is Van Hausen and she sells houses. It's like a dentist named Payne or . . ."

"Or Larry Speakes," said Eric—and then he realized the name didn't mean anything to her. "He was the White House spokesman for Ronald Reagan."

She smiled. "Exactly. There's a name for that. It's called—"

and as she said it, it came to Eric, but not from his memory—he'd never heard the term before—but from hers: "nominative determinism."

"Cool," he said, making an impressed face.

"They talk about it in *New Scientist* all the time," she said.

"You read *New Scientist?*" And then: "Oh, so you do. You subscribe."

"I adore it," she said. "Great magazine."

He looked at her in the dim light of the bar. She was absolutely lovely, but she was eighteen years younger than him. Which was crazy. Which was *nuts*.

The waitress appeared. "Another round?"

Eric gestured at Jan; it was up to her.

"Sure," she said. "Why not?"

"HI, Darryl," Susan said as she entered the conference room on the first floor, just down the corridor from Trauma.

Darryl Hudkins was sipping a coffee. His shaved head was showing a faint stubble, and his face was showing even more. "Hey, Sue."

"The president wants me to send you on a trip tomorrow morning."

"Somewhere warm and exotic, I hope."

"Well, it'll be warm, anyway. And he wants you to take Bessie Stilwell with you."

"Oh," said Darryl, sounding not at all enthusiastic now. "Does it have to be me?"

Susan looked at him. "You're the one linked to her so, yeah. There's no one who knows her mind better than you do. After all, she's still a security risk."

"Lucky me," said Darryl.

"Look, I think I have an inkling of what's eating you," Susan said, "but there'd be no respite for you in just staying here if we sent her somewhere else. You'd still be linked. Singh says—well, okay, he didn't *say* it, but he *knows* it: quantum entanglement works even across light-years of separation." She tried to lighten his mood. "All those geeks at the Pentagon who have been working on remote communication are going to love this."

But Darryl shook his head. "The problem is that when I see the way she looks at me, it triggers *me* to remember *her* past—and her feelings."

Susan smiled sympathetically. "I'm sorry, Darryl, but it's got to be you."

CHAPTER 29

Saturday

TONY Falconi came home drunk. Again.

Janis sat on the couch, afraid to say a word. Anything could trigger his anger, and—

And he was looking around the living room. Janis's pulse quickened. She knew what he was doing: seeking something—anything—to find fault with. Something that she hadn't cleaned properly, something that hadn't been put away, something that hadn't been done to his satisfaction. It didn't matter that she'd been locked up at the hospital until late, it didn't matter how much she'd done right; he'd find the one thing she'd done wrong, and—

"I thought I told you to get rid of that chair," he said, pointing.

Janis's stomach was churning. What he'd actually said was he was thinking they should get rid of that chair—it was an old kitchen-table-style chair and had a rip in the vinyl uphol-stery; it wasn't worth repairing. But she knew contradicting him would be a mistake.

But so, apparently, was silence. "Didn't I?" he snapped.

And then, without waiting for her answer, he said, "So why the fuck is it still here?"

"I'm sorry," Janis said softly.

"You're always sorry," Tony said. He surged forward, grabbed her arm—the one with the tiger tattoo—and roughly pulled her to her feet. "You stupid bitch," he said, shoving her now toward the chair, and—

—and Eric Redekop shook his head violently, trying to fling the memory away.

But he couldn't. This one or ones like it kept coming back to him.

Eric was lying on his bed, staring at the ceiling, as the morning sun poured in around his blinds. Janis had headed home around 10:00 P.M.—he'd paid for a cab to take her from the pub—and Tony had staggered in an hour later.

He rolled onto his side, drawing in a deep breath, then letting it out slowly.

He couldn't take this. And *she* shouldn't have to.

The old memories of events like this would always be there. But he could at least make sure that no similar new ones were ever laid down.

It wasn't his place. It wasn't his responsibility. It wasn't his duty.

But he'd saved the president of the United States. Surely, he could save this woman, too.

And suddenly it came to him. A memory from a month ago, forcing itself into his awareness, and . . .

No. Not *one* memory; a series of memories. Memories of . . . of *every* month—the . . . yes: the fourth Saturday morning of every month. Jan went to play Dungeons & Dragons at . . .

He'd never heard of it, but apparently the Bronze Shield was the largest gaming store in the capital district. It was her one day out a month; Tony almost never came—he preferred to stay home and watch TV. But Jan's brother Rudy was usually there; in fact—ah, yes—that's why she was allowed to go at all: keeping up the appearance of freedom in front of her family, lest eyebrows be raised.

And—yes, *today* was the fourth Saturday. Still, he asked himself if the event had been canceled in light of what had happened yesterday, but it hadn't been as far as she knew—which meant she would indeed be at the Bronze Shield this morning.

All right then. All right.

SUSAN Dawson had grabbed some sleep in the conference room downstairs; she figured she got maybe five hours. When she woke up, she went to check with Ranjip Singh, who also hadn't gone home.

It was odd not having to ask him for an update; she *knew* what he'd been doing. Before he'd gone to bed, he'd contacted his colleagues back in Toronto, as well as those at the Montreal Neurological Institute, the Center for Cognitive Neuroscience at Penn, and the Center for Consciousness Studies at the University of Arizona, providing copies of his data to them, hoping someone somewhere might have an idea how to break the linkages.

And this morning, the weird happenings here at LT had finally merited some time on the news, after almost continuous coverage of the assassination attempt and the bomb explosion at the White House; Singh and a few of the affected people had been interviewed here in Singh's lab.

But the TV crew was gone now, and Singh was plugging away at his computer.

"Good morning, Agent Dawson," he said as Susan entered.

"Ranjip."

At that moment, a uniformed hospital security guard entered. He had two holsters, one holding a walkie-talkie and the other a gun.

"Professor Singh?" the man said.

"Yes?"

"I'm Ivan Tarasov." Susan remembered him from yesterday; he had been affected by Singh's equipment, and had found David January for Susan, and, later on, she'd interviewed him. She glanced at the whiteboard: Tarasov could read Dora Hennessey, the kidney donor, and in turn was read by Orrin Gillett, the lawyer.

"You have to do something about these links," Tarasov continued. He must be addressing Singh, Susan thought, but he wasn't actually looking at him, or at her.

Singh gestured at his computer screen. "I am trying."

"You have to do more than try. This is driving me crazy."

"How do you mean?" asked Singh.

Tarasov did glance briefly in Susan's direction, but, again, didn't actually meet her gaze.

"Every time I look at my daughter, I see images of a little girl being molested."

"My . . . God," said Singh. "You're linked to Dora Hennessey, right?"

"Yes."

"So it's her memories of being molested?"

"I guess."

Singh's mouth fell open. "That's . . . horrible."

"It's disgusting. That poor little girl."

"How old was Dora when this happened to her?"

"I think she was the same age my daughter is now. Three."

Singh consulted a document on his computer. "Miss Hennessey is thirty-seven." He looked up. "The person abusing her—do you know who it was?"

"I'd never have recognized him today, but yes. It was her father, Josh Latimer."

"The fellow she's giving the kidney to?" Singh said, surprised.

"I don't think she remembers the abuse," said Tarasov, still not actually looking at Singh. "I can't recall her ever discussing it with anyone."

Susan saw Singh's eyebrows go up. "That's . . . fascinating."

"What is?"

"You remember something from her past that she doesn't. I wonder why."

Tarasov frowned. "Maybe the memories are so traumatic, she's blocked them out."

"That's *one* possibility," said Singh, "but . . ."

"Yes?"

"You said you thought she was three when this happened."

"It had to be," said Tarasov. "Three, or earlier. Dora's mother and father split when she was three. She didn't see him again until this past year, when he tracked her down, hoping she'd be a good tissue match—and that she might agree to the donation."

"Three . . . or younger," said Singh.

"Yes."

"Most adults remember almost nothing from before they were three and a half or even four. But . . ."

"Yes?"

Singh said, "I've seen you around the hospital—before all this, I mean. You are . . . a bit of a loner."

"So?"

"And you tend not to meet people's gaze. In fact, you avert your eyes."

"Are you accusing me of something, Mr. Singh?"

"No, no. Not at all. But if I may ask: are you on the autism spectrum?"

"I'm an Aspie," said Tarasov.

"Asperger's syndrome," said Singh, nodding. "Do you think in pictures?"

"Yes."

"Pictures, not words?"

"Most of the time."

"And do you remember your own very early life?"

"I remember my *birth*," Tarasov said. "Lots of people on the spectrum do."

"Well, there it is," said Singh, looking at Susan then back at Tarasov. "Everyone starts out life thinking in pictures; they have to, of course—we don't get language until much later. When we *do* acquire language, our indexing system for memories changes: words, rather than images, become the principal triggers of recall, and we can no longer recall things from before we had sophisticated linguistic abilities. It's been argued that the memories are still there, but they're inaccessible. But you, Mr. Tarasov, can access Miss Hennessey's original indexing system, the prelinguistic one, because you think in pictures. You can remember things from her past that she herself no longer can. In fact . . . can you remember *her* birth?"

He thought about it. "I was born in Russia, at home, years before my family came here. But Dora . . . she'd been born— yes, I can see it now—in a hospital room with blue walls, and—the details are fuzzy; I guess infants don't focus well— and the doctor doing the delivery was a woman with short black hair."

"Incredible," said Singh, his voice full of awe. "Fascinating."

"This isn't an academic point," said Tarasov, sharply. "I can't get the memories of her being molested out of my mind. They keep coming to me every time I look at my own daughter. It's like having horrific child pornography constantly shoved in my face."

"I'm sorry," said Singh. "I am so sorry."

"Sorry doesn't fix it," said Tarasov, and for once he looked directly at Singh. "This needs to be solved, right away."

CHAPTER 30

DARRYL Hudkins had never flown business class, and he'd assumed he never would. But the president had, for some reason, insisted they take a commercial airliner to their destination, and the next flight heading there had nothing but premium seats available.

All of which was fine, except . . .

Except it *was* a long flight, and . . .

And *he* could read Bessie's memories.

He swallowed and tried to be calm, tried to ignore them, but . . .

But she was *nervous,* damn it all. She was nervous traveling with him because—

Because he was black.

Because she'd heard awful things about black men.

Because both in DC and back where she lived in Mississippi, most of the crime—or so she thought—was committed by black men.

He tried not to think about what *she* was thinking about, tried to put her thoughts out of his mind, but—

But it came back to him. She'd thought the n-word.

The fucking n-word!

He leafed through the in-flight magazine, noting another petty indignity—the almost complete lack of black people in the ads. He looked around at the other passengers: a fat white guy softly snoring, a prim white woman reading on a Nook, two white men chatting softly about some sort of investment.

And, damn it all, he couldn't help wondering what experience Bessie had had with black men, and—

And to wonder was to *know*.

Bessie had grown up in Memphis. Lots of blacks there, of course, but even after all this time, not much mixing; even after all this time, separate but not equal; even after all this time, people thinking, even if they never said it, "colored" and "Negro" and worse.

His stomach churned, and not just because the plane was experiencing turbulence.

NO sooner had Ivan Tarasov left Singh's lab than two more people came in.

Oh, joy, thought Susan. The people were Rachel Cohen, the woman who worked in accounts receivable at LT, and Orrin Gillett, the lawyer who'd tried to get out as the lockdown was being initiated yesterday. Susan was surprised to see them back here—surely Rachel didn't normally work weekends, and Orrin had made it crystal clear that this was the last place he wanted to be.

"Professor Singh," Rachel said. "I was hoping you'd be in today."

"And Agent Dawson," said Gillett, dryly. "Always a pleasure."

"Is everything okay?" Singh asked. "Miss Cohen, you can read Mr. Gillett, I believe? Has anything changed in that regard overnight?"

Susan thought he sounded hopeful; if their link had weakened or broken of its own accord, of course that would be wonderful.

"No," said Rachel. "It's still exactly like yesterday."

"I am so sorry," said Singh. "Believe me, I had no idea—"

"I saw you on TV earlier this morning," Rachel said, cutting him off. "The interview you gave."

"Ah, yes. I hear they subtitled me! Really, my accent isn't that thick, is it?"

"You said you were trying to break the linkages."

"Yes, of course."

"You can't," Rachel said simply.

Singh smiled. "You do wonders for my confidence, Miss Cohen. I admit I don't yet have any clue how—"

"I mean you *can't,*" Rachel said. "I won't allow it."

"Pardon?"

She reached over and took Orrin Gillett's hand in hers. "I *like* being linked to Orrin. I don't want you to break the link."

Susan was surprised, and so, quite clearly, was Ranjip. "But, Ms. Cohen," he said, "once I figure it out, I suspect *all* the links will break simultaneously."

"I don't care about the other links, but you can't break mine. It's important to me. And it's important to Orrin, too, isn't that right?"

"Yes," Gillett said.

Susan was baffled. "But why?"

Gillett looked at her. Rachel squeezed his hand, and said, "It's okay."

"Because," Gillett said, "it makes this woman the perfect lover. Don't you see? She knows *exactly* what I like; she knows everything there is to know about me."

"And," said Rachel, "I get to recall us making love from his point of view—him seeing me, feeling what it's like for him being inside me."

Singh's complexion didn't let him visibly blush, but he nonetheless looked embarrassed. "Well, as my son would say . . ." Ranjip began, and it came to Susan before he completed his sentence exactly what Harpreet would say: "'Whatever floats your boat.'" But then Ranjip shook his head. "But, as I said, I believe it is an all-or-nothing proposition as far as the network of linkages is concerned."

"Be that as it may," said Gillett, "Rachel does not consent to the procedure."

"What?" said Susan—but she could see Singh frowning.

Gillett faced her. "Before this hospital, or any other, may perform an experimental procedure on someone, that someone has to provide informed consent. And Rachel chooses not to."

"The others want the links severed," said Singh.

"I don't care what the others want," said Rachel. "You are talking about making a fundamental change to my mind, my mental processes—and I forbid it."

"But it was an accident—"

"That's right: what you did to me before was an accident. But what you're talking about doing now is premeditated, and I won't allow it."

"Really, Ms. Cohen—"

Gillett folded his arms in front of his chest. "Listen to her, Professor Singh. Without informed patient consent, you can't conduct *any* procedure on her—and you know that. And you categorically do *not* have my—my *client's* consent."

"This is a national-security matter," Susan said.

"Why?" said Gillett, wheeling on her. "Because you say so? *Puh-leeze.* Rachel's reading me, and I'm reading a security guard, for God's sake. There's no national-security issue involving us—but you can bet that we'll bring one hell of a lawsuit if you wreck this for us."

THE flight attendants were coming through the cabin, offering beverages. Darryl got himself a Pepsi, and Bessie had a coffee, and—

And when the attendant asked her how she wanted it, she hesitated, that same silly hesitancy he'd seen a million times from white people who never once would have associated race with a phrase like "a white Christmas."

"Black," she said at last.

Bessie had the window seat. They brought down the seat-back trays—effectively trapping them until their beverages were consumed—and so this seemed like the perfect time; she couldn't just excuse herself to go to the lavatory. Darryl took a deep breath. He didn't want to speak loudly—he didn't want others on the plane overhearing. "You know I know what you know," he said.

She looked puzzled for a moment, perhaps trying to disentangle all the "knows," but then she lifted her head, and her chin stuck out defiantly. "There is no law against having thoughts," she said. "This isn't the Soviet Union."

He frowned; she *was* old. He tried to make a joke. "Or China, either."

But she was buoyed. "Exactly. I can think whatever I want to think."

"Yes, ma'am, you can. I can't stop you. But . . ."

Bessie seemed content to let him trail off; she turned and looked out at the clouds—perhaps pleased to see nothing but whiteness.

"But," continued Darryl, "I'm a good man, ma'am. I serve my country every day. I'm good to my mother, and to my brothers and sisters. I'm not what you think I am—think *we* are."

"I don't know anything about you," Bessie said.

"That's exactly right, ma'am. You don't. You *think* you do, but you don't. But I know everything about you. It's none of my business—I understand that. But I can't help it. And, you know what, ma'am? I've been searching—forgive me, but I have. Searching for when a black man hurt you, or dissed you, or maybe stole something from you. Searching for when one of us did something to make you feel the way you do."

She turned back to face him. "Well, one of you is violating me right now."

"Yes, ma'am, I understand that. It isn't right, what I'm doing, is it? But like you said, there's no law against having thoughts, and, to tell you the truth, I don't even know how *not* to think about things." He paused. "And not to be the pot calling the kettle black"—he smiled gently to let her know that he was conscious of what he was saying—"but I've no doubt you're doing the same thing with Prospector—President Jerrison. I doubt you can help yourself any more than I can."

That, at least, got the barest of nods.

"So, I've tried to recall stuff about unpleasant experiences with black people. And, well, I can't find it. So, I thought maybe you just hadn't *stored* that they were black folk, although that seemed strange that you wouldn't. And, well, I'm sorry about that guy at high school and what he did to you . . . but I don't think he was black; I don't think there were *any* blacks in your school. And I'm sorry about the way Cletus treated you—but with a name like that, there's no way he's black. And I'm sorry about all the other bad things that I can recall that happened to you."

"They . . ."

She stopped herself, but he could guess. "They weren't my fault—that's what you were going to say, right? And you're right—they weren't. But they weren't the fault of any black person. Yet you don't like being around black people."

"I really would rather not have this conversation," she said.

"Honestly? I'd rather we didn't *need* to have it, ma'am. But I think we do. Stuff happens for a reason. I think the Good Lord set this up on purpose."

Bessie seemed to consider this for a few moments, and then, at last, she nodded. "Perhaps he did, at that."

"I know you believe in God, ma'am."

"Yes, I do."

"I do, too. And there's only one God, ma'am. He made us all."

She nodded again. "Yes, I suppose he did."

"So, I guess all I'm saying, ma'am, is I don't think you've ever had a black friend."

"That's not true," she said at once, the words coming quickly. But it was a reflex response, Darryl knew, and at least she halted herself before getting out, "Some of my best friends are black."

Darryl decided not to challenge the statement directly; instead, he just let it pass as if he hadn't heard it—after all, on reflection, she had to know that he knew what she'd said wasn't true. "And so," he continued, his tone even, "I'd like to be your first." He held out his hand.

She looked at it for several seconds, as if not sure what to do. And then she lifted her own hand and took his. This surely, he thought, must be a memorable moment for her: as far as he'd been able to determine, one of the few times she'd ever shaken hands with a black man. And so, as he released her hand, and she returned hers to—no, not all the way to her lap, where it had been, but just to the armrest between them—he let his mind search for the memory that had just been laid down, the one of that moment where his flesh had touched hers.

And he saw himself as she had coded him; of course, his mind couldn't help but impose his actual face on whatever cues she'd stored. But it wasn't himself that he was curious about, it was her thoughts, her feelings.

And they came to him. She'd been surprised by the feel of his hand, the roughness of his skin—and she'd been surprised, even though she'd noted such things before, by how light-colored his palm was. She'd also been surprised that he wore an analog watch—nothing to do with his skin color, and everything to do with his age; she'd expected all young people to wear digital ones if they bothered with a watch at all. He'd let go of her hand—and she'd noted him smiling at her. And, yes, she'd actually thought about whether to bring her hand all the way back to her lap, but, with a small effort of will, she'd stopped herself from doing that. And included with the memory, a part of it, a part of her, and now a part of him, were four small words.

That wasn't so bad.

It was a start.

CHAPTER 31

DR. Eric Redekop parked his Mercedes out front of the Bronze Shield, which was a much larger building than he'd expected it to be; Jan was used to its size, he guessed, and so her memories hadn't really encoded it as remarkable. He knew in a vague way that gaming was big business, but it still surprised him that the store was so large, and—

And it was closed! The front door was locked; he almost snapped the fingers off his hand in the cold yanking on the handle. He looked at the business hours; they didn't open until noon on Saturday. He blew out air, watching it form a cloud in front of him.

And then it hit him, a memory—the memory he needed. The *store* opened at noon, but the gaming room opened at 10:00 A.M., with players coming and going by the back door.

He looked left and right, recognized left, and headed that way, and—ah!—there it was, a door painted in a pinkish beige that his old pencil-crayon set had called, back in the days of easy racism, "flesh." He closed the distance and pulled, gingerly this time, on the handle. But, crap, this door was locked, too.

Another memory came to him: you had to knock. He did.

About ten seconds later, a guy in his twenties with long, greasy hair, wearing a T-shirt depicting Robot Chicken (Jan knew it, even if he didn't) pushed the door open. Eric was prepared to have to explain himself, but the guy just held the door until Eric stepped into the large back room, which had five long tables set up with people seated around them, and—

And there she was: Janis Falconi.

Her back was to him, but there was no mistaking the tiger tattoo covering her left shoulder and continuing down her arm.

It was odd to be in a room that he'd never been in before and yet to *know* it. The washroom was over there, behind the door with the poster of The Incredible Hulk taped to it. The vending machine, next to it, was famous for running out of Diet Coke.

The guys sitting at Jan's table all had nicknames: Luckless, Bazinga (in truth, her brother Rudy), and Optimus Prime; even Jan didn't know the real name of the last of those.

She was laughing—he could hear her, and see her shoulders going up and down. He changed his position slightly so he could get just a glimpse of her profile; it was so good to see her being happy. He wondered if any of those she was playing with knew that this one day a month was just about the only time she *was* happy when she wasn't at work.

All the players seemed absorbed in what they were doing. At one table, they had boxes of donuts spread out. At another, some boisterous discussion was going on about something that had just happened in the game.

There were other chairs—metal-frame stacking ones with gray carpetlike upholstery, the kind you bought at Staples— stacked against the pale green wall. Several more tables whose legs had been folded up were leaning against the wall. Eric removed a chair from the stack and sat down, waiting for Jan's game to end; everyone was so intent on what they were doing, they simply ignored him. He pulled out his iPhone, flicked until the screen displaying the Kobo app was shown, tapped on it, and opened the new book he'd bought recently, the latest Jack McDevitt novel, and tried to lose himself in it, but—

But it all seemed so . . . so familiar. Granted, it was another installment in McDevitt's Alex Benedict series, but . . .

But that wasn't it. He'd read this already, and—

No, no. *Jan* had read it. He scrolled through his list of books, looking for something else to read.

Suddenly, the D&D game at Jan's table was over. Bazinga was leaning back in his chair, chatting animatedly with Luckless. Optimus Prime was putting away all the polyhedral dice and lead miniatures. Jan stood and picked up her chair, ready to add it to a stack against the wall, and, as she turned, she saw Eric, and her eyes went wide, and her mouth dropped open into a perfect O. She came over to him. "Eric, what are you doing here?"

Others were milling about as they put chairs away. Bazinga and Luckless came near, carrying the table they'd been using over to the wall.

He didn't know if this was the right moment—didn't know if there'd ever be the right moment—didn't want to shatter the happiness she seemed to be feeling just now. "Umm, Jan, can I speak to you for a second?"

Her eyebrows went up, but she nodded. He led her across the room, over to near the door with the Hulk on it.

"Yes?" she prodded.

He took a deep breath, then: "There's a women's shelter in Bethesda. They'll take you in, give you counseling, protect you. And I'll help you get a lawyer."

She started slowly shaking her head. "I can't."

"Can't what? Can't leave him? Jan, I *know* he hits you. I know what happened last night."

"Eric—Dr. Redekop—it's none of your business."

"I wish that were so, but I can't stop reading your memories."

"That doesn't give you the right to change things," she said.

Eric tilted his head. "I'm not trying to change things; I'm trying to help."

"I don't need help," Jan said.

Another memory of Tony yelling at her came to him: *You think you can just leave me? You're a fucking addict! I tell them that, and you'll never work as a nurse again.*

"He can't ruin your career," said Eric. "There are treatment programs—you know that. I'll see you get the help you need."

Jan was trembling. "You should go," she said softly.

"No," said Eric. *"We* should go. Jan, please, let me help."

Luckless came over to them. "Everything all right?" he asked, then, looking at Eric: "Who are you?"

Eric looked at him, pissed off, but Jan's memories came rushing in. Luckless knew all about Tony's treatment of Janis. He was interested in her—hell, *all* of the guys here were interested in her—but although Janis had literally cried on his shoulder more than once, Luckless had never taken advantage of her being despondent; Eric had to give him points for that.

"I'm Eric Redekop."

Luckless's eyes went wide. "You're the guy who saved Jerrison."

"I work with Jan," Eric said simply.

"Whatcha doing here?"

Eric looked at Janis, then back at Luckless. It wasn't violating a confidence; Luckless *knew* Tony was abusive. "I want to take her to a women's shelter."

And suddenly he knew things about Luckless, including why he was called that: it didn't just have to do with his unerring ability to get the wrong numbers to come up on the dice, but also with his sad history of going to work for small computing companies that folded almost as soon as he'd been hired; he had been out of work for eight months now.

Luckless looked at Jan. "You should do it," he said.

Someone was knocking on the outside door. The same fellow who'd opened the door earlier for Eric opened it again and—

Oh, shit.

Eric's stomach knotted, and he tasted bile at the back of his throat.

He'd never seen him in the flesh before, but he knew him at once. Hair buzzed short, jug ears, brown eyes, and a long, thin face. There was no doubt: it was Tony. But what the hell was he doing here?

Eric never paid any attention to clothing; without looking down, he couldn't say what clothes he himself was wearing right now. But Jan *did,* and what Tony was wearing now was doubtless what he'd also been wearing earlier this morning when he'd left the house. Eric concentrated on the clothes: a red plaid work shirt with a sky-blue T-shirt underneath visible through the open collar of the other shirt, and denim jeans, but brown not blue, and—

And it came to him: Jan's memories of this morning. A tense conversation with Tony over breakfast. Tony saying the job site he was going to be at today was only a few blocks from the Bronze Shield, so he'd drop her off . . . and come by to join them for lunch. What Tony presumably hadn't seen, because Jan had fought so hard to hide it, was her disappointment at this. She'd wanted to say please don't come; she'd wanted to say it was her one time out a month; she wanted to say they were *her* friends; she even wanted to say that none of them liked him—because, of course, most of them had previously seen the way she deflated in his presence. But she hadn't said any of that; she'd just nodded meekly and gone back to eating her Rice Krispies—a taste that came now to Eric, one he himself hadn't experienced since childhood.

Eric thought about leaving; after all, there'd be other opportunities to get Jan to the shelter. But seeing Tony triggered more memories.

Of him screaming.

Of him throwing a can of soup at her.

Of him berating her for the house being a mess.

Of him choking her during sex.

And he *was* going to drink again tonight; he was doubtless going to get drunk.

Meaning he would hit her again tonight.

And Eric could not let that happen. He took a deep breath, then: "Jan, let's go."

"Go where?" demanded Tony, crossing over to stand near Jan.

Eric looked him straight in the eyes—in the small, mean-spirited eyes. "To where she'll be safe."

Jan's gaming group had formed a sparse semicircle around them now, and people at the other tables, where games were still being played, had started looking up.

Jan looked at Eric with pleading eyes. "Please, Eric. Go home. You're just making things—"

He turned to her. *"Worse?* How could they possibly be worse?" He felt his arms shaking. Damn it! He truly hated confrontations although normally he could handle himself well enough during them. But every time he looked at Tony, he had another flashback to him humiliating or abusing or ignoring Jan, and it was making him livid. He spread his arms a bit, indicating the people around them. "I don't want to violate Jan's privacy, but—"

"But what?" demanded Tony.

"But I'm linked to Jan; I know what she knows. And I know *everything* you've ever done to her."

Tony narrowed his eyes. "Linked?" He wheeled on Janis. "That shit that was on the news? You didn't tell me you were part of that."

"It doesn't matter," Janis said meekly.

Tony looked at Eric, but he was still speaking to Jan. "He can read your mind?"

"My memories, yes," said Jan, staring down at the hard-wood floor.

Tony's eyes were tracking left and right, as if reviewing his past with Janis. His mouth dropped open a bit, showing yellow teeth.

Eric crossed his arms in front of his chest. "That's right," he said. "Her memories—of you." Eric watched Tony's face with a mixture of interest and disgust. It was almost as if Tony had discovered that what he'd thought had been done in private had really been recorded by security cameras. He briefly looked like a trapped animal. But then he rallied some inner strength. "None of that matters," he said defiantly. "She's my *wife.*"

"Only if she wants to be," said Eric, trying to keep his tone even.

"She's my wife!" Tony said again, as if that were sufficient justification for everything he'd done.

Eric couldn't take looking at him any longer. He shifted his gaze back to Jan. "Come with me," he said.

"If you do," Tony said to Janis, "you know what'll happen."

"No," said Eric. "It won't. We'll get her help for that. She'll keep her job."

Tony's face did an odd dance of expressions   he was still coming to grips with the notion that Eric had some special insight; Tony had clearly intended his threat just now to be a private one.

Jan looked at some of the other faces—the gamers, her

friends, her hapless brother, the people she saw once a month. And as Eric followed her gaze, memories of them came to him, too. Tony didn't show up often, it was true, but most of them had met him before. Of course, what they'd said to Jan might not be what they really felt; Eric himself had made plenty of polite noises over the years about friends' and colleagues' spouses, and—

And Optimus Prime spoke up. He was thin, pencil-necked, in his late twenties, with pale white skin and reddish blond hair. "Go with him," he said, indicating Eric with a movement of his head.

Jan shook her head, ever so slightly, and Tony snapped, "Shut up!"

But Optimus Prime stood his ground. "Jan, it's your turn—and it's your best move."

"Stay out of this, asshole!" Tony said.

It *was* Jan's move, Eric knew, but he couldn't keep quiet. "Jan," he said, "choose to be safe."

"You're going to regret this," Tony said through clenched teeth.

"No," said Eric. "She's not." He looked at her. "Jan?"

The tableau held for perhaps fifteen seconds, although Eric's pulse, pounding in his ears, was too accelerated to be a reliable timekeeper. And then Jan took a deep breath and started walking toward the door.

Tony surged forward and grabbed her arm, the one with the intricate tattoo of a tiger. And that did it—contact, the grip, right where he'd bruised her before. *"Don't!"* snapped Jan. "Don't you dare touch me."

Tony's eyes went wide. No memories came to Eric; Janis had never spoken to her husband like that before. She continued marching forward, and Eric fell in next to her. He still had his coat on, and she grabbed her coat and her purse, both of which were by the door.

"Jan," said Tony, pleading now. "I—I'm sorry, okay? I'm sorry. Things will be different."

Janis turned around, and for a second Eric thought she was changing her mind, but then he realized the truth: she wanted to see Tony like this, remember his face at the moment he lost her—a memory to savor, a memory for all time. No words were necessary, and she said none. Instead, she just turned, and Eric opened the heavy door for her, and they headed out into the November day. Eric was so pumped with adrenaline that he didn't feel the chill at all, but Jan soon started shivering—as much, he suspected, from emotional turmoil as from the cold. This time he did put his arm around her shoulders, and they walked toward his car.

CHAPTER 32

SECURITY at LAX was the most stringent Darryl had ever seen—after all, it had only been eleven days since an al-Sajada operative had been arrested in a parking lot here with one of those hexagonal bombs in his trunk. Still, as a Secret Service agent, Darryl could see dozens of holes in the procedures.

Once they got out of the secure area, they were greeted by a uniformed limousine driver holding a sign that said "Hudkins"—which was a first for Darryl, who was much more used to running alongside limos than riding in them.

Bessie and Darryl sat in the back, separated from the driver by a pane of smoked glass. Darryl suspected Bessie was thinking that in the good old days, it would have been the black man driving the white man, not the other way around. And speaking of the other way around, why did it have to be *him* reading *her*—or why couldn't Obama have still been in office, if she were destined to read the president's memories?

The limo took them through the Los Angeles traffic all the way out to Burbank. It had been years since Darryl had visited L.A., and he'd forgotten how horrible the congestion was, but Bessie was thrilled to catch a glimpse of the Hollywood sign high above the city. When they arrived at their destination, they had to go through more security—this with even more holes—handing photo ID through the car window to the gate guard. Darryl was stunned at how time-consuming and inefficient the process of getting in here was; he thought of five easy ways he could have gotten past the guards.

He'd never been on a studio lot before, and he hadn't known much about corporate mergers, but apparently Disney owned ABC Studios, and so, in addition to traditional Disney fare, lots of sitcoms and adult dramas were produced here. The soundstages were giant cubical buildings the color of cheese with huge billboards for ABC or Disney programming on their sides—who knew that *Chadwick's Place* was still in production?

The driver hopped out of the car and held the rear door open for Bessie. Darryl got out from his side, and a brown-haired white woman in her mid-twenties came driving up to them in a golf cart; the driver had called her to let her know they'd arrived.

"Hello," the woman said. "I'm Megan; I'm the assistant to Jessika Borsiczky. Won't you come with me?" She drove them down a series of paved paths between buildings and past some giant trucks until they came to the entrance to one of the stages. A sign on the door said, "Do Not Enter When Red Light Is Flashing." But it wasn't—and so they did.

They walked along a narrow space between the wall of the stage and the plywood backs of whatever set was on the other side. Giant black cables ran along the floor, and they occasionally had to squeeze against the wall to let people pass in the other direction; it was a long, arduous journey for Bessie. Finally, they came to the end of the plywood, and Megan turned. Craft-services tables—Darryl was pleased with himself for knowing that term—were spread out in front of them, covered with coffee urns, plates of sandwiches and pastries, and wicker bowls full of packaged snacks. A couple of people were standing by the table, chatting softly. They walked on, and came to more plywood, but this wall was *curved* . . .

They continued around to the other side, and there it was: The Oval Office.

Granted, it was a reconstruction, but except for the fact that it had an overhead grid of lights instead of a ceiling, it was *perfect*. And, Darryl supposed, it pretty much *had* to be: over the years, most Americans had seen countless pictures of the real Oval Office and had a good sense of what it had looked like before it had been destroyed. The Secret Service agent in him thought it ridiculous that the room the president had spent most of his waking hours in had been so publicly documented: its location, its exact dimensions, its every nook and cranny. But it had been, and this was a near-perfect duplicate. He wasn't surprised, though; lots of people in Washington loved *Inside the Beltway,* calling it the most accurate White House drama since *The West Wing*.

A smile broke out on Darryl's face. Here he was thinking about the *set,* when right there in front of him, sitting behind a flawless reproduction of the *Resolute* desk, was Courtney B. Vance, who starred as President Maxwell Doncaster. Vance was one of Darryl's favorite actors; Darryl had been thrilled when he'd won an NAACP Image Award earlier this year. He was looking off in the distance, apparently waiting for something.

"They'll be breaking for lunch in just a minute," Megan said.

"Can we do one more, Courtney?" asked a woman's voice; from this angle, Darryl couldn't see the speaker.

Vance nodded. He picked up the phone on the desk and spoke into the mouthpiece. "Get me the Russian president right away," he said, "and if he's not awake, wake him!" He slammed the phone down, and, in what the scriptwriters had doubtless written as "off the president's determined expression," the shot came to an end.

"Perfect," said the woman's voice. "All right, everyone, that's lunch!"

"Is it okay if we go onto the set now?" Darryl asked Megan.

Bessie, who looked more excited than Darryl had ever seen her, said, "And can I meet Mr. Vance?"

Megan smiled. "Of course." Vance was just getting out from behind the desk. "Come with me."

Bessie looked like she was going to burst. Darryl followed her.

"Courtney," said Megan, after they'd closed the distance,

"this is Mrs. Stilwell and Mr. Hudkins—Mr. Hudkins is a real Secret Service agent."

Vance was gallant. He took Bessie's hand gently in his, and said, "A pleasure to meet you, ma'am." Darryl smiled: two handshakes from African-Americans in one day; it probably was a record for Bessie. Vance then took Darryl's hand and shook it much more firmly. "Agent Hudkins, what an honor, sir."

"Thank you," said Darryl.

"Are you here consulting on the show?" Vance asked.

"Not exactly."

"Well, I hope you enjoy your visit."

Megan must have heard a cue in that. "Mr. Vance has only a short time for lunch, and he has to do a wardrobe change before he comes back, so if you'll forgive him . . ."

Vance smiled and moved off. Having an African-American president had become a cliché in movies and TV before Barack Obama had ever come to office. Darryl had enjoyed the joke that had been everywhere when Obama had been elected: "A black president? Crap, that means the Earth is about to be hit by an asteroid!" But he could tell that Bessie had been genuinely thrilled to meet Vance; then again, blacks as entertainers had always been welcomed, even by bigots.

Although he'd shown it to her repeatedly before, Darryl again fished out the picture he'd been carrying of Leon Hexley, the director of the Secret Service. The print was a still frame from security-camera footage taken on the day in question; Hexley had on a dark blue suit and a tie much more colorful than any he would have let his subordinates wear.

Bessie squinted as she studied it, then she nodded, and started to explore the set. There were cameras they had to walk around, but the rest of it was uncannily like the real thing. The lighting wasn't quite right, though—it was brighter than the real Oval. And the translight visible through the window was not exactly the view one got from the president's window—which, of course, made sense: the photographer who had taken the image probably had done so from out on the Ellipse.

Darryl was fond of the movie *Working Girl,* and particularly liked the ending, because he loved Carly Simon singing "Let the River Run." When he was young, you could count on seeing that movie every few months on TV, but nobody showed it anymore; Melanie Griffith's character had worked in the World Trade Center, and the movie ended with a pullout of her in her office fading into a loving long shot of the Twin Towers—it was just unbearably sad to watch now.

He wondered how the writers for *Inside the Beltway* were going to deal with the loss of the White House; would it continue to exist in their series? That, too, would probably be unbearably sad to see.

Darryl watched as Bessie slowly circumnavigated the room, looking at things that might jog her memory: the portrait of George Washington over the mantel at the north end flanked by potted Swedish ivy (a tradition that went back to the Kennedy administration), the bronze horse sculptures, the grandfather clock, the Norman Rockwell painting of the Statue of Liberty, the two high-back chairs in front of the fireplace, the coffee table, and the presidential seal in the carpet.

But Bessie kept shaking her head. Darryl was tired—it had been a long day already—and so he decided to sit in the one place he'd never been able to in the real Oval: the president's red leather chair behind the *Resolute* desk.

"Anything?" said Darryl. "Ignore the cameras; ignore the cables."

"Not yet."

Darryl looked around the room, and—

And of course he spotted it at once, although a casual visitor—or viewer!—would miss it altogether: the plain panel that was the door to the president's private study, just east of the Oval Office.

Darryl walked over to it. It had no handle, and it popped open when one pressed against it, just like the real thing had.

"Jerrison was here," Darryl said. "He came through this door into the Oval Office from his study."

Bessie shuffled over to be next to Darryl. He motioned for her to go into the study, and he sidled along the curving wall of the Oval Office so she could look back through the hidden doorway without having him, an extraneous element, as part of her view.

"Anything?" called Darryl. "Think about Jerrison in that room, walking through that door, finding Leon Hexley stand-

ing here, his back to the president at first, talking on his Black-
Berry, and saying . . . what?"

"I don't know," said Bessie. "There are so many memories
of this place, and of meetings here with Mr. Hexley. To find
the precise one you want . . ."

"It was Wednesday, about four in the afternoon. Hexley
said, 'Tell Gordo to aim' . . . ?" He let the unfinished sentence
float in the air, hoping she'd fill in the rest.

She shook her head but repeated, "Tell Gordo to aim" out
loud five times, each time in a slightly different way—and
finally her voice brightened. "He said, 'Tell Gordo to aim
4-2-4-7-4 the echo.'"

Darryl scrambled for a pen and paper. There was a pad
with the presidential seal on the desk, and a fountain pen in a
fancy stand. He desperately hoped it was a real pen, and not a
nonfunctional prop—and it was. He quickly wrote out what
Bessie had said.

"Are you sure?" he said. "Are you positive?"

"That's what he said, all right," Bessie replied. "He must
have heard the president then because he stopped talking and
turned around. What does it mean?"

Darryl shook his head. "I don't know. But let's hope to God
someone does."

CHAPTER 33

ERIC Redekop and Janis Falconi got into Eric's maroon Mercedes, out front of the Bronze Shield. He buckled up and waited for her to do so, then gently said, "You're doing the right thing, Jan. The shelter is open even on weekends. We'll have no trouble getting you in."

"No," replied Jan softly.

Eric had his hand on the ignition key. "Sorry?"

"Don't take me to a shelter."

"You need help, Jan. You need support."

"Tomorrow, maybe. But not today. You can't just abandon me."

Whatever they were going to do, sitting outside the gaming store wasn't prudent. Jan's husband might come after them, after all. Eric turned the key and drove, heading nowhere in particular. "Okay," he said. "Let's get some lunch, then. Do you like—" But merely thinking the question was enough to know the answer. She loved Italian food; memories of her at various restaurants popped into his head. "There's a great Italian place not far from here."

"Thanks," Jan said.

They drove in silence for a time; the roads weren't busy on a normal Saturday and were even more sparsely filled today.

"You're recalling my memories," Jan said. "Right now. Aren't you?"

Eric nodded. He was trying not to do it, but they came anyway.

"You know I like you," she said. He was keeping his eyes on the road but was aware that she had turned her head and was looking at him.

"Yes," he said softly.

"And I thought, before all this craziness," she said, "that perhaps you liked me."

"Yes," he said again, signaling a turn.

"But that was *before*," she said. She was quiet for another block, and so was he, but then she asked, "What about now?"

And *that* was the question, Eric realized. It was one thing to know someone on the outside, but to know them on the inside! He'd never known anyone but himself this well before. He knew what her childhood had been like. A memory came to him of her at maybe eight years old, unable to sleep, coming down to the kitchen in her family's little house and telling her mother that she was scared about dying, and her mom comforting her and saying that everyone dies eventually, but it would be a long, long time before either of them did.

And he knew what she'd been like at college, including the one and only time she'd cheated on a test, desperate to get into nursing school.

And he knew what she'd been like on her wedding day, walking down the aisle, thinking, *This is the biggest mistake of my life*—but being too afraid of making a scene to put a halt to the whole damn thing.

He knew it *all*. And she was right to wonder what effect that had on his perception of her.

The car rolled on; shops and restaurants passed by.

And the answer came to him. Not from his mind and not from hers—but from his heart.

He did still like her.

He liked her *a lot*.

But . . .

"Jan," he said. "I'm a doctor. I can't . . ."

"Can't what?" she replied. "Get involved with a patient? I'm not your patient, Eric."

She was right. "True."

"And, yes, you're older than me, but I like older men."

He thought about this; she did indeed. "Ah."

"Or," she said, "is it that you can't get involved with a nurse? Because, like, this would be the first time in history *that* has ever happened."

He smiled and drove on.

SUSAN Dawson was waiting down in the lobby of Luther Terry for Paul to show up. They'd been dating for six months, and he'd had a key to her place for the last three. He had kindly gone there to pick up a change of clothes for her.

And there he was! She ran over and hugged him, holding on tighter than usual; she surprised herself by how much she needed the contact, needed the stability.

When they separated, he gently swept her hair away from her face. "You managing okay?"

"Yeah," she replied. "You?"

He lifted his shoulders slightly and tipped his head toward the glass doors leading out of the lobby, leading back to the crazy world outside. "As well as anyone, I suppose. Couldn't sleep last night."

She nodded. "Me, neither."

He had a big cloth bag with him. In addition to a dark suit and white blouse, he'd also brought along her red ski jacket, since the blood-soaked coat she'd used yesterday was too horrific to wear.

She desperately wanted to have a coffee with him at the Starbucks here in the lobby, but her BlackBerry vibrated. She pulled it out and read the message from Darryl. Bessie Stilwell had remembered what Leon Hexley had said. Darryl had typed it in, but the words and numbers didn't make any sense to Susan. Still, she was delighted that the memory had been recovered.

Darryl's message noted that they were going to take a military jet back. Susan thought about texting that Jerrison had wanted them to take civilian flights, but then, now that she thought about it, he'd actually only said to make sure they flew to L.A. on a commercial plane; he hadn't said anything about the return, and—

"Everything okay?" Paul asked, indicating her BlackBerry.

She looked up and smiled at him. He worked in security at the Smithsonian; they often went jogging together on the Mall. "Yes, baby—it's fine. But I gotta go." She quickly kissed him and headed out of the lobby, taking the bag he'd brought. She went by Singh's office, which was empty—the Canadian was down the hall in his lab—and quickly changed into the fresh clothes, feeling a little more civilized for having done so. She then took a yellow pad—this one had some of Kadeem's doodles on the top sheet, which she tore off—and wrote out in big letters the words and numbers Bessie had remembered Hexley saying. Then she hurried back down to visit the president.

When the lockdown had ended yesterday, she'd sent a number of the Secret Service agents who had been here home and ordered others to come take their places. The two on duty out front of Prospector's door were ones she'd had transferred from the detail that looked after visiting dignitaries—in other words, ones who would never normally have direct access to the president and thus were less likely to be involved in any conspiracy against him. She'd also had two FBI agents brought in, and they were there as well—watching the watchers.

"HELLO, may I please speak to Maria Ramirez?"

"Speaking."

"This is—"

"Hello, Professor Singh."

"Is my voice that distinctive?"

"I'm afraid so, Professor. Is there— is something wrong?"

"No, no. But I have a question, if I may."

"*Sí.*"

"You can read the memories of Darryl Hudkins, one of the Secret Service agents, correct?"

"*Sí.*"

"Do you recall him meeting anyone . . . interesting, shall we say, today?"

"No."

"Are you sure, Maria?"

"Nothing comes to mind."

"An actor, perhaps . . . ?"

"Oh! *Sí! ¡Qué emocionante!* Darryl is in Hollywood, no? And he met Courtney B. Vance!"

"Yes, he did."

"But . . . but why is this important?"

"Just confirming something. It proves that the links remain intact even over distances of thousands of kilometers."

"*¡Dios mio!*"

"My thought exactly."

SETH Jerrison's previous nurse Sheila had been replaced by one named Kelly. He liked her better. She wasn't as stern, and she laughed at his little jokes. Earlier, she'd read him the most recent batch of get-well-soon and sympathy messages from foreign leaders, and she was now rearranging the vast collection of flowers that had been placed on a table by the window; they were a tiny fraction of those that had been delivered to the hospital since the shooting.

The press had been making noises about a transfer of power under the Twenty-Fifth while Seth was recuperating. Seth would be damned if he'd let that happen; this was a time of crisis, and he intended to lead. He'd insisted on being given another stimulant half an hour ago, and he was feeling, if not chipper, at least more alert and energetic than he had when he woke up.

The door to the room opened, and in came Susan Dawson. "Pay dirt," she said.

"Kelly, will you excuse us?" Seth asked.

The nurse nodded. "I'll be just outside."

"That's fine."

Susan took the vinyl-covered chair next to Seth's bed and she held up a lined yellow notepad so he could see it. "Yes, yes!" he said once. "That's it—that's it exactly. 'Tell Gordo to aim 4-2-4-7-4 the echo.'"

"The 'aim' part is certainly suspicious," Susan said. "But it's not conclusive."

"True," Seth said. "Call it in to the NSA decoding desk; see what they make of it."

Susan nodded and took a minute to do that. When she was off the phone, Seth motioned for her to show him the sheet again. "What do you make of the '4-2-4-7-4' bit?" he asked.

"Forty-two thousand four hundred and seventy-four," said Susan. "Does that mean anything to you?"

"No."

"It's not some sort of reference to you? Maybe your old ZIP code or something?" She pulled out her BlackBerry and went to the USPS site. "Huh," she said. "It's not a valid ZIP code. Well, maybe that first 'four' isn't the number. Maybe its, um, the . . ."

"Preposition," Seth provided.

"Right. Maybe it's 'aim for 2-4-7-4.'"

"Well, 2-4-7-4 doesn't mean anything to me. But if the final 'four' is also the preposition—aim for 2-4-7 for the echo—then maybe it's a time. You know, 2:47?"

"But surely you'd say 'two-forty-seven,' then. And, besides, you were shot in the morning."

"What about 24/7—you know, seven days a week?"

"But he said 'two-four,' not 'twenty-four.'"

Seth frowned. "And what's this about echoing?"

"That *is* strange. Danbury shot you from inside the Lincoln Memorial. With all that marble around him, it was bound to echo loudly no matter when he took the shot."

"'Echo,'" Seth said. "Suppose it's not the word; suppose it's the phonetic alphabet. You know: alpha, bravo, um . . ."

"Charlie," said Susan, "delta, echo."

"Right. So maybe it stands for something that begins with *E*."

"Executive?" offered Susan. "Execute? Eliminate?"

Seth's heart pounded—which hurt like hell. "God," he said.

"What is it?"

"Two-four-seven. They add up to thirteen."

"Yes. So?"

He hesitated. Did he really want to reveal the 13 Code to a Secret Service agent? But, of course, in this day of RSA encryption, no one except school kids bothered with simple substitution ciphers. He took a moment to explain how his code worked and talked her through writing up the conversion table on her yellow pad so she could see what he meant:

A=C	E=I	M=T
B=D	F=J	N=U
	G=K	O=V
	H=L	P=W
		Q=X
		R=Y
		S=Z

"There," he said, when she was done. "A decryption table for the key two-four-seven."

Susan looked at him like he was crazy. Seth nodded sagely. "They called me mad at the university."

She smiled. "I'm sure they did, sir."

CHAPTER 34

AFTER leaving Professor Singh's lab, Ivan Tarasov had intended to simply get through his day, trying to think of nothing but his duties as a security guard here at the hospital. He was good at his job, and he liked its repetitive quality: at *this* time, walk down *this* corridor, check that the doors to *these* rooms were properly locked, and—

And *there he was*. Ivan caught sight of Josh Latimer walking toward him. Seeing him, even from a distance, brought back a flood of Dora's memories, including the awkward call, months ago, when he'd phoned her—him here in Washington, her over in London, the father who had missed all her school plays and her move to England and her wedding and even the funeral of her mother, calling up to make sure he'd tracked down the right Dora, checking that her maiden name had been Latimer, that she'd been born in Maryland, that her birthday was August 6, and then, once he was sure, explaining that he was her long-lost father, and arranging to come visit her for a face-to-face meeting. And in a little restaurant off Piccadilly Circus, after they'd each tried to compress three decades of life into an hour, he told her why he'd sought her out and what he needed from her.

Memories of what had happened after they'd parted came to him, too. Of her talking it over with her doctor, her best friend Mandy, and her minister, and ultimately deciding she had to do this; she couldn't deny him.

Latimer was wearing a green hospital gown but blue jeans underneath. As Ivan watched, he turned and entered a room. Ivan's own path took him by the same room, and suddenly he found himself pushing the door open, entering, and closing the door behind him.

Latimer was sitting in the chair by his bed. Across the street, through the window, George Washington University's Jacqueline Kennedy Onassis dorm was visible. Latimer looked up, clearly startled to see a security guard entering.

Ivan felt his blood boiling; the mere sight of Latimer infuriated him. "How could you?" Ivan demanded.

Latimer frowned. "What?"

"After what you did to Dora, to ask her to let herself be cut open for you, to give a piece of her own body to you—how could you?"

Latimer groped on the table next to his chair for his eyeglasses, unfolded them, and put them on. "I don't know you," he said. "And you don't know me. The person reading my memories is a woman—a nurse. Janis something."

"Falconi," said Ivan, nodding; he knew the names of all the nurses and doctors here. "I'm not reading you. I'm reading your daughter Dora."

Latimer said nothing.

"You're thinking she can't possibly remember—because if she *did,* she'd never have agreed to help you. And maybe she doesn't remember. But *I* do."

"I don't know what you're talking about," said Latimer.

That further infuriated Ivan. "Don't lie to me," he said, moving closer. "Don't you dare lie to me."

"What are you going to do?" asked Latimer.

"I'm going to tell Dora," Ivan said. "She deserves to know."

"You can't," said Latimer, rising now.

"Oh?" said Ivan, turning now to exit, and—

Sound, movement, a tugging, and—

And Latimer grabbed the gun out of Ivan's holster. Ivan spun around and saw the pistol aimed at his chest. "I'll die without that transplant," Latimer said. "You're going to keep your mouth shut—about *everything.*"

"Or what?" asked Ivan, proud of himself for managing to briefly meet Latimer's gaze.

"Or I'll shoot you," said Latimer.

"You'll go to jail."

"Wanna bet? I was just talking to that guy Gillett, the lawyer. He said this was the *perfect* time to do something crazy because any competent attorney could get you off. Scrambled brains? Other people's memories? No one's fault. It's *carte* fucking *blanche.*"

"No judge is going to buy that," said Ivan.

"No?" said Latimer, waving the gun. "You came in here threatening me. There was a struggle; I got your gun, and it went off. Simple as that . . ."

AFTER leaving President Jerrison, Susan headed up to four, and was surprised to see that Orrin Gillett was still in the building. "What are you still doing here?"

"I had an appointment with Josh Latimer," he replied.

"Oh? And does he want to prevent Singh from severing the links, too?"

"Well, no. But that wasn't why I was seeing him. I'm representing him in his action against this hospital, related to his aborted kidney transplant."

"I heard they rescheduled that for Monday," Susan said.

"Be that as it may," said Gillett. "My client has suffered enormously. And I might as well tell you that we'll want to question you in relation to that."

Susan rubbed her eyes. "I am so *tired,*" she said. "I'm tired of all of this. I just want it to be *over*—and you aren't making it any easier, you and Rachel Cohen, with your demand that Singh not sever the links."

"We do have rights, Agent Dawson."

"So do the other people who were affected," said Susan, "myself included. The needs of the many outweigh the needs of the few."

"This isn't *Star Trek,*" Gillett said. "Individuals have individual rights."

"Who are you linked to again?"

"A security guard here."

"Oh, right," said Susan. "Ivan Tarasov. Well, I can tell you that he came to see Singh earlier this morning, and *he* wants the exact opposite: he wants the links severed as quickly as possible."

Gillett frowned, presumably recalling this. "So he did. And I do understand he's having a rough time; I'm truly glad the links are only—what did Singh call it? First-order. I'd hate to be seeing what Ivan is seeing, and—*fuck!*"

"What?"

"I just recalled one of his memories. Ivan with my client, Josh Latimer, and—Jesus!"

"What?"

Gillett considered for a moment. "He's my client, but—damn. I can't let him do this. Josh grabbed the guard's gun and has it aimed at him."

"What? When? When's that memory from?"

"Today. Sometime since I left Josh—so, the past fifteen minutes."

"What room are they in?"

"I don't know. I met Josh in the waiting area over there, but his room is somewhere on this floor."

Susan spoke into her sleeve. "Dawson to Central. I need to know the room number for Josh Latimer, a patient here at Lima Tango."

"Two secs, Sue," said the voice in her ear. Then: "Room 411."

"I need backup in that room," Susan said as she started running. She read the room numbers: 419, 417, 415, 413, and—

She unholstered her SIG P229, holding it in two hands vertically beside her face, then kicked open the door to 411.

"Drop it!" Susan barked, taking in the scene. Latimer must have heard the pounding footfalls: he had his left arm around Tarasov's neck, pulling him back against himself in the classic hostage-taking stance. The gun—a .38, Sue saw—was aimed at Tarasov's right temple.

"I said drop it!" Susan said again. If Latimer had been aiming at a protectee, there'd be no question; she'd have already taken him out. But she thought she might be able to talk Latimer out of this. Susan was blocking the only exit. She could hear sounds of panic in the corridor; her entry into Latimer's room had not been subtle. She stepped fully into the room and, with a backward kick, sent the door swinging shut behind her. A voice in her earpiece said, "Backup is on the way."

"You're not giving me any choice, Mr. Latimer," Susan said. "Drop the gun."

"And what?" said Latimer.

"We just forget about all this."

"Forget," repeated Latimer, as if it were the punch line to a joke. "That's the whole fucking problem, isn't it? Nobody can forget anything."

"Just put down the gun," Susan said.

Ivan Tarasov had been motionless, a statue, during all of this, although Susan could see that his forehead was glistening, and his eyes were showing white all around.

"Everything was going fine," Latimer said. "I'd found my daughter."

And then Tarasov spoke. Susan thought he was going to plead for his life, but he didn't. "You know what he did," Tarasov said to Susan. "I told you."

"Tarasov!" Susan snapped. "Shut up!"

"He *molested* his daughter," Tarasov said. "You know that."

"You don't know *anything,"* Latimer said. "You can't prove any of it."

"She may not remember, but I do," said Tarasov. "I'll testify against you."

"Shut up!" Susan barked. "Latimer, it'll be okay. No one is going to accept linked memories in court; there's no case law to support using them as evidence. Put the gun down, and we all walk away from this."

"He's going to tell Dora," Latimer said. "He's going to ruin *everything."*

Tarasov twisted now against Latimer's grip. "She deserves to know."

"Don't!" said Latimer and Susan simultaneously, and Susan added, "Damn it, Tarasov, shut up and let me protect you."

"Like you protected Jerrison?" Tarasov said. "You have no

idea what I'm seeing right now! *Right now!* The horrible things that little girl saw—the things that he did to her!"

Before this, Latimer had relaxed his grip a bit and had let the gun lower slightly, but now, in that slow motion that happens in times of real crisis, Susan saw him lifting the pistol, closing his grip, and moving his finger, and—

Blam!

Susan felt herself being slammed backward—

Oh my God!

—by the recoil of her own gun.

There'd been no way to hit Latimer in the chest; Tarasov's torso was covering it. And so she'd shot Latimer just above the right eye, blowing that side of his head open, blood and bone flying.

Latimer's blood splattered across the side of Tarasov's face. The security guard looked as though he was unsure who'd been hit, and Latimer—

Latimer's eyes were still open—wide, wide open—and tracking; his mouth opened as if to say something. Susan looked for an opportunity to get another shot off, but then Latimer collapsed, falling backward to the floor.

Tarasov wheeled around and recovered his gun.

Susan's heart was pounding ferociously. She had trained for this, and trained for it, and trained for it—but she'd never killed a man before. Her hand was shaking as she reholstered her own weapon.

Tarasov moved partway across the room and found a chair; he dropped himself into it and put his blood-spattered head in his hands.

Susan lifted her arm to speak into her wrist microphone, but it wasn't necessary. The door to the room was kicked open, and two agents, guns out, appeared at either side of it. They quickly surveyed the situation, then entered.

"Sue," said one of the agents, while the other one rushed over to Latimer's fallen form. "What went down?"

Susan looked at them then and at the ruined side of Josh Latimer's head, lying now in a widening pool of blood. She found herself unable to speak as she groped for a chair.

CHAPTER 35

AFTER they'd had lunch, Eric Redekop had taken Janis Falconi to his luxury condo, which was just a few blocks from LT, overlooking the Potomac. Jan was amazed. She knew top surgeons made a lot of money, but she'd never quite realized how much; Eric's place was gorgeous, with a sumptuous marble entryway. He gave her a quick tour: separate kitchen and dining room, two full bathrooms, and four bedrooms. He used one as an office, another as a TV room, and a third was set up as a bedroom for when his son Quentin visited; Quentin was twenty-one, and was studying genetics at UC Berkeley. They came out to the living room, which opened on a wide balcony and had pristine white walls, a white leather couch, and a matching chair. Janis opened her mouth to say something complimentary, and—

And she heard a deafening sound, like a car backfiring right beside her, and she had a brief flash of—well, of light, and she saw the face of a woman. An *"Ooof!"* came out of her as she staggered backward.

"Jan?" said Eric wheeling around.

Agony. More pain than she'd ever felt—ever thought she *could* feel.

Jan reached out with her right arm, flailing for something to grab on to, but found nothing. She tumbled backward, falling to the hardwood floor.

"Jan!" shouted Eric, dropping onto one knee next to her. He touched her wrist, feeling for a pulse.

The pain continued to shoot through her; it wasn't localized—it was *everywhere*. She couldn't focus or turn her head. She thought—as much as she could think *anything* through the agony—that perhaps she was having a heart attack.

"Jan, what is it?" asked Eric. "Where does it hurt?"

With a massive effort, and although it felt like her neck was snapping to do so, she managed to turn her head to face him, but—

But her vision was receding into a long tunnel, and the person at the end of the tunnel was—well, she didn't know *who* it was, but it wasn't Eric. The face she saw there, in the distance, was terrified, and—

She felt herself being lifted up in Eric's arms, and he carried her a short distance and set her down—ah, it must be on the white leather couch she'd been admiring a few moments before. But she couldn't see it; all she could see was the tunnel—and it was narrowing. And yet she knew she wasn't dead: her pulse was pounding in her ears.

Eric was holding her hand and feeling her forehead. The tunnel was constricting even more, and there were colored forms running past her peripheral vision. People. Faces. An old man. An even older woman. A little girl.

Events. Snowboarding. Riding a dirt bike. Scuba diving. None of which she'd ever done . . .

And—thank God!—the pain was abating, fading, dissipating. The images were being replaced by a pure, bright, brilliant light, absolutely white, brighter than the sun but not at all uncomfortable to look at.

Her pulse was fading in her ears now. Everything except the light was fading.

"Jan!" Eric, sounding a million miles away. "Jan!"

The light was so enticing, but . . .

"Jan!"

But she wanted to be with Eric. She struggled mightily to open her eyes—and finally succeeded. She was indeed in his living room, looking up at the stippled plaster of the ceiling. "Eric . . ." she said, but her voice sounded faint to her.

He loomed in and held up his key fob, which had an LED light on it. He pointed it first into her left eye, then her right; the bright light she'd seen at the end of the tunnel hadn't hurt at all, but *this* did.

"I'm fine," she said, her voice raw.

"We've got to take you to the hospital, find out what's wrong with you."

"I'm fine," she said again and closed her eyes, part of her hoping the pure white light and the calming euphoria would come back.

REPORTERS were still camped out in front of Luther Terry Memorial Hospital when Eric and Jan tried to enter. Eric kept his head down, and they'd almost made it to the staff entrance when a female journalist called out, "Wait! Wait! You're Eric Redekop, aren't you?"

"I've got no comment," Eric said. He cupped Jan's elbow and propelled her toward the doorway.

"What was it like performing surgery on the president?" called the same reporter, and, "Any update on Jerrison's condition?" shouted another.

Eric and Jan kept walking, but then another reporter called out, "Dr. Redekop, what about these memory linkages? They say *you* were affected."

"And that woman!" called another reporter, pointing now at Jan. "Is that who you're linked to? What's it like?"

Eric pushed the door open, and they entered the building.

"Jesus," said Jan.

"It'll be okay," Eric said. He led them to the elevator, and they headed up to Singh's lab on three. When they got there, they found Singh in his room, working at his computer. Susan Dawson was also there, sitting with her face in her hands.

"Dr. Redekop," Singh said. "And Nurse Falconi. I thought you both had today off."

Eric saw Susan look up. She appeared devastated over

something. Jan took a step backward and her eyes went wide. "Oh my God," Jan said softly.

"What?" said Eric and Singh simultaneously.

"It's you," Jan said, looking at Susan.

Eric knew that Jan had been interviewed by Professor Singh, not Agent Dawson; there was no particular reason she should recognize Susan.

"Yes?" Susan said.

"You're the one who killed me."

"Pardon?" said Singh.

"I mean, who killed Josh."

Susan put her head back in her hands.

"Jan collapsed," Eric said. "She was having some sort of horrible memory."

"You were reading Josh Latimer," Singh said to Jan, "and, yes, you're right, Mr. Latimer is no longer with us."

"Because she blew him away," Jan said softly, looking at Susan. "But it felt like *I* was the one dying."

"Can you recall Mr. Latimer's memories now?" asked Singh.

Jan nodded meekly.

"Are you sure? Umm, did he have any pets as a child?"

"Benny," she said at once. "An iguana."

"And the name of the street he lived on when he was ten?"

"Fenwick Avenue."

"Fascinating," said Singh. "He's dead, but you can still access his memories."

"I guess," said Jan.

Singh frowned again. "Then I wonder . . ."

"Yes?"

"Does he have any new memories?"

Eric crossed his arms in front of his chest. "He's *dead,* Mr. Singh."

"Yes, I know, but, well, if she can still access his memories from before, they must be *somewhere,* no? And so it's worth asking—"

"Asking what?" said Eric. "Whether she can recall angels?"

"It's worth a try," said Singh. "Or if not angels, maybe . . . well, I don't know what."

Janis made a long-faced frown, as though this was the most

bizarre idea she'd ever heard. But she closed her eyes—indeed, scrunched them tightly shut in concentration. "Okay," she said after a moment, "I'm thinking about angels. Nothing. Heaven, clouds. Nothing. And—um, my God, Josh tried to kill somebody, didn't he?"

Ranjip nodded.

"All right, then," said Janis. "Given that, I'm thinking of fire and brimstone. Well, not brimstone; I don't know what that is."

"Sulfur," said Ranjip.

"Okay," said Janis. "But it's not bringing anything to mind."

"This is bullshit," said Eric.

"Perhaps," said Singh. "But—"

"He's dead," said Eric. "He's *gone*. And Jan felt him die. We should be worried about *her,* not him."

"I understand that," said Singh. "And, if there is an after-life, I doubt that any of the symbolism from Christianity—or from Sikhism, for that matter—appropriately captures it. It may just be that the right trigger hasn't come along to let Mrs. Falconi access Mr. Latimer's new memories."

"I don't care about Latimer," said Eric, firmly. "What caused Jan to feel this?"

"That's a very good question," said Singh, looking at her. "Something must have triggered you to recall Mr. Latimer's death shortly after it happened, Mrs. Falconi. What were you doing when you had the flashback?"

"Eric was showing me around his condo. It's just a few blocks from here."

Singh frowned. "There was no—I don't know—hunting rifle on the wall, or bloody roast defrosting in the sink?"

"No," said Jan. "I was just admiring Eric's furniture."

"That seems unlikely as a trigger for this," Singh said. "I wonder how long after Latimer died that the memory of it came to you."

"Jan collapsed at 12:17 P.M.," said Eric. Singh looked at him. "I'm a doctor," Eric added. "You always note when a seizure or anything similar starts and how long it lasts."

"Agent Dawson," Singh said, "when did you, ah, um—when did you shoot Mr. Latimer?"

Susan looked up again. Her voice was small. "I don't know. Sometime shortly after noon, but . . ."

"Hospital security will know," Singh said. "They must have recorded the sound of the gunshot; I heard it even down here." He picked up the phone on his desk and pounded out four digits. "It's Ranjip Singh. I need to know the time the gun was discharged this past hour. Yes. No. Really? Are you sure? Are you positive? Thank you. Good-bye." He put down the phone. "The gunshot was recorded at 12:17 P.M."

"But memories are recalled after the fact," Eric said. "That's what *recall* means."

"This wasn't like the other memories of Josh's I'd recalled," Jan said. "It felt more real, more . . ."

"Immediate?" offered Singh.

Jan nodded.

"So you accessed Mr. Latimer's memories not *after* they'd been laid down," Singh said, "but in real time, *as* he was experiencing the event?" He looked at Susan and lowered his voice a bit. "Did your seizure, as Dr. Redekop called it, start with the gunshot?"

"Yes," said Jan, "although I didn't know what it was at the time. There was a flash of light and unbelievable pain, and then I saw her"—she pointed at Susan—"and then I was fading away bit by bit."

"Amazing," said Singh. His eyes were wide with excitement. "Amazing."

"How so?" asked Jan.

"Until this point, people in our linked circle had been accessing memories randomly, and not in synchrony. What I was thinking about or doing had nothing to do with what Agent Dawson was recalling from my memories. But what happened to you was different. At the moment Mr. Latimer was being shot, *you* experienced what he was feeling, exactly when he felt it." Singh shook his head slowly, and his voice was filled with wonder. "You weren't just reading his memory, Mrs. Falconi. You were reading his *thoughts*."

CHAPTER 36

SUSAN Dawson continued to sit in Singh's lab with her head in her hands. That she'd done everything properly didn't matter; she'd never get this image—her own memory—out of her mind: the bullet hitting Josh Latimer's head, his blood geysering out, and him crumpling to the floor.

She'd studied the Zapruder film during training, of course—including the frames not usually shown that depicted JFK's head blowing open. She remembered her instructor at Rowley saying that it was actually Kennedy's bad back that had killed him. Oswald's first, nonfatal shot should have caused the president to pitch forward, out of Oswald's line of fire from the School Book Depository, but the back brace he wore had kept Kennedy upright, letting Oswald get the subsequent killing shot in.

She'd always remembered those grainy images, but this—this!—was so much more vivid, with vibrant colors, deafening sound, the stench of gunpowder, and the recoil of the weapon. She'd been prepared to take a bullet for Jerrison—she really had been. But killing someone herself turned out to be a very different matter. She couldn't bring herself to participate in the discussion going on around her, but she listened.

"You weren't just reading his memory," Singh had just said to Janis Falconi. "You were reading his *thoughts.*"

"But why?" Eric Redekop asked. "The intensity of the feelings?"

Susan looked up in time to see Singh make his trademark shrug. "Maybe. But this raises a new level of concern. Fortunately, Mrs. Falconi wasn't injured—but she could have been. Indeed, if she'd been operating a motor vehicle, or even just walking down a tall staircase, she could have been killed."

Killed.

Susan thought again about her pistol firing, Latimer's blood spraying, and bits of his skull flying—and she thought about his *eyes*. Still tracking, still alive, still *thinking* for several seconds, like the severed heads of French guillotine victims looking up at their executioners.

"Sadly," continued Singh, "we've learned something else. I'd been hoping that the daisy chain might be like the wiring of Christmas lights—if one went out, the whole chain would go, and all the memory linkages would break."

Susan briefly wondered what experience a Sikh could have had with Christmas decorations. "But that's not what happened," she said.

"No," replied Singh. "I can still read Dr. Jono, and I take it, Agent Dawson, that you can still read me."

Susan concentrated for a moment; Singh had had two hard-boiled eggs for breakfast; he, she suddenly knew, always kept a few on hand in that small refrigerator over there. "Yes."

"And Dr. Redekop, can you still access Mrs. Falconi's memories?" Singh asked.

Eric tilted his head sideways, then: "Yes. No problem. It's exactly the same as before." He turned to Janis, and it looked to Susan as though an idea had just occurred to him. "But you got Latimer's memories in real time at the end."

"Yes," said Janis.

"Obviously, being shot was traumatic for Latimer," Eric said, "but, well—forgive me, Agent Dawson, I don't know about people in your line of work, but . . ."

"But I do," said Singh, apparently realizing whatever Eric

was getting at. "I spend most of my day dealing with people who've had to kill—even when it's their job, even when it's in the line of duty." He looked at Susan. "It's not easy, is it?"

Susan thought about saying something, but simply shook her head.

"What's the normal procedure following such an incident?" Singh asked.

"Paperwork," said Susan. "Forms, reports."

"And counseling?"

It was mandatory. "Yes."

"Looking at you, Agent Dawson, it's obvious that killing Latimer was traumatic for you, wasn't it?"

Susan drew a deep breath, glanced at each of the others in turn, then blew the air out. "It was horrifying."

Singh's tone was kind. "I'm sure it was. Do you see our point?"

She shook her head.

"It's this," said Eric. "If you were severely traumatized by the shooting, maybe the person who is linked to you got your memory—your thoughts—in real time, too."

RANJIP Singh entered the room first, followed by Eric Redekop and Janis Falconi; Susan Dawson had been bringing up the rear, but she'd been detained by someone calling her over her earpiece.

"Hello, Kadeem," said Ranjip.

"Hey, guru," said Kadeem.

"This is Janis Falconi; she's a nurse here. And this is Dr. Redekop."

"Another memory researcher?" asked Kadeem.

"Actually, I'm a surgeon" said Eric, "but—" He stopped short as Kadeem's eyes went wide in horror.

Ranjip wheeled around to see what Kadeem was looking at. It was Agent Dawson, who had just now entered the room. "My God, Sue," said Kadeem. "My God. You blew that motherfucker away."

She nodded but said nothing.

"Did you just realize that?" asked Ranjip. "Did the memory just come to you?"

"Yes," said Kadeem. Ranjip looked at Eric; it had seemed like such an interesting idea, but—

"Again," added Kadeem.

"*Again?*" said Ranjip at once, looking back to Kadeem.

"Yes."

"When did you first recall this?"

"While ago."

"When?"

"Don't know."

"What room were you in when you recalled it?"

"This one."

"And what time did you come into this room?"

"I don't know. Does it matter?"

"Yes," said Ranjip. "Is there anything that can help you pin down when you accessed that memory?"

"Like what?"

"Did you look at the clock?" asked Eric.

Kadeem gestured to encompass the room; there was no clock.

"What about a phone call?" asked Janis.

"Yes!" said Kadeem. "Yes, now you mention it, it was just after I called Kristah." He pulled out his phone, and ran his fingertip along the touch screen. "The call lasted three minutes twenty seconds and"—another touch—"it began at 12:03."

Ranjip frowned. "And how long after that did the memory of—of what Agent Dawson did—hit you?"

"Couple of minutes."

"It can't be just a couple of minutes," said Eric, looking at Janis. "Not unless we're dealing with precognition now."

"Could it be longer than that?" asked Ranjip. "Ten minutes, say?"

"Sure," said Kadeem.

"Or twenty?"

"Maybe. I guess."

"Thirty?"

"Not that long, man."

"How did the memory begin?" asked Ranjip.

"What?"

Ranjip frowned. He knew the dangers of priming recollections, but he needed to get to the bottom of this. "What's the first thing you remember? Was it Agent Dawson bursting into the room? Her confronting that man who was holding the hostage? Her attempts to talk him out of what he was going to do?"

Kadeem shook his head. "I don't remember any of that—or, I didn't at the time; I do now, now you mention it." He looked sympathetically at Susan. "You did your best, Sue; it's not your fault."

"But what about the first time?" asked Ranjip. "What popped into your mind initially?"

Kadeem actually shuddered. "Agent Dawson pulling the trigger."

Eric and Ranjip exchanged glances. "There it is," said Ranjip. "Simultaneity—minds linked in real time during a moment of crisis."

"But this whole thing *began* with a moment of crisis," Eric said. "The electromagnetic pulse when the White House was destroyed. What will happen if there's another crisis that affects all of us at the same time?"

Ranjip shrugged. "That's a very good question."

CHAPTER 37

SUSAN Dawson and Mark Griffin enlisted three LT psychologists to brief the affected people about the dangerous possibility that they might experience direct real-time linkages during moments of crisis, perhaps with debilitating effects. The psychologists spoke face-to-face to the people still in the hospital and phoned the ones who had left.

Meanwhile, Ranjip Singh ordered an MRI scan of nurse Janis Falconi but was told there was nothing unusual about her brain; no matter how vivid the pain had been when she'd tapped into Josh Latimer's mind at the moment of his death, there didn't seem to have been any gross permanent change.

He then got Eric Redekop into a second MRI scanner and looked to see if there was any interesting activity in Janis's brain while he was recalling her memories. It would have been fascinating if corresponding spots in, say, their right temporal lobes had lit up at the same time—but nothing like that happened. That just added fuel to the notion that the linkages were indeed based on quantum entanglement, a realm beyond the resolution of the brain scanners.

He also ordered an MRI of Kadeem Adams. The private

had been scanned just before undergoing Ranjip's procedure. The aborted attempt at memory-erasing shouldn't have altered Kadeem's brain in any way an MRI scanner could see, but Ranjip had wanted to check if there was any structural change that could be attributed to the mind linkings. Again, the results were negative; his earlier MRI and the new one showed no appreciable difference.

But, still, something had changed.

As Kadeem was pulled out of the MRI tunnel, he looked up at Ranjip and the MRI technician, and said, "Sue's with Prospector."

Ranjip tilted his head slightly; he'd never heard Kadeem refer to the president by his code name before. "Oh?"

"She's with Prospector right now," said Kadeem.

"Probably," said Ranjip.

"I see it," said Kadeem. "Him. His room. I see it, right now."

"Instead of me?" asked Ranjip.

"No, I see you, too, guru. You're more vivid, but I see . . . I'm seeing what she's seeing, too. Like a faint double exposure, or an afterimage, or something."

"Superimposed over your vision?"

"Yeah."

"How long has this been going on?"

"I don't know. Not long. It's faint, like I said. Couldn't make it out in the MRI machine, but here, lying on my back, looking up at the ceiling—it's a plain white roof, see?" He pointed; Ranjip glanced up and confirmed it. "So, my own vision's not showing much, and I can—damn, it's strange—I can see what she's seeing, faint, ghostlike, but *clear.*"

"Memories don't contain a lot of visual information," Ranjip said.

"Ain't no memory, guru. I can jump around in her memories. What'd she have for dinner last night? Bunless hamburger, down in the cafeteria here. What'd she have for lunch? Protein bar. Where'd she go after dinner? Woman's room, off the lobby—had something in her eye, took a bit to get it out. Memories I can get in any order, and from any time. This is playing out like a movie—I can't skip ahead, or go back, or anything."

"And it's from her point of view? You're sure?"

"Yeah. Prospector just asked, 'Any update on the matter we were discussing earlier?'"

"You can *hear* what she's hearing, too?"

"If it's quiet around me. Volume's really low—like, you know, if you left your iPod on but have taken off the earbuds. You hear that faint music, and you think, damn, where that be coming from? It's like that. We're talking now—you and me—so I can't make it out, and when I look at you, or over at all that equipment over there, the background is too messy and complex for me to really see what she be seeing, but if I really concentrate, it's there."

The MRI technician—a petite white woman with bright red hair—spoke. "Like floaters, sort of?"

Kadeem frowned. "What?"

"Lots of people have them," said the technician. "Bits of junk in the vitreous humor of the eye; you see them when looking at a clear blue sky, or a plain sheet of paper, or whatever, but can't make them out the rest of the time."

"Yeah," said Kadeem. "Kinda like that. But way more detailed." He looked up at the blank ceiling again. "I can see Prospector right now—like he's looking right at me—and he doesn't have that breathing thing in his nose anymore."

"Are you just getting her sensory stream," asked Ranjip, "or can you also read Agent Dawson's thoughts?"

"Hard to say. There are some *words*, and they ain't Prospector's. But I don't hear them—and they're not a steady stream. But, yeah, must be Sue. 'Check with Darryl . . .' '. . . something something keycard access.' Fragments, but I hear them."

"Give me a moment," Ranjip said. There was a gurney nearby. He stretched out on it, reflecting, not for the first time, that it was nice to have a turban that doubled as a portable pillow. He looked up at the same blank ceiling Kadeem had been staring at and tried to discern any faint images of Lucius Jono's life—not memories of the redheaded surgeon but the sights that Jono himself might currently be seeing. He also strained to listen for any sounds Jono might be hearing. Of course, it was possible that Jono was asleep, even though it was now well past noon, but . . .

Nothing. Nothing at all. Ranjip got off the gurney.

"Power nap, guru?" asked Kadeem.

"Just trying to see if I was linked in the same way, but I'm not. Still, let's check our facts." He pulled out his BlackBerry and a small Bluetooth earpiece for it, then walked across the room, far enough away that Kadeem couldn't possibly hear what the earpiece was conveying. Then he placed a call. "Agent Dawson. It's Ranjip. Can you talk?"

"Yes."

"You are with President Jerrison?"

"Yes, that's right."

"Tell me: does he still have a respirator on?"

"No, they removed that about an hour ago."

Ranjip felt his heart pounding. Still, it didn't prove anything other than that Kadeem had Agent Dawson's memories, as before. "I need your help to conduct an experiment."

"Sure," Susan said. "Two seconds." He heard her begging President Jerrison's indulgence. Ranjip happened to be looking over at Kadeem when he heard Jerrison say, "I'm not going anywhere," and he saw Kadeem smile in amusement—but was it at the president's quip or something else?

When Susan was back, Ranjip spoke loudly so Kadeem could hear from across the room. "Private Adams?"

"Yo."

"I'm going to ask Agent Dawson to think of a series of numbers from one to ten. As she thinks of them, please hold up the right number of fingers, okay?"

Kadeem nodded.

"All right, Agent Dawson, you heard what I said. Give me a series of numbers, from one to ten. Not any sequence you know by heart, like your social security number, but random numbers, one per second. Just whisper them to me, starting . . . now."

"Four," said Susan, and Kadeem held up his left hand with the fingers splayed and the thumb tucked against his palm.

"Two," said Susan, and Kadeem made a peace sign.

"Seven," she said; he kept the peace sign up and added a full hand with all five fingers.

"Six." Kadeem made the polite choice about which finger to drop from the peace sign.

"Ten." Both hands, all fingers splayed, like a child showing he'd successfully washed.

"Amazing," said Ranjip.

"What?" asked Susan.

"That real-time link that Private Adams had with you at the moment you shot Latimer? It's persisting. He can still read your thoughts."

"Oh, shit," Susan said.

And, from across the room, Kadeem added, "She's wondering what'll happen if Bessie Stilwell ends up being able to do the same thing with Prospector."

DORA Hennessey's internal clock wasn't adjusting properly to the five-hour time-zone change between London and Washington: although it was only 3:00 P.M. here, it was already 8:00 P.M. back home. And it hadn't helped that they'd made an incision in her side on Friday morning; the stitches itched. Still, she didn't like just lying in the hospital bed, and so instead was sitting in a chair by the window, looking out at the November afternoon.

Dora and her father each had a private room, which was all to the good. She'd be ready to go to sleep in a few hours; the last thing she needed was a roommate who'd want to watch television in the evening.

Dora could read the memories of Ann January, a nurse who had been part of the team that had saved the president. She still wasn't happy about having her own surgery postponed to accommodate him, but she did know, because Ann knew it, just how close they'd come to losing Jerrison, and although her father was thinking of suing, she couldn't bring herself to contemplate that.

There was a knock on her door. "Yes?" she called.

The door swung inward revealing Dr. Mark Griffin. She'd met him on Friday; he'd come to see her after she woke up from the anesthetic to explain why the surgery had been halted. "Hello, Dora," he said. "May I come in?"

"Sure."

There was another chair in the room, a smaller one. He turned it around, and straddled it, facing her, his arms folded across the top of its back. "Dora," he said, "I'm so sorry, but I've got some bad news."

"You're not postponing the transplant again," she said. Did he have any idea how nerve-racking all this was for her?

"There won't be a transplant."

"Why not? The tissue match was perfect."

Griffin took a deep breath. "Dora, your father is dead."

"What?"

"I'm so, so sorry."

"Dead?"

"Yes."

She was quiet for a time, then: "If this is because you post-poned giving him my kidney—"

"It's not that. It's not that at all. Dora, your father tried to kill someone this afternoon—and he was shot by a federal agent."

She'd heard a sound earlier, but—*God*—she'd thought it had been a car backfiring.

"What . . . what happens now?"

"One of our surgeons will have a look at your incision; we'd planned to reopen it, of course, so the closure was done to accommodate that. We'll get you fixed up."

Her head was spinning. "I—I don't know if I can take all this," she said.

Griffin nodded. "I understand. We're hoping you'll stay here. We're advising all those who were affected by the memory linking to stay under our care until we get that sorted out, and, well, with everything you've been through . . ."

Dora looked out the window again, but her vision blurred as tears welled in her eyes.

CHAPTER 38

AFTER having the MRI scans, Eric and Jan went by Jan's locker at the hospital. She kept a change of clothing there—you never knew when a patient was going to vomit on you, she said. She put the clothes in a plastic bag, and they headed back to Eric's apartment, stopping at a CVS along the way to buy her a toothbrush and a few other things. The sky was cloudy.

Events hadn't gone the way Eric had intended. He'd wanted to help Jan, yes, but he'd really only planned to get her to a shelter.

But now she was here, in his home.

And he knew more about her than anyone else in his life. More than he knew about his parents, his sisters, his son, his ex-wife.

He thought back to this morning, back to when he'd come to get her at the Bronze Shield, her setting up to play, rolling the characters, and—

No. No, those were *her* memories, not his; he hadn't been there at the beginning of the game. God, they came to him just like his own memories now . . . like she was a part of him.

Like they were a couple.

Huh. Funny phrase that. "A couple." A singular noun for two individuals. Except . . .

Except they weren't *quite* individuals anymore. He was linked to her, and for events they had shared—the MRI session this afternoon, her collapsing before that, what went down at the gaming store, their interaction yesterday—the memories were hopelessly intertwined. He couldn't think about any joint experience they'd had without her perspective mixing with his own.

Time was passing. It would be evening in a few hours. And then night, and—

And he did care about her.

And she did like him.

And she was very, very beautiful.

But—

But when they'd come into the living room now, and he'd sat on the long white couch, he'd expected her to sit down beside him. Instead, she took the matching chair that faced the couch and sat with her knees tucked up toward her chin.

"Can I get you anything to drink?" he asked. "Coffee? Beer?"

She just sat there.

He lifted his eyebrows. "Jan? Did you hear me? Would you like something to drink?"

"I heard you," she said. "I just figured you'd answer your question."

"Jan, I can't read your mind—just your memories. This isn't a time of crisis." *So far, anyway* . . .

"Oh, right. Sorry."

He tried to move to more neutral ground. "It's strange that the linkages can, at least some of the time, connect not just memories but thoughts, too."

"Why's that strange?" she asked. "It's all just brain activity, right?"

"Yeah, but memories involve permanent changes in the brain—an actual physical alteration in its structure. Thoughts are evanescent."

"I wish I *could* read your memories," she said, and she gave him the faintest of smiles. "That would save me the embarrassment of having to ask you what that word means."

"Evanescent?" said Eric. "Fleeting. Vanishing like vapor. Unlike the laying down of memories, there's no permanent structural change in the brain associated with having thoughts." He shifted on the couch and looked across the glass-topped coffee table at her. "You know, it's funny. If someone attacked you with a knife and scarred you, the courts would assess the physical damage—how long a scar, how many stitches it took to close the wound, whatever—and they'd come up with a figure that you'd be entitled to in compensation. But hurting someone with words that they'll always remember? With an act they'll never forget? *That's* physical damage, too—it changes you just as permanently as a scar. But instead of tallying up what the compensation should be, we just say, 'Get over it,' or 'You should develop a thicker skin,' or—and this is ironic, given that it's the one thing that's impossible—'you should just forget about it.'" He shook his head, thinking about the things Tony had said to her, had done to her.

She was quiet for a time, then, so softly that he wasn't sure he'd heard every word correctly, she said, "I can't take it."

"Take what?" asked Eric.

"The memory thing."

He nodded; it was unequal, it was unfair, it was *unbalanced*. "I'm sorry," he said. "Really, I am—I don't mean to invade your privacy."

But Jan shook her head. "It's not that; it's not *you*. It's *her*."

"Who?" asked Eric.

"*Her.* That woman who is linked to you—the one who sells houses. Um, Nikki Van Hausen."

"What about her?" asked Eric.

"She knows everything that's happened between us, everything that happened today." Jan looked away. "And everything that will happen later."

"But she's gone from our lives," Eric said. "She left LT when the lockdown ended. I'll probably never see her again."

"She's *not* gone," said Jan. "She's right *here*. She'll recall this conversation, recall what happened with Tony at the Bronze Shield, and if we ever—if we ever make . . ." She shook her head a bit and fell silent.

Eric looked around his living room—familiar surroundings to him, alien ones to Jan, but, yes, doubtless recallable by Nikki Van Hausen even though she'd never been here. It was easy to forget that the intimate way he knew Jan was echoed by the way Nikki knew *him*.

But it wasn't the same, God damn it. It *wasn't*. Nikki was a complete stranger to him, just as he was to her. Oh, sure, it was probably interesting to her in an abstract way that she had someone else's memories, but there was no emotional connection between him and her.

"Sweetheart," said Eric—and a memory, or rather a lack of a memory, hit him; Tony had never called Jan that, or any other term of endearment. He went on: "It's okay. We never have to see her again, or even think about her."

But Jan shook her head once more. "She knows—or will know—what you just said. And she'll resent it—she'll think you're insulting her. Don't you see? She's got the same level of access to you that you have to me; she can't help but be fascinated by your life."

"I'm sure she just wants to get on with her own," Eric said.

"Just like you did?" Jan replied, looking at him across the intervening coffee table.

"It's different," he said again.

"I don't know," Jan said sadly.

"Just don't think about it," Eric said. "As one of my favorite writers once said, 'Learning to ignore things is one of the great paths to inner peace.'"

"I don't think I can ignore *this*."

He hesitated for a moment, then got up, crossed over to her, perched himself on the wide padded arm of the chair, and reached to stroke her tattooed shoulder. But she flinched, and he stopped.

After a moment, she rose and walked out of the living room, heading to the second bedroom, the one that was there for when Quentin visited, leaving Eric wondering at what point in the future—the next day, the next week, the next year, the next decade—Nikki Van Hausen would recall what him having his heart broken felt like.

CHAPTER 39

UNDER normal circumstances, Bessie Stilwell might have wished to spend more time in Los Angeles. She'd always wanted to see the Walk of Fame, and find the stars there for Cary Grant and Christopher Plummer and James Dean. And it certainly was nice to be somewhere warm after Washington. But her son was still in the hospital, and although she'd seen him first thing this morning before she and Darryl had flown here, she needed to get back, to be there for him.

They left the TV studio and headed straight for the Los Angeles Air Force Base. Bessie was put in a secure waiting room, with two uniformed Air Force guards standing outside the door, while Darryl went off to speak to the base commander. She lowered herself slowly, painfully, onto a wooden seat and picked up a magazine off a table—but the type was much too small for her to read.

At last, Agent Hudkins returned. "Okay, ma'am," he said. "Everything's set. I'm sorry we have to make two big flights in one day."

"That's all right," Bessie said. "I need to get back to my son, anyway."

"Yes, ma'am. Shall we go?"

JANIS was lying on the bed in the guest room, in a fetal position, her eyes closed, thinking about what she'd done. Part of her was elated at having left Tony. And part of her was terrified, wondering what the future held.

And, of course, there were the memories of Josh Latimer being shot. They were still vivid, but they weren't *real* anymore; they felt like any memory felt, with no sense that the thing was happening again right now. The soldier she'd met today, Kadeem Adams, had post-traumatic stress disorder; his flashbacks felt like the horrific things were really happening again. But, thankfully, it seemed Jan wasn't going to be experiencing that immediacy every time she recalled Josh being shot.

"Jan . . . ?" Eric's voice, not much above a whisper—the kind of tentative uttering of a name one uses when testing if someone is asleep.

She opened her eyes. He was silhouetted in the doorway, a thin, bald man, leaning against the jamb. "Hmmm?" she said.

"Dr. Griffin called. There's going to be a press conference about Jerrison's condition at 4:00 P.M. He wants me to be part of it."

"Ah, okay."

"Do you want to come?"

"How long will it take?"

"Could be a couple of hours. He wants us all to go over what we're going to say first, before we face the reporters."

She hadn't been part of the surgery. "Can I stay here?"

"Of course," and although he didn't say it, she heard in his tone and was grateful for it, "For as long as you like."

"Thanks," she said.

"I'm going to head out. Help yourself to anything in the fridge. You like Chinese." She'd never told him that, but he knew. "There's some leftover kung pao chicken."

"Thanks."

Jan soon heard him leave the apartment. She lay there a

while longer, hugging her knees, but at last she got up, left Quentin's bedroom, and headed into the living room.

The furniture was nicer than any she'd ever owned; everything in her place had been named for some damn Swedish lake or river and had been assembled with an Allen key. But this stuff—the coffee table, the bookcases, the cabinets, all in what she guessed was cherrywood—was *expensive*.

Besides numerous hardcover books—a luxury Tony had never let her buy—there were objects on the bookshelves: an Eskimo soapstone carving of a bird, a quill pen, a bronze medallion with the word "Champ" engraved into it, a white marble chess piece. Each of them doubtless had a story behind it—they were keepsakes, mementos—but they meant nothing to her.

But there *was* someone besides Eric who could tell the story behind each one: Nikki Van Hausen.

It was a distinctive-enough name, Jan thought, although, if she were married, it might be her husband's first name that was in the phone book.

Jan exhaled noisily. *If she were married.* This Nikki woman knew everything about Eric, but Jan didn't know even the most basic facts about Nikki.

She went into Eric's office. He had a MacBook Air sitting on a glass-topped workstation, with a Safari browser window open. She typed "Nicky Van Hausen" into Google, but that produced too many hits to be useful. But adding "real estate" to the string quickly turned up pay dirt, thanks to Google's offering the correct spelling of the first name: her website, but also, Jan was surprised to see, an article from this morning's *Washington Post*. Upon getting word of the memory linkages that had occurred at LT, a clever reporter had interviewed Nikki, since *she* remembered the operation as clearly as Eric himself did.

Her website—which offered "2% commissions" and "free home market evaluations"—gave her phone number. Jan picked up the handset in this room, then set it back down; she didn't want the Caller ID to show Eric's name. She went to the marble entryway, got her purse, dug out her cell—and saw that she had four voice messages from Tony. She shuddered, ignored them, and placed the call.

"Nikki Van Hausen Realty," said a perky voice.

"Is this—" Christ, she still didn't know if it was Miss or Mrs. "Um, is this Nikki?"

"Speaking."

"Nikki, this is Janis Falconi."

There was silence for three or four seconds. "Oh."

"I need to talk to you," Jan said.

"What about?"

Jan's turn to hesitate. "Sharing Eric's memories."

"Look, about that article, I didn't—"

"No, no. I don't care about the article; I don't care that you know *that* stuff. It's just—I just . . . I don't know, I thought maybe I'd be more comfortable with all this if I met you."

"Umm. Okay. Maybe."

"Could we get together this afternoon?"

"Um, where?"

"Well, I'm sure you know I'm staying at Eric's place, and I don't have a car or a key. Could you—could you come by his home?"

"Ah, will he be there?"

"No. No."

Nikki sounded relieved. "Yeah, I guess I could do that." A pause. "He's in the Potomac Palace, right?" she said, naming his condo development. "Penthouse two?"

Jan shivered slightly. "Yes."

"I'm showing a place near there this afternoon. About 4:30, okay?"

"Fine," said Jan. "Thanks." They ended the call, and she held her cell phone in her trembling hand.

BESSIE hadn't had much to do with the military since her husband had come back from Korea all those years ago. She was amazed at how high-tech everything had become: here at the base there were all sorts of computers, complex screen displays, and sundry gadgets that she couldn't begin to identify, and—

And, well, no, that wasn't right. She *did* know what a bunch of them were, now that she thought about it: she knew because Seth Jerrison knew, having learned about them since coming to office—although a lot of them still didn't really make sense to him, either, what with being a history professor and all. As she and Darryl walked toward the plane, they passed soldier after soldier, and out on the airfield, near the jet that was going to take them, she saw what had to be a bomber, and . . .

And the word *Counterpunch* popped into her head.

And as they continued on into the plane and were shown to their seats, details about it came to her—horrible, horrific details. Her hands were shaking so much that she had to ask Darryl to do up her seat belt for her.

Yes, the US had been pushed too far by terrorists; there was no doubt about that. But this—this was . . .

Of course, a response was necessary; yes, leaders had to lead.

But *this!*

The plane started rolling down the runway. She had four hours until they'd land.

Four hours to decide what she was going to do.

CHAPTER 40

AT 4:54 P.M., Eric's phone emitted a strange double tone. Jan had heard his phone ring earlier, when Dr. Griffin had called, and it had made a normal sound, but—

Ah! It must be one of those Enterphone things, like at Rodger's place; Rodger was Tony's best friend. She picked up the handset. "Hello?"

"It's Nikki Van Hausen. I'm downstairs."

"Ah, okay. Um, damn, I don't know what to do to let you in."

"Press six," said Nikki—like she'd been here a million times before, like she fucking *lived* here.

Jan did so. She heard an electric whine through the handset and then that connection, at least, broke. She straightened her hair in the mirrored door to the entryway closet, then looked through the peephole in Eric's front door, and saw—

It was like the tunnel vision she'd had when Josh Latimer was dying. She saw a woman, impossibly small, impossibly far away, coming toward her, closer and closer and—

And Jan opened the door. There'd been a picture of Nikki on her website. In it, Nikki had reddish hair, but now she had light brown hair with blonde streaks—and she was a few years older; she looked to be in her mid-thirties.

"Sorry I'm late," Nikki said. "Weather's getting hairy out there." But then she stopped and just stared at Janis. "Wow," she said softly.

"What?"

"I'm sorry. It's just that it's strange seeing you. Eric's memories of you are flashes, you know? Your smile, your teeth, you tossing your head a certain way, the tattoo—he loves the tattoo. But to see it all brought together is . . ."

"What?"

"He remembers you as being beautiful, of course. But, well, beauty is in the eye of the beholder, and . . ." She shrugged a little. "And, well, it's interesting to see, that's all."

"Oh?" said Janis, a little defensively.

Nikki lifted a hand. "Sorry, I'm not saying this right. What I mean is, you are absolutely lovely. I can see why Eric fell for you so hard."

Jan's heart skipped a beat. "Fell for me?"

"He's crazy about you," Nikki said. "But he knows you're vulnerable, and he doesn't want to take advantage. Plus, there's the age thing."

"Who cares about that?" Jan said.

"*He* does. It really bothers him."

"It shouldn't."

They were still standing in the entryway. Jan took Nikki's coat and motioned for her to go into the apartment proper. As Nikki walked ahead, Jan said, "Can I offer you a drink? Coffee?"

"I'm fine," Nikki said, entering the living room—but she came to a stop so suddenly that Jan actually bumped into her from behind.

"Sorry!" Nikki said. "I'm sorry. It's just that . . ."

Jan moved to stand beside her and saw the wonder on Nikki's face. "Yes?"

"It's like I know this place," Nikki said. "Like I've been here before." She began walking again, looking around the living room. When she came to the bookshelf with the "Champ" medallion on it, she gently picked it up.

"What's it for?" Jan asked.

"Hmmm?" said Nikki. "Oh. He got it at the hospital, five years ago. He brought in the most donations for the Christmas charity drive."

Jan half smiled. That was Eric, all right: forever trying to help those in need. But the smile quickly faded. This woman would always know him better than Jan ever could. "It's cruel," she said.

"What?"

"This—this *thing* that's happened to us. Why couldn't it have been reciprocal? Why couldn't you be linked to the same person that's linked to you?"

"I don't know," Nikki said. "It is what it is."

"Yeah," said Jan, very softly.

"Why did you want to see me?"

Jan looked at her, then looked away. "I'm sorry, it was stupid. I just didn't know what to do. I, um, you—you know everything Eric knows, and, well . . ."

"He really does care about you, if that's what you're asking me."

Jan did manage to meet her eyes. "Actually, no. I don't have any doubts about that."

"But you keep asking yourself, how can he like me when he knows *this* about me, or *that* about my past, or that I did *whatever,* right?"

Jan nodded.

"Different people react differently, I guess," said Nikki. "I know comparable stuff about Eric. But he and I didn't know each other before the linkages, so, um, like . . . okay, you ever read *People?*"

"What?"

"People, the magazine. Or *Us.* Or any of those. The magazines that tell you all about the private lives of celebrities."

"Sometimes in my dentist's waiting room, I guess," said Jan.

"Well, Eric is like that to me. He's like Angelina Jolie or Johnny Depp or some other celebrity that I don't know personally, but I know everything about. Yes, I know his dirty secrets—minor though they are—including all kinds of stuff I'm sure he wishes really was private. But so what? It doesn't affect me, and it's not like I'm going to do anything with the information."

"I know, but . . ." Jan blew out air. "Sorry. I have no idea how to deal with this."

"But surely you must be going through the same thing, no?" asked Nikki. "You must be linked to somebody else, right?"

"I was," said Jan, softly. "He died."

"Oh!" said Nikki, and Jan saw her eyes flicking left and right rapidly as she assimilated Eric's memories related to that. "Oh my God—just this afternoon. I'm so sorry."

"I'm trying not to think about it."

"Sure, of course. Sorry. But, Jan, it's like that with me and Eric. I don't like to dwell on my *own* past, let alone anyone else's."

Jan. Every little thing Nikki did reminded Jan of just how much Nikki did know about her private life. "I know, but it's like he's gossiping about us, like he's talking about me behind my back."

"He *isn't.* And I don't know your details, you know. I know what he remembers, not what *you* remember. But I do know he really does like you. And, yeah, there is the age difference, obviously. And, sure, people are going to gossip about that. They're going to say he's having a midlife crisis—but you know what? He already *did,* five years ago. Ask him about it; it's no big deal, and he's *over* that; it's in the past. He's not attracted to you because of your age; he's attracted to you *despite* your age, and—"

Nikki fell silent.

"Yes?" said Jan.

"He wants to have sex with you."

Jan looked away. "Oh."

"But it's not because he's horny—although he *is.* It's because he's scared. You're thirty-two; he's fifty. He's afraid you're going to be turned off by his half-century-old body."

"What? That's silly."

"Maybe. But that's what he thinks."

"How do you know? I thought all you could do is read his memories, not his thoughts?"

"That's all I *can* do. But he told someone that, and I can recall the conversation."

"He was gossiping about me?"

"More like seeking advice. He's at Luther Terry now, right? He ran into—well, I know him, too; I met him earlier and went a little nuts, I have to say. He's been talking with Jurgen Sturgess, another doctor there." Nikki shook her head then went on. "It's funny; I shouldn't even *care*. All of this is really none of my business."

"So what did Dr. Sturgess say?"

"He wasn't one to give advice. He mostly just listened. But, well, I guess *I* have a vested interest in seeing Eric be happy. No point in my having to share a bunch of unhappy memories, after all. So let me give you some advice: don't let me stand in the way of you being happy with Eric. He's a good guy. Believe me—I *know*."

AT Seth Jerrison's insistence, they'd set up a computer for him in his hospital room. A forty-two-inch LCD monitor had been mounted on a small table at the foot of his bed, and he'd been given a Bluetooth ergonomic keyboard with a little trackpad attached. Despite lying on his back with his chest only propped up slightly, it was actually pretty comfortable to use, although he had to slide his bifocals way down his hooked nose to get the screen in focus.

Seth had always been a news junkie, and while Nurse Kelly watched him attentively from her seat, he used the computer to read about the assassination attempt. It was fascinating, in a macabre way, and it gave him a small taste of what the coverage might have been like had the attempt succeeded—although he supposed if he *had* died, the *Huffington Post* would not be grousing that "You'd think Jerrison would know how to give a speech in a presidential way instead of sounding like a tenured academic who doesn't have to worry about job security. The RNC would do well to hire him a media coach."

Damn it all, he *had* a media coach. And he really had tried to pay attention to her. She'd gone over everything with him time and again, including the way he held his head, when to use a hand gesture for emphasis, and the speed at which he should read from the teleprompter. He'd initially spoken much too quickly, she'd said, clocking him at 11,000 words per hour. He'd told her that was a holdover from his days at Columbia;

there was an awful lot of history to cover, and only so many classroom hours to cram it into. She said a dignified pace, and one that most people could comfortably follow, was more like 8,500 words an hour, and he'd practiced slowing down. For instance, the speech he'd been giving at the Lincoln Memorial was 1,734 words, and when he'd rehearsed it, he'd come in bang at twelve minutes, not counting time for applause. Of course, he hadn't gotten far into it when, as an article on MSNBC said, "the crack of a would-be assassin's rifle split the cold November air, and—"

And a thought came to him. He opened the document containing his speech and highlighted everything from the beginning to the point at which he'd been shot; he'd seen the clip repeatedly now on the news (and found it oddly compelling to watch—Kadeem had seen the news coverage before he had, and so Seth remembered it the first time he saw it; it felt an awful lot like he was viewing it from outside his own body). He searched the menus until he found the word-count command. "Words: 281" appeared on the screen along with some other statistics. Oh, well. It had been a good thought, but—

But he'd marked it from the beginning, including the title and other things. He scrolled back to the top of the document and redid the highlighting starting after the words "Speech to be delivered by POTUS at Lincoln Memorial re the Chicago bombing. Check against delivery." Then he issued the word-count command again. "Words: 247."

Tell Gordo to aim for 2-4-7 . . .

He went down to the end of the marked block and read aloud the last sentence he'd said before the bullet hit: "If my students could take away only a single lesson, I always hoped it would be the famous maxim that those who fail to learn from history are doomed to repeat it."

Repeat it. Like an echo.

Tell Gordo to aim for 2-4-7 for the echo . . .

Lots of people had access to his speeches before he gave them; it would have been easy for Secret Service Director Hexley to have seen the text in advance and have gotten copies to other people, including Gordo Danbury—copies marked up with each word numbered so they could plan precisely. Hexley had been telling someone to convey to Danbury that the perfect echo—the perfect blast from the past—would be to take down the current president, as he was standing in front of a statue of the first president to have been assassinated, while he was reflecting on history repeating itself.

And, Seth thought, history almost had.

Just then, Susan Dawson entered. "Good afternoon, Mr. President. Bessie Stilwell and Agent Hudkins are in the air. They should be at Andrews by 10:00 P.M."

"Andrews?" asked Seth. "Not Reagan?"

"No, Mr. President. They're taking an Air Force jet back."

"I said they should travel on a civilian plane."

Susan's eyebrows went up. "Um, sorry, sir—what you actually said was they should fly out to L.A. on the next commercial flight. You didn't say anything about the return, and Darryl figured you wanted Bessie to be protected as much as possible, so they're coming back on an Air Force plane."

"Damn," said Seth.

"What's wrong, sir? I apologize if—"

"No, no. What's done is done. But . . . *damn.*"

CHAPTER 41

NIKKI Van Hausen was driving home from her meeting with Jan Falconi; she hoped the poor girl could find some peace. In her trunk were a couple of "Open House" signs that she'd need tomorrow; Sunday was a big day for such things.

Open house.

Letting strangers in, letting them poke around, letting them imagine their own lives superimposed on the bare bones of a building: *this* place, but with *their* furniture. People would come in and try to decide whether this was a suitable spot for laying down years of new memories.

It was snowing. Nikki turned on her windshield wipers. As she drove along, she was distracted by Eric's memories—a press conference this afternoon, the surgery yesterday morning. So much had happened in such a short time!

And those were just his *new* memories. Eric was fifteen years older than Nikki. It was strange to think that she now had more memories in her head of his life than of her own—a decade and a half more, to be precise: another fifteen Christmases, a dozen more vacations, the big bash when he'd turned forty, the more subdued one when he'd turned fifty, splitting from his wife, burying his parents, watching his son head off to college.

Despite the fact that the streets were slick and wet, the traffic was sailing along. She had her radio set to DC101. The current song was "Don't Cha" by the Pussycat Dolls, and she realized as it played that Eric didn't know it at all; it didn't conjure up any memories for him—he was the wrong generation.

A car cut in front of Nikki, bringing her attention fully back to the road. She hated aggressive drivers at the best of times, and when it was snowing, there really was no excuse for it.

The Pussycat Dolls sang their final refrain and a traffic report came on. Things were moving surprisingly well, and—

And another maniac came careening past her, cutting in and out of traffic, and—

And the car in front of her, a white Ford Focus, swerved to make room. Nikki hit her horn, two other cars veered, she heard the squeal of tires and the sound of a high-speed impact, and she saw the Focus roll over as another car plowed into it. She pumped her brakes, but—

Damn! She hit the car in front of her, and her air bag deployed. She pitched forward into it and heard more groaning metal plus the sound of shattering glass, and, muffled by the air bag, screams.

She was dazed for a few moments, then the air bag deflated, and she saw a red carnation bloom of blood on it as it pulled away from her face. She reached a hand up and it came away wet; she looked down and saw blood dripping onto her pantsuit.

Nikki turned off her car, then flipped down the visor and looked at herself in the mirror on the back of it. Her nose didn't seem to be broken, thank God, although it was certainly bleeding.

Her back hurt, but not severely. Her windshield had cracked in a thousand places, and that made it almost impossible to see what was in front of her. She went to check her rearview mirror—and saw only the stem that had attached it to the window; the mirror itself must have gone flying in the impact.

She used her sleeve to wipe the blood from her nose; she

really needed something to stanch the flow, though, and her purse had gone flying, too, apparently.

Nikki looked out her side window. Another crashed car was right up against her door—she couldn't get out that way. And so she undid the seat belt and hauled herself across to the passenger seat. As she made her way over the center hump, she saw her purse way in the back, on the shelf beneath the rear window. She continued across the front and tried to open the passenger door. It was stuck and she was afraid that it had been damaged in the crash, but—

But no; it wasn't stuck—it was just *locked*. She never used this door, and it took her a second to find the release, blood falling like rain from her nose onto the tan upholstery.

The door opened. She hauled herself out into the early-evening darkness and surveyed the damage to her own car. The front end had accordioned. She had the presence of mind to worry about whether the gas in the tank was going to explode, and she bent down—an action that sent daggers of pain through her—and looked underneath to see if gasoline was leaking out. It was hard to tell in the darkness, but she didn't think so.

And then, hands on hips, she surveyed the scene. In front of her, all three lanes of traffic were blocked by smashed vehicles that were now skewed across the road. The asphalt glistened in the streetlamps, and snow continued to sift down. She went over to the guardrail on the right side and climbed on it so she could have a better view.

Another wrecked car and a smashed pickup truck were blocking the road in front of the three cars she'd already seen. Some of the other drivers and passengers were out of their vehicles now, too. She looked behind her and saw cars backed up as far as she could see. Horns were blaring, and there was another sound: someone screaming, "Help! Help!"

The source was off to her left: the furthest of the three cars blocking the highway. She headed over to see what was going on, and—

Damn! Her feet almost went out from under her, and she felt a jolt of pain; the road was slick with ice. She steadied herself by grabbing onto the side of one of the other wrecked cars. Its driver was now outside, too, but he was just leaning against his front fender, looking dazed, his face bloodied. She made her way over to the car the screams were coming from—and, as she got closer, she saw that the entire windshield had shattered and fallen away, and the front end of the car was pushed in even more than her own had been. She approached from the car's right side. There were two people within: a male driver and a female passenger, both white, both in their forties.

"Are you okay?" Nikki said.

"My legs!" the woman shouted. "They're pinned!"

Nikki craned to look inside; the car had been compacted enough that the dashboard was right up against the woman's chest; there was no way to get her out.

"And my husband," the woman said, imploringly. "My husband!"

The only way to get to the other side of the car was by clambering over the trunk, which was still reasonably intact. Nikki did so and made her way along the driver's side to the front door.

"It's locked!" Nikki called out. She tried to reach through the space where the windshield used to be, and the pinned woman stretched as much as she could, trying to reach the unlock button; it was the passenger who got to it first, and the door unbolted with a sound like a gunshot.

Nikki opened the ruined door—it took all her strength to get it to swing outward, given how twisted it was. The steering column was bent downward. The male driver had been thrown forward and his neck had smashed against the top of the steering wheel; the car either was too old to have a driver's-side air bag, or it had malfunctioned.

The man had been exposed to the elements longer than Nikki had, and he wasn't wearing a winter coat; Nikki could see his parka draped across the backseat. Still, she thought, it wasn't *that* cold; he shouldn't be turning blue from the chill, and—

And it wasn't from the chill; it was from lack of oxygen! She didn't want to move him—he might well have a neck injury, but if he wasn't breathing, then any other injury wouldn't matter in a few minutes. She steadied his head and neck as much as she could with her hands as she gently tipped his whole body backward into the seat.

His throat was caved in, right below the jawline.

Nikki stood up and looked around again, but nothing had changed. There was no way an ambulance could get to them.

"Help!" she shouted. Perhaps eight or nine people, in various states of injury, were visible outside their vehicles, some bloodied, a couple lying down on the asphalt. "This man needs help! Are any of you doctors?"

A few of the people looked at her. One man shouted, "No," and a woman called out, "Let me know if you find one!"

Nikki inhaled deeply then let the air out; it was cold enough that she could easily see her own breath, and that of the woman pinned in the passenger seat—but there was no sign of any breath coming from the driver.

She felt herself beginning to panic. Christ, what to do? What to do? She rubbed her hands together, trying to warm them. Then she brought them to her face to blow on them, and saw them—covered with blood.

And it came to her: this man needed a crike—an emergency cricothyrotomy—right away. No, no, not right away: *stat*.

And—yes, yes, yes—Eric knew how to perform one, and so *she* knew how to do it, too.

But he—she!—needed a scalpel, or at least something really sharp.

"Oh, God!" said the pinned woman, looking now at her husband, whose blue color was becoming more pronounced. "Oh, God—he's dying!"

Nikki undid the man's seat belt, and, with great effort, pulled him out onto the cold wet pavement, laying him on his back. She didn't have a razor blade or knife—not even back in her purse. But there were shards from the car's broken mirrors, and she found one that was long, narrow, and pointed.

The top part of the man's Adam's apple was crushed. She moved her fingers down about an inch until she felt the bulge of the cricoid cartilage. She backed up a bit, finding the valley between it and the Adam's apple—the cricothyroid membrane.

She knew she should sterilize the mirror fragment and the man's skin, but there was no way—and no time!—to do that. She held the shard as firmly as she could without cutting herself, and she drew it horizontally down the man's neck, above the membrane, but—

But she didn't even break the skin. Knowing how to do it wasn't the same as having the guts *to* do it, it seemed.

"What are you doing?" shouted the man's wife, who could only see that Nikki was on her knees at the side of her husband; her husband's body was mostly out of view.

It was a good question. What the hell *was* she doing?

What she had to do. What she—what Eric—had trained to do.

She took another deep breath, then tried the cut again, this time at least breaking the skin. But she had to go twelve millimeters deep—except she had no idea how much twelve millimeters was. Damn! It was—it was—

About half an inch.

She pushed the glass in further, making the incision. Blood welled up, thick and dark, and—

Damn! The glass broke; the sharp tip was now stuck in the wound. Nikki threw the rest of her impromptu scalpel away and it clattered against the pavement. She used her thumb and forefinger to dig out the piece of glass, tossing it aside as well. The tissues pressed together, closing the incision.

Nikki reached into her jacket pocket and pulled out a ball-point stick pen—one with her firm's name emblazoned across it; a good real-estate agent always had a pen handy to close the deal. She pulled out the writing tip and its attached tube of ink, and fumbled in the cold to pry off the blue end cap until, at last, she had a plastic tube open at both ends.

She was supposed to insert the tube about twenty millimeters, and, well, if twelve was half an inch, then . . .

She pushed the tube into the incision. And then she blew into the tube and placed her palm flat on his chest. It rose! She paused for five seconds, blew in again, waited another five seconds, exhaled once more, counted off five more Mississippis, again and—

And the man's eyes fluttered open.

She waited to see if he was breathing well on his own—and he seemed to be; she was pleased to see puffs of condensation blowing out of the end of the tube.

Nikki rolled back on her rump, drew her knees up to her chest and hugged them, and just sat there, waiting for her own breathing to stabilize. After a minute or two, she reached up to touch her nose to see if it was still bleeding; it wasn't—but it certainly was tender to the touch.

Off in the distance, she heard sirens; God only knew when trained medics would get here, but . . .

But *she* was a trained medic now, it seemed. And as much as she'd freaked out at the hospital, as much as she really didn't wish to intrude on Eric's and Jan's lives, as much as she just wanted things to be the way they had been before this craziness began, she had just saved a person's life.

And that was something she'd always remember.

CHAPTER 42

"I need to get back in action," Seth said to Susan Dawson.

Susan spread her arms to encompass the drip bags, the vital-signs monitor, and more. "You're still recovering, Mr. President."

"I can lie in bed anywhere. I need to go home."

Susan's voice was gentle. "Sir, the White House is gone."

"Yes, I know. It's—yes." He closed his eyes for a moment. "I know. But the country needs to see that it has a leader, and . . ."

He trailed off, and after a while Susan prodded him with, "Sir?"

He considered how much to tell her. It was Saturday, and Counterpunch was scheduled to commence Monday morning Washington time, "There's something big coming up, Susan, and I need to be available for it. I can't lead from here."

"Nothing is more important than your health, sir."

"*This* is."

She nodded. "All right. Where would you like to go?"

"Camp David."

Camp David was located sixty miles north-northwest of DC, in Frederick County, Maryland. Following in the footsteps of George W. Bush and Barack Obama, Seth had named the camp's Evergreen Chapel as his primary place of worship—neatly sidestepping the need to be seen at a public church each week. The site of the historic peace talks between Anwar Sadat and Menachem Begin, and of numerous meetings between Bill Clinton and Tony Blair, Camp David was one of the most secure facilities in the nation, guarded by an elite unit of Marines.

"What if something goes wrong?" asked Susan. "What if you need medical attention?"

"It's a military facility," Seth said. "It's got an excellent infirmary, and Dr. Snow and the rest of the White House medical team will relocate there. And the First Lady is on her way there now to get things set up for me; she's flying in from Oregon."

"What about Mount Weather?" Susan asked. "Isn't that where most of the White House staff are now?"

Seth really wanted to take a long pause before he went on, but that was hardly the way to demonstrate that he was fit to be moved. "Camp David is the designated fallback location for the Executive Office of the President under the Continuity of Operations plan. And that's where I want to lead from."

"Yes, sir," Susan said.

"I want Singh and his equipment relocated there, too. Both he and it are far too valuable to be anywhere but a secure installation."

"Very well, sir. Will do."

"Oh, and one more thing," Seth said. "Make sure that Leon Hexley is moved there, as well."

Susan frowned. "Are you sure that's wise, sir, given his contact with Gordo Danbury?"

"One of the foremost lessons of history, Agent Dawson: keep your friends close and your enemies even closer."

BESSIE Stilwell was exhausted. She wished her son had taken better care of his health, wished that he'd had a less stressful job, wished that he'd stayed in Mississippi.

But Mike had done none of those things, and so she'd been pulled into all this craziness. Linked minds! Meeting the president! A trip to Los Angeles! Visiting a TV studio! And now a flight back to Washington on a military jet. It was all much too much.

Darryl Hudkins had dozed for most of the return flight so far—and that had let Bessie relax. At least when he was unconscious, he presumably wasn't riffling through her memories.

Memories. Of a life that was almost over, a life nearing its end, and—

And that was *something,* she realized. Mike had bugged her for years to write her memoirs, commit her recollections to paper, set down what it had been like to go work in a factory during World War II, to lose a son—Mike's elder brother, in Vietnam—to watch the first man go into space.

Eighty-seven years of life.

She'd seen endless footage of the Lincoln Memorial on TV these last couple of days, and, of course, she knew the words of Lincoln's most famous address, even though it was an artifact of the War of Northern Aggression.

Fourscore and seven years . . .

A lifetime. Her lifetime.

The world will little note nor long remember . . .

Her.

And it was true.

Her husband was gone.

Her elder son Robert was gone.

Yes, Mike had survived this heart attack, but he had his father's genes; he'd be—it was tragic to think it, but she was a realist, she always had been—he'd be gone soon, too.

But Darryl was—well, he'd never said, and she had little experience judging the age of colored men—but he couldn't be more than thirty-one or thirty-two.

More than half a century younger than her. And he'd told her, earlier in the long flight back, that one of the linked people had been killed but the person he was linked to—a nurse—had retained his memories.

That man was gone.

But not forgotten.

And if that's the way these things worked, she decided she was pleased: a half century from now or more—and maybe, what with all the things medical science was doing, much, much more—*someone* would remember her life, someone would recall what it had been like to be her.

The Gettysburg Address had been a eulogy: *from these honored dead we take increased devotion to that cause for which they gave the last full measure of devotion . . .*

She'd heard dozens of eulogies over the years, for family, for friends, for neighbors. And they all had said some version of what Lincoln had observed, although rarely as eloquently. They're not really dead—so long as we remember them.

In that sense, at least, the events of the last two days had given her a new lease on life. Darryl Hudkins would remember her. He shifted a bit in his seat next to her, and Bessie smiled at him.

A short while later, the military jet started its nighttime approach toward Andrews Air Force Base. Bessie was grateful for the darkness; she'd rather not see the ruins of the White House off in the distance.

But she did see one building that she recognized—indeed, that she imagined *everyone* recognized, although its form could really only be appreciated from the air.

The Pentagon.

It sat there like a monstrous snowflake. And on the other side of South Washington Boulevard from it was a vast black area, and she knew, because *he* knew, what it was: Arlington National Cemetery, where 30,000 souls were trying to rest in peace.

The site of the Pentagon focused her attention, bringing back memories of . . .

Peter Muilenburg, the secretary of defense, meeting with President Jerrison and first proposing Counterpunch.

And, to his credit, Seth reacting with horror, and outrage and shock.

Yes, Seth had said, they'd attacked Philadelphia, destroying the Liberty Bell, and so much more.

Yes, they'd bombed San Francisco, taking out the Golden Gate Bridge.

And, yes, the tallest tower in Chicago had been brought tumbling down.

But *this* couldn't be contemplated, *this* was unthinkable, *this* was un-American.

But Muilenburg had continued to make his case, to outline his plan, to show how it could be done with negligible American casualties, to show that it would *work* . . .

And, at last, Seth Jerrison, the history professor turned president, had said, "Do it."

Bessie could feel the air pressure changing as the plane descended. She took out her hearing aid to help things equalize.

She was in a tizzy, still not clear what she should do. Should she tell Darryl about Counterpunch? Ah, but he worked for President Jerrison and—it came to her: he was one of two Secret Service agents that Seth still trusted.

Besides, even if she told people, would anyone believe her? Back in Pascagoula, she'd seen how folks looked at Mabel Simmons, laughing at her stories of seeing aliens and ghosts, calling her "that crazy old bat" and "Unstable Mabel."

But no. It had been in the press: memory linkages at Luther Terry Memorial Hospital. And there'd been much speculation about who, if anyone, was linked to President Jerrison.

The press.

She thought back to her hotel room at the Watergate, and about what that building was famous for.

The press. The people who could blow the lid off things—even those things the president of the United States was desperate to keep secret.

She looked out the window and took a deep breath, trying to calm herself. And, at last, she found the strength she needed. She knew what she had to do.

All those reporters in front of the hospital: they'd doubtless still be there, waiting for any update about the president's condition. And as soon as she arrived, she'd run up to them, and she'd tell them, with their cameras rolling, that she was linked to President Jerrison, and she'd let them know all about the horrible thing that he was planning to do.

JAN was sitting on the white couch in Eric's living room. The ornate wall clock sounded a chime; she'd discovered that it did that every hour on the hour.

Jan was reading the just-published new edition of *Time* on his iPad. The cover image showed separate maps of the west and east coasts of the United States, with pillars of black smoke coming up from San Francisco, Chicago, Philadelphia, Washington, and, harking back to 9/11, Manhattan. Above that in stark black letters was the text, "Will it ever end?"

The door to the penthouse opened, and Eric came in. She went over to greet him—and there was an awkward moment during which she wasn't sure *how* to greet him. And so she did nothing: no hug, no physical contact at all. But she did ask, "How was the press conference?"

Eric took off his jacket—which was wet; he must have walked the few blocks back from LT—and hung it on the doorknob so that it would drip on the marble instead of inside the closet. "It was all right, but I hate doing stuff like that. Doctor-patient relations are supposed to be confidential. I know we get VIP patients to sign consent forms, but it still makes me uncomfortable discussing a procedure with anyone who isn't a colleague." He stepped into the living room. "I mean, I get that he's the president and all, but still, it feels wrong."

They continued on into the kitchen, and he opened the fridge and pulled out a bottle of microbrewery beer. "Want one?"

"No, thanks."

"It's like 9-1-1 calls," he said. "I hate it when you hear one of those go public. I remember a bunch of years ago when William Shatner's wife drowned; his call to 9-1-1 was all over the news. That's just *wrong.*"

Jan nodded. "Yeah, I agree. I think it makes people reluctant to call."

"How was your afternoon?" asked Eric. They headed to the living room, and Eric sat on the leather couch. Jan sat next to him, and she saw on his face that he was pleased by that. She was about to answer his question when he answered it himself. "You had Nikki Van Hausen over."

She nodded.

"How is she?" Eric asked. "She was pretty messed up when I first met her; the memory linkage was freaking her out."

Jan knew she didn't have to answer; Eric now knew what Jan remembered of the afternoon, and—

And suddenly he was averting his eyes. Ah, of course: he was probably recalling Nikki telling Jan how he felt about her.

"I had to know," Jan said gently. "I mean, this is all happening so fast, and, well, I needed to know if you were everything you seemed to be."

He did meet her gaze now. "And?"

She got up, stood in front of him, and reached down to take his hands, pulling him to his feet. "And let's go give Nikki Van Hausen a memory she'll never forget."

THE Air Force jet landed at Andrews. It was dark, and Bessie couldn't see much of the surroundings, but she was glad to be getting off the plane. Although the flight had been smooth, it had also been long, and apparently most soldiers didn't have hemorrhoids; the chairs were uncomfortable. She'd had the window seat, so Darryl had to get out first—and, she realized, it had probably been a pretty uncomfortable flight for him, too, given how long his legs were.

Darryl took Bessie's arm as they went down the metal staircase that had been parked at the side of the plane, and she was grateful for it; the last thing she needed was to fall and break her hip.

Andrews was fifteen miles southeast of Luther Terry, Bessie knew—because Seth knew it. On a Saturday evening, it should be an easy drive up Branch Avenue to the Suitland Parkway and then along I-295.

As they entered one of the buildings, they were met by a man in a green Army uniform. He was six-six and muscular. "Agent Hudkins?" he said. "And Mrs. Stilwell?"

"Yes," said Darryl, and "That's right," said Bessie.

"I'm Colonel Barstow," he said. "I'm an aide to the SecDef."

"The what?" asked Bessie, but it came to her from Seth's memories even before Barstow answered.

"The secretary of defense, ma'am. The two of you have been placed in my custody."

"Custody!" exclaimed Darryl.

"Yes, sir." Barstow looked at Bessie. "If I may, ma'am, you might want to visit the ladies' room before we head out."

"I'm fine," Bessie said. "It's a short trip."

"No, ma'am, it isn't," said Barstow.

Darryl raised his eyebrows. "We're going back to Luther Terry."

"No," Barstow said, and his hand went to his sidearm. "You're not."

CHAPTER 43

Sunday

JAN and Tony Falconi had had blackout curtains in their bedroom; Tony sometimes worked nights and needed to sleep during the day.

Eric might have had blackout curtains, too, for all Jan knew, but they'd tumbled into bed without having drawn them; no one could look into Eric's bedroom, which was on the top floor of the condo and looked west over the Potomac. She couldn't see the sun, which was rising on the other side of the building, but the brightening sky had awoken her.

It was Sunday morning, and neither of them had to be back at work until Monday. Oh, he was on call in case anything happened to Jerrison, but that's why God invented the Black-Berry. She lay there, looking at him, his eyes closed, his mouth open a bit, and she listened to the soft sound of his breathing. She felt something she hadn't felt for a long time. She felt safe.

And yet—

And yet, Washington was *not* a safe place these days. In the last forty-eight hours, there'd been an attempt on the life of the president, and a terrorist bomb had destroyed the White House.

Of course, she thought, *nowhere* was safe. There'd been the bomb in Chicago before that, and San Francisco—a city she'd always wanted to visit—and Philadelphia, where her uncle lived, not to mention terrorist attacks in London and Milan and Cairo and Nairobi and Mexico City, and the list went on and on.

Eric stirred a bit, and his eyes opened. "Hey," he said.

Jan smiled and touched his cheek. "Hey yourself."

"What do you want to do today?" he asked.

She looked out the window; it wasn't snowing, and the sky looked cloudless; a nice change from yesterday. "Let's go for a walk on the Mall."

"Really?"

She nodded. "See the monuments, the Smithsonian." She lifted her shoulders slightly. "I think I need to be reminded of America's greatness."

ERIC and Jan left his apartment just before 10:00 A.M. Under her coat, Jan was wearing the spare set of clothes she'd retrieved from LT yesterday, as well as a Harvard sweatshirt that belonged to Eric, and she had on her bright red ski mittens, which had been tucked in her coat pockets. Rather than hike the six blocks to the Mall, they took a cab over; Jan was pleased to see that Eric was a generous tipper.

The cab let them off near the Arlington Bridge Equestrian Statues. Everything was beautiful: a classic winter wonderland, with pristine snow caked on tree limbs and statues. They walked to the Lincoln Memorial, approaching it from behind and keeping to the pathways, which had already been plowed—the National Park Service had its own snow-removal teams. Once there, they headed around to the front. The wooden platform and podium that had been set up for Jerrison's speech, which they'd both seen on the news now, had been taken down. There was no obvious sign of where the president had been shot, but two young men were arguing on the steps about whether he'd been hit *here* or *here*. Jan thought that was a bit morbid, but still, she and Eric walked up the steps to look, too.

"I once went to Dealey Plaza," Eric said.

Her face must have conveyed that he'd lost her. "In Dallas. Where Kennedy was shot."

"Ah," she said.

"There's no commemorative plaque, no marker. But there is a white X painted on the roadway. If you wait for the light to turn red, you can go out into the middle of the street and stand on the spot where Oswald's killing shot got him."

The two people arguing about where Jerrison had been hit had come to an agreement. They took turns standing in the middle of one of the broad steps, each photographing the other. When they moved away, Jan and Eric walked to the same spot and gazed out at what, had the bullet taken a slightly altered trajectory, would have been the last sight Seth Jerrison had ever seen. Of course, it was different now: there were only a few dozen people around instead of the thousands who had been here for the speech, there was snow on the ground, and the sky was clear instead of the overcast it had been on Friday. But the Reflecting Pool stretched out in front of them, leading to the Washington Monument.

Unlike the boisterous pair who had preceded them in this spot, Eric and Jan stood in silence, but he did put his arm around her shoulders. When they'd had their fill, they walked up into the memorial and stared for a few minutes at the statue of the Great Emancipator. They then headed down the marble steps and started walking east. There were two paths they could take: along the south side of the Reflecting Pool or along the north; they opted for the north. A few other people were out strolling, and some joggers came toward them. They reached the World War II Memorial—which was Jan's least favorite of the various war memorials; it was the most recently built, and the Vietnam and Korea ones were tough acts to follow. Then they headed up 17th Avenue to the corner of Constitution, and made their way around the gentle curve of Ellipse Road.

And there it was.

Or, more precisely, there it had been, on the other side of what was left of the metal fence.

The White House.

Jan had seen pictures on the news, but that wasn't the same

as beholding the ruins in real life. She found herself shaking her head. Her breath, visible in the chill air, gave a faint reminder of the smoke that had been billowing from the ruins two days ago.

She looked at Eric to see if he wanted to go closer; he nodded.

SECRETARY of Defense Peter Muilenburg studied the giant display in the windowless room. The aircraft carriers were on station, or right on schedule to reach their stations. As he watched, the red digital timer changed from "1 day 0 hours 0 minutes" to "0 days 23 hours 59 minutes." There was no seconds display, but his pulse, which he was feeling with a finger on his left radial artery, served well enough: he was the conductor for this orchestra, and his heartbeat the metronome.

IT was hard to take his eyes off the destruction in front of him, but Eric Redekop turned to look at Janis. She was just thirty-two, for God's sake—by the time she was his age, what crazy weapons would the world be facing? How small would they be? How much damage would they be able to do? It was almost inconceivable the amount of destructive power that would be in the hands of individuals by then.

The part of him that was anchored in the here and now had been worried about where this relationship might eventually lead—about whether he'd leave her a widow in her sixties.

The part of him that half—but only half—believed all the stuff he read in science magazines and medical journals had thought that surely they'd pass the tipping point sometime in the next couple of decades and the average human life span would increase by more than a year for every year that passed, meaning that he and Jan would both have much, much longer lives than their parents or grandparents, and that, as the decades, and maybe even centuries, rolled by, an eighteen-year age difference would seem utterly trivial.

But the part of him that came to the fore now was the one that had been lurking at the back of his mind since 9/11, and had been reinforced so many times since, including when the

Sears Tower went down. Now that Jerrison was safe, and Eric finally had time to take it all in, he realized it didn't matter what miracles future medical science might hold; the planet was *fucked*. The world had transitioned from a place where wars were fought between nations, declared in legislative assemblies and concluded with negotiated treaties, to a place where small cabals and even individuals could wreak havoc on a massive scale. And *scale* was indeed the issue: the weapons kept getting smaller, and the damage they were capable of kept getting larger.

And *that* meant that the age difference between him and Jan didn't matter; none of it mattered. The world wasn't going to last long enough for him to get really old or for Jan to collect a pension. It was over; they were *done*—it was only a matter of time before someone wrecked *everything* for *everyone*.

He looked at her lovely, youthful face—horrified though it was right now as it studied the caved-in ruins of what had been the home of the most powerful man in the world.

"Do you know who the Great Gazoo is?" he said.

She looked at him, tilting her head slightly in a way that made him think she was sifting memories, but whether the answer came from her own childhood or from Josh Latimer's he had no way to tell. "A cartoon character," she said. "From *The Flintstones.*"

He nodded. "He was from the planet Zetox," he said, pleased, despite the circumstances, for knowing that bit of trivia. "Do you know why he was exiled to primitive Earth?"

She tilted her head again; he rather suspected that hardly anyone besides him remembered the answer to that—but he did; it had chilled him when it had first been explained in the episode in which Gazoo was introduced, and he'd never forgotten it.

The Great Gazoo—the smug little flying green guy whose introduction for so many indicated the point at which *The Flintstones* had jumped the shark—had been *precisely* the kind of terrorist Eric now feared the world would soon face. "He'd invented the ultimate weapon," he said to Jan. "A button that if pressed would destroy the entire universe. So his people sent him somewhere with primitive technology so he could never build anything like that again."

She looked at him, getting it. "But it doesn't have to turn out that way," she said.

He gestured at the White House: the central mansion reduced to blackened ruins, the east and west wings gutted by fire. "How else can it turn out?"

She let out a sigh. "I don't know. But that *can't* be the only way."

Others had tarried here to look at the wreckage. A small knot of Japanese tourists was standing a short distance away, listening to a guide; Eric didn't understand anything she was saying, but she sounded sad.

At least it hadn't been a nuclear weapon, Eric thought. But those were easy enough to ferret out with Geiger counters and other techniques; these new bombs were hard to detect.

More memories came to him—his own, from his childhood. The doomsday device going off at the end of *Dr. Strangelove,* and his mother always making him call her for the ending whenever it was on TV, because, despite the horrific succession of nuclear explosions, she loved hearing Vera Lynn sing "We'll Meet Again."

And Colonel Taylor—Charlton Heston himself—pushing down on the crystalline control panel at the end of *Beneath the Planet of the Apes,* setting off the Alpha-Omega bomb: one man destroying an entire world, so that it cracked like an egg in space.

And the end of the novel *2001,* which he'd struggled to read after seeing the film for the first time when he was ten, with the Star Child detonating all the nuclear bombs in orbit around Earth, bringing a false dawn to the planet below.

And on and on and on, the collective memory of humanity, the pop culture created by people of his parents' generation, a generation—he looked over at the Japanese tourists—who remembered Hiroshima and Nagasaki.

And the horrors of his own generation, oh so terribly real: 9/11 and everything since.

And, now, in front of them, yet another echo, another aftershock, another flashback, the latest example of the ongoing, never-ending wave, the sick inversion of the old adage: the wants of the evil few outweighing the desires, the hopes, the dreams, the *lives,* of the many.

"It can't go on like this," Eric said, as much to himself as to Jan.

"It won't," Jan said, and he marveled for a moment at the notion of her—the young one—comforting him about the future.

They walked closer to the White House, making their way around the snow-covered Ellipse to stand by the brown metal fence at the south end. Lots of workers were scurrying about the spacious grounds, looking through rubble, collecting the countless scraps of paper, trying, Eric supposed, to make sure no fragment of a classified document could be recovered by souvenir-seekers. It was such an odd view: the ruins of the White House framed by picture-perfect trees with beautiful snow on their boughs.

Eric was startled by a rough voice. "Guess I'm not the only one."

A man in tattered clothes, a filthy blanket around his shoulders, and a worn parka beneath that, had sidled up to stand next to Jan. He was rubbing his hands together for warmth.

She looked at him. "Pardon?"

The man indicated the White House with a movement of his head. His hair was long and might have been white if it were clean. "The only homeless one," he said. He wasn't making a joke, it seemed; he sounded genuinely sad.

Jan nodded, and so did Eric. On a normal day, he might have ignored the man, or briskly walked away. But this was not a normal day.

"Don't you have any gloves?" Jan said.

"Did," the man said. "Don't."

Jan pulled off her bright red ski mittens and proffered them. "Here."

His scraggly eyebrows went up. "Seriously?"

"Sure. I can get another pair."

Eric put his arm around her shoulder.

The man took them with his left hand and with his right he grasped Jan's now-naked hand and shook it. "Thank you, miss. Thank you."

Jan didn't flinch; she didn't pull away from the contact. She let him hold her hand for a few seconds. "You're welcome."

"Well," he said, looking again at the wreckage, "just

wanted to see how the cleanup was going. Gotta get back to my usual spot."

Eric looked at Jan just in time to see her eyebrows go up. "The Vietnam Veterans Memorial," she said.

"Yup. I was one of the last to go over there. Just eighteen."

Eric was intrigued. "And you're there every day?"

The old man nodded. "With my friends."

"Other vets?"

"No," he said. "My friends. On the wall. Their names. I point 'em out to people, tell 'em stories about them—those that need to hear 'em. Young folk, folk that don't know what it was like. Can't let people forget."

"Darby," said Jan. "And David. And Bob."

The man looked just as surprised as Eric felt. "And Jimbo," he said. "Don't forget big Jimbo."

Jan nodded. "And Jimbo, too."

The old man looked like he wanted to ask her a million questions—but then his face changed, and he nodded, as if the questions had been answered. "You're a good person, miss."

"So are you," she said, and then Eric's heart skipped a beat when she added one more word, a name—*his* name: "Jack."

Jack looked startled, but then an almost beatific calm came over his face. He smiled, put on his new mittens, and started shuffling away.

"You've never met him," Eric said. He'd formulated it in his mind as a question but it came out as a statement.

She shook her head.

"But you know him now."

"As well as you know me."

Eric turned and looked back across the Ellipse, toward the Washington Monument. Jack was getting further away.

"Why do you suppose that happened?" he asked.

Jan put her hands in her coat pockets, presumably to keep them warm, but then she pulled them out again and looked them over, turning them palm up then palm down. "He touched me," she said. And then: "I touched him."

Eric frowned. "When Josh Latimer died, the chain was broken. I was connected to you, but you weren't connected to anyone. And so—"

"And so my mind sought a new connection," said Jan.

"But he wasn't the first person to touch you since Latimer died," Eric said.

Jan frowned, considering this, and Eric frowned, too, recalling her memories, and then they both said, simultaneously, "No, he wasn't."

And Jan went on: "But he was the first *unlinked* person. Everyone else who touched me—you, Nikki Van Hausen, and Professor Singh—was already linked to somebody."

"What about the MRI technician?"

"He was wearing blue latex gloves. And, anyway, I'm not sure he touched me."

"We should go after Jack," Eric said and he started to walk south.

Jan reached out with her arm—the one with the tiger tattoo hidden beneath her clothes, although they both knew it was there—and stopped him. "No," she said, turning to look at where the White House had been, "we shouldn't."

CHAPTER 44

MARINE One—the president's helicopter—landed on LT's rooftop helipad. Seth was strapped to a gurney and loaded on board for the flight to Camp David. He was accompanied by Dr. Alyssa Snow and Secret Service agent Susan Dawson, and was met by a Marine honor guard upon landing.

Mrs. Jerrison was already at Camp David. Seth insisted on being taken to Aspen Lodge—the presidential residence—rather than the infirmary, and was gently transferred to the king-sized four-poster bed there. A roaring fire was already going in the bedroom's fireplace. The large window had its curtains drawn back, giving a magnificent view of the countryside, even if most of the trees—poplars and birches and maples—had long since lost their leaves.

Seth lay in the bed, his head propped up enough that he could stare into the flames, thinking about the speech he was going to give later today.

One must learn from history, Seth had often told his students—and sometimes not even from American history. In 1963, a terrorist group called the *Front de Libération du Qué-bec* planted bombs in several Canadian military facilities and in an English-language neighborhood of Montreal. Later FLQ attacks included bombings at McGill University, the Montreal Stock Exchange, and the home of Montreal Mayor Jean Drapeau. Then, in October 1970, the FLQ kidnapped the British trade commissioner, James Cross, and the Québec minister of labor, Pierre Laporte.

Pierre Trudeau, Canada's charismatic prime minister— who had been a thorn in the side of Johnson and Nixon—had finally had enough. When asked how far he'd go to put down the terrorists, he said, "Just watch me." And the world did, as he invoked Canada's War Measures Act, rolled out tanks and troops, suspended civil liberties, and arrested 465 people without charge or trial.

Laporte was ultimately found dead: the FLQ had slashed his wrists, put a bullet through his skull, *and* strangled him— in the first political assassination in Canada since 1868. But it never happened again: in all the decades since, there'd never been another significant terrorist event on Canadian soil. Lone crazed gunmen, yes, but organized acts by terrorist cells, no.

Just watch me.

Seth continued to stare into the flames.

JACK was back at his station, back at the Vietnam Veterans Memorial. The place's name was the one thing that bothered him about it: you usually think of vets as soldiers who survived a battle, but the 58,272 names engraved here were the Americans who had died in that swampy nation, fighting a pointless war.

Jack was grateful for the nice new ski mittens that pretty woman had given him, and he was wearing them now. He didn't know why she had his memories, but he was glad she did. The dead soldiers named here understood, and so did those who'd survived, and, he imagined, many of those who'd been to Afghanistan or Iraq or Libya understood, too—but it was so hard to share what it had been like with those who had never seen combat, those who had never tasted war. At least that woman, Janis, understood now, too.

There were always people on the Mall, but Jack imagined fewer would stop at the Vietnam Memorial today. Instead, just as he himself had earlier, they'd hang around the places that had been in the news lately: the Lincoln Memorial and the charred rubble that had been the White House.

The main part of the Victnam Vctcrans Memorial con sisted of two polished black stone walls that joined at an oblique angle. The west wall pointed to the Lincoln Memorial and the east one to the Washington Monument. The walls were only eight inches high at their ends but rose along their 250-foot lengths to be over ten feet tall where they met.

Someone was approaching now. Jack always waited to see what each person needed. Some people knew how the wall worked—the soldiers were listed chronologically by date of death—and could find their loved one's name incised in the stone. Others needed help, and if they seemed lost, he'd show them how to use the index books that told you which of the 144 panels had a particular name on it. Others still needed someone to listen, or someone to talk to. Whatever they needed, Jack tried to provide it. And for those who didn't know, who didn't understand, he told stories.

The approaching man was black and about Jack's age— maybe a vet himself or maybe the brother of one. Jack watched as the man found the name he was looking for—it was about shoulder-high on the wall. Not many people left flowers in the winter, but this fellow did, a small bouquet of roses. Jack waited a minute then walked over to speak to him.

"Someone special?" Jack asked.

And, of course, the answer was "yes." It was always "yes"—everyone listed here was special.

"My best friend," the man said. "Tyrone. His number came up, and he had to go. I was lucky; mine never did."

"Tell me about him," Jack said.

The man lifted his shoulders a bit as if daunted by the task. "I don't know where to begin."

Jack nodded. He took the bright red mitten off his right hand and offered that hand to the man. "My name's Jack. I was there in 1971 and '72."

The man wasn't wearing gloves. "Frank," he said. He shook Jack's hand for several seconds.

"Tell me about the last time you saw Tyrone," Jack said. The memory of that event—Tyrone's farewell party, at his favorite bar—came to Jack as soon as he asked about it, but he let Frank recount the story anyway, listening to every word.

BESSIE Stilwell was scared. The Army colonel who had intercepted her and Darryl at Andrews Air Force Base had taken them to Camp David—and then locked them in Dogwood, a large guest cottage on the grounds there. She hadn't been allowed to go to Luther Terry Memorial Hospital to see her son, and hadn't been allowed to speak to anyone except Colonel Barstow and Darryl.

She understood what was going on: as soon as Barstow had gotten her and Darryl into his car, the memories of President Jerrison's phone call to Secretary Muilenburg asking him to have his staff intercept them had come back to her. They were prisoners here, cut off from the rest of the world. The president was going to go ahead with his plan; he wasn't about to let a little old lady interfere.

According to the framed photos on the walls, German chancellor Helmut Kohl had stayed in this cottage during the Clinton administration, Japanese prime minister Yasuo Fukuda had stayed here during the Bush years, and British prime minister David Cameron had used this place when Obama was president. The cottage had a large, luxuriously appointed living area and four giant bedrooms, so she couldn't really complain about the quality of the accommodations. But her cell phone had been confiscated, and so had Darryl's BlackBerry, there were no computers—although Darryl had pointed out where they had previously been installed—and the phone could only reach the Camp David operator. And, of course, the doors were guarded, so they couldn't leave.

Bessie didn't need much sleep—five hours a night was all she normally took since her husband had died. And so she woke up before Darryl emerged from his room, and she went into the living area and sat in a nice rocking chair, looking through a window at the beautiful countryside. She concentrated on Seth's memories, trying to find something—anything—in them she could use. But it was, she had learned, all about triggers: unless something brought forth a memory, the memory was hidden. Ask her what she knew about Seth

Jerrison and the answer was nothing; ask her what his birthday was, or what make his first car had been, or whether he preferred his toilet paper to hang over or under the roll, and she could dredge the answer up.

She hunted and hunted, thinking about *this,* about *that,* then about something else, again and again.

At last, frustrated, she did what she always did when she needed guidance. She prayed. God, she knew, understood that she had arthritis and wouldn't mind that she didn't go down on her knees. She just sat in the chair, closed her eyes, and said, "O Lord, I need your help . . ."

And after a moment, her eyes opened wide.

Ask and ye shall receive.

She'd already been told she couldn't speak with President Jerrison. But maybe, somehow, there was a way to get a message to him—and him alone.

Perhaps a letter? She got up from the chair and shuffled over to the elegant antique writing desk—it pleased her that it was probably older than she herself was. She found some stationery in a drawer, and a retractable ballpoint pen, but—

But she couldn't trust that anything she wrote down, even if she put it in a sealed envelope, wouldn't be read by others before the president saw it. If only there was some way to send him a private message . . .

And it came to her.

Of course.

So simple.

You take any three numbers that add up to thirteen . . .

CHAPTER 45

BESSIE opened the door to the cottage, letting in a blast of cool morning air. The blond, brown-eyed Army officer stationed outside spun on his heel, and said, "Can I help you with something, ma'am?"

"Are you normally here, young man?"

"Someone will be on guard all day, ma'am."

"No, I mean, are you normally part of the Camp David staff?"

"No, ma'am. I've been temporarily assigned here; I'm usually stationed at the Pentagon."

"Ah," said Bessie. They weren't going to let her talk to anyone who wasn't already in the know, it seemed. "I need you to deliver this to the president," she said, handing him a sealed envelope; she'd found some nice linen ones in the same drawer as the Camp David stationery.

"I can't leave my post, ma'am, but I'll call for someone else to come and get it." He took the envelope from her.

"It'll go straight to the president himself?"

"Well, ma'am, I'm sure there's a process. It'll be turned over to his staff."

Bessie shook her head. "That's not good enough, young man. I want you to take it to him—you personally. Call for someone else to stand here, but you deliver it yourself, do you understand?"

"I—that's not how it's normally done, ma'am."

Bessie rallied all her strength. "These aren't normal times, are they? Surely you understand that the president brought me here for a reason. You wouldn't want to be the one responsible for him not getting an important message from me in time, now, would you?"

He seemed to consider this, then: "No, ma'am."

"So you'll personally see that he gets it?"

"Yes, ma'am. I'll take it directly to the residence."

"You promise?"

"Yes, ma'am."

Bessie smiled. "Thank you." She closed the door and turned around just in time to see Darryl Hudkins emerging from his room. He was wearing the same clothes he'd had on yesterday, although Bessie's luggage had been waiting for her when she'd arrived here; someone had fetched her things from the Watergate.

"Good morning, Mrs. Stilwell," he said. "Sorry I slept in so long."

"Nothing else to do," Bessie said.

"True. Did you sleep all right?"

"As well as can be expected."

"Have you called for breakfast yet?" They'd been told whatever they needed would be brought to them.

"No," Bessie said. "I'm usually not hungry when I get up." She thought for a moment, made a decision, then pointed to the living area. "Won't you sit down? There's something I need to tell you."

She imagined his eyebrows went up, but, from this distance, she really couldn't see. He went to the sink, got himself a glass of water, asked her if she wanted one, then went and took a seat on the ornately upholstered couch facing a giant window.

"We have to talk, Darryl. Or, well, maybe we *don't*. I'm still getting used to how this all works, but . . ."

"Yes, ma'am?"

She paused, again having second thoughts. After all, Darryl was one of Jerrison's trusted associates; the president had chosen him to go with her to California. She searched Jerrison's memories for any indication that he'd taken Darryl into his confidence about Counterpunch.

Nothing.

Of course, Darryl might still be in on it; Bessie doubted the president briefed members of his protective detail personally. And so, she decided, she'd find out the old-fashioned way: she'd ask. "Darryl, does the name Counterpunch mean anything special to you?"

"No, ma'am."

"It didn't to me either, until yesterday, but . . . God, I don't even know where to begin. Can you—can you pluck it from my mind?"

There was a pause, then: "I'm not finding anything, ma'am."

"Counterpunch? Are you sure? I know all about it."

"Nothing is coming to me. Where did you hear about it?"

"Well, I didn't, actually. It's something I learned about from the president's memories."

"Oh," said Darryl. "Well, if I understand what Dr. Singh said, ma'am, the linking of minds is what he called 'first-order.' You can read the president's memories, and I can read your memories, but I can't read through you to his memories."

"Oh, I see," said Bessie. "Then I guess I just have to tell you."

"That'd be simplest, ma'am."

She took a deep breath. "Operation Counterpunch is what they're planning to do," she said.

"Who?"

"The president. The military."

"When?"

"Tomorrow."

"And, ma'am, what is it they're planning?"

"To destroy Pakistan."

"I—what?"

"To destroy Pakistan," she said again, and this time she did clearly see Darryl's eyebrows go up. "To wipe all hundred and seventy million people there off the face of the Earth."

"God," he said, although it was more breath than voice. "Why?"

"I—I don't know how to put this."

"Was it Jerrison's idea?"

"No. No, it was presented to him two months ago, by um . . ." She had trouble with the name; she'd recalled it repeatedly now, but wasn't quite sure how to make the initial sounds for it. "Um, Mr. Muilenburg. He's the, um—"

"The secretary of defense," said Darryl. "Go on."

"That's right. He came to see the president, and laid it all out for him. Their conversation went something like this . . ."

SILVER-HAIRED Peter Muilenburg sat on one of the short couches in the Oval Office, and Seth Jerrison sat on the other one, facing him, the presidential seal on the carpet between them.

"And so," Muilenburg said, "our recommendation is simply this: we wipe Pakistan off the map."

Seth's mouth dropped open a bit. "You can't do that."

"Of course we can, sir," replied Muilenburg. "The question is whether we should."

"No," said Seth. "I mean, you *can't*. Nuclear weapons are dirty; if you take out Pakistan, you're bound to send fallout into the surrounding countries. Iran and Afghanistan to the west, China to the north, India to the east."

Muilenburg nodded. "That would be true if we were proposing using nukes. But the new Magma-class bombs don't give off any appreciable radiation, and the electromagnetic pulse they produce is much less devastating than that generated by a nuke."

"It sounds like those terrorist bombs," Seth said.

"Where do you think they got the technology?" Muilenburg replied evenly. He held up a hand. "Not that we gave it to them, of course. The initial research was another one of those cold-fusion notions, coupled with some interesting new physics out of Brookhaven. No one quite realized the destructive potential at first; when we did, it was classified beyond top secret, but enough hints and clues had already gotten out."

"So the Chinese have this, too? And the Russians?"

"Not big bombs, like we've got, sir—at least, as far as we know. Which is why we have to do it now—an immediate counterpunch."

Seth shook his head. "It's not a proportionate response, Peter."

"Was nuking Hiroshima and Nagasaki a proportionate response to Pearl Harbor?" asked Muilenburg. "Two whole cities, full of civilians, for one Navy base? At Pearl Harbor, twenty-four hundred people died, of whom just fifty-seven were civilians; the bombs dropped on Hiroshima and Nagasaki killed a hundred times as many—almost a quarter of a million people, almost all of them civilians. Was *that* proportionate? No—but it ended the war. It stopped it cold. When we had the clear upper hand in 1945 against the Japanese, we used it—and we never had to fear the Japanese again."

"But the terrorists aren't just in Pakistan," Seth said.

"True. But most of the al-Sajada leaders are there. And Pakistan shielded bin Laden for years; their ISI knew he was there. Yes, there are terrorists in Afghanistan and Iraq and elsewhere, but the message will be clear: if there's another attack on American soil, we'll take out another nation that harbors terrorists."

"No," said Seth. "I mean the terrorists are *here*. In the United States, and London, and elsewhere. They're already here; that's how these attacks can happen."

"Foot soldiers. The leaders are back there."

"In the Islamic world?" Seth said. "This isn't a war against Islam."

"No, it's not," Muilenburg said. "There are 1.6 billion Muslims in the world, and fifty countries in which Muslims are the majority of the population. Pakistan is just a tiny part of Islam."

"This is horrific," Seth said. "Abominable."

"What's been done to us is horrific," replied Muilenburg. "And it will go on and on unless we force them to stop, unless we show them that we will not tolerate it. We're the last remaining superpower. It's time we used our superpowers and put an end to this."

• • •

DARRYL listened intently as Bessie recounted the meeting between Secretary of Defense Muilenburg and the president. "And Jerrison bought into this?" he said when she was done.

Bessie nodded. "And it's going ahead on Monday. Tomorrow."

Darryl looked around the luxurious cottage—but a gilded cage is still a cage. "I guess there's nothing we can do about it, is there?"

"Well," said Bessie, "there's not much." She searched the president's memories to see if he had received her letter yet; it didn't seem so. "But," she added, looking out the window at the snow-covered forested ground, "at least I've given it my best shot."

CHAPTER 46

SETH Jerrison was still lying on the bed in the presidential residence at Camp David. The First Lady—Jasmine Jerrison, tall, sophisticated, refined—was sitting nearby, working on her laptop computer, which was perched on a little desk. With the exception of Agent Susan Dawson, Seth had dismissed the Secret Service from providing his protection here; he was now relying on Navy and Marine officers who had been screened by Peter Muilenburg's staff.

There was a knock at the door. Jasmine got up and opened it. One of the Marine guards saluted her crisply. "Ma'am, an envelope for the president."

Seth couldn't see her face from here, but he imagined she was narrowing her green eyes. "Who's it from?"

"Ma'am, Mrs. Stilwell insisted that it be delivered to your husband."

"I'll take it."

"I promised Mrs. Stilwell that it would go to the president."

"I'll give it to him. Thank you." She took the envelope. The young man saluted and left, and Jasmine brought the envelope over to Seth. He nodded, and she got the ornate letter opener off the desk and slit the flap, put on her reading glasses, and pulled out the single sheet.

"It's gibberish," she said.

"What?"

She held it so he could see. He was already wearing his Ben Franklin glasses, and he tipped his head so that he could look through the lenses at the paper. It was a piece of Camp David stationery with a long message written on it in a shaky hand. The letter began:

    5-2-6
    IJFXK XVXJY DIJLZ . . .

"What's it mean?" Jasmine asked.

The First Lady was privy to all his secrets—personal and professional—although he'd never had cause to explain the 13 Code to her before. He did so now. It took only a few seconds for her to write up a decryption table for the key 5-2-6, but converting the message was tedious—just as, Seth imagined, it had been tedious for Bessie to write it out.

He dictated Bessie's note one letter at a time, and Jasmine typed the corresponding decoded characters into her laptop. She then put in the proper spacing and added punctuation.

"'Dear Mr. President,'" Jasmine read aloud. "'You've kidnapped me and are preventing me from seeing my ailing son.'"

"'Kidnapped' seems a bit strong," Seth said.

Jasmine, who, he supposed, had taken in the gist of the letter while typing it up, lifted her eyebrows. "It gets stronger. She writes, 'I believe in God. I read the Bible every day. I do believe in an eye for an eye. But what you're planning is a million eyes for one. I can't hold with that.'"

Seth shifted a bit on the bed. The fire continued to crackle. "'I prayed to God for advice, and discovered that you had no similar memories, that you'd never prayed, that you don't believe in the Lord. I'm shocked and saddened. It's another thing you lied about on the campaign trail. But I also know, because you discussed it with your campaign director Rusty, that you think it's possible to be moral without God, that you believe an atheist can be a good person.'"

Seth closed his eyes but continued to listen.

"'I can't argue politics or national security with you. I don't know enough about them. But I do know this. You told Rusty that after you leave office, you're planning to come out as an atheist. Your political career would be over, anyway, but you wanted to show the world that an atheist had successfully led a democratic nation. You wanted to strike a blow for the acceptance of atheists in American society. But if you do what you're planning to do, you will hurt the cause of atheism, Mr. President. People will say only someone who didn't fear God could have done something so monstrous.'"

Jasmine scrolled her screen, then went on. "'It's a small argument, I suppose—but it's the best one I can give you. If you go ahead with Counterpunch, you will damage your cause beyond repair.'"

Jasmine looked up. "And then she closes with, 'God bless the United States, and God bless you, too, Mr. President.'"

Jasmine put the laptop back on the desk and came over to sit on the edge of their bed. She took her husband's hand, the back of which had a little cotton ball taped to it, covering where Dr. Snow had inserted a needle a short time ago.

President Jerrison and the First Lady sat in silence for a time. "No," said Seth at last.

"Pardon, dear?"

"No. I can't do what Bessie wants. Sweetheart, something happened while you were in Oregon."

"I'll say."

"Yes," said Seth, "but there was something else." She'd been briefed by her staff about the memory linkages, of course. Seth went on. "A young Army vet made me experience something. He'd been with Operation Iraqi Freedom." Seth knew all the facts and figures, of course. The war had begun under George W. Bush on March 20, 2003, in large part as a response to the 9/11 attacks; it had ended, more or less, under Barack Obama, on August 31, 2010—except that for Kadeem Adams, and thousands like him, it had *never* ended.

"Yes?" said Jasmine.

"He made me share a flashback to that war, to Iraq."

"God," said Jasmine.

"It was horrific. I can't put our soldiers through anything like that ever again." He looked into his wife's eyes. "We have to end this. We have to stop it, once and for all. Counterpunch is going ahead."

DOGWOOD, the cottage at Camp David that Darryl and Bessie were being held in, had two well-stocked bathrooms. Darryl had shaved, removing the stubble from his face and head, and he and Bessie were now eating the elegant dinner that had been brought to them.

No matter how hard he tried, he couldn't keep from being inundated by her memories—after all, there were so many more of hers than of his own. He knew now what it was like to be white, as well as to be a little girl, a teenaged girl, a grown woman, a middle-aged woman, a woman of a certain age, and, yes, at last, what it was like to be old. The being-old part was worse than he'd ever imagined it would be: constant pains, fading vision, failing hearing, a melancholy sense that one had once been so much more vigorous, more acute, more attractive, more *everything*—and, always in the background, a haunting awareness that time was running out.

Perhaps it was the last of those that prompted Bessie to speak. "Everything is going to change soon," she said, "what with what Jerrison is planning to do."

"Yes, ma'am," said Darryl.

"Things will be different."

Darryl sipped his coffee. "Yes, ma'am."

"And, well, if it's all going to come to an end, then I need to say something."

"Ma'am?"

"I owe you an apology."

"For what?"

"For the things I've thought all these years. You're right. I've never really known—known someone like you. You're a good . . ." She trailed off, looking embarrassed.

"You were going to say 'boy,' weren't you, ma'am?"

"I'm sorry."

"What would you call a white man who was more than fifty years younger than you? Would you say he was a good boy?"

"Well . . . yes."

"Then it's *fine,* ma'am—and thank you." Darryl glanced at

the wall clock, which, like everything here, was ornate and beautiful. "It's almost 8:00 P.M.," he said. "Time for the president's speech," he said. "It's going to be televised—want to watch it?"

But Bessie shook her head slowly, sadly. "No." She looked out the large window at the forested grounds, which were shrouded in snow. "I already know what he's going to say."

CHAPTER 47

"I am not happy about this, sir," Dr. Alyssa Snow said.

Seth Jerrison shifted slightly on his bed. "I'm not going to address the nation lying down, Alyssa. Now, come on, help me."

Dr. Snow, who had changed into her Air Force captain's uniform, and the First Lady, who was wearing a stylish salmon-colored dress, helped Seth out of the four-poster bed and into the wheelchair that had been brought here. He was wearing a blue suit—Jasmine and Dr. Snow had struggled to get him into it an hour ago. Susan Dawson stood to one side.

Seth grunted repeatedly as they moved him. His chest hurt, and his head swam for a moment; it was, he realized, the first time he'd sat up since they'd taken him out of the Beast on Friday morning.

The presidential bedroom was on the ground floor, and the residence had a direct connection to the press center. Susan Dawson wheeled him along, with Jasmine on his left and Dr. Snow on his right. The corridor had been cleared: there would be no photos of him arriving in a wheelchair.

They reached the green room, which was small but

comfortable. Seth briefly looked up at the official portrait of himself, hanging on the wall: smiling, confident, healthy. The makeup lady glanced at the photo, too, as if assessing the magnitude of her task. She then set about getting him ready to go on camera.

When his makeup was completed, he thanked the woman. Dr. Snow touched Seth's wrist to check his pulse, felt his forehead, and then reluctantly nodded. She and Jasmine helped him to his feet, and Susan Dawson handed him an ornate cane. He nodded his thanks and immediately shifted much of his weight to it.

Jasmine put a hand lightly on each of his shoulders and looked into his eyes. "I won't say break a leg, sweetheart, because that's the last thing we need. But good luck." She kissed him gently and then exited through the other door, heading out into the press room. Seth took a few moments to compose himself, then started walking. Each step was painful, but he refused to grimace. "Hail to the Chief" began to play over the speakers, and as he stepped out into the press room, everyone rose and spontaneously applauded. When he made it to the podium, he gripped its sides for support—his media coach be damned.

The roof was angled, and the walls were paneled halfway up with dark wood; the rest of their height was painted beige. An audience had been brought in for the speech; Seth was still a university professor at heart, and he spoke better when there were warm bodies in front of him. The twenty-four people— more like a graduate colloquium, he thought, than a freshman lecture—were seated in six rows of chairs split by a central aisle that contained the camera and its operator. Vice President Flaherty was in the front row, and Jasmine was sitting next to him. The rest of the audience members were uniformed Navy and Marine officers, drawn from the camp's staff. Seth nodded to let them know they could sit down. The teleprompter screen was mounted in front of the camera lens, and he read from it.

"My fellow Americans," he began, as all presidents always did. "We are faced with an unrelenting enemy, but we cannot allow the terrorists to win. We either cower in fear, or we march forward with our heads high—and the American people, I know, opt for the latter. This country, the greatest the world has ever seen, will not be held hostage by the demands of the disgruntled few. I say here resoundingly and definitively, on behalf of us all, to those in every corner of the world: we will not tolerate terrorism, and we will treat with equal severity terrorists, those who harbor terrorists, and those who ignore terrorists in their midsts. There is no friend we will not protect, no ally we will not help make secure—and no foe we will not oppose with all the resources at our disposal. This is not a battle between civilizations; rather, it is a battle to save the very notion *of* civilization, and—"

And he felt himself faltering. The teleprompter continued to roll for a few lines before the woman operating it realized he'd stopped speaking. Seth tightened his grip on the sides of the podium. The members of the audience—those here and the countless millions watching worldwide—were doubtless waiting anxiously for him to go on.

And Seth *wanted* to go on, but to talk was suddenly beyond him—and yet it would make headlines all over the planet if he didn't: "Jerrison Hesitates During First Post-Shooting Speech." "Is US President Unfit to Lead?"

But the words on the teleprompter were too much for him. Not that he hadn't rehearsed them, not that he didn't know what they meant, not that any were tricky to pronounce, but every term suddenly triggered a dozen vivid memories. He was supposed to say, "We will rise to this challenge as we have risen to every challenge since the days of the Founding Fathers." But the word *fathers* brought to mind countless recollections of his own dad, who'd been an expansive storyteller and womanizer, and of a handsome black man he recognized as Kadeem's most-recent stepfather.

He wanted to shake his head, to fling the images from his mind, but he knew he'd lose his balance altogether if he did that. These memories were every bit as vivid and immediate as those he'd experienced while sharing Kadeem's post-traumatic flashback.

He summoned his will and tried to resume his speech, but he suddenly became conscious not of the teleprompter but rather of the TV camera behind it, and—

And images of other cameras came to him: old-style TV

cameras, motion-picture cameras on cranes, tiny digital cameras, Polaroid cameras, SLR cameras, all of them superimposed. And each camera had a story to tell; indeed, he suddenly recalled his visit to the Sixth Floor Museum at Dealey Plaza, where Abraham Zapruder's Bell & Howell 8mm, or one just like it, had been on display.

"Mr. President?" said Dr. Snow, *sotto voce*. She had stepped into the press room but had stopped short of entering the camera's field of view. "Are you okay?"

Seth couldn't find the words to reply to her. More memories came at him, and the deluge made him think of Professor Singh, whose equipment had started all this, and that brought to mind Kadeem meeting Singh for the first time, with the young private listening oh-so-skeptically to what the Canadian had to say.

His heart pounded painfully. Some audience members were whispering among themselves, clearly wondering what was going on. Seth wanted to slide his hand across his throat in a cut gesture, but he still lacked motor control.

His faltering finally proved too much for the vice president. Paddy Flaherty got up and moved to the podium, doing what he was supposed to do: acting for the president when the president himself could not. "Ladies and gentlemen," he said, standing next to Seth and leaning into the microphone, "President Jerrison has, of course, undergone a great deal lately. I'm sure we are all grateful for . . ."

Seth felt his legs going out from under him. Dr. Snow surged in, catching him and putting an arm around his waist, helping to hold him up. Seconds later, Jasmine was at his side, too.

More images—and sounds—and smells—came to him, some from his own past and some from Kadeem's, piled on top of each other. He closed his eyes, hoping to shut all the images out, but that reminded him of horror films and trying to get to sleep and a dust storm in Iraq and countless other things. Now that he was being supported, Seth did try to fling everything from his head with a violent shake—but that just brought to mind memories of whiplash and comic double takes and watching tennis games.

The First Lady carefully walked Seth toward the green

room. He was surprised that Agent Dawson hadn't brought his wheelchair close, but as they entered the room, the reason became clear: Susan, who perhaps had been leaning against the wall when Seth had started his speech, had slipped down onto her rump, her back still against the wall and her head tipped toward her chest.

Dr. Snow quickly got the wheelchair and she and Jasmine helped Seth into it. Seth tried to make out what Flaherty was saying in the other room, but the present was overwhelmed by the cacophony of the past.

Susan looked up, and it seemed to take a moment for her eyes to focus. "Sir," she said, and then a second later she added, ". . . 'kay?," presumably as much of, "Are you okay?" as she could get out.

He nodded, or at least thought he did.

Suddenly, Susan's eyes went wide and she managed to say, "Ranjip's in trouble."

NIKKI Van Hausen had finished showing her last house for the day. It had probably been a lost cause—indeed, the whole day had likely been a waste. She'd often told those wanting to sell homes that they should bake cookies and put flowers in vases—but she herself was still bruised and bandaged from yesterday's accident, not to mention exhausted—hardly the sort of sight that made people feel good about buying a house. Hopefully she wouldn't look quite so mangled by next weekend.

Nikki was driving a rented Toyota. Her car had been a total write-off, but it had also been seven years old; she was still contemplating what she would purchase with the stingy amount her insurance company would eventually cough up.

She pulled into a 7-Eleven, got a coffee, and, as she walked up to the cash register, the cardboard cup slipped from her hand and hit the floor. The plastic lid she'd put on moments ago popped off, and coffee splayed out in front of her.

She saw the middle-aged man behind the counter make a pained expression, half oh-shit-I-have-to-clean-that-up and half Christ-if-she-scalded-herself-will-she-sue?

"Sorry!" said Nikki. "I'm sorry!" She staggered forward,

almost slipping on the now-wet floor, and grabbed the counter, right next to the hot-dog roaster. Her head was swimming.

"Geez, lady," the clerk said. He doubtless saw the bandage on her left hand and the one on her forehead; perhaps he simply took her for a klutz. But then he added, "You okay?"

Nikki issued a reflexive, "I'm fine"—but she wasn't, and she knew it. Her head was pounding. It was like back at Luther Terry when she'd first been linked to Eric Redekop, magnified a hundredfold. Images of his life ran through her mind as though she were flipping through a magazine. She took a deep breath, but doing so seemed to draw the strength from elsewhere in her body, and she slumped down onto the tiled, wet floor, next to the counter.

Another customer thought better of his planned purchase and just put it down on the nearest shelf and left the store. The clerk came around from behind the counter. "Lady, what's wrong?"

Nikki tried to speak again, but no words came out.

"Should I call 9-1-1?" asked the man. When Nikki didn't respond, he started backing away. "I'm calling 9-1-1," he said decisively.

Memories kept coming forth, more vividly than ever before: scenes from her life and Eric's, depicting other convenience stores, spilled beverages, open houses, and—*bam! bam! bam!*—multi-car pileups.

She vaguely heard the clerk talking on the phone, and then his footfalls returning. But she was having flashes in her vision, like a migraine was coming on, and she didn't dare lift her head to look at him since it would mean also looking into the overhead lighting panels.

"An ambulance is coming, miss," he said, crouching down beside her. "Can I get you anything?"

She shook her head—as much to fling out the invading memories as to answer his question.

"Do you want to stand up?" he asked.

Another wave of memories washed over her—of getting to her feet after falling while skating, of Eric being stood up for a date decades ago, of stand-up comedians she'd seen in the past. She wanted to say no, but still couldn't find her voice.

"Here, come on," the clerk said, and she felt his hands

grabbing her naked wrists. But after he'd lifted her bottom a few inches off the ground, he suddenly let go of her, and she dropped back to the floor—and he tumbled backward into a rack holding snack cakes. She heard him say, "What the fuck?" over and over again.

Chimes sounded as the door to the store slid open. "Oh my God!" said a male voice. "Are you guys okay?"

Nikki still couldn't bring herself to look up, but the new customer approached. "What happened? Was it a robbery?"

The clerk said, "No. God, it's like . . . like . . . *shit!* It's like someone else is inside my head."

At last Nikki managed to speak. "Join the club."

CHAPTER 48

AT Camp David, leaning into the microphone on the podium, Vice President Flaherty came to the end of the speech. ". . . and so this government will protect its citizens and its allies today, tomorrow, and forever. God bless America. Good night."

There should have been applause, and indeed there was a smattering, but there was also an immediate din of conversation.

In the adjoining room, Seth leaned back in the wheelchair, grateful for it. Memories of his life and Kadeem's continued to overwhelm him, involving basic training, and press conferences, and *Ironside* reruns, and a hundred other things.

Dr. Snow's BlackBerry rang. "Hello?" There was quiet while she listened, then: "All right. Bring them to the infirmary. We're heading there now." She ended the call. "It's official," she said. "Bessie Stilwell, Agent Hudkins, and Professor Singh are all affected, too—everyone here who was part of the linked group at LT."

"What about the others?" asked Jasmine. "Those who *aren't* here?"

Dr. Snow crouched in front of Susan Dawson. "Susan, where's the contact list for the others who were affected?"

Susan managed to meet Alyssa's gaze but still couldn't speak. After a moment, Alyssa gave up; the president was her number-one priority. She rose, positioned herself behind Seth's wheelchair, and began pushing it. They entered the hallway, which reminded Seth of each time he'd been down it before, and of a hundred other similar corridors, and of so many other things: long narrow streets in South Central L.A., and soccer fields, and the underground tunnels that connected government buildings in Washington, and—yes—the tunnel of light he'd seen when he'd thought he was dying.

They had to go outside to get to the infirmary building; it was cold and dark—the sun was down—but no one bothered to put on coats, and Seth found that the chill helped him focus. The links had suddenly become much, much stronger, and the distinction between himself and Kadeem seemed to be . . .

There was no doubt. He wasn't just accessing Kadeem's memories. He felt, even more than he had when sharing Kadeem's traumatic flashback, that he *was* Kadeem. He was still Seth, too; he was *both* of them.

They entered the low building that contained the infirmary, and soon Seth's wheelchair was brought up next to one of the beds and rotated 180 degrees, which revealed the surprising sight of Bessie Stilwell being carried in. She was seated in what was presumably a rocking chair from the cottage she'd been held in. Two uniformed Marine officers had taken the simple expedient of picking it up by its seat and carrying her here in it.

The sight triggered a thousand memories for Seth, drawn from the vast intermingled pool of his and Kadeem's joint pasts: chairs, and chairlifts, and old ladies, and football players being hoisted on the shoulders of teammates, and so much more.

A moment later, Darryl Hudkins entered, two female Marines flanking him and helping to keep him on his feet. Meanwhile, someone had apparently found a spare wheelchair, and a Marine had used it to transport Susan Dawson here; she was being wheeled in now.

"All right," said Dr. Snow. "Thanks for your help getting

these people here. You can go; it's getting too crowded. Dismissed!"

The Marines departed, and Seth looked at who was left: his wife Jasmine, Alyssa Snow, agents Darryl and Susan, and Bessie Stilwell.

At that moment, Singh entered. A bald Asian man wearing a Navy lieutenant's uniform was holding on to his elbow, and somewhere along the line they'd picked up a cane for him; he was leaning on it. Another man—a Marine with a blond crew cut—followed behind. They found a chair for Singh, who currently seemed incapable of speech.

Jasmine Jerrison crouched so that she was at her husband's eye level. Seth managed to lift his right hand ever so slightly, and she took it and intertwined her fingers with his, and she smiled that smile he'd fallen in love with thirty-five years ago.

And suddenly he had *her* memories, too. Every part of her face—her green eyes, her wide mouth, her small nose, her freckles, her laugh lines—triggered flashbacks to events he and she both remembered, but these flashbacks were even more vivid. If what he'd originally experienced was like grainy television, and what he'd seen since he faltered during the speech was akin to Imax, then these memories, the ones he shared with Jasmine, were like Imax 3D.

Perhaps that made sense: he didn't have to confabulate a dining room if she remembered him in the one at their old apartment in Manhattan; he knew what it looked like, too. He didn't have to make up their children's faces; he knew precisely what his own now-grown kids had looked like at every stage of their lives.

As he held her hand, he concentrated on her, on *just* her, on the memories—the life!—they'd shared, trying to shut out everything else, if only for a minute, trying to regain his equilibrium, his focus, his self. And as he looked at her, he saw her eyes go wide, showing whites all around the iris. He managed to say, "What's wrong?"

Jasmine opened her mouth, but no sound emerged.

Seth tried to shout "Alyssa!" but it came out softly. Still, it was enough to get the physician to react. "Mrs. Jerrison," Dr. Snow said at once, "are you all right?"

His wife still looked terrified. Seth thought perhaps she

was accessing his memories of being shot. He flexed his hand, trying to disengage his fingers, in hopes that might sever whatever link they'd suddenly forged, but she brought her other hand up and laid it over the two that were intertwined, her diamond ring sparkling in the room light.

"Mrs. Jerrison," Alyssa said again, and then all her medical training seemed to drain from her, and she fell back on a movie cliché. "Snap out of it!"

Jasmine managed to shift her head to the left and up, looking at the doctor. "It's . . . it's *amazing.*"

Seth was still in the wheelchair, Jasmine was still crouched next to him, and Alyssa was bent at the waist so she could better tend to them both. Jasmine lifted her left hand and reached to take Alyssa's hand, but the doctor pulled back and stood up straight. "No," she said. "No, if it's contagious . . ."

From across the room, Agent Darryl Hudkins, who was now lying on one of the infirmary beds, spoke for the first time. "It's not a disease," he said, the words protracted and his volume low. "It's a miracle."

But Dr. Snow was now backing away, and she spoke to the Asian lieutenant and the Marine with the blond crew cut. "Are you two okay?"

They nodded.

"Good," said Alyssa. "It doesn't seem to be transmissible through touching clothes—it happened to the First Lady through skin contact. So don't touch anyone, understood?"

"Yes, Captain Snow," said the lieutenant, and the blond Marine—who had a thick Southern accent—added, "Whatever you say, ma'am."

Alyssa looked at Singh, who was slumped over in a padded chair. "Professor Singh, I need you to focus. I'm in way over my head here."

He slowly lifted his bearded face, but that was all.

"Professor Singh," she said again. "I need you. The president needs you."

Ranjip blinked repeatedly but said nothing, and Seth imagined that he was overwhelmed by—who was it now? Ah, yes, the redheaded clown in the clown car: he'd be overwhelmed by Lucius Jono's memories, vividly intermingling with his own.

Seth turned his attention back to Jasmine and found that he, at least, was regaining his strength, perhaps thanks to all the stimulants that had been pumped into him prior to starting his speech. "It's okay, sweetheart," he said to his wife. "It's going to be dandy."

The First Lady nodded, and a memory came to him in out-of-synch stereo: him saying the exact same words after he'd won the Republican nomination.

Across the room, he saw Bessie slump down again in her chair. Dr. Snow began to surge toward the elderly woman, but checked herself, presumably again not wanting to touch one of the infected.

Seth put his hands on the large gray tires of his wheelchair and started pushing himself forward. Jasmine caught his intent and stood behind the wheelchair, but ended up using it as a walker to support herself rather than helping propel it along.

"What are you doing?" Alyssa asked.

The president ignored his doctor and continued to roll until his chair was up against the wall, next to Bessie's rocker, with the two of them facing in opposite directions. She looked wan and weak, like her life was slipping away. Seth took Bessie's wrinkled, liver-spotted hand in his, and Jasmine leaned in and placed her hands on top of theirs. The physical connection with Bessie brought Seth a flood of her memories: growing up in rural Mississippi, her father speaking out in favor of segregation, a blisteringly hot summer's night.

"Bessie," he said softly.

She stirred slightly, but her eyes were still closed.

"Come on, Bessie," he said, and he squeezed her hand a bit more tightly.

At last her eyes fluttered open, and they locked on his. He nodded encouragingly, and she smiled slightly at him.

Alyssa Snow came closer. "Mrs. Stilwell, are you okay?"

Bessie nodded and, as Alyssa turned, Bessie reached out with her free hand and clasped Alyssa's wrist. Seth saw the doctor try to shake the hand loose, but Bessie somehow managed to hold her grip for several seconds.

Alyssa half turned, and Seth, craning his neck, thought she

looked unsteady on her feet. He couldn't get up to help her, but the lieutenant rushed forward and caught her before she toppled, his hands touching hers. He gently lowered her to the floor by holding on to her wrists, letting her back rest against the door of a cabinet. It was only after she was safely down that he realized what he'd done. "Oh, shit," he said, looking at his hands.

Alyssa's eyes had gone wide. "My God," she said softly, and then she mouthed the words once more, but no sound came out.

There was a sink at one side of the room. Seth saw the lieutenant walk toward it, as if the contagion could be washed off with soap and water. But he made it just halfway before he stumbled and went down on his knees.

The Marine with the blond crew cut apparently realized he was the only unaffected person in the room. "What's happening to y'all?"

Seth found himself marveling at the pronoun so often needed but not existing in most English dialects: *y'all*. You all. All of you together. All of you as one.

And they had, at least in part, apparently become just that, because in unison he and Ranjip and Darryl said, "Something wonderful."

Vice President Paddy Flaherty entered the room. "Seth," he said, starting toward the president.

Susan Dawson, still in the spare wheelchair, rallied some strength and spoke for the first time since they'd arrived at the infirmary. "Mr. Vice President, sir, turn around and walk out that door."

"What's wrong?" Flaherty asked.

"You have to get out of here," Susan said.

Flaherty continued to close the distance between himself and Jerrison.

Susan drew her sidearm and aimed it at Flaherty. "Mr. Vice President, *freeze!*"

Paddy Flaherty stopped. "Are you insane, Agent Dawson? Stand down."

"No, sir," said Susan. "The president is compromised, and so my job is to protect the line of succession. Leave this room at once."

"Young lady," Flaherty said, "you are making a huge

mistake. Director Hexley will deal with you personally, no doubt, and—"

"Get him," said Seth.

Flaherty turned to look at the president. "What?"

"Get him," Seth said again. "Get Leon Hexley—right now."

CHAPTER 49

A Boeing E-4 Advanced Airborne Command Post had been dispatched to Andrews from the 1st Airborne Control Squadron out of Offutt Air Force Base, near Omaha. Secretary of Defense Peter Muilenburg saluted the soldiers he passed as he walked toward the plane.

Normally, an E-4 was simply used as a "looking glass"—mirroring operations at the primary command site on the ground, in case that site was destroyed. But given the successful terrorist attack on the White House, Secretary Muilenburg had chosen *Pteranodon*—the call sign being used today for this plane—as his primary base for overseeing Operation Counterpunch.

The E-4 was built on a modified 747 airframe. Muilenburg stuck his head into the cockpit on the upper deck and said a few words to the commander—who was a friend of his—as well as the copilot, navigator, and flight engineer. Their flight plan would take them clear across the continental United States and out over the Pacific.

Muilenburg then headed down to the middle deck and walked to the conference room, which was in the center of the fuselage, with wide aisles on either side. The room's walls were covered with monitors showing maps of Pakistan and the surrounding countries, as well as the positioning of the air-craft carriers, flight telemetry from the B-52s, satellite views of specific cities, and spreadsheets and charts detailing equipment-deployment status. Muilenburg's operations staff was already on board, seated in swivel seats at the long work-table. He took his position, strapped in, and gave a thumbs-up to one of the crew.

The giant plane began to roll down the runway.

ERIC Redekop and Janis Falconi were back in his luxurious condo, watching the president's speech on Eric's wall-mounted TV. They'd both been stunned that Jerrison was standing up; after the sort of surgery he'd had, he should still have been in bed. When Jerrison first started to falter, Eric declared, "See!" as if he'd been vindicated. But then, moments later, Eric became unsteady himself as he was overwhelmed by vivid memories from Jan's life, as well as memories of his own past coming back with stunning clarity.

Jan had been leaning her head against his shoulder as they sat on the white leather couch; it took a few moments for Eric to realize that she had slumped against him. But despite feeling physically weak, mentally he felt something he never had before: an exhilarating sense that he was larger than he'd ever been. For a moment, he thought he was recalling one of Jan's memories of being high, but it wasn't that—this wasn't a mem-ory. Rather, it was how he felt—how *they* felt—right now, right here.

Jan spoke, her voice small. "It's expanding," she said. And then, *"We're* expanding."

"But why?" Eric managed to ask. "Why so fast now, so easily?"

"Why does a boulder roll downhill faster than a pebble?" Jan replied, and he knew what she meant; so many were affected now—and more were joining in each moment. The pressure, the force, the strength was increasing exponentially.

Eric leaned back into the couch—or maybe, he thought, he was pushed back into it by the headlong rush.

• • •

SETH Jerrison imagined that the Secret Service director expected to lose his job: after all, his agency had manifestly failed in its mission to protect the president, and, indeed, two Secret Service agents had been involved in the attempt on Seth's life.

Seth had had Leon Hexley sequestered in a cottage here at Camp David. They were all named after trees, and it had amused the president to assign Hexley to the one called Hemlock. They'd sent one of the Marines who had been in the press-room audience to get Hexley, and—

Ah, and here he was. Hexley entered the infirmary, but instantly stopped in his tracks; the accompanying Marine stopped, too.

"Agent Dawson!" Hexley exclaimed. Seth was sure that Hexley, like any good Secret Service man, must have immediately taken in everything about the scene, including that Susan Dawson, sitting in a wheelchair, had a gun aimed at the vice president's chest. "What the hell is going on?"

Seth spoke before Susan could answer. He looked at the Marine with the blond crew cut. "You, there. What's your name?"

"Collins, sir."

"Collins, arrest Director Hexley. Agent Dawson has handcuffs. Take them from her and put them on him."

The young Marine instantly drew his sidearm. Susan, still in the spare wheelchair, let him take her handcuffs, and he quickly snapped them onto Hexley's wrists, trapping his arms behind his back.

"What the hell is going on?" Hexley asked again. He was forty-seven, with hair like Reed Richards: brown except for silver-gray at the temples. As always, he was wearing a blue suit and a conservative tie, and he had on horn-rim glasses and a fancy Swiss wristwatch.

Seth wondered how best to accomplish what he wanted. He could simply take hold of one of Hexley's hands—even if they were now cuffed. But although as a politician he'd shaken the hands of a lot of people he didn't like, having to touch the man who had presumably organized the attempt on his life was more than he could bear.

Or, he thought, he could try to sock the bastard in the jaw. But he doubted he was currently strong enough to manage it.

As he looked at Leon Hexley—*my God, yes!*—the man's memories became accessible to him; links were apparently forming now without physical contact.

Memories unveiled; secrets revealed. Hexley had been in Afghanistan, along with Gordo Danbury and Dirk Jenks. All three of them had been converted there, wooed with real riches in this life and the promise of so much more in the next.

Leon Hexley was older than the other two men, and had been with the CIA before the Afghan war; it had been easy enough for him to get a senior position in the Secret Service upon his return to the States, and eventually to become its director, promoting and deploying Danbury and Jenks as he saw fit.

But they had waited until the time was right—until the US had been demoralized by attacks on San Francisco and Philadelphia and Chicago—to strike at the very heart of the American government. Danbury was to have gone out in a blaze of martyrdom killing Jerrison. Then Jenks was supposed to take out Flaherty, or whatever surviving presidential successor became commander in chief after the White House was destroyed: two dead presidents in a matter of hours.

Seth was relieved to learn from Hexley's memories that only three members of the Secret Service had been compromised; tomorrow, he'd go back to having its agents protect him and his family. But for now . . .

The Secret Service had originally been part of the Treasury Department; Seth had used that bit of trivia in his classes at Columbia. Since 2003, it had been an agency of the Department of Homeland Security, and DHS was a cabinet department under his direct jurisdiction as leader of the executive branch. "Agent Dawson?" he said.

She was still holding her gun. "Sir?"

"I'm giving you a promotion. Effective immediately, you are the new director of the United States Secret Service."

• • •

JAN Falconi was lying down now on the couch, her head in Eric's lap. She was listening to all the voices and reliving all the memories: hers, and those of the veteran named Jack, and those of everyone he'd touched at the Vietnam Memorial, and—

Ah, yes, it was a cold night, and Jack had gone to a homeless shelter. He'd brought in dozens more there, first by touching them, but then, after the total number had reached some critical threshold, merely by looking at them.

Eric's ornate wall clock made its hourly chime; it was midnight. The TV was still on, and a new program began. Jan laughed, and Eric, who was linked to her, did, too, and so did Nikki, safely back at her house, since she was linked to Eric, and so did Lucius Jono, who was linked to Nikki, and on and on: the laughter cascading not just down the chain, for it was no longer a simple series of links, but out onto the branching, growing network.

The new TV program Jan was watching, and so therefore were all the others, was an infomercial—for a surefire technique guaranteed to improve memory.

CHAPTER 50

Monday

TRIGGERS.

Stimuli that invoke memories.

So idiosyncratic: a fragrance, the way someone holds their head, a pattern woven into cloth, a few bars of music, a taste, a touch, a word. For one person, a memory might be brought to the fore; for another, nothing.

History provides shared triggers. Where were you when you heard President Kennedy had been shot? When Armstrong took that first small step, that first giant leap? When the Twin Towers fell? When they blew up the White House?

But even those were only triggers for a fraction of the world's population. Still, there were a few general triggers— universally shared experiences—that focused most minds, putting people on the same page, the same wavelength.

The circle had originally been closed.

Then—with triggers figurative and literal—it had opened. More and more individuals were drawn in. A few dozen minds, then a few hundred, then a few thousand, then more still.

Many of those in the original circle had had trouble adapting to it, but now each new mind that joined in was greeted, boosted, buoyed, embraced by countless others who had already experienced the first moments of connection, who had survived it, and who were now reveling in it all. Calming waves and swelling euphoria washed over the newcomers, enticing them, relaxing them, welcoming them.

And yet, despite the peace felt by those who were linked, despite the tranquility of shared joy, of banished loneliness, there was still something dark, something evil, something outside.

Those who were already linked considered, contemplated, cogitated, until . . .

A realization, a revelation—and a resolution.

This madness—the insanity that had cost humanity so much for so long—could not go on.

It could not, or the world would not long endure.

Things had to change—and they had to change now.

But for the next step, the next leap, a trigger was still needed: a general trigger, a shared trigger, a trigger that would sweep the globe . . .

DORA Hennessey had fallen asleep at Luther Terry Memorial Hospital just after 6:00 P.M.; she still wasn't dealing well with the time-zone change. A part of her had wanted to stay up to see President Jerrison's speech on TV, but she'd been too tired.

Dora had been so distraught over the aborted transplant operation and the death of her father—not to mention dealing with Ann January's memories—that she wasn't surprised to find she'd slept for twelve hours. But by 6:00 A.M., she was wide-awake and so decided to go for an early-morning walk.

Her stitches had been redone yesterday, and she'd been told they would hold nicely until the incision healed. She slowly got dressed, put on the winter jacket that had taken up half of her suitcase when she'd brought it over from England, and headed down through the lobby and out into the dim pre-dawn light. There were already quite a few cars on the road, and several other pedestrians walking briskly along.

She ambled south on 23rd Street, passing the Foggy Bottom metro station and a Dunkin' Donuts and the beige edifice of the Department of State. She turned left when she got to

Constitution Avenue and was surprised to find, nestled in a grove of trees, a huge bronze statue of a seated Albert Einstein; she hadn't known there was a memorial to him in Washington. She looked up at his sad eyes. *Everything is relative,* she thought; she felt like a little girl next to this giant man.

Dora had assumed it wouldn't be safe to go onto the National Mall this early, but there seemed to be a fair number of joggers about, so she crossed to the south side of Constitution Avenue. She knew from the tour she'd taken when she'd first arrived that the Vietnam Veterans Memorial was just to her right, but she continued south, toward the Reflecting Pool. The sun would be up very soon, and she thought it would be fun to watch it rise behind the tapered obelisk of the Washington Monument.

She got in position just in time: a tiny point of brilliance appeared on the horizon, slowly widening into a dome. The monument cast a long shadow pointing toward her. She'd left her phone back at the hospital, which was too bad—she'd have loved to have snapped a picture of this.

The sun quickly became too bright for her to look at directly, but it brought back memories of other sunrises over London's skyline, over the English Channel, over the desert. Some of the memories were her own: she had indeed pulled all-nighters at college, seeing the sun rise as she hurried to finish essays.

And some of the memories were clearly Ann January's, including one of her and David watching the sun come up from the deck of a cruise ship during their honeymoon.

But she was startled to also have memories that were neither hers nor Ann's: neither of them had ever been to Australia, but she had a vivid recollection of the sun coming up over the Sydney Opera House. And neither of them had ever seen a solar eclipse, but she clearly recalled the sun clearing the horizon with a bite already taken out of its disk.

The shadow of the monument gradually shortened as the new day continued to dawn.

SUSAN Dawson soon realized what Seth Jerrison already had: links were now forming spontaneously, without physical contact. As she looked at Vice President Flaherty, his memories opened up to her, and as she looked at Seth Jerrison, he, too, became an open book. She lowered her weapon; there was no point any longer in keeping the two of them apart.

Soon, everyone at Camp David ended up with their memories intertwined. But even the linked had to sleep, and although some few managed to stay up all night, dealing with the flood of media inquiries after Jerrison's aborted attempt to address the nation, most had nodded off by midnight. The president, of course, had been through an enormous trauma. Bessie Stilwell normally didn't need much sleep, but the round-trip to California had left her fatigued. Ranjip Singh never managed to rally much strength that night, and was out cold by 1:00 A.M., and Darryl Hudkins was asleep by 2:00.

Susan did manage to stay up all night, sitting in her wheelchair, but she knew it was pointless: the vast majority of those in DC, in Maryland, and in Virginia were asleep, and although that didn't impede accessing the memories of those who were already linked, those who were unconscious couldn't reach out to others.

The infirmary had a big window that happened to look east. Although the view was partially obscured by trees, Susan was nonetheless drawn by the rising sun. A memory came to her of a sunrise over the Taj Mahal—seen by Ranjip Singh on one of his trips to India.

Another sunrise came to her, one familiar and yet alien. Familiar, because it was a view through the windows in the East Wing of the White House, looking across East Executive Avenue toward the Treasury Department—a window she'd often enough looked out herself. But alien because she'd never looked out those windows at dawn, and—ah, more of the memory came to her: and certainly not with the First Lady standing next to . . . to *him*. It was the morning after their first night in the White House, and Seth Jerrison and his wife had come here to watch the day break.

Ranjip Singh was waking up—they'd eased him onto one of the infirmary beds. The sleep had done him good, it seemed: he was capable of speech again. He looked at Susan, and the first words out of his mouth were, "You can read President Jerrison's memories."

"Yes."

He sounded amazed. "I can recall you recalling *him* recalling a wonderful sunrise seen from the White House."

Susan nodded. "The beginning of his first full day in office. Yes, it just came to me."

"This is . . . is . . ."

"'Major league,' as your son would say," said Susan.

Singh smiled. "That it is."

Darryl Hudkins was lying on one of the other infirmary beds. His eyes fluttered open. "Good morning, Miss Susan," he said, softly, looking at her. But Darryl never *called* her that; in fact, the only person who'd called her that recently was . . .

Bessie Stilwell.

Susan found she no longer needed the wheelchair. She rose from it and walked over to him. "Bessie?" she said, looking into Darryl's brown eyes.

"Yes, dear?" he—or she—replied.

Susan swallowed. "Bessie, where's Darryl?"

"Darryl? Such a nice young . . . young man." A frown. "I don't know. I haven't seen him."

Susan called over her shoulder. "Ranjip! Ranjip!"

He hopped off the bed and joined her. "What?"

She gestured at Darryl. "His body is awake, but it's as if Bessie is answering my questions."

Singh looked at Darryl. "Agent Hudkins?"

"Yes?" said a voice.

"And Mrs. Stilwell?"

"Yes?" said the same voice.

Seth Jerrison woke next, sitting up straight in his wheelchair. His eyes seemed alert.

"Mr. President," Susan asked, "are you all right?"

"No," he said. "No, it's—it's like when I was dying. I feel distant from my body."

Dr. Snow must have rallied at some point, because she soon appeared at his side. "Sir, you're here at Camp David, in the infirmary. You're *here*. Is there any pain?"

That seemed to be the wrong question. Suddenly, Jerrison's eyes went wide and his mouth dropped open and he let out a grunt as if he'd been punched in the stomach—or shot in the back.

"Damn," said Snow, under her breath. "Sir, it's all right. It's all right."

But it wasn't. Susan suddenly felt a sharp pain in her chest, too. The sight of Jerrison echoing what had happened on the steps of the Lincoln Memorial was triggering her to access that memory, too. And the pain of *being* shot brought back the different pain of *having* shot—the shock and nausea she'd felt after gunning down Josh Latimer.

Perhaps in response to the pain, her consciousness *fled*. She was suddenly in a fancy apartment somewhere, and there was a woman she recognized: Janis Falconi—which meant she perhaps was in the mind of Dr. Redekop. She tried to speak, but before the words could get out she was somewhere else yet again, outdoors, in the cold, brushing snow off a car.

And then her vision split in two, as if her left eye were in one place and her right another. The left showed an outdoor scene—the sun rising above some more trees that had lost their leaves for the winter. And the right showed an interior of someone's house, with beat-up furniture and piles of old newspapers. But there was no harsh line between the two realities, no clear demarcation. She could contemplate either or— yes!—*both* simultaneously. And each object in each scene triggered memories: a cavalcade of images and sensations and feelings.

And then Susan's vision seemed to split horizontally, showing her four images: the original two in the top quadrants, a view through a car's windshield driving on a highway in the lower left, and a bouncing view of a TV set in the lower right that she soon realized was the perspective of someone watching a morning news show while treadmilling.

The images split again, each quadrant dividing into four smaller views, for a total of sixteen. She felt like she was equally in all those places, indoors and out, warm and cold.

She turned her head—at least, she thought she was turning it—and the views shifted, revealing new squares to the left; and as she tilted her head up and down, more squares appeared above and below.

All the images split again; each one was now quite small, and yet, despite that, there was absolute clarity. After a moment, they divided yet again—and her whole field of view was filled with hundreds of squares. But despite their small size, she could make out minute details: reading a headline on that commuter's newspaper; admiring the engagement ring on that woman's finger; seeing the time on the clock in this one—and the clock on that one—and the watch on this one—and the iPhone display on that one. And they all said the same time: 7:32 A.M., which was *now*. It wasn't just in times of crisis anymore; she was reading minds in real time. *Lots of minds*.

She was still Susan Louise Dawson—but she was also all those other people. She was white and black and Asian. Female and male. Straight and gay. Christian and Jewish and Sikh and Muslim and atheist. Young and old. Fit and not. Brilliant, average, and dull. Both a believer and a skeptic; at once a scientific genius and a scientific illiterate.

She tried to assert her individuality: she was . . . was . . .

No, surely she was still . . .

But it *was* getting harder to stay separate. All the elements of who she was were still there, but they were juxtaposed with components of other minds, other lives. And she was a smaller part of the whole with each passing second.

Suddenly, she became conscious of geography. All of the minds touched so far were nearby, part of the wave front, the leading edge.

A song from her youth—from everyone's youth—came to her, to them: *We don't stop for nobody! We don't stop for nobody!* And as the world spun on its axis, as the sun came up, the wave front moved inexorably westward. But she was baffled about why South American cities weren't included. Parts of Colombia, Ecuador, and Peru were due south of Washington, and yet there seemed to be no mental contact with anyone from there. Could it be that South America was too far away to be included?

No, no—that wasn't it. Lessons from her college studies of geography came back, reinforced by the memories of countless others who knew the same thing. Earth's axis was tilted 23.5 degrees to the plane of the solar system. The swath of the Earth being affected was following the dawn line, the terminator. None of South America had yet been included.

The dawn, Susan thought, and *the dawn* echoed a thousand others. As people looked up, or woke up, as they recalled previous sunrises, they were brought in—and if they didn't note the dawn, they were soon brought in anyway, as others willed links to them.

She'd almost expected everyone to topple over; there had been much wooziness during the early stages yesterday, after all. But it seemed that each new mind that came on board—and thousands were popping in every minute now—brought new strength and stability. Agent Dawson (she found herself thinking of her in the third person), Agent Hudkins, President Jerrison, Professor Singh, and all the rest seemed to be capable of going about their normal tasks, but—

But she looked on in fascination, as if from a great height now; perhaps—ah, yes, she was linked to a traffic reporter in a helicopter over Washington, giving an update on the morning commute. Everything was flowing smoothly. Despite icy conditions on I-295 and Ridge Road Southeast, there had not been a single accident reported so far, and all roads, including the Beltway, were moving well. It was as if the combined vision and reflexes of all the drivers were enough to overcome any potential problems. It was precisely what one might expect of a . . .

Susan herself didn't know the phrase, but others did, and they shared it. *Group mind:* a collective consciousness, the aggregate will of countless people, each one still separate, each a nexus, an individual, but each also linked, connected, networked. Unlike a hive with expendable drones, those who were joined now composed a vast mosaic, every stone precious, each member cherished, no one ignored or discarded or forgotten.

The world continued to turn. Dawn broke over Ottawa, Ontario; over Rochester, New York; over Pittsburgh, Pennsylvania; over Atlanta, Georgia. The squares were subdividing so quickly they seemed to flicker.

She thought again about the motorways and their myriad drivers. Those individuals spurring their cars to action were . . . a term she'd learned from Singh's memories: *excitatory inputs.* Those that counseled inaction were *inhibitory inputs.* And, in a true democracy, greater than what Washington or any other place had ever seen or could hope to aspire to, the excitatory and inhibitory inputs were summed, and the whole—the collective, the *gestalt*—acted, or not, depending on the result.

Sudbury, Ontario, saw first light, as did Saginaw, Michigan; Indianapolis, Indiana; and Memphis, Tennessee. Millions of additional voices joined the choir.

But surely, Susan and countless others thought, *a species could not operate that way.* Individual will was necessary! Individual will was what made life worth living!

It was individual will that let someone try to assassinate me.

It was individual will that let someone abuse me.

It was individual will that let someone kill my child.

It was individual will that let someone set off a bomb in my city.

The sun rose over Green Bay, Wisconsin; Columbia, Missouri; and Dallas, Texas. Daylight was spreading across the continent. Tens of millions were now interconnected. And with each passing second, more who weren't yet connected turned to face east, face the dawn, face the new day, and they recalled a dozen, a hundred, a thousand similar mornings as the Earth spun on.

ON any given day, about 150,000 people die, almost all peacefully from natural causes. When Josh Latimer had been shot, only Janis Falconi had been linked to him. But behind each person dying now stood millions of others, all connected to him or her. As lives slipped away, the gestalt strained to hold on to the expiring individuals: first this woman; then this man; then, tragically, this child. With the attention brought by millions, with the scrutiny of the legions, each demise was examined in detail and seen for what it was: the piecemeal dissolution of self. It didn't depart all at once, it didn't transfer from *here* to *there,* it didn't go *anywhere.* Rather, it decayed, crumbled, disintegrated, and ultimately vanished.

And so, reluctantly, sadly, the majority began to accept what the minority had always known. The dead hadn't passed on; they were *gone.*

But, at least now, they would never, ever be forgotten.

CHAPTER 51

PTERANODON—the E-4 Advanced Airborne Command Post—continued its westward flight through the darkness, the black waters of the Pacific far below.

SUSAN Dawson—the physical body of the Secret Service agent—was still in President Jerrison's office at Camp David. She had previously doubled over in pain but now fought to dismiss it from her mind.

Alyssa Snow—again, the body called by that name—was attending to the form called Seth Jerrison, who also had been experiencing great pain.

Susan felt herself simultaneously inside and outside her body, and what Singh knew about observer and field memories came to her: sometimes you remembered things as your eyes had seen them, and sometimes you saw yourself in your memories, as if observing from a distance. But this was *both* simultaneously—both an in-body and an out-of-body experience. She looked at Dr. Snow—and looked at herself looking at Dr. Snow—and saw in Alyssa's eyes that she must be experiencing the same duality.

The president's face was a battleground, with grimaces coming into existence and then being suppressed. Susan watched for a moment in concerned fascination, but then saw a preternatural calm come over Prospector's face, as if he was now drawing strength from all the linked minds. "My God," he said. "It's wonderful."

Perhaps fifty million people were linked together now—but there were still seven billion who weren't. The daybreak line would continue to sweep across Canada, the US, and Mexico, but it would be four hours until New Zealand—the first non–North American landmass of any size—saw the dawn, at about the same time that Ketchikan, Alaska, did. If it really was going to take a full day for the effect to circle the globe, covering fifteen degrees every hour, then the United States would be fully absorbed long before Russia or China or North Korea.

"We're not safe," Susan said. "If those who aren't linked decide that we're an abomination, they could nuke us. We have to maintain the appearance of normalcy until tomorrow morning—until the transition is complete."

"But how?" asked Jerrison. "Everyone would have to act in concert to maintain the illusion, and . . . oh."

Susan nodded. "Exactly. We're linked; we're one."

"E pluribus unum," said Jerrison, his voice full of awe. He looked at Singh, then back at Susan. "Still, it can't be that everyone wants this. Why's it happening?"

"It's like my kirpan," Singh said. "An instrument of *ahimsa*—of nonviolence; a way to prevent violence from being done to the defenseless when all other methods have failed."

Susan looked at him, and he went on. "In the ancient past, a crazed human could only kill one other person at a time. Then we developed the ability to kill small groups, and then larger groups, and still larger groups, and so on, until now a person can take out a major portion of a city, or"—and Singh glanced at Jerrison—"even a whole country, and soon after that, the whole wide world."

"And so *this* is happening?" Susan said. "We're linking together as a survival strategy?"

"I think so," said Singh. "Once again, the needs of the many *will* outweigh the needs of the few; the human race in aggregate will do the things that are best for the human race. The individuals will still exist, in a way, and those that need to do work to support the collective still can: farming and maintaining the infrastructure of civilization, but—do you feel it? Any of you?"

Darryl Hudkins spoke up. "I do," he said, and then, "We do."

Singh looked at him and nodded. "It's *gone,* isn't it? Racism, prejudice. *Gone.* Hatred, abuse. *Gone.* They were never the majority state of the human race—or, at least, hadn't been for decades and maybe longer—and they're being diluted away into nothingness as the gestalt grows."

Susan looked out the window. The sun wasn't directly visible anymore, but the trees were still casting long shadows. It had been perhaps two hours since daybreak, meaning it would presumably take another twenty-two hours for the process to finish. She was worried that someone here who had ties to people in Russia or China or another nation with nuclear weapons would alert them, urging them to stop the expansion in the only way they could.

But no—no. This was too good to wreck, this was too wonderful to derail, this was too *necessary* to stop.

On that point, all those who had been affected were of one mind.

DAY came to Montana and Wyoming and Colorado and New Mexico. And then to Washington state and Idaho and Utah and Arizona. And, at last, it swept west into California, the sun clearing the Sierra Nevada mountains.

PTERANODON continued its nighttime flight. Peter Muilenburg was pleased that the aircraft carriers and B-52s were all now on station, right on schedule. Of course, the E-4 wasn't going all the way to South Asia; there was no need for the command post to be proximate to the theater of operations. He wanted it positioned where it could get ground support, and there really was nowhere more appropriate, the secretary of defense thought, than west of Honolulu, high above Pearl Harbor—still the headquarters of the United States Pacific Fleet.

SUSAN Dawson now knew things she had never known.

The complete works of William Shakespeare.

Every verse of the Bible, and the Qu'ran, and every other religious text.

How to identify thousands of species of birds and thousands of kinds of minerals.

She knew calculus and how to play the stock market. She understood rainbows and tides. She knew why Pluto wasn't a planet.

She could play hundreds of musical instruments and speak many dozens of languages.

And she remembered countless lives: millions of first days at school, millions of first kisses, starting millions of new jobs, and millions of dreams about a better tomorrow.

Yes, there were unpleasant memories, too, but it came to her—it came to *everyone*—that there was no need to add to their number. How much better it was to share contented, positive, *happy* memories—and the best way to ensure that most of the new ones recorded from now on were just that was to help rather than hurt, to share rather than hoard, to support rather than belittle, and, of course, to love rather than hate.

"MR. Secretary?" said a uniformed aide coming into the conference room aboard *Pteranodon*.

"Yes?" replied Peter Muilenburg.

"We're on station above Pearl Harbor and circling. The commander invites you up to the cockpit. He says the view should be spectacular."

Muilenburg got out of his swivel chair, walked past the long table, and exited the room. He took the staircase to the upper deck, entered the cockpit, and stood with one arm on the back of the commander's chair and the other on the back of the copilot's.

The sky was brightening. He watched from high above as the sun climbed up from the gently curving ocean horizon, spilling color and warmth and light all around.

"Beautiful," Muilenburg said, when he'd seen his fill. "Thank you."

"You're welcome," replied the commander. "Perfect day for an operation, isn't it?"

The secretary of defense replied, "I'm aborting Counterpunch."

"But sir!" said the navigator, who hadn't been looking out the window, hadn't yet gazed upon the dawn, hadn't yet seen the light. "The president said you have to go through with it."

Muilenburg shook his head, "As my son would say, 'Let's not, and say we did.'"

"Peter," said the commander, turning now in his seat, "you don't have a son."

"True," replied Muilenburg. "But someone I know—or, at least, I know *now*—does."

SUSAN had never heard the term before, or, if she had, it hadn't registered; it was nowhere in her memory. Indeed, it was, she discovered, absent from most people's memories: *the Singularity*. But some knew it, and so now she did, too: the moment at which machine intelligence would supposedly exceed human intelligence, sparking lightning-fast technological progress that would leave plain old *Homo sapiens* far behind.

But what the partisans of the Singularity had glossed over was that machines were *not* getting more intelligent as time went on; they had *zero* intelligence and no consciousness, and no matter how fast they got at crunching numbers, they were still *empty*.

And yet the predicted surge *had* come: the vast, all-encompassing, world-changing *whooosh* of accelerating power. It was a chain reaction, an unstoppable cascade. But rather than machines, it was human beings amplifying each other, the wisdom of crowds writ large, the society of minds spreading far and wide.

To know everything, to understand all, to appreciate the totality of nature, of literature, of mathematics, of the arts. And to be free, at last, of duplicity and mendacity, of concerns about reputation, of establishing hierarchies, of all the game playing that had gone with petty individuality. It liberated so much of the intellect, so much energy—and it brought *peace*.

Susan Dawson didn't regret the old life she'd lived—a life she, and everyone, would always remember—but this new existence was so much greater, so much more fulfilling, so much more stimulating.

And it had only just begun.

EPILOGUE

IT'S an odd coincidence, the gestalt thinks, that here, at the end of November, if you start the day with sunrise in Washington, DC, the last place to see the dawn, twenty-four hours later, is a group of storied islands.

But odd coincidences abound in geography. For instance, those islands, out in the Pacific, happen to straddle the equator, and they are on the same meridian as the crater at Chicxulub, formed when an asteroid slammed into Earth sixty-five million years ago, triggering the worldwide climate change that killed the dinosaurs and paved the way for the ascent of mammals.

Finally, though, the archipelago Charles Darwin arrived at in 1835 is being kissed by the nascent day. Here now great tortoises—those from each island boasting a distinctive shell—are rousing from their sleep, their blood warming with the arrival of the sun. Here now the calls of finches—those from each island sporting a distinctive beak—herald the dawn. Here now black iguanas, the world's only extant marine lizards, slip into a sea stained orange and pink by the rising daystar.

And here now all those who call the Galápagos home, as

well as the visiting biologists and geologists and science-oriented tourists, join in, the last group to fuse with the collective. It is appropriate, judges the gestalt, that the place that taught the human race the most about evolution is the site of the completion of humanity's transcendence into its next stage of existence.

Darwin's closing words from *The Origin of Species* swirl through the collective consciousness:

> There is grandeur in this view of life, with its several powers, having been originally breathed into a few forms or into one; and that, whilst this planet has gone cycling on according to the fixed law of gravity, from so simple a beginning endless forms most beautiful and most wonderful have been, and are being, evolved.

The gestalt recasts the words ever so slightly: there is indeed grandeur in this view of life, with its combined power breathing now as one, and that, while this planet completes its most recent cycle according to the fixed law of gravity, from so simple a beginning a new form most beautiful and most wonderful has now evolved.

ABOUT THE AUTHOR

Robert J. Sawyer's novel *FlashForward* was the basis for the ABC TV series of the same name. He is one of only eight writers ever to win all three of the world's top awards for best science fiction novel of the year: the Hugo (which he won for *Hominids*), the Nebula (which he won for *The Terminal Experiment*), and the John W. Campbell Memorial Award (which he won for *Mindscan*). According to the *Locus Index to Science Fiction Awards*, he has won more awards for his novels than anyone else in the history of the science fiction and fantasy fields.

In total, Rob has won forty-six national and international awards for his fiction, including twelve Canadian Science Fiction and Fantasy Awards ("Auroras"), as well as *Analog* magazine's Analytical Laboratory Award, *Science Fiction Chronicle*'s Reader Award, and the Crime Writers of Canada's Arthur Ellis Award, all for best short story of the year.

Rob has won the world's largest cash prize for SF writing, Spain's 6,000-euro Premio UPC de Ciencia Ficción, an unprecedented three times. He's also won the Hal Clement Award (for *Watch*, the middle volume of his WWW trilogy) and a trio of Japanese Seiun Awards for Best Foreign Novel of the Year (for *End of an Era, Frameshift,* and *Illegal Alien),* as well as China's Galaxy Award for "Most Popular Foreign Science Fiction Writer."

In addition, he's received an honorary doctorate from Laurentian University and the Alumni Award of Distinction from Ryerson University. *Quill & Quire,* the Canadian publishing trade journal, calls him "one of the thirty most influential, innovative, and just plain powerful people in Canadian publishing."

Rob lives in Mississauga, Ontario, Canada, with his wife, poet Carolyn Clink. His website and blog are at **sfwriter.com**, and on Twitter and Facebook he's **RobertJSawyer**.

Don't miss the first book in the WWW trilogy
from Hugo and Nebula award–winning author

ROBERT J. SAWYER

0001110010101010000000010111111101010000000101000101010000001011101010 0101010

WWW:WAKE

0001110010101010000000010111111101010000000101000101010000001011101010 0101010

Caitlin Decter is young, pretty, feisty, a genius at
math—and blind. Still, she can surf the net with the
best of them, following its complex paths clearly
in her mind. When a Japanese researcher develops
a new signal-processing implant that may give her
sight, she jumps at the chance, flying to Tokyo for the
operation. But Caitlin's brain long ago co-opted her
primary visual cortex to help her navigate online.
Once the implant is activated, instead of seeing reality, the landscape of the World Wide Web explodes
into her consciousness, spreading out all around
her in a riot of colors and shapes. While exploring
this amazing realm, she discovers something—some
other—lurking in the background. And it's getting
smarter . . .

M794T1110

From award-winning author
ROBERT J. SAWYER

00011100101010100000000010111111101010000000101000101010000001011101010010101 0

WWW:WATCH

00011100101010100000000010111111101010000000101000101010000001011101010010101 0

Webmind is an emerging consciousness that has befriended Caitlin Decter and grown eager to learn about her world. But Webmind has also come to the attention of WATCH—the secret government agency that monitors the Internet for any threat to the United States—and the agents are fully aware of Caitlin's involvement in its awakening.

WATCH is convinced that Webmind represents a risk to national security and wants it purged from cyberspace. But Caitlin believes in Webmind's capacity for compassion—and she will do anything and everything necessary to protect her friend.

M603T1111

Now available from
CHARLES STROSS

**"Stross gives his readers a British superspy
with a long-term girlfriend, no fashion sense,
and an aversion to martinis."**
—*San Francisco Chronicle*

THE FULLER MEMORANDUM
A Laundry Files Novel

When a top secret dossier known as the Fuller Memorandum vanishes—along with his boss—Bob Howard is
determined to discover exactly what the memorandum
contained (and perhaps clear his boss's name). But Bob
runs afoul of Russian agents, ancient demons, and the
apostles of a hideous faith who have plans to raise a very
unpleasant undead entity known as the Eater of Souls.

Now Bob must use all of his skills to learn the secret of
the Fuller Memorandum in order to save the world—and
avoid becoming an item on the Eater of Souls's dinner
menu . . .

M652T0311